A LANDSCAPE OF SHADOWS

A LANDSCAPE OF SHADOWS

Julie Upshur

Published by Blazon Publishing
www.blazonpublishing.com

First Printing, 2024

ISBN: 978-1-963148-00-8

Cover Design: GetCovers

Printed in the USA.

For Nana

Solara Barthelme knew her thoughts were not her own. It was not her own will that commanded her legs as she walked down the dark alleyway, holding her breath against its stink of piss and mold. Solara knew better than to come here alone. Yet, she felt no panic, only a constant urging toward something or someone that waited on the other end.

"You're being a bitch, Nikara."

The voice, low-pitched and aggravated, was one Solara, or the thoughts in her head, knew well, and she dismissed it. It wasn't her quarry. She came to the end of the alleyway and stepped into the street, which was dimly illuminated by moonlight and smelled precious little better than the alley. The fourth ring of Diadem City – and the three rings that followed it – was poorly cared for, its occupants too busy breaking their backs for the comfort of the noblemen and women living in the three inner rings.

"You thought she was pretty."

"I never said that."

"It was obvious from the way you were staring at her."

     Julie Upshur

It was the second voice that tugged at Solara. As careless as its predecessor was grim, it made Solara feel weightless. Euphoric. There, across the street. Two figures in the dark.

"Here she is," the woman said. "I drew her all this way. Come here, pretty thing."

Solara nearly tripped over her feet in her haste to obey, until she stood before the woman. Nikara. Even her name had a richness to it, a regal bearing. Nikara was tall, her body narrow and muscled in its sleek fitting black clothing. She had a row of rubies in her left ear, each monstrously large jewel shining like a drop of blood. Her thick, dark hair hung in braids past her hips.

She smiled at Solara with a sweet look in her hazel eyes. In that moment, Solara would have died for her. No hesitation.

"She is a little pretty," Nikara said, lifting Solara's chin. Her leather gloves were damp and warm. "But equal parts feral. Look at her, Tessan."

"Leave her alone." Tessan sounded sullen.

Solara had no sooner had the thought then it was brushed away, her focus drawn back to Nikara. Her beauty. Her grace. The brilliant gleam in her smile as she stroked Solara's chin as if petting a doting dog.

"Should I make her beg for you?" Nikara suggested.

"Let. Her. Alone."

Solara turned toward him at the barely leashed anger in his voice, but Nikara tightened her grip on Solara's chin. Amusement danced over the woman's face. "Oh, she is a fighter. Look at me, little pretty. Pay him no mind."

"As you wish," Solara said. The words were prompted to her lips.

"Do you never tire of these ridiculous games?" Tessan snapped.

"Not when it makes you squirm like this," Nikara said. "I could make her crawl on her hands and knees. Don't you wish you had even a fraction of my gift?"

"Not if it made me act like you."

Solara turned her head. Nikara wasn't quick enough to stop her again. The scowling Tessan towered above Nikara, a mountain of a man. He wore similar nondescript black clothing, but his dark gold hair was loose and wild as a lion's mane.

Their eyes met, his dark gray like the sky before rain, and his jaw tightened as he looked away. "Let her go," he said.

"Very well," Nikara said, sounding disappointed. "If you're going to be a bore." She gave Solara's chin a gentle squeeze. "Tell him your name."

"Solara Barthelme," Solara said before Nikara had even finished the command.

Tessan shot Nikara a vile look, and a wicked grin flashed over her features. "Kiss him goodbye, Sol."

Tessan jerked backward, but Nikara's order was swift and Solara's obedience swifter still. He was head and shoulders above her, but she caught the front of his shirt and pulled him down to her. Their mouths met abruptly, with a clash of lips and teeth, and then Solara had cupped his face in her hands and steadied them both.

He tasted faintly of sweat, and his skin was hot to the touch as Solara slid her fingers into his hair, pressing their bodies together almost in desperation, and then–

And then Solara came back to herself.

She hadn't felt it when Nikara took control of her mind, but she felt it distinctly as Nikara vacated, releasing her thoughts like someone spitting out something foul. Solara reared backward so violently she stumbled and fell, her palms grating against the uneven cobblestones.

For a moment, she was so confused she couldn't understand what she was seeing. What had happened.

Tessan stared at her, too shocked to move.

Fear propelled Solara up, and she turned and bolted back the way she'd come, the way Nikara had drawn her, as Nikara's harsh laughter rang out. "Bye, Sol! Think of him often!"

CHAPTER ONE

Ten days of rain had reminded Diadem City of the status quo. The city's first three rings, with their glass spires and drainage systems, had been polished to a near unbearable sheen. The gold-tinted cobblestones and copious stained-glass windows amplified the blinding effect. But in the four remaining rings, everything had turned to sludge.

Solara muttered no fewer than twelve curses per city block as she made her way through the fourth ring toward work, dodging puddles of unidentifiable muck. It was a relief when she passed through the gates into the third ring, automatically ducking her head to avoid the stern, piercing gazes of the soldiers on duty.

Yes, please don't get arrested. Her twin brother's psychic voice was *almost* always welcome in her head, except in moments like these, when he thought he was much funnier than she did.

I didn't ask you, Lu, she retorted, and her brother laughed. She could see him in her mind's eye as she'd left him that morning, sitting beneath the sole window in their dingy apartment, hands busy with sewing.

That's the trick, isn't it? Lunaro said. *You never have to.*

Solara rolled her eyes and ignored him. It was a bright, beautiful day, but the air was taut with electricity, and people rushed about their business, heads low and shoulders high as if to protect themselves from impending rain. There were servants in dull raincoats and nobles under brightly colored umbrellas or rattling by in carriages. Here, nobility and the help mingled, twisting and twining around one another like intricate stitching. Solara had to squint in the brightness, but she knew her route by heart. She'd tired of the view ages ago, though she never tired of the smells. She passed through the baker's district and her mouth watered at the aroma of fresh baked bread and frosted pastries.

Sometimes she wished she were a baker instead of a seamstress, though her current job paid better. She passed through the millinery and then into the seamstress' section, which was one of the largest. Over thirty shops lined the roads, each one with its windows full of fabrics in every color.

Solara's place of work was not the largest, but it was the most imposing. Its front windows were red glass etched with a borderline grotesque scene from *Storybook of War*, where two women were in the process of gutting a battalion of man-beast hybrids. Above the door, a cut wood sign read "BJORN'S BATTLEMENTS, because clothing is armor."

The well-educated children of nobility were probably not raised on the storybook of gore and heroes, as Solara had been, so she didn't know how many of the shop's patrons knew the image. But it always made her smile as she passed beneath the sign and entered the shop. "Good morning, ma'am," she said cheerfully.

Bjorn herself stood at the front counter, a slim woman in her late fifties with a braid of salt and pepper hair down her back. Age and sun had faded her tattoos, of which she had many, so they were barely visible against her dark skin. "Hm," Bjorn said. She wasn't much of a talker, though her thoughts were loud enough.

She looks shaky today, Bjorn thought. *That child will waste away before my eyes.*

"Almost late," Bjorn added. She polished her counter, her head lowered and her long lashes hiding her eyes.

"I come bearing gifts." Solara brandished the satchel hung across her shoulder and chest. Between her and Lunaro, they had mended two raincoats, a lady's skirt, and half a dozen blouses last night.

She looks so gray this morning, Bjorn mused. *He must be hunting her again.*

Solara's throat tightened, but she kept her smile plastered on her face. Bjorn had no idea the strength of Solara's gift, how easy it was for Solara to hear the woman's thoughts. Bjorn was a private person. She wouldn't want such a gift around her, no matter how lucrative Solara had proven for the odd little business.

Bjorn's Battlements had begun as a costume shop, but Bjorn's skill with a needle and thread was unparalleled, no matter what she plied them to. Bjorn hired Solara three years ago specifically to assist her with a fairytale wedding gown for a costume party in the first ring, the Center, but when the job was done, Solara had just never left.

"More projects in the box," Bjorn said.

Solara nodded and went to the intake box, where mending jobs were dropped off. She gathered the armful of projects, each wrapped in brown paper and tied with twine. One smelled of a delicate floral perfume, and Solara resisted the urge to hold it to her nose as she carried the packages into the back room.

The storefront was Bjorn's domain, with its shelves and racks full of finished product. She stood behind her large wooden counter like a queen. But here in the back room, everything was raw. A dozen dummies stood in soldier-like rows, each one clothed in a half-finished dress or coat, polka dotted with pins. Behind them, fifty bolts of fabric hung on bars welded to the wall.

Amidst it was Solara's chair, surrounded by three worktables, each one hidden beneath scraps of cloth, spools of thread, and cases upon cases of needles. She settled into her seat. Its cushion was rounded to the imprint of her body; she'd spent hundreds, maybe thousands of hours here, her thoughts moving as swiftly as her needle.

Out in the front room, Bjorn puttered, her movements as practiced as a dance. She was comfortable here, as Solara had been, once upon a time. Tessan had changed that.

She didn't have time to dwell on it – as she would have, no matter how hard she tried otherwise. The bell chimed over the front door, and Solara's thoughts shifted toward the three new presences. High-pitched, female thoughts, though these were not full of ribbons and hemlines and nightgowns, as patrons' thoughts usually were.

"If I were her," one girl said, "I would have killed myself long before he got the chance."

The second girl laughed. "You would have at least tried to kill him first. They can say what they like about wild animals. I bet Tessan carved her up and ate her himself."

Solara grimaced. It wasn't rare for customers to come in discussing Tessan Manfalon's latest exploits, but these were not just any customers. The voices belonged to his sisters. Roga and Maliq. Their thoughts screamed it, proud of their lineage.

The third presence hadn't spoken. It was muted and colorless like sand. Solara lowered her head over her work as if she could shut that shell of a soul away from herself.

"Solara," Bjorn called.

Damn. Solara stood, spilling her armful of fabric into her vacated chair, and returned to the front room, brushing nonexistent wrinkles from her skirt. Three girls stood at the front counter. Roga and Maliq were smaller versions of Nikara, with the same long dark hair; Roga's was braided, and Maliq's was in locs. They had the same chiseled cheekbones, hazel eyes, and full lips.

"Good morning, ladies." Solara swept a curtsy. "How may I help you today?" She couldn't look at the third girl.

Roga, the elder sister, twisted one braid around her index finger, her head tilted. "I have a complaint to make."

"I can't imagine my work was subpar in any way, but I am here to serve," Solara said, knowing full well she was overstepping. Maliq smirked, but Roga's lip curled in an ugly snarl.

"Aliss," Roga said, and the third girl stepped forward. Solara had no choice but to look at her. Aliss was emaciated, red haired, with vacant eyes. Her hair hung loose and tangled; it clearly had not seen a comb in some time. She had a distinct, heart-shaped scar on her breastbone, pale against her ochre skin. "Aliss," Roga said again. "Show the little shop girl what happened this morning."

Aliss lifted her silky scarlet sundress over her head and dropped it in a pool on the floor.

Bjorn tsked her disapproval. Beneath the dress, Aliss wore a white nightgown with red embroidery. Solara's handiwork, hours of it. The side seam had torn, leaving a gash open along her side, and exposing a violent purple bruise on the girl's ribs.

Solara's gaze snapped back to Roga, but Roga just tipped her head the other way, a bored smile on her lips. "And this was just ordinary use. Imagine if I'd actually had to beat the girl."

Steady, Sol, Lunaro said. He could feel her fury rising.

What had Roga done to Aliss? Beat her with a poker? Aliss stood dumbly, staring at nothing. Such was the life of a well maintained Second. Their job went by many definitions, but Solara had never thought of them as anything other than psychic slaves.

It was simple, really. Horribly so. Someone with a greater psychic gift – in this case, the bitchy Roga – consumed the Second's will, until they controlled their thoughts and actions like a puppeteer making a puppet dance. The stronger the Master, the more of a hollowed-out shell the Second became.

"Shall I have her take it off for you to repair?" Roga said. She would probably enjoy stripping Aliss naked in public. Solara glanced out the front windows. People hurried by on the streets, not bothering to look in at the debacle.

"Take her into the back, Solara," Bjorn said. "It won't take long, my ladies."

Solara picked up Aliss's discarded dress with a shaking hand. "Come with me, Aliss." She took the girl's arm and led her away. Aliss's steps were awkward and halting, unsure without her Master ordering her movement. They made it into the back room and Solara closed the door. She pressed her fisted palm against the door for a moment, fighting for composure.

Aliss stood in the center of the room with perfect posture. She didn't have the presence of mind to be ashamed of her nakedness or her bruises; the one on her side was not the only one, Solara discovered. Aliss's torso was a maze of injuries in various states of healing.

Goddamn the Manfalon family. Roga and Maliq, and who knew who else, had beaten Aliss within an inch of her life. Aliss only blinked, thoughtless, not even flinching as Solara worked around her. There were no laws to protect Seconds, not once they had surrendered their will. As far as officials were concerned, Aliss belonged to her Master. There was no one to tell, no one to go to for the help Aliss clearly needed.

"Does it hurt?" Solara asked, looking into the girl's dull eyes.

Aliss didn't react, but Solara felt a surge of anger, of hate, so blinding and burning that she had to catch her breath, dizzied by it. It hadn't come from Aliss. The girl was too far gone. But before Solara could pinpoint its origin, it disappeared.

It didn't take her long to finish her work. She dressed Aliss again, lifting her arms and sliding them through the sleeves. Aliss may as well have been one of the mannequins in the corner. Solara had seen hundreds of Seconds before, but none this empty. Roga must have been an impressive psychic, to hold Aliss so tightly.

"Solara!" Bjorn barked, as if she could sense Solara dragging her feet.

"I am so sorry," Solara whispered. In all likelihood, Roga could hear her. She could access Aliss's senses as easily as opening a book to read. But Solara had to say *something*. She took Aliss by the hand and led her into the front room. Maliq puttered amongst a rack of walking coats, and Roga stood at the front windows, looking out at something.

"I'm here, my lady," Solara said. "It's finished."

"You're slow," Roga said without turning around. She was being petty. Even dallying, Solara was quick. She thought Roga might be able to feel Solara's hate radiating out of her, because Roga turned around with a sickening smile on her lips. "Come along, Aliss."

Aliss didn't move. She looked, if anything, more vacant than ever, a dreamy expression on her face as she stared out the front windows. Solara followed her glazed stare.

Across the street was a man. He was the only one standing still on the sidewalk, so it was easy to mark him.

"Aliss!" Roga shouted.

Everyone jumped. Aliss's fingers went limp and slid out of Solara's hand. She lowered her head and followed Roga out of the shop. The door hit her in the shoulder, but she didn't seem to notice. Maliq, looking uneasy, followed them. The man had vanished.

Bjorn put one hand to her chest.

Solara exhaled a long, shuddery breath. She shouldn't ask any questions. It was none of her business. But she turned to Bjorn. "Who was that girl?"

Bjorn gave her a reprimanding look. "Roga Manfalon?"

Solara started to explain that she was asking about Aliss, but at the last second, she closed her mouth. Bjorn probably didn't know, and her thoughts were growing irritated with Solara.

She is always causing some trouble with that family, Bjorn thought. *It's as if they all seek her out.* Her thoughts flickered to Tessan, and Solara ducked her head and went back to her room.

CHAPTER TWO

Solara hadn't hated the nobility of the Diadem until Nikara Manfalon. At twenty-one years old, it felt like her only concern for her entire life had been her and Lunaro's survival. She hadn't known enough about nobility to care one way or another. Nikara had certainly made her care.

There were so many things about that night that had terrified her. Nikara's smile, saccharine and deceptive. Her calm cruelty. The thoughts, not Solara's own, had been frightening enough. But it was the false emotion, shoved into her like stuffing a pillow, that had shaken Solara to the center of her being. She had looked at Nikara and loved her with every bit of her heart.

Sometimes, when Solara closed her eyes, she saw Nikara's face and those old, twisted lies tried to assert themselves: Nikara was beautiful and graceful and generous. But those thoughts weren't Solara's. Nikara was dangerous. She was a Manfalon. And the Manfalon's owned the city.

Then there was Tessan. Thinking about him made Solara walk faster toward home, holding her satchel against her chest like a shield against the falling dusk.

He must be hunting her again, Bjorn had thought that morning, and that was precisely what Tessan had done.

Two weeks after that night, Solara had been at work, manning the counter while Bjorn was out to lunch. She had heard the bell chime and lifted her head, a cheery greeting on her tongue that had instantly died.

Tessan was as massive as she'd remembered, filling the doorway and then some. He was every bit as attractive as his sister, which Solara had not needed to be reminded of; she'd followed Nikara's order. She'd thought of him often. He'd stood in the doorway for a moment, his eyes adjusting to the muted light. Through the red windows she had seen his bodyguards, two of the infamous Scarlet Guard in their crimson armor.

"Solara," he'd said. As if they had known each other forever. As if they were important to each other.

It had been cruel, Nikara forcing Solara to tell them her name. It had made it easy for Tessan to find her. That day, he'd merely greeted her and asked after her health. She hadn't been able to answer without stammering, her heart dancing against her ribs. But he'd given her many chances to improve her conversation skills by coming to visit once a week. It was never the same day, and the unpredictability had her on constant edge. He never came under any pretense. Bjorn, and anyone who happened to be in the shop, knew he came to see her. He'd stand at one end of the counter and talk to her between customers: about his horse, the weather, his younger sisters. If Solara was in the back room, he'd stand in the doorway, one shoulder braced against the jamb.

It had gone on for months. But abruptly as it all began, it ended. Five months later, he stopped coming. It had taken weeks for Solara to stop expecting him every time she heard the bell jingle. He must have found someone else to hound, some other unlucky girl he thought pretty.

It was then that Solara had begun to pay attention. She listened to what the wealthy talked and thought about as they rummaged the store and passed her on the street. Walking down the street tonight, she had to be hyper-aware, not just because her chances of being robbed grew greater as she approached the fourth ring, but because if she had the gall to bump into a nobleman, she could be beaten for that infraction.

Solara had had many unfortunate encounters with nobility, though she'd been lucky enough that they didn't end in beatings. The customers who could afford her and Bjorn's work were highborn, used to having their own way, without delay. She had been scolded, screamed at, and a few times, they would even lift a hand to strike her, although no one had ever followed through. None had quite the impact as the Manfalon siblings, but altogether, they had forged a new hate in Solara's heart.

And now this, today. Aliss.

Solara's footsteps slowed to a halt. Was it her imagination, or had Aliss squeezed her hand before letting go? How much of that poor girl's mind remained beneath her blank façade?

Across the street, a group of women walking home called out to her. "Better hurry home, little chick! It's going to rain!"

Solara shook herself, forcing a smile to her lips. "I will. Goodnight!" She watched them go, grateful to be disturbed from her morbid thoughts. *I hope you're cooking a twelve-course meal,* she thought at Lunaro. *I'm starving.*

Her brother didn't respond. There was a stark emptiness in her thoughts where normally she could sense him.

In the same instant, someone seized her from behind, a rough hand clamping down on her mouth. Solara screamed, but it was muted in the thick leather glove, and her attacker snaked an arm around her midsection, pinning her arms to her sides.

"Don't make this difficult," he said. "If you want to see your brother, come with me. *Quietly.*"

She stopped struggling.

"Are you going to behave?"

Shaking, Solara nodded. The man let go of her mouth, then took her by the wrist and pulled her after him. He took Solara down a succession of alleys until they came to a carriage parked on the side of the road beneath a stand of trees. He opened the door and hoisted her up by one arm, stuffing her inside, and shut the door behind her. A small lamp in the corner illuminated the claustrophobic space and the lump on the floor. Lunaro. Solara dropped to her knees next to her twin, shoving his dark tangled hair back until she could press two fingertips to his pulse.

"I'd be a poor negotiator if I killed my trump card."

Solara lifted her head. Sitting on the bench was the man from the street. She hadn't gotten a good look at him earlier, but she recognized him immediately. He had the same long red hair as Aliss, the same soft gaze. He, however, was alert. His eyes held a calculative look that put her instantly on guard.

That wasn't the worst of it, though. She couldn't hear his thoughts. Solara could hear *everyone's* thoughts. It was as easy as walking into a room. Sometimes, if they were a stronger psychic, the door would stick a little, but she could open it, if she wanted to. This man, however, was a vault. It wasn't that she couldn't open the door. There was no door.

"Who are you?" she said hoarsely. He was nobility. This was an obscenely expensive carriage. The seats were upholstered in silk, and the lantern base was pure gold. The man himself wore several diamond rings, and his clothes had been tailored to suit him.

"My name is Lord Faisal," he said.

Solara wilted. Lord Faisal Casarriba, of the Casarriba empire. The Casarriba family owned water. All of it. The river. Water puddles. Raindrops. It was part of the deal made amongst the six lords who founded the Diadem over a century before. Of the original six families, only two remained – Manfalon, Casarriba – and the Casarribas had always been known as the kinder ones, until Faisal.

"I see my reputation precedes me," Faisal said, smiling dryly.

Lunaro was out cold, and even if he hadn't been, there was no escape route. Lunaro was paralyzed from the waist down. Running wasn't an option. Solara tried not to think of how scared he must have been. Had men burst into the house? Dragged him from his chair? Hate constricted her throat. Why hadn't she sensed something was wrong?

"I plucked your name from your mistress's head, when it was clear I could not pluck it from yours, Solara Barthelme," Faisal said.

"How do you know me?" she said. "Why does it matter what my name is?"

Faisal studied her, and Solara lowered her eyes. Her brother, who'd always been significantly larger than her, seemed small on the floorboards. His pulse was steady, but he was heavily drugged. She couldn't sense a whisper of his thoughts.

"You're an incredibly powerful psychic, Solara," Faisal said.

"There are lots of powerful psychics," Solara said.

"I said incredibly," Faisal said. She supposed he would know. Faisal Casarriba went by another name. The Dancemaster. According to the rumors in the dress shop, he had once taken control of eight assassins sent to kill him and forced them to dance a ballet until they dropped dead of exhaustion. Eight. No one had ever controlled that many before.

Faisal had never taken a Second, although with his strength he was probably capable of maintaining several. Nikara, his nearest rival, kept six, and judging from the gossip in the shop, it never seemed debatable that he was stronger than her. The rumor around the city was that he'd never taken a Second because he could enslave any mind that went past him. The other hypothesis was that he trusted no one, certainly not a weak-minded slave, to keep his secrets.

When all was said and done, it really didn't matter. He was strong enough and rich enough to do whatever he wanted to her, and no one could help her. No one would want to cross him.

"What do you want with us?" Solara said, her voice smaller.

"I have no interest in your brother," he said. "Just in you." His tone grew brisk. "I have a proposition for you, and I will make it simple. I want to hire you."

"I will never be a Second." She breathed the words, but he heard her. Solara hunched her shoulders, prepared for blowback.

"You don't have a choice," Faisal said. "I did my research on you, Solara Barthelme. Your parents died when you were young. Your brother had a short but successful run as a cage fighter until he lost the use of his legs two years ago. You've been the breadwinner ever since. You're scraping by, but barely. Bjorn debates daily whether she can afford to keep you when you attract so much negative attention in her store. They're predicting a harsh winter this year, and you barely survived the last one."

The first sentence out of his mouth made the hair rise on the back of Solara's neck. She stared at her brother, fighting the tears that gathered in the corners of her eyes. Lunaro looked peaceful, but she couldn't deny that his cheekbones were more apparent than they'd been last year. His collarbones jutted out a little farther.

"I don't want you forever," Faisal said. "I want you for a year. And in exchange, I will see to it that you and your brother are comfortable for the rest of your lives."

"And if I say no?" she said quietly.

"Then your brother doesn't wake up."

Solara's head shot up. Faisal gazed down at her, unperturbed. He had a harsh face, as if he had never truly smiled.

"There's a minute difference between killing someone and allowing them to die," Faisal said. "I prefer to do the latter. It makes sleeping easier." He nodded at Lunaro. "Your brother is trapped inside his mind. If I never let him out–"

"Let him out," she snarled.

"I will," Faisal said. "When you take the bond." He watched her, a glint of amusement in his eyes. "You're sitting on a lot of rage, Miss Barthelme. Choose your next move carefully."

"Wake him up," she said. "Or I swear–"

"What do you swear?" Faisal interrupted. "Are you going to attack me? I did my combat training like every good little noble boy, and I was good at it. You can try to turn that powerful mind on me, but you're talented, not trained. I'm very well trained."

Lunaro wasn't moving. Even in his wheelchair, he was always moving. Sewing. Gesturing. Wheeling around their tiny apartment at top speed. He didn't like to be still. Solara swallowed hard. "Wake him up first."

Faisal shook his head. "The bond first."

Solara laid her hands against Lunaro's arm and imagined the words he always said when she was afraid. *Build me a wall, Sol.* Solara closed her eyes. In her mind, the mental barrier rose, a behemoth of white marble veined with pink. It was a hundred feet tall, its top coated in shards of pink glass large enough to cut a man in half. Gritting her teeth in concentration, Solara began to build. She dug a moat as deep as the wall was tall and filled it first with black water, then the monsters of her childhood, horrific man-beasts from the *Storybook of War* with so many teeth they could barely fit in their gaping maws.

Next, she grew a dark forest to surround her citadel with twisting, malevolent trees. She filled the forest with more beasts that could run and howl and shred an intruder to pieces.

When she opened her eyes, Faisal was smiling. "Do we have an agreement?"

Could she do it for Lunaro? Solara looked at her brother again, his face identical to her own. He'd said once they would never become so desperate as to sell her mind. They'd do anything and everything else first. But his life hadn't been in the balance then. She leaned down and pressed a kiss against his tangled hair. "I'll do it."

CHAPTER THREE

The carriage carried them to the Casarriba mansion, the river house. Solara stayed on the floor beside Lunaro, clinging to his limp hand. She'd never laid eyes on the river house, and as they pulled into the driveway, she couldn't help but sit up straight, craning her neck to see out the window.

The house was built over a massive underground river that provided all the running water in the Diadem. Solara, like most people, had never seen the river and didn't expect to. The house itself was a spectacle of white stone and black glass, towering four stories into the night sky. The first level was built entirely of stone, sprawling out for tens of thousands of square feet. Each ascending layer was more glass and less stone, until it reached its crowning glory, a round glass tower that even in the pitiful starlight shone like a bolt of lightning.

The carriage halted. Faisal disembarked first, and then the man from before – his name was Markan – lifted Lunaro's unconscious form. Solara almost tripped over her skirt as she climbed down, sticking close to Lunaro.

Faisal led them into the house through a long, damp hall. The walls seemed to hum, but it was too dark for Solara to see anything. She followed Markan and Faisal's footsteps, her shoulders drawn close. She told herself not to violate Markan by reaching out for his thoughts, but they were right there for her.

Not much of a thing, but less wretched than the last one.

The last one?

Solara held her own hand since she couldn't reach Lunaro's. Her ring, their father's wedding band, cut into her palm. But she couldn't make herself let go. They made their way up an ascending hall and entered the house proper: a bright room lined with gilt torches. It took Solara a

moment to realize the walls were made of glass. They were in a glass tunnel that arched over a courtyard below.

They passed back into a stone section of the house. A flight of intricate stairs led up to a glass landing, and Markan stopped at the foot of them. They were unlike any stairs Solara had ever seen; each step was a perfectly round glass disc attached to the wall with metal bars.

"Those don't look very sturdy," she said.

Faisal was already ascending. "Come along, Miss Barthelme."

She looked at her unconscious brother, willing his thoughts to stir and make their way to her through the secret tunnel she kept in her wall. But Lunaro was silent. And then… something had come in through the tunnel, shimmied through the crack in the wall, and it was like winter settling over her mind. It coated Solara's thoughts with frost.

Faisal reached the landing and turned to face her, his face blank but his voice amused as he whispered straight into her head, *Hello, Solara.*

Solara recoiled and nearly fell on top of Markan, who caught her with the flat of his arm and held her on her feet.

Don't fall.

Solara took a step backward.

"That will be all, Markan," Faisal said. The guard nodded and beat a hasty retreat, taking Lunaro with him. Solara tried to protest, but she was disoriented, disturbed by Faisal's presence in her head. No one had forced their way into her mind since Nikara, and she'd sworn that night it would never happen again. But it was happening. Right now.

In Solara's head, Faisal marveled, taking in the battlements. *What an extraordinary mind you have, Solara Barthelme.*

Solara had frozen like a startled deer.

Faisal strolled through Solara's head. He saw her house, the packages of work she brought home, their little table. He saw Lunaro in the combat cage, heard the sickening crunch of her brother's spine, and how she had screamed for him. She'd dragged her brother home on a tree branch. He'd blacked out from the pain.

Then Faisal reached for another memory, and like hitting a locked door, he stopped. He tugged. With physical eyes, he studied her. "What's in the shadows, Sol?" Her nickname rolled off his tongue with disturbing ease.

The Manfalon siblings were in the shadows. But that was a locked-down box of her mind that no one, not even this man, could force. And that emboldened her. Solara began slamming doors in her head, twisting the locks, throwing bolts, sweeping out the snow. Faisal grinned and pushed back. They flung their weight at the same door, and it held.

"Come now, Solara," he said. "Don't be selfish."

She'd promised herself. Never again.

The door slammed, foisting Faisal out, and her head was hers again. Solara's heart pounded, but Faisal was unfazed. "Do you have any idea the strength it requires to push me out of your head?" He didn't wait for an answer. "Come with me."

Did she really have a choice? Solara started up the stairs.

"Have you always been this strong?" Faisal asked. He strode down the hallway.

Solara dug her fingernails into her palm, forcing her voice to come out flat. "No."

Faisal paused, glanced back at her. His keen gaze missed nothing, and she stared stonily. He resumed walking. This hallway was built of etched glass, a hunting scene unfurling before them as they walked. "And your brother?"

Solara hesitated but answered truthfully. "His only power is in the twin-bond." People said the twin-bond was how psychic ability had begun, a union in its purest form.

Faisal reached out, finding the thread that ran between her and Lunaro. "Uncommonly strong," he said.

They had come to another flight of stairs, and Solara balked. She could see a well-lit room at the top, but it might as well have been a dungeon. He was taking her farther and farther away from her brother. Faisal said, "I am not going to hurt you, Solara, although I will drag you up these stairs if you're going to be difficult. I won't keep you from your brother for long."

Solara felt the third presence join them.

"Is she supposed to be my replacement?" At the far end of the hall, a small girl, perhaps fifteen or sixteen years old, stood with arms crossed. Her short hair was shaved nearly to the scalp. What remained was bright blue. It made for quite the statement, and it was certainly not the hair of a noble girl, but her tone was not the deferential one of a servant.

"No one replaces you, Mage," Faisal said without even looking at her.

"Was it that impressive?" Mage demanded. She sounded offended.

"She kicked me out," he said.

"She had to let you in first," Mage shot back.

"She's untrained," he said.

"And let me guess," Mage said. "You could train her. Faisal–"

"Solara, come," Faisal said and resumed his climb. Solara glanced at Mage and was surprised again by the utter disgust in the girl's eyes. She was no ally.

Solara hurried up the stairs after Faisal. They were now in the glass turret, in a circular office with a round table in the center. A few books and papers lay spilled over its polished surface, and a wine decanter and several glasses sat at one end. The view was beautiful: the city to the left, a garden of light; the forest to the right, a landscape of shadows. Faisal gestured to a chair, but Solara made no move to sit.

He sat on the edge of the table, crossing his ankles. He kept a psychic hand on her fortress walls, steady pressure. Was this a game to him? Did he find strong psychics and use them for practice? Was she going to last a year?

Mage stepped into the room but stayed near the doorway. Her presence joined Faisal's in Solara's head, pacing the boundaries.

"She's a vault," Faisal said with relish.

Mage scoffed. She seemed too young to sound so scornful. "That doesn't mean she's trustworthy."

"With a Second's bond, she won't have a choice."

Solara set her teeth, and Mage smirked. "She doesn't look like she takes no for an answer. She's worse than me."

"She knows the price for disobedience," Faisal said. "The longer you stall, the greater the chance I can't wake your brother back up. I've given you your choices, Miss Barthelme. If you'd like to change your mind–"

"Better not," Mage counseled. "You don't want to make the Dancemaster angry."

Faisal shot her an irritated look, and the girl flashed a feral grin. "Mage, if you're going to be dramatic, get out." Then he turned to Solara once more. "Are you ready?"

No. Solara had heard it wasn't painful. She'd also heard it was like ripping your soul out of your body. Faisal straightened and went to the wine tray. Solara's courage almost gave out. She'd seen this moment before, in Seconds' heads. They never forgot this part – the moment they lost themselves. Faisal poured a glass of wine.

"Sit down," Mage said. She was taking pleasure in this. There was a hard, almost bitter look in her eyes. Replacement, she'd called Solara. What did that mean? "Have a drink."

Solara sat in the chair Mage nudged out for her. She twisted her brass ring on her finger, filling her head with images of Lunaro. Awake. Talking, reading, swatting her hands away when she tried to brush his hair. But never again in the cage. Never again subject to the mercy of some monster who enjoyed inflicting pain.

"I think she's having second thoughts." Mage's dark eyes sparkled.

"Mage, stop being a pain," Faisal said. He took Solara's hand and put the wine glass in it. The scent was overwhelming. It wouldn't take much of it to compromise her, which was the whole point. *Forgive me, Lu.* Solara picked up the wine glass and swallowed the contents in one breath. It was much, much stronger than any liquor she'd ever had. It burned her throat and made her eyes water. She set the glass down, her hand still gripping the stem. Whatever it was, it worked quickly, softening her limbs, making her vision glossy and unclear.

A cool wind stirred at her barriers, but the walls, the moat, the spikes, held.

"Look how she fights it," Mage murmured condescendingly. "I hope you're not getting in over your head, Faisal."

Through her haze, Solara felt Faisal step up behind her, steadying her head. The powerful scent of the wine hit her again. "Swallow slowly," Faisal said. He held a second cup to her lips, and Solara did as she was told.

In theory, all the walls came down. The doors flew open. Everything was laid bare, and the Master seized control. But it didn't happen that way. Solara opened a single, small door through the wall, and Faisal entered.

She was two people: the girl slumped barely conscious on the table, and her mind-self, who stood in the fortress and watched Faisal prowl the corridors. The doors were open. He went where he pleased, and she stood, and she watched. He saw that when she was nine, her father had placed this brass ring on her finger and a kiss on her forehead. He saw her mother, tucking Solara and Lunaro into bed, each with a baked sweet potato to warm their hands, and for a snack, because otherwise they would both crawl out of bed and go to raid the kitchen on their own.

Lunaro, breaking, in the cage.

Bjorn, her approval and scorn and jealousy.

Then, the door. The locked door. Some part of her struggled to keep it closed but it was too late. Faisal saw Nikara, felt her silken laughter and the hand she'd tucked under Solara's chin.

Solara cried out – whether in the memory or in reality, she wasn't sure. It was happening again. Someone had broken in. And on pure instinct, she struck. Like a viper, she went after Faisal. The path between

Master and Second was supposed to be one way, but she drove down the bond between them and speared straight back into his own thoughts.

Shock.

Fear.

And then a scrambling, walls coming up, enclosing that blank space, but it was too late. Faisal's mind was a palace, a twisting, mirrored palace that sent her reflection back to her a million times over. But his reflection, too. She saw a boy, barely sixteen, sitting at the bedside of his mother wasting away.

She saw Mage, even younger in the memory, a starving thing in rags, trying to mind-control Faisal into giving her his money. How he'd laughed at her before scooping her up, a screaming ball of rage, and bringing her to the river house.

She saw him standing on the other side of the road earlier that day, seeing her in the shop, as she stood bristling between Aliss and the Manfalon girls. He'd thought Solara looked fierce.

She saw… Aliss? Laughing, in a garden, turning back and saying, *You're my brother, Faisal. You're not allowed to bully me. You're supposed to protect me.*

And then rage, blinding and searing and all encompassing, like what she'd felt that morning. It blew her backward out of his head, and she snapped conscious, almost falling out of her chair as she vomited.

Mage shook Faisal, who had slumped over the table. "Faisal! Faisal, wake up!"

Solara's head ached. It felt like her boundaries had stretched, doubling the size of her.

"Faisal!" Mage screamed.

He jerked awake, and their gazes locked. A shudder ran through them both.

Hello, Faisal.

His lip curled. There. There were her boundaries, on the other side of him. A palace of glass and mirrors to complement a castle of glass and stone.

What have you done?

Solara didn't know.

"What's happened?" Mage's voice trembled. Her gaze flitted back and forth between the two of them.

Faisal stood. Solara stood, too, in perfect sync. He tipped his head one way, and she went the other. Or perhaps she went one way, and he went the other. Where had the thought originated? Somewhere in the center of them. She was herself, but she was also a cold wind, a dusting of snow.

"You made me a promise," Solara said. Faisal mouthed the words with her, not a second behind.

"I know what I said," he said. Solara knew his words before he spoke them. Mage gripped his arm, her eyes wide and frightened. Rightly frightened, Faisal thought. Something had gone wrong. He didn't know who was in control. Who was Master, and who was Second?

"Faisal, what is going on?" Mage hissed.

"Mage, it's long past your bedtime," he said. "Go to your room." She started to protest. "Go now."

Mage glowered but whirled and stalked out, slamming the door behind her.

Faisal tipped his head. Solara mirrored.

"What did you do?" he said quietly.

"I don't know," she said. She tipped her head the other way. This time, he didn't move. "I must have been stronger than we thought."

"Tell me–"

"What you're thinking? That you've made a mistake and–"

They finished the thought together. "Solara cannot be allowed to live."

She felt no fear at the pronouncement because she knew the rest of his thought process, too. Wondering how this could work. If she could be trusted. If this, perhaps, was not a superior bond to a simple one-way path. She marveled at the ease with which she slipped between their thoughts. Theirs, not hers and his. More doors in her house.

Then he said, "Tessan."

A shudder roiled down her spine. Through both of their spines, because he, too, felt her disgust.

"You must have a talent for attracting the rich and powerful," he said. She withdrew from their tangled thoughts, finding safety in her own. "A useful talent."

She couldn't see what he was thinking now. "I'm tired."

"Yes," he said, studying her. She could still taste the bitter alcohol. "You should rest." A smile ghosted over his lips. "We have a lot to do tomorrow. Goodnight, Sol."

CHAPTER FOUR

arkan took Solara to her brother. It was a short walk, and although each step took her farther from Faisal, she could still feel him. Markan took her to a pair of bedrooms joined by a cozy sitting room. There were at least a dozen windows. When the sun rose, this light-filled space would be the opposite of their apartment.

"He's in there," Markan said, nodding at one of the bedroom doors. "I'll leave you to him." He didn't lock them in when he left, but Solara supposed he didn't have to.

She went to the bedroom. Markan, or whoever had done the kidnapping, had brought along Lunaro's wheelchair. It sat in a corner of the room. Lunaro was on the bed, beginning to stir. Solara crossed the room and sat on the edge of the bed. "Lu?"

He lifted one hand to rub his face. "Sol?"

"Are you all right?"

His hand dropped to the covers. He squinted in the dark, confused. "Where are we? What happened? I was in the apartment and then…" He sat up, taking in the room. "Sol?"

Any other day, she could have simply given him her memories, instantly catching him up on everything that had happened. But she couldn't make herself open the crack in the wall. She had always kept that passageway for him, and no one had ever found it. It was too late to protect herself from Faisal now, and yet she was still tense, defensive.

"We're in the river house," she said. "Lord Faisal… took us. He wanted me as a Second."

Lunaro stared at her. "What did he do when you said no?"

Solara could already picture her brother's reaction. "I didn't say no, Lu."

His expression was disappointed, then angry. "Whatever they promised you, it's not worth it," he said. "We're not that bad off, Sol. I can work more. I barely need to sleep. I–"

"Lunaro, stop."

"We'll take on more projects," he said, frantically. "Magdalen at the butcher's shop will let me work for her. She's already said so. We can make this work."

"It's just for a year. And he's going to pay me really well, and we never have to worry about anything ever again."

Lunaro went silent. She felt how badly he wanted it to be true. Then, his voice hard, he said, "This is insane, and you know it. And even if it wasn't–"

"What if it isn't?" she said. "We're getting by, Lu. But what if something happens? What if I get hurt or you get sick? What then? One thing goes wrong, and we're ruined."

Lunaro leaned closer, looking intently into her eyes. "You'll be a *shell*. What is the point of having money if the only person I care about ceases to exist?"

She wanted to promise that it wouldn't happen that way, that she was strong enough to fight back. But was she? There was nothing she wouldn't do for Lunaro. He had gone into the cages to fight for her. Bruised and bloody and broken, every night, so that she could eat and go to school. The fights had scarred him, but he was still as handsome as he'd been as a carefree boy. *Little boy Lu, pretty as the moon*, their mother used to sing.

"Stop it," Lunaro said stonily. "Stop looking at me like that."

"It's a good agreement," she said. "A roof over our heads. Enough to eat. I'd do it for that alone."

"Then you're an idiot," he snapped. "A stupid, wishful idiot."

"I don't care," she said.

"Sol, *please*." He took her hands. His own hands had grown soft, the scars of the cages worn away. "This isn't the way."

Solara gently pulled away. "It is now. It's already done." Lunaro's shoulders slumped, and Solara felt like she'd slapped him. She stood up, blinking rapidly. "Try to get some sleep, Lu. I'll see you in the morning."

She left the room quickly, holding her breath so she wouldn't cry.

Solara slept like the dead. Two placid-faced servants woke her late the next day. One drew a bath, the other laid out some clothes, and they left her alone. She sat on the bed for several long, silent minutes, alone with her thoughts. But not alone. Because there was Faisal, a small presence, like a cat lounging on a windowsill.

She got up and went to bathe. The water was chilly, and she didn't stay in it for long before rising to dress. Seconds were dressed in all manner of ways according to the whims of their Masters. Faisal, it seemed, was purely practical. Breeches, polished boots, and a sleeveless white blouse. Solara re-braided her hair and then went to check on Lunaro. He was asleep, his thoughts foggy with dreams.

He'd always worked as hard, if not harder, than her, insisting he wasn't tired. She couldn't remember the last time she'd seen him sleeping.

Nearly two hours later, a soft knock came at the door. She slipped away from Lunaro and went out into the hall. It was Faisal. He wore an elegant white suit and situated in the curve of his throat was an obscenely large diamond.

Faisal looked her over. "Are you ready?"

"For what?" she said curtly. Any pretense at manners had gone out the window overnight. Besides, she knew he didn't care. Not really. Not when every incensed thought she had moved freely between their heads. He already knew she wanted to shred his face.

"Today is my birthday party," he said. "I've invited all the so-called best the Diadem has to offer. Your job is to watch and learn. Learn their faces. Their voices. Their mannerisms. When the party is over, I'm going to ask you a lot of questions, and if you can't answer them all, that will be unfortunate, for you and for your brother. Give me your hand."

She already knew his intention, and she offered him her left hand. He removed a diamond ring from his pocket. The stone was as big as her thumbnail. "All of my important servants wear one," Faisal said, slipping it onto her ring finger. Her father's brass band looked pitiful beside the gold, and Faisal grimaced but said nothing. He knew she wouldn't take it off.

"People are going to ask you endless questions," he said. "You are Solara, my Second. Nothing more. Nothing less. Keep your walls up."

"I don't need to be told that," she snapped.

His lips quirked. "No, Solara. You do not."

"What's going to happen to Lu?"

"Servants will attend him," Faisal said. He didn't care about Lunaro. He'd made that clear enough. She fell into step behind him as he began walking. They passed servants, their thoughts loud but orderly, focused on tasks. They were people Solara had never seen before, but now she knew their faces and names.

"What is Mage?" she said suddenly, slowing her steps.

"Mage is my ward," he said, because he could sense her apprehension. "She's gifted, as you are, but too bold and stupid for her own good."

He thought Mage would have died if he'd left her on the street, using her gift recklessly. Solara caught something else, too, a stab of concern that Mage was out of control, but he dismissed the thought.

Would Solara be like Mage if she hadn't had Lunaro? The streets were a hard place when you were alone. Solara had seen her classmates, the friends of her happy childhood, in places and positions she never wanted to see again. The Diadem was built for the rich, everyone else be damned.

Solara had a thousand more questions, but she set them aside. For now. She began to watch.

Faisal had a long, swaggering step, chin up, eyes hard. She could hear voices, and she felt a swell of thoughts as they neared the ballroom. Mage was already there. So were a dozen other psychics at least as strong as Mage. The air felt heavy with their power.

Miss nothing, Faisal said, and they entered the ballroom. At least three hundred guests were packed into the massive room, a rainbow of colors and fabrics.

The first thing Solara saw were the Seconds. Men and women, some children, of every ethnicity, height, and coloring. Some were dressed extravagantly enough to rival their Masters. Some wore plain black shifts that were little more than a square with head and arm holes. Some wore bruises as openly as jewelry. One man kept his hand very low on his Second's exposed back, despite his glowering wife's presence. All of them had varying levels of their own identity remaining.

If Solara had one, all-powerful wish, it would be to end the practice of Seconds. Maybe to strip psychic ability from everyone, so it wouldn't even be possible.

Her vehemence amused Faisal, but he didn't comment. A man in a blue suit stopped them, his wrinkled face wreathed in a disingenuous smile. "Faisal," he said, taking his hand. He winced at the strength in Faisal's grip. "Happiest of birthdays, my lord."

"Thank you," Faisal said. His tone was nothing short of contempt.

The man's gaze skated over Solara. "Who is this sweet creature?"

The moniker rankled her, but Solara started to bow. Faisal's wrath froze her in place. She straightened her spine. "Solara," she said. "A pleasure."

Bow to no one, Faisal said frigidly. *And it is* not *a pleasure.*

Then he moved on, and she moved after him, two steps behind, committing the face to memory. Lord Kaiser. Faisal's third cousin. And, judging by the hateful thoughts Kaiser sent after them both, no friend.

They made their way around delicacy-laden tables and towering floral monoliths, greeting false friends and grim politicians. Faisal didn't appear to be truly attached to any of these people whatsoever, although for the most part he kept his more vicious thoughts to himself. No one seemed surprised by her presence, dismissing her as a servant.

They approached a group of men with their backs to them.

"Good afternoon, gentlemen," Faisal said, and the men turned.

Solara recoiled. Tessan Manfalon. The others didn't matter. All she saw was Tessan.

"The birthday boy himself," one said. He clasped hands with Faisal, the warmth faked.

Tessan, too, had gone still, his gaze locked on Solara. It had been six or seven months since his last visit to the seamstress shop, but she would never forget the details of him. He stood a head taller than the others, the sharp cut of his muscles apparent even beneath his well-tailored suit. It infuriated Solara that she couldn't *not* notice. His smile, when he flashed it at Faisal, was tight and joyless.

After her first shocked glance, Solara stared at an empty space between the men. The smallest man watched her with curiosity, and he prodded at her defenses, surprised by her strength.

The other two men were inconsequential beside Tessan, and in her panicked state she was incapable of gleaning their identities, although they both watched her with great interest as Faisal introduced her. "My Second, Solara," he said, gesturing for her to step forward.

But that would be one step closer to Tessan, and Solara didn't move.

Disbelief flashed over their faces. Doubly wary now, Solara shifted minutely closer to Faisal, although she had no misconceptions about what protection he'd offer. *Remember these faces,* Faisal told her. *These names.* He introduced her to each of them, finishing with Tessan, as if an introduction were required.

"A Second?" one of the other men said. "I thought you frowned upon it."

"I frown upon the linking of a superior mind to an inferior one," Faisal said. Solara wondered if he was trying to sound like a pompous ass. "Solara is suitably extraordinary." They all studied her harder, and she made herself stand very still, giving no indication of her discomfort. "She won't be a burden."

"God forbid someone burden you," Tessan said. His voice was cold. Solara glanced at him once more and then locked her frigid gaze on Faisal.

It isn't my face you need to remember, Solara. Watch.

She wanted to claw his face into ribbons. She lifted her chin and thought of her brother. She could do anything for Lunaro.

The quartet struck up a song, and Tessan said, "Do you keep your Second like a slave, Faisal, or is she allowed to dance?"

No no no no no no no.

"If she wishes," Faisal said.

I will kill you, you bastard, she fired at him.

Watch your language.

Tessan held out his hand to Solara. Solara had the sickening thought that he could crush her skull in his palm. "I'm a terrible dancer," she said.

"I'm talented enough for the both of us," he said and took her by the wrist.

Faisal, please *don't let him.*

But Faisal merely smiled, and Tessan pulled her onto the dance floor. The floor was crowded with dancers, but everyone made room for Tessan. Perhaps it was deference. Perhaps it was fear. He put his hand on Solara's waist, and she tensed, a passive resistance, but he didn't need her cooperation to move her effortlessly across the dance floor.

The music sounded far away, and the two of them moved in silence. Tessan was very comfortable with silence. He could spend an hour in the shop without saying a word, simply watching. Quiet made other people nervous, but not him. It must have been because of what he was: a stone mind. No psychic ability whatsoever. No amount of training or effort would ever allow him to hear another person's thoughts, and no one would ever hear his. Solara couldn't imagine the volume of such emptiness inside your own head.

It was a rare phenomenon, and the favorite explanation for Tessan – who came from a family of such strong psychics – was that he'd consumed his twin in the womb, destroying his ability to connect to anyone. Roga was known to say he still enjoyed the taste of human flesh. It was a stupid, petty story that Solara didn't believe. Mostly.

Tessan twirled her once, then drew her back close. He smelled like expensive ink and peppermint, and his body heat was overwhelming. Solara had never been able to tell if his temperature ran hotter than the average person or if her heightened emotional state was playing tricks on her. Her legs were leaden, but he moved her easily. She felt like a child, standing on the toes of her father's boots while he taught her basic steps.

"Why are you here?" Tessan said abruptly.

Solara startled. "I didn't have any choice in the matter," she said and then immediately wished she'd given a more straightforward answer.

"He dragged you here against your will?" Tessan's hand on her back tightened. She could feel each individual fingertip in the divot of her spine.

This was the longest song in the world. He twirled her again, and she saw Faisal in her peripheral, greeting Mage without a care in the world. "One way or the other, it is none of your concern, Lord Tessan." She tried to sound unbothered, but he had always bothered her and seemed unaware of it. The warmth of his hand seeped through the thin material of her shirt. She could feel the ring he wore. She wished she was not so aware of it all.

Tessan's gaze bored into her, and she stared stubbornly at his chest, refusing to look him in the eye. "Being a Second doesn't ever end well," he said. "I think that's especially true if you're the first of Faisal's."

Solara glanced up. She couldn't help it. Did he know what Faisal was planning to do with her?

"You aren't safe there, Solara," Tessan said.

With a last twirl of flute notes, the song ended. Several dancers clapped, and the sound ended their staring match. Solara stepped backward out of Tessan's arms, inclined her head, and walked swiftly off the dance floor. She went to a table and, although she didn't know the rules about this, upended a thimble glass of whiskey into her mouth.

Pay attention, Faisal said.

Kiss my ass.

The whiskey was a terrible idea. Her head ached already. She scanned the room, aware now of the attention she'd drawn to herself. That Tessan had drawn to them. Faisal's cousin. The small man and the other two, whose faces she'd forgotten and now had to remember. Several shrewd-faced women nibbling on little cakes.

See who's watching you. Remember those faces.

The small man's eyes were keen on her, taking in her every move. Jas, a Manfalon cousin. He didn't know exactly who she was, though he had heard Tessan mention her name twice before. The women. Two of them turned to each other now, hands moving as they spoke. Solara pushed herself out of her own shaking thoughts and focused on theirs.

Plain-faced sow. She's the one? The common bitch Tessan chased after?

Solara bristled, and, across the room, Faisal laughed. She set her empty glass down, a little dizzy now, and made her way toward Faisal. He warned her away, and she casually changed direction and went to the table full of cakes. A gaggle of women stood there, chatting amongst themselves.

"Hello, pretty thing," one said.

Thing. Solara bit back a snarl, already sick to death of everyone in the house. "Good afternoon," she said.

"Were you and Tess having a bit of a spat on the dance floor?"

"I told him I was a terrible dancer, but he insisted on attempting it," Solara said. She picked up a delicate glass plate with a round yellow cake. The lemon pastry melted on her tongue. "My name is Solara. I am Lord Faisal's Second."

The woman's painted eyebrows rose. "What an honor."

"It hasn't been a day yet. I have a lot to learn." She finished the cake in another bite, and then, although she knew it would be frowned upon, picked up another, this one beautifully iced with pink and red. Let them look down their noses at her. She'd never had anything that tasted this delicious.

"Where do you come from, Solara?" another woman asked. "I can't place your accent."

Yes, she probably knew very little about the fourth ring, unless she was of the crowd that enjoyed slumming it on the weekends. "Here and there," Solara said blandly. The other ladies introduced themselves. Solara stored away their names and faces, the evolution of their expressions as they explained where their families were from, how they were connected to Faisal. A friend's cousin. A golfing partner's sister. They were all several stages removed; no one introduced themselves as a friend outright, which did not surprise her in the least.

When Solara had gleaned everything she could, she moved on to another group, this one a mixture of men and women both young and old. She introduced herself, and they made room for her in the circle, but warily. They weighed their words, studied her face, gazes flitting from her to Faisal, who was across the room and paying her no attention. They wondered how tightly wound this bond was. If Solara had any control of herself, or if they were simply speaking to Faisal through a different face.

This was a whole new world, but as the evening wore on, it didn't feel new. A side effect, Solara assumed, of having so much of Faisal's memory and emotion at her fingertips. He was comfortable here, so she was, as well. She wondered if the discomfort she should have felt had been displaced onto him.

The party dragged on, and as the clock chimed midnight, Solara drifted back to the table of alcohol. She reached for a glass, but another hand darted in and snatched it.

"Should you be drinking that?" Mage said.

Solara deliberately took another cup. "You're still up? Your governess should have taken you to bed."

Mage breathed a laugh. "So, you do have a little bit of spine. Or is that him?"

"It's hard to tell." Solara sipped her drink, trying not to grimace at the bitterness. "Tell me. Have I made any egregious errors in my deportment tonight?"

"You have an impressive vocabulary for a common bitch," Mage said. She'd been listening to the gossip, too. Solara wondered how strong Mage's gift was, but she was hesitant to push her. There was a street-born savagery in the girl that she couldn't hide, even while pretending to be part of high society. "Although I suppose I should have expected it," Mage went on. "Faisal only chooses the most talented of us, you know."

"And here I thought he chose you for your complete lack of manners," Solara said.

Mage flushed. "It's none of your business why he chose me," she snapped. "It's your business to be good at what you do, and drinking yourself under the table isn't it." She turned and stalked off, flinging back psychically, *Uppity whore.*

Solara blinked at the hate in the girl's tone, then her lip curled with distaste.

You will need to learn to control your face, Solara.

Faisal had kept his distance all night, and the sudden appearance of his voice startled her. She drained her glass, set it down, and turned to face the room. The quartet was playing a melancholy song, the flutist starring. Across the room on a dais, Faisal lounged in the chair of honor. His posture was relaxed, but there was no disguising the watchfulness in his eyes.

Why don't you want me near you? she asked.

He smirked. *Did that offend you?*

I want to understand this game we're playing. Solara followed his wandering attention, hoping she hadn't missed something he would question her on later.

You'll understand soon enough. You have an admirer.

She glanced left. Tessan and Jas sat at a small table. Jas was speaking, but Tessan wasn't listening. He was watching Solara. He had a very intent gaze that seemed to pull not only her attention but most of the people in the room, because the moment their eyes met everyone noticed. A flurry of thoughts filled Solara's head, but it was Jas's who rose above the noise, as they were intended specifically for her.

You made a mistake coming into his world, little girl.

Solara turned away, not even attempting to control her expression, both hot and cold from the combined threat and attention. Faisal had been in every recess of her mind. He knew how she felt about Tessan. It was cruel of him to put her in this situation.

This is your training, Solara, Faisal told her. *Control your fear. You will face much more terrifying enemies than him before this is over.*

CHAPTER FIVE

It was two in the morning before Faisal left the party. Twelve hours of revelry was exhausting. Solara was so tired she was barely conscious. Tessan had left over an hour ago, a boisterous entourage with him, clamoring about a bar. He'd looked around for her before he left, but she'd ducked behind a table, and she didn't care who'd seen her do it.

Mage had retired shortly after her rude exchange with Solara. She'd gone up to Faisal to say goodnight, and he'd dismissed her with a cool wave of the hand. Mage accepted the insult with a smirk because she knew it was all a game. He cared more for a single hair on her head than he did for the rest of the people in the room combined.

Faisal made his exit swiftly, and Solara scampered after him, her thoughts on her bed and her brother. They left the ballroom behind and ascended a flight of stairs. At the top, in the quiet of the landing, Solara said rudely, "Are you finished with me yet?"

Faisal turned around, loosening the collar of his shirt. "Lady Merisande."

"Redhead, with pearls in her ears. She's terrified of Mage and lusts after you."

That amused him, though his expression didn't change. "The dark-haired man with the gray tie."

"Regus Coffer, a consultant for Lord Roon Manfalon. He decides how much money is spent on armor, and he believes the Manfalon family spends too much on a show of might."

Faisal leaned against the wall, arms crossed. "Tessan Manfalon."

Solara's jaw tightened. "Second eldest of Roon Manfalon. Twenty-three. Commander of a battalion in his father's army. Not exceedingly bright."

"On the contrary," Faisal said. "He scored top marks in primary school and later in the military academy. He's exceedingly intelligent. People too often equate weak psychic ability with a weak mind. Don't let your personal issues cloud your judgment." He straightened, letting his arms fall to his sides. "Me."

Solara didn't hesitate. "Lord Faisal Casarriba, heir to the Casarriba empire. Watchful. A good liar." She cocked her head, and he mirrored the movement instantly. "You're hiding something from me. I can feel the weight of it, the secret, but you're keeping it from me somehow, like a room within a room."

Faisal laughed. "You do not disappoint me, Solara."

"Good," she said. And she meant it. "Are we done?"

Faisal beckoned for her to follow. He led her all the way back to the apartment, though she could have found her own way. It was close to the river; she hadn't noticed that yesterday, but she could hear the water rushing somewhere below their feet. Faisal lifted his hand to knock on the ornate door, but Solara suddenly reached out and caught his arm, stopping him. Faisal lifted his eyebrows in question.

She knew this door. She had seen it in his memories when they bonded. "Aliss," she said, and the muscles in Faisal's arm went rigid. "Your sister, Aliss."

"A servant will collect you in the morning." He shrugged her off. "Goodnight, Solara." He left.

Solara watched him go, her exhaustion temporarily replaced by curiosity. What was a highborn lady doing as a slave? And did Tessan

Manfalon have no soul at all, to come to Faisal's birthday party while one man's sister enslaved the other? And, finally, was it a coincidence that Solara had met brother and sister in the same day? She entered the room, seeing again in her mind's eye Aliss's face and the light in her eyes.

Lunaro sat in his chair at the window. He was a strange picture, his hands idle in his lap.

"Lu." It felt like a lifetime since she'd last seen him.

He looked at her, his expression cold. "You snuck off like a rat and left me here."

She sank onto the couch. "Don't scold me."

"You're still alive."

"Of course. I'm fine. Are you?" She looked him over. He wore the same clothes he'd been in that morning, although his chair had been scrubbed clean. Solara wondered if someone had tried to bathe him and gotten the brunt of his fury, as she had many times before.

Lunaro studied her. "You look... strange. Clean."

Their smiles were simultaneous. "It is strange, isn't it?" For work, Solara had kept her hands immaculate, but the rest of her body was fair game for grime. She looked at her clean nails, and Lunaro saw the ring.

"What is that?"

"Apparently all of the high ranking Casarriba servants wear a diamond." Her voice had the taint of Faisal's dry humor.

"Where's mine?" he said lightly, but anger swirled in his thoughts. He was offended for her, for the desecration of their father's ring.

They sat silently.

"Did it hurt?" he asked.

She wanted to lie, but he knew her too well. "Yes." She toed off her boots and drew her knees to her chest. "It's bizarre. Another voice in my head, as loud as my own."

"You still sound like you."

"I am still me." Solara glanced at him. "You should take a bath. Did they bring you clean clothes?" She fingered the soft material of her shirt. "They're really nice."

"Your price is an expensive shirt? It doesn't even have sleeves."

Solara laughed. "It's summer, Lu. I don't need sleeves." She got up and began exploring the apartment again, this time with new eyes. Which of these bedrooms had belonged to Aliss? "It's really beautiful here," she called back to her brother.

"What do you think he wants from you?"

"I don't know." She came back into the sitting room and collapsed on the couch once more. "But I'm not as afraid as I was." His sister had adored him. Surely, he couldn't be all monster.

"He might be controlling your thoughts already."

She shot him a testy look. "I think I would know."

"That's the danger of it, Sol," he said. "You wouldn't know. None of us would know, not until it was too late."

"Trust me."

"I do. I'm just..." He exhaled hard. "It's not like they locked me in this room, but..." But he felt trapped, and she couldn't blame him.

Solara rested her chin on her knees. "I'm sorry, Lu."

"Don't bother being sorry," he grumbled.

"I think I'm going to be summoned very early in the morning. I need to sleep." She came over and kissed Lunaro's cheek. "I love you."

"I love you, too." He muttered it.

Solara went into her bedroom, tossed her new clothes in a pile on the floor, and then crawled under the soft coverlet. Despite her restless thoughts, she was out in an instant, deep into a dreamless sleep that lasted until the precise moment that Faisal, wherever he was in the house, woke the next morning.

She took a moment to remember where she was and why. Then she got up. There was a fire in the fireplace. Yesterday's clothes had been removed, and a fresh set lay folded on a chair.

By the time Solara had bathed and dressed, she could sense the servant coming to the door, and she went out to intercept before their knock could rouse Lunaro, whose thoughts were slurred in sleep. He'd stayed up so late last night, worrying, he'd probably sleep the day away. Again. She had a moment of concern, wondering if his deep sleeps were of his own choosing. Who knew how much power Faisal held over him?

She dismissed the thought as paranoia and opened the door just as the servant lifted her hand to knock.

"Good morning," Solara said. The girl was afraid of her, wondering what mind was behind Solara's dark eyes.

She gestured for Solara to follow and started down the hall. The sun was just rising, and the house was aglow. Despite the heat outside, the house itself remained cool. The walls hummed with the movement of the river below. Servants moved silently through the halls, carrying breakfast trays, towels, and firewood. They passed at least twenty on their swift trip, and none wore a diamond ring. There was one other servant in black breeches and a white shirt like Solara's. He did not project the distant aura of a Second, but there was something not quite right in his thoughts, and Solara twisted back to watch him go.

Mind your own business, Solara.

Faisal's voice made her shudder. She faced forward, but only because the man had turned the corner. *Do you match us all in these pretty clothes?* she said sarcastically.

This city enjoys dressing its Seconds in disgustingly overblown outfits. I have no wish to be associated with that frippery. So, yes. You match.

He looks like a doll.

They came around a corner into a lovely breakfast room, and Faisal rose from the round table, saying, "So do you."

The servant girl dipped a curtsy and fled. Were the servants terrified of Faisal or the combination of her and Faisal?

"Am I to be subjected to another interrogation?" Solara asked.

"Mage is right. Your vocabulary is rather impressive for your humble beginnings. Is that a product of your eavesdropping or did your parents teach you to read before they died?" Faisal said it snidely, and Solara started to flip him off but then thought better of it, although by then he'd already read her intent in her thoughts. He smiled, more a baring of teeth. "Don't forget your place, Second."

"Don't be so hasty to put a name on this bond, Master," Solara said. The faintest of snarls curled his lip. He knew as well as she did that this, this was not quite right. Something had gone crooked when she surged back into his mind. Perhaps she was his Second, subjected to his will. But perhaps not. And the moment she decided to push that theory, one way or another, the status quo would shatter.

They stared at each other testily. Then she moved to the other chair at the table and sat down without being invited.

He debated checking her impudence. But then he exhaled softly and sat down. "I'm taking you into the city."

"More watching?" She picked up the glass of water. The rest of the table's contents looked much too sweet for breakfast, and she had a headache from last night.

"This time, you'll be watched." He sat back in his chair. Even at rest, Faisal was rigid, elbows at perfect right angles on the armrests. "Do you have something against food, Solara?"

She shrugged.

"You didn't eat last night."

"I was nervous," she said. "Are we going somewhere specific to be watched?"

"I have a golfing match with Lord Manfalon."

She coughed on her water. Some of it spewed over the table, and Faisal moved her embroidered napkin within easy reach. Solara snatched it up to dab at the moisture on her lap. "What is your business with him?" she demanded. "And why am I a part of it?"

"You don't even know which Manfalon I meant," he said.

Solara waited.

"Although I did, in fact, mean Tessan," he said, and her eyes narrowed. "But I'll explain my business when I'm ready, and not a moment before, so wipe that insolent look off your face."

The chill in his voice matched the chill through the bond, as if he'd laid a frozen hand on her physical body. She schooled her features, her teeth grinding as she struggled to contain her anger. When her face was blank, Faisal smiled.

"Much better. You're useless to me if you can't control yourself." He gestured, and a servant appeared from nowhere to collect her untouched plate. "Bring Miss Solara something to settle her stomach. Quickly. We have somewhere to be."

The servant bobbed and left.

Attempting a civil tone, Solara said, "Are you taking me just to be cruel, or to unsettle Tessan?"

Faisal shook his head. Her question disappointed him. "Your mind is only as useful as its security, Solara, and if you're going to fall apart every time you look a Manfalon in the eye, it will be difficult to trust you." The servant returned, and Faisal paused as the girl set the plate on the table and then disappeared once more. He studied Solara as she ate her plain toast. "There was a rumor for months that Tessan had a paramour–"

Solara choked on her toast and had to grab her water once more.

"–and we were all curious," he said, frowning. "I can't imagine he's so delusional as to have been referring to you."

"He stalked me," Solara said. That was possibly unfair. Tessan seemed happily oblivious of his effect on her, but that just meant she could despise him for being stupid. "But that's been done with for months."

"Tessan," Faisal said. And Solara knew the instant her face curled into a snarl that he was proving a point. "Control. Your. Face."

She snatched a piece of fruit off her plate. "I despise him."

"One would think the bulk of your hatred was reserved for Nikara."

It was Solara's fear over which Nikara had a monopoly, but Solara didn't want to admit it, even if Faisal already knew. "Does it not make you uncomfortable, too? The silence?"

Faisal looked curious. "What do you mean?"

"Around him," Solara said. "I always thought stone minds just meant you wouldn't hear their thoughts, but I can hear his silence, when I pay attention."

"I don't understand the difference," Faisal said.

Solara didn't know how to explain it any better. Maybe she was too sensitive when it came to Tessan. She changed the subject. "Am I expected to be civil at this meeting?"

"Yes."

She smiled. "You have very high expectations of me, Lord Faisal."

"Do I? You didn't look nearly as afraid of him last night as I expected," he said. Solara bit the insides of her cheeks to keep her expression neutral. "And he is certainly enamored by you. Eat your breakfast."

Solara didn't touch it.

"Don't cut off your nose to spite your face, Solara," he said. He turned his head slightly, as if he'd heard something, but then he said, "Your brother is up."

"I. Know." She had felt Lunaro stir a second before.

"Tell me about your bond with your brother."

Solara lifted her fork and speared a slice of pineapple. "I imagine it's much the same as yours with your sister, Aliss."

Faisal's cool expression didn't change. "It's always been speculated the bond between twins is the strongest equal bond one can have," he said. "Though the power does seem to tip in your direction."

The accusation – was it one? – made Solara wrinkle her nose. She shrugged her shoulders. "I don't know how to explain it."

"You've given your brother orders before."

Solara ripped her bread in half. "Not intentionally."

"So, you're an unintentional dictator." They glowered at each other. Solara didn't know how far she'd be able to push him without consequences, although it seemed to keep happening.

The door opened. Mage stepped in, halted when she saw them, and then shook her head. "The two of you make me feel uncomfortable," she said.

The tension eased out of Faisal. "Is that so?"

Mage sauntered into the room and leaned against the back of Faisal's chair. She scrutinized Solara over Faisal's head. "Do you really think this is a good idea?"

"It's never been a good idea," Faisal said. "That doesn't mean it can't be successful."

The infant is allowed to know your intentions for me but I'm not? Solara demanded.

I hope it's no reflection on me that my chosen prodigies are both so infantile, he returned, unconcerned.

Mage straightened. There was a hard look in her eyes. "I know you're talking to each other and it's eerie."

Faisal removed his napkin from his lap and laid it over his plate. "I'm going golfing. Are you going to behave for your lessons, Mage, or are you getting in trouble when I get back?"

Mage flashed an angelic smile. "Well..."

"Your mind is a waste if you won't use it," he said sternly.

"I'm brilliant and I don't need dull lessons to prove it," she said. "I came to tell you I was going into the city, and" – here she turned to Solara – "I'm taking your brother."

Solara and Faisal were both surprised.

"I'm taking him to the physician," she clarified. "Anyone with a drop of gift can see how sad he is about his legs, so I'm taking him to a specialist to see if they can be salvaged. Your presence isn't necessary. I'm taking some guards to look after him, so don't fuss."

Solara stared at her.

Mage looked embarrassed. "Faisal said we were giving him a good life. Don't get excited. He's probably crippled forever, but I thought I'd try."

The twins had assumed he was paralyzed forever. They hadn't been able to afford a proper doctor, not then and certainly not now. Solara glanced at Faisal, trying to gauge how much she should trust the child holding her brother hostage. "I'd rather be there with him."

Mage won't hurt him, Faisal said. *She has her orders.*

"We don't need you," Mage said, the flicker of irritation in her eyes indicating she knew they were, once more, conversing beyond her hearing. Solara tried to imagine someone intruding on her twin-bond with Lunaro and the mere thought discomfited her.

"My brother doesn't–"

"Faisal," Mage said slowly. Solara had hit her limit. "Are you going to tell me I can't go just to keep your project happy?"

Faisal sighed. It was a sound of defeat, because Faisal knew he was overindulging Mage and simply didn't care enough to fight her on it. "Be careful, Mage," he said, and the girl shot Solara a triumphant look. "And do your lessons," he called after her as she flounced out of the room. He couldn't meet Solara's eye as he pushed his chair into the table.

"What a lovely child you've raised," Solara said. "Who would ever know she was common when she fits in with the Manfalon sisters so well?"

Faisal went still, and Solara regretted her words. She shouldn't have said that. Not when those same sisters were holding Aliss.

"Finish your breakfast," he said curtly. "We need to go."

CHAPTER SIX

An hour later, as they made their way toward the golf course on horseback, Solara said, "I apologize for what I said." The road they traveled was covered with arching, flowering trees, its soft dirt footing muting the horses' hoofbeats. This was her first time ever on a horse, but it felt like she'd done it a thousand times before. A perk of shared thoughts with a great horseman. Their trip thus far had been in silence.

"I do not require your apology," Faisal said.

"Regardless, I'm giving you one. I think that child's a monster, but she's hardly as bad as they are." It wouldn't be long until she was, though. The terms of the agreement had seemed straightforward when it came to Lunaro. He was in no way beholden to Faisal. Faisal had no control over him. And yet, here they were, with Mage whisking him away for her amusement, cutting Solara out of it entirely.

She wanted to tell Lunaro she was sorry, but she didn't dare open that link.

"Mage is young," Faisal said. "Her power's gone to her head, and she can be difficult. But you'll learn the particulars of her temper soon enough."

His nonchalance pissed her off. "If I don't beat her senseless first."

Faisal wheeled his horse around so fast that Solara's horse startled, nearly tripping over itself to get out of the way of the larger mare. Solara shrank back from the hateful expression on Faisal's face, her ire sputtering.

Faisal steadied his breath. "Believe it or not, Miss Barthelme, I understand the difficulty of the situation I've placed you in. And I consider myself a temperate man. But I will have no mercy on anyone who lays a hand on that child."

A flicker through the bond. A memory. He tried to brush it off, but Solara latched onto it too quickly. There was Mage as the filthy child he'd met on the street, fighting him like a feral thing when he hauled her back to the river house. He'd handed her off to a trio of maids to clean up, and later one had come to him, her head bowed. *My lord, the girl is… someone has been beating her. For a long time.*

And then the memory surged into that tsunami of hate she'd come to know so well, and all she heard was a man – Mage's father – screaming.

Solara let go of the memory, even as she winced at the sound. It seemed to reverberate through her bones. "I don't care about Mage," Solara said. Faisal was still glaring at her. "My only interest in her is that her pettiness doesn't hurt my brother."

Faisal jerked his horse straight once more, and it gave an angry shake of its head at the abuse. "Mage will honor my promises."

"That's supposed to relieve my fears?"

"It's a fact. I don't care about your fears."

Solara was going to injure her jaw from the amount of teeth-grinding she saw in her future. But she had pushed enough for one morning. She didn't want to see Faisal really lose his temper. She forced herself to think of other things: straight, perfect stitches; Lunaro's window and the lovely view he had from the river house; the grace and beauty of the two horses.

The road widened into the vast, grassy field of the golf course. Immaculately kept lawns spread over rolling green hills, and in the distance was the clubhouse, which was a tall white stone building.

They arrived at the clubhouse several minutes later. A man in livery took both horses at the front door, and Faisal strode inside, Solara falling in behind. He'd given her no further instructions about this latest test. Inside was a large yet homey room filled with solid oak furniture. Two gentlemen sat beside an empty fireplace, one smoking a foul-smelling cigar and the other taking a late breakfast. Although the room could have comfortably sat some sixty people, the two men were the only ones there.

Both came to attention when they saw Faisal. The cigar smoker was well into his sixties, and the other was somewhere in his early twenties, but they both bowed low.

"Lord Faisal," the elder man said. "This is a surprise."

"Welcome, I hope," Faisal said. They shook hands. "Who is this?"

"My grandson," the man said. "Cote."

"It's an honor, sir," Cote said. He sounded eager and childish, and Solara was embarrassed for him.

Then Faisal gestured for her to step forward. "My Second, Solara. Solara, this is Mr. Goodwin. He worked for my father."

Ah. A genuine relationship, at last.

Don't presume to know anything, Faisal said mildly.

Solara bowed to Mr. Goodwin and nodded at Cote. The latter had a gentle, unguarded mind, and for that reason alone she tried not to listen to his thoughts. But he was of the unfortunate majority that seemed to be shouting them at the top of his lungs. He found her attractive and thought it a pity she was tethered to Faisal, and then he wondered if they were both reading his thoughts right now, and his face flushed as he scrambled to think of a blank wall.

"Golfing so early?" Faisal said, gesturing for the men to resume their activities. "Wander off, Solara," he said. "Don't get lost."

Bite me, she thought.

Continue to aggravate me and I might.

Holding back an irreverent smile, Solara began to explore the room. There were several private nooks and crannies, and she found one a safe distance away, surrounded by tall bookshelves filled with ancient-looking books, many of them in foreign languages. She ran her fingers over the well-conditioned leather bindings, sounding out the words silently.

Such wealth around her. She was used to it only in bits and pieces, in the expensive clothing that passed through her hands at the seamstress shop. Solara felt a pang of homesickness for her little back room. Was Bjorn worried about her? Did she even care that Solara had vanished? So much had happened in such a short span that her other life felt a world away. Here she was, Solara the seamstress, tethered to the second wealthiest family in the city. Family. The word made her thoughts flicker back to Aliss, but she couldn't begin to puzzle out that mystery.

She picked a book from the shelf, then made herself comfortable in one of the overly large leather chairs. It was a book of faraway lands, filled with engravings of exotic animals. She paged through it slowly, running her fingers over the fine ink, as if she could feel the texture of the strange beasts, their feathers and furs and claws. She was so engrossed in the images that it took her a moment to realize the men had gone silent in the other room.

Solara lifted her head and listened. Cote's rambling thoughts had faded away. The three of them had gone out on the green. Faisal hadn't summoned her, so she resumed reading.

Control your face, Solara, Faisal warned.

You can't even see me.

"Hello, Solara."

She shrieked. While she was absorbed in her book, Tessan had arrived. Such was the danger of someone with a stone mind. She couldn't hear his thoughts coming, and she'd completely forgotten they were there to meet him.

He stood in the opening of her nook, his hands in his pockets, looking startled at her outburst.

Faisal had left her here on purpose. Like bait.

"I didn't mean to scare you," Tessan said, self-conscious.

Solara closed her book and held it to her chest. "I was so caught up in my book I didn't hear you arrive, Lord Tessan." Perhaps she couldn't control her face, but her voice was calm.

He stayed in the doorway. Studied her. Studied the books. Everything. "Are you enjoying it?"

"The book?"

Tessan gave a slight shake of his head. "I saw the way you looked at Seconds in the dress shop all those weeks," he said. "You always had such disgust in your eyes. And now, here you are. You don't look unhappy."

He was capable of being observant when it suited his interests. "I don't think you read my face very well, Lord Tessan."

Tessan took a step into the space, and her grip on the book tightened. He came no closer.

"Shouldn't you be on the green?" she asked. Control. Control.

"Faisal told me you were here," he said. "I suppose he knows our history, if your bond was successful."

What, exactly, is our history? Solara wanted to say. But even if he'd been willing to answer, she wasn't willing to hear his side of the story.

"You seem afraid of him," Tessan said. When she remained silent, Tessan took another step toward her. Perhaps the worst thing about him was that his face was kind. But if he did possess any great kindness, Solara had never seen it, and neither had anyone else. The Diadem knew Tessan as cruel and calculating. In the market, Solara would hear people gossiping about when – never if – he was going to murder Nikara to take her place as heir to the family's empire. And of course, there had been his fiancé, dead in the woods, half eaten by forest creatures. She had had one predecessor, and that woman had out of the blue flatly refused to marry him. The theories as to what scared her were many and horrible.

"Solara?" Tessan said quietly.

What am I supposed to tell him, Faisal?

Silence.

Abandoned again. She didn't know what he wanted from her, what either of them wanted from her, and it was making her ill. Her breakfast swam dangerously in her stomach, and suddenly the closeness of the room, of the heavy books and shelves, made her want to bolt, as she had that night. *Think of him often, Sol.* Nikara had chosen her parting blow well. Solara couldn't claw this man out of her head. "I should see if I'm needed." She rose, set her book on its proper shelf, and turned to go, but

Tessan stood between her and the exit, and she didn't want to pass that close to him.

"You're a Second, Solara," Tessan said, a hint of anger in his voice. "I'm sure the great Lord Faisal will summon you with a dog whistle straight into your mind."

She drew herself up to her full height, although it was laughably small compared to him. "Do you expect me to apologize for doing what's necessary to survive?"

He took a step forward, and she took a step backward. "Do you understand that this bond can't be broken?" he said. "Not by you. You're his to command until he decides otherwise, no matter what he may have promised you."

"It's none of your concern," she said.

Tessan took another step. He towered over her, solid as a wall. Was he unaware of the sheer power like an aura around him? Was it intentional? Solara didn't know whether to hate him for being stupid or for being a bully. With forced nonchalance, she said, "None of my life is any of your concern."

"Am I not allowed to care about what happens to you?" he said harshly.

"You've never cared before about what happens to a Second." The words lashed out of her too quickly to stop, and Tessan's eyes narrowed. *I'm scared.* The thought escaped, winnowed off to Faisal, but she couldn't sense him, and he didn't answer. Tessan must have been taking all the air in the cubby because Solara struggled to breathe, her chest so tight it ached.

A shrill whistle split the air.

"Come, little doggy," Faisal called. "We're going home."

Solara shoved past Tessan and tore out into the main room.

Control your face, Solara.

She didn't acknowledge Faisal as she flew past him, just stormed out into the sunlight, shaking, her eyes welling. She heard him speaking to Tessan, but she didn't wait. She made her way to the stable where their horses waited.

Her mare nickered a greeting, and Solara leaned against her warm neck, pressing her eyes closed to staunch the tears. She would not cry. She would not.

Footsteps. She whirled around, saw Faisal through her tears, and lashed out. He caught her wrist before her palm connected with his face, but even their conjoined thoughts were not enough to warn him before she lifted her leg and slammed her knee between his legs. He cursed and doubled over.

Solara's words were a hiss. "How *dare* you–"

He stood upright, face flushed with pain, and snapped, "Lay a hand on me again–"

"Don't you dare threaten me." She didn't know if she was speaking audibly or searing the words into his brain. "Why are you doing this to me? Why in the hell–"

"Because." He didn't speak the rest, just flung a series of images and emotions into her head that stopped her, because she had been going to strike him again.

She stood there, stunned. "What?"

We. He fought back a grimace. *You. And I. Are going to kill his sister.*

C H A P T E R
S E V E N

They made the ride back to the river house in silence. She trailed Faisal dumbly into the house, and they went up to the glass office. Faisal sat on the edge of the table. "The day I saw you in the dress shop, I was following Roga and Maliq Manfalon." Speaking their names pained him.

"Because of Aliss," Solara said.

Faisal nodded. "The Manfalon family has more money and more manpower than any other single entity or syndicate in the city. In the territory. Roon Manfalon pays the Scarlet Guard, effectively making the police his own. His title may not be official, but he is essentially king of the city."

There had never been a king of the Diadem, but everyone knew who ran the city.

Faisal stared out the window. He softened the hard line of his jaw. Relaxed his fists. This was the closest she'd ever seen him come to losing control. "As you can imagine, the Manfalon children are not used to being told no."

Solara nodded once.

He laid out the specifics in a dull voice, as if reciting a history lesson. Fourteen months ago, Roga Manfalon, in a bid for her father's favor, had offered her hand in marriage to Faisal. He knew her intention was to take his empire and leave him dead, so he refused. She insisted. He refused again. "She took the matter very personally," Faisal said. "She sent eight assassins to teach me a lesson."

Solara's eyes widened. She'd mostly believed the story, but it was something else to hear Faisal confirm it.

Faisal smiled faintly. "That story, at least, was rooted in truth."

He'd taken control of all eight and made them dance a ballet all the way up to the gate into the Center, where they'd collapsed in exhaustion, and then promptly been dispatched by guards. But there had been too many witnesses to keep the story secret.

"My sister paid the price for my arrogance," Faisal went on. "The next day, Aliss disappeared. And the day after that, she was at Roga's side. Aliss is strong, but Roga used Nikara to force the bond."

Solara didn't know that was possible.

"Aliss has been Roga's prisoner for over a year," Faisal said. "I don't know how much of her is left." His voice wavered, and he looked down. "I've tried to usurp the bond. To overwhelm it. I'm not strong enough, not with Roga *and* Nikara holding the reins. But–"

Solara spoke softly. "If you kill Roga, Aliss will die."

Faisal's jaw tightened. "I am aware."

He couldn't leave Aliss there to be beaten and abused, not when he didn't know how aware she was. Did she feel the pain? Did she miss her home? All questions he couldn't answer. And if she were simply a simulacrum of her old self, even still, he couldn't leave her there to be mistreated. He would bring her home and bury her with the honor she deserved.

Solara took a hesitant step toward him, then rested her hand on his shoulder. He had no desire to be touched or comforted in any way, and it surprised Solara, how strongly she felt for him. "If it takes Roga and Nikara to hold the bond, maybe you and I could break it," she said. As she spoke the words, she knew he'd tried that, too.

Mage.

"Mage isn't strong enough," Faisal said, his volume dropping, as if his ward might hear and be offended. "I overwhelm her. Perhaps if she were older–"

"I'm stronger than Mage," Solara said.

Faisal looked her in the eye, a faint smile tugging at his lips. "Yes, you are. But I don't know if I trust you."

It wasn't about keeping his secret. Despite herself, Solara grinned. He was worried she was stronger than him. "You have my utmost loyalty, Master."

He knocked her hand off his shoulder and stood, going to the window. "No third person has ever broken a bond between two people before. If we attempt it and are unsuccessful, I don't know what Roga would do to Aliss."

"Take control of both of them," Solara said.

Faisal shook his head. "I can't."

"Why?"

"I have never been able to control Aliss. Believe me, when I was a child, I tried. And Roga, whether she realizes it or not, is already partially subject to Nikara. It's a cascading effect, and it's difficult to disrupt. I'm stronger than Nikara on paper but overcoming three sets of such strong wills is proving impossible." He turned to look at her. Though his expression was neutral, his eyes were full of anguish. "Nikara will know if she loses control of Roga, and she'll know exactly who to blame, and how to punish me."

He'd thought long and hard about this. Of course, he had. He couldn't just take them. Nikara would sense it, and she could obliterate their minds in an instant. And besides, you didn't kidnap a Manfalon and walk away from it. They were too well guarded. And it was clear Faisal had no intention of joining his sister in the afterlife. Probably didn't want to abandon his darling Mage. "So," Solara said. "You want to use me to get close to Tessan and then into the palace."

Faisal nodded, almost regretfully.

"And then what? I cut Roga's throat and then she, Aliss, and I all die together?" Solara's cheeks flushed. "No, they'd die together. I'd be tortured for who knows how long before they finally put me out of my misery."

"I wouldn't leave you there," Faisal said, dismissively enough that she knew he hadn't thought that far. All he cared about was rescuing Aliss.

"Yes, you would."

"Rescuing my sister is my primary concern," Faisal said. "The rest of our welfare is somewhere on the list." He shook his head. "If you think Tessan and Nikara are evil, then you cannot begin to imagine Roga. I grew up alongside the Manfalon children. I know them far too well. Nikara Manfalon is a general in her father's army. She rose to power by poisoning her predecessor with a sprinkle of arsenic over his breakfast every morning, after she'd shared his bed. I'll spare you the list of Tessan's crimes. But Roga–"

"Enough," Solara whispered. Her stomach churned. No, she did not want the list of the Manfalon crimes. She had a good enough concept of their idea of sport. Perhaps that was cruel of her. Perhaps stubbornness and stupidity were Tessan's only shortcomings where she was concerned.

Hardly, Solara. He is smart enough to know you fear him. He simply chooses to ignore it because he wishes it wasn't true.

"Are you any better?" she said.

"You and I have an agreement."

"You weren't upfront about its particulars."

"You should have asked more questions." He smiled at her vicious glance. "Your mind might be a fortress, but your face is a window."

"Stop talking about my face. If we're caught..." She stopped, corrected herself. "When you're caught–"

"Do I strike you as a careless man?" he interrupted. Unwillingly, Solara shook her head. "Do I strike you as a man who would haphazardly plot something like this?"

"No." In fact, if anyone were able to pull it off, Solara would have placed her bets on Faisal. "You pluck a girl from the streets to..." She shook her head again. "To do this."

"Solara," he said, "I want to be very straightforward with you, if only because I appreciate your intelligence and your abilities. You're going to help me, or I'm going to tie up my loose ends."

Solara waited to feel fear but felt nothing.

His expression was rueful. "I have never told anyone this. Mage knows I'm attempting to get Aliss back, but she doesn't know the extent to which I'm willing to go. I've assured her again and again that I will do nothing rash."

"You lied."

"Precisely." He did not hesitate. "The only way you and I have a chance at surviving is if no one else knows. So, if you are not with me, I am going to cut your throat from here to here." He traced a line across his throat from ear to ear. "You'll bleed out instantly and feel no pain. Then I will go and do the same to your brother."

She wondered if her face was a window now, exposing the varied emotions swirling through her.

"I realize there is no way to classify this as anything but a threat, but I don't mean to scare you," he said. As insane as it sounded, he meant it. "I want your help," he said. "Your connection to Tessan is invaluable, as painful as it is for you, and I will exploit it. But I am also dedicated to my purpose, and it means far more to me than you do."

Solara ran her hand over her face. Laughed a soft, bitter laugh. How had this happened? How had this shitty situation gotten so much shittier? How had she gone from stitching dresses to planning murder? She looked Faisal in the eye, searching for something she couldn't quantify. Something to put her faith in.

They were both defensive now, walls up in their mind. She wanted to laugh incredulously at herself. Their mind. Singular. Because an uncomfortable melding had occurred, instead of the overtaking that should have happened.

"Do you expect me to choose the painless death?" she said finally.

"I have no idea what you'll choose," he said. "And I'm trying not to make assumptions."

"You don't care to just read my mind?"

"This bond isn't as straightforward as that." He cocked his head, and so did she. "You have hidden doors of your own."

She didn't know how long they'd sat here in this room. As open, as bright as it was, she felt trapped. "I'm no spy."

"I don't need a spy," he said.

In the far reach of her mind, she felt Lunaro stir. For a moment, she'd forgotten she had a brother. She'd forgotten anything outside of this rock and hard place. Her brother was waking from a deep, drug-induced sleep. He was worried. He reached out for her, but she didn't respond. She hadn't opened the crack in her walls since Faisal had slipped through, and now she doubted she ever would.

She imagined Faisal going to her brother, drawing a blade across his throat. Would it be easier for them? Better?

No. No, she was not ready to give up like that.

"You'd better hope this works." Solara breathed the words.

Faisal only nodded.

Mage had given Lunaro a new wheelchair. It was sleek and polished, and so was he, bathed and wearing the same crisp uniform as Solara. He had been subjected to a haircut, as well, and looked livid about it as Solara entered the apartment.

"I'm sorry," she said, and he scowled at her teasing tone. "I'm looking for my brother? Have you seen a bedraggled boy, rat's nest on his head?"

"And I'm looking for my sister, an actual rat," he fired back.

Solara laughed. She didn't know how her throat could even form the sound after that meeting in the glass office. The armrest of this new chair was too slender for her to sit on, so she propped on the chair opposite him at the window. "You look handsome. Good care suits you."

"We took plenty good care of ourselves." He was reading her face. "What's wrong?"

She couldn't tell him. She couldn't drag him deeper into this. They had never kept secrets from each other. Certainly nothing like this. Solara chose her words carefully. "It weighs on me, more than I thought it would."

"I haven't laid eyes on him since we got here. Is it that hard?"

Solara nodded. Shook her head. Nodded again. "I don't know."

Lunaro tipped his head back and closed his eyes. "There's no way out of this, is there?"

"Not until he breaks the bond. A year, if he's honest." She rose and started to pace. "But never mind about me. How did it go with the physician today?"

He inhaled. "I don't know. They gave me this nasty medicine as soon as I arrived, and I didn't wake up until we were back here." His lip curled. "They'd washed me up and put me in this slave suit while I was unconscious."

She felt his anger. Felt a surge of her own. He despised being helped. She didn't know the last time he'd bathed. Her attempts to cut his hair had been met with him chucking the nearest weapon at her, and she'd give up rather than attempt to overpower him. Wrestling matches had gone poorly for her in the past. The fond memories soothed her.

Yes. As wild, as dangerous, as insane as all of this was, she could do it for Lunaro. He'd given up his body to protect them. She could give up this bit of her mind for them. For him to get back some of what he'd lost.

"She didn't tell you anything?" Solara said.

"It's an ongoing process, apparently," he said, disdain in his voice. "I've been told to expect miracles, but in due time."

"You won't even hope, will you?"

Lunaro smiled wryly. "I gave up praying and wishing some time ago, and it would take an extended series of miracles to get my hopes up now."

Solara sighed. "Let's go exploring."

They were limited to this floor, as she couldn't get him down the long, narrow flights of stairs, but there was still plenty to see. The house was gigantic, twisting and turning around on itself. They found a sunny corridor that overlooked a grassy hillock spotted with daisies.

"It's beautiful here," Lunaro said. "Have you seen the river?"

"No." She put her hand on the window glass, felt the slight tremor. "You can feel it, though. Through everything."

"Like a heartbeat."

She nodded. They watched the wind draw trails in the deep grass, like invisible fingers running through it. Solara leaned against the window jamb. Lunaro leaned back in his chair. It was a precious quiet between them, one free of any other presence, psychic or physical.

"It's odd." He lifted his empty hands. "Not to have anything to do."

"I know." Nothing but these games Faisal was playing.

"What is our life now?" Lunaro said. "What's the point of it?"

"Right now? To put you back on your feet. To make all of this" – she indicated the house – "a part of our past."

Is that even a possibility? he asked, grimly.

He'd realized she wasn't speaking psychically to him, and she could feel his sadness at the loss of that intimacy they'd always shared. He blamed Faisal, which was fair. He blamed her a little bit. That was fair, too.

CHAPTER EIGHT

Faisal, Mage, and the twins all sat down to dinner together. And the other servant Solara had noticed, the boy who matched her, joined them. He had an eerily serene expression as he sat there, and she could feel again that something wasn't quite right with him.

Leave it alone, Faisal warned.

Solara hadn't even looked at him, sitting at the head of the polished table, or Mage, for that matter, sitting to his right. Lunaro had. He studied Faisal as one would study a venomous snake.

Faisal's eyes narrowed. *You should teach your brother to shield his mind.*

Solara smirked, pulling her gaze away from the boy. *He wanted you to hear that.*

"Sit," Mage said. A command, not an invitation. The girl's audacity was flooring. The table would sit eight, and one of the chairs had been removed so Lunaro could roll his wheelchair into its place. He and Solara sat side by side, wary. The servant boy was across from Solara, and he gazed at her but didn't seem to see her.

"Does Gaius make you uncomfortable?" Mage said. Solara willed herself not to react to the humor in the girl's tone, and Faisal sighed. "He's my Second of sorts," Mage went on. Beneath the table, Lunaro gave Solara a warning jab in the thigh. "Not long after I got here, I thought I'd try forging a bond, and it didn't go right. Faisal keeps him around to punish me."

Now Solara's incredulous gaze turned on Faisal, but he'd turned to gesture to a servant. "Serve the plates."

Any sympathy she'd felt for him since their conversation earlier that day evaporated. It wasn't surprising that someone as far removed from the masses as Faisal could be immune to the inhumanity of being a Second, but his own sister had been enslaved. How could he bear looking at anyone under control of someone else? Especially like this?

Mage wasn't finished. "Gaius has never been the same, but he doesn't take orders, either. Faisal says I did quite a number on him."

Through all of this, Gaius did not react in any way. He blinked at Solara, his hands folded on the tabletop. Solara had never sensed anyone like him. He was there; mind and soul, he was still there, but somewhere far off. "It does seem to be a new level of barbary," Solara said.

Mage chuckled, but even that felt vaguely threatening. "I'm nothing if not innovative."

Solara tensed, and Faisal murmured, *Perhaps this dinner table is all the lesson in self-control you'll ever need.*

Mage must have felt it, sensed the current between them, because she said, "Don't scold her on my behalf, Faisal. You barely seem capable of controlling the beast as it is."

"Watch your mouth," Lunaro said softly.

Mage glanced at him, prepared to keep going, but something in his face gave her pause. Faisal laid a hand on his ward's arm and said, "As tangled as Miss Barthelme and I have become, I would rather you not antagonize both twins at once. Be a dear and stop."

Her jaw went rigid. Then she smiled. "Very well. If I must."

"You must," Faisal said.

Servants returned bearing plates of food. Attention was redirected, even if the tension was not. Solara gave her brother a thin smile as a thank you. When she looked away from him, she found herself looking directly into Gaius' eyes. He methodically cut his meat into manageable bites without even looking at his work.

Stifling a shudder, Solara focused on her own plate and the luxurious foods she could barely identify. For several moments there was thick silence. Lunaro broke it. "May I ask how we're to be treated?"

Mage rolled her eyes.

Lunaro ignored her, his eyes on Faisal. "I can't tell if we're servants or slaves or guests."

"You are a guest, Mr. Barthelme," Faisal said. "That was the agreement your sister and I made. Solara is something else."

"What?" Lunaro said.

"I don't know that I can explain it," Faisal said.

"Try."

Solara snorted a laugh into her glass, and Mage shot her a vicious look. On the one hand, Solara could easily understand the rivalry between them. Mage felt she had been replaced, and in a way, she had. She wasn't a strong enough psychic for what Faisal wanted to do. But she was also clearly a member of his family, a position Solara had no desire to take from her. Mage was young; she couldn't see that. But she was also powerful and overindulged, so Solara had no qualms treating her like the enemy she was.

Faisal said, "If your sister wishes you to know her business, I'm sure she'll tell you. It's not my job to soothe your fears."

Lunaro's mouth opened, and it was Solara's turn to nudge him, willing him to be quiet. *What?* he said curtly. *I'm expected to sit here quietly and not worry about you?*

He was trying to goad her into answering psychically. Solara just picked up her fork. Again, Gaius caught her eye. He looked to be in his late teens, but there was a childlike innocence in his brown eyes. How many years had he been like this?

"What's on the agenda for tomorrow?" Mage asked Faisal.

"Lady Rankin is coming to visit," he said. "I said we'd make time for her in the afternoon."

"With that awful daughter of hers?"

"Maliah is the sweetest human being I've ever known. Your behavior towards her is deplorable."

Why are we here for this? Lunaro questioned Solara.

She shrugged.

Mage kept glancing at Solara as she spoke. "If Rankin ever convinces you to marry that cow, I'm going to make her life a living hell. She'll never have a moment's peace in this house."

"There is no peace in this house," Faisal said. "And what of our guest? What did the physician have to say?"

Solara's breath held.

Mage made a dismissive gesture. "We're going to see Kaia in two days. She wanted to hunt down some needle or herb. She seems optimistic."

"Did she give you a timetable?" Faisal pushed.

"Six months," Mage said. "Six months until he's walking."

Solara could feel how hard Lunaro tried to be neutral, but his breath whooshed out of him at Mage's casual pronouncement. Six months. A lifetime, but also nothing at all. Nothing compared to the last two years. "How confident was she in that timetable?" Solara said, because Lunaro wanted to ask and couldn't.

"Confident enough," Mage said. "Kaia's never wrong."

Solara nodded slowly.

Mage bared her teeth. "Smile, pretty thing. And say thank you."

"I am not a thing," Solara snapped.

"Solara," Faisal said, just condescending enough that she bristled. "Please eat your dinner. You didn't eat anything at breakfast."

Mage and Lunaro both looked confused by the sudden change of subject. Solara's fingers dug into the shiny silver of the fork she'd been gripping the past five minutes. She wanted to snap at him, but deep in their shared mind she could feel his honest concern. It was hard to hate someone you could understand so well. She picked up her knife and began carving up her meat.

"In the meantime, what do guests normally fill their days with?" Lunaro asked.

"You enjoy reading," Faisal said. Lunaro bristled – he must have known Faisal had plucked the information from his head – but nodded. "I have the best library in the Diadem, and a dozen scribes and a librarian up to their necks in books that need cataloguing. If you want a job, you have one. I'll assign you an attendant to get you up and down the stairs."

"I don't need–"

Faisal cut him off. "Regardless of what you think, you are a cripple for at least six more months, and you need the help."

Lunaro's face flushed.

"And me?" Solara said, redirecting. "What are my duties for tomorrow?"

Faisal motioned to her plate. "You and I have errands to run."

In the morning, a different set of clothes had been laid out: a sweeping turquoise skirt, its pleats like ripples in water; and a very snug corset with black lace sleeves. Solara dressed warily, and a servant girl detangled her hair but left it down. Solara had forgotten how long her hair was, so accustomed to tucking it up out of her way while she worked. The dense curls only lay flat when well saturated, and the servant girl had not held back on moisturizing cream.

Lunaro was having breakfast in the sitting room, and his eyebrows rose quite high when he saw her. "Off to a ball?"

"I don't know what I'm off to," Solara said. The servant girl didn't know, either. Solara picked a slice of toast off his tray. "Are you going to become a librarian?"

"I want to say no to spite him, but I can't sit here for days on end doing nothing."

"At least we'll have stories to tell when we see each other again." She devoured the last bite of toast. "See you later."

He waved, although he couldn't quite hide his worried frown as she and her long skirt floated out of the room. She didn't want him to get a good read on how she felt. He wouldn't have liked the answer – she felt wonderful. The skirt was so soft and light and cool. Her hair was free of knots and tangles for the first time in weeks.

This extravagance wasn't for her, and she shouldn't get used to it, but she wanted to. She followed the servant out of the house and into the courtyard, where a lacquered black carriage waited. Faisal was speaking with the driver, a sallow-faced man who gave Solara a furtive, frightened glance.

Why is everyone so afraid of me? she asked Faisal.

Because you're close to me, and you're not afraid. He opened the carriage door, took her hand, and handed her up into it. She'd never worn a skirt so long and nearly stumbled, but he braced a hand on her elbow, and she made it up and half fell onto the plush leather bench inside. Then he closed the door, saying, "Try to look confident, Solara."

Solara had so many questions, but he strode off, mounted his mare, and they were off. The ride was short, and before Solara could even work up too much anxiety about their destination, the carriage stopped. A moment later, Faisal opened the door and held out his hand to her.

You've watched enough ladies to pretend to be one, he said. *Don't be afraid.*

Was she to behave like an entitled brat? Solara tried not to roll her eyes. He helped her down, discreetly flipping the tail of her skirt so she wouldn't trip over it again and make a fool of herself.

The carriage had stopped in the circular gravel driveway of a stately country mansion. Except they had not traveled nearly far enough to have cleared the seventh ring and made it to the priceless country homes in the green acres beyond. No. They had gone inward, to the jewel of the city. The Center. It was the smallest ring of all, home to the Manfalon and only their most loyal followers.

Solara froze for several seconds, gripping Faisal's hand.

She had no idea who this home might belong to. It was surrounded by forest on three sides, and a statue of a stag in a fountain marked the middle of the round driveway. The home itself was not as large as the river house. It had a cozier, homier feel. The front walk was lined with seashells as large as Solara's head, and the double doors that made up the front entrance were painted a cheerful blue.

Faisal tugged her forward, and when her legs were moving reliably on their own, he released her hand. "Try not to let your jaw hang," he said.

She snapped her mouth shut. They'd made it halfway up the front walk when the doors opened, and a tall, gray-haired woman in severe black waved. "Come in, come in! Look at you, Faisal, striding up like you own the place. You're terrible. Come in!"

This woman's mind was ironclad. Not a whisper of her thoughts escaped. Of course not, if she was influential enough to have a home in the Center. Solara could feel the woman reaching out, as well, testing Solara's defenses, and her eyes widened just slightly at the utter silence she encountered.

"Lady Gao," Faisal said warmly. He took her hands and kissed her cheek. Her light brown skin was thin enough to show blue veins. "You weren't at my birthday celebration. I was hurt."

She scowled at him. "These old bones travel for business only, and you know that well, Faisal Casarriba. This is the one I've heard so much about? The Second? I can see why you like her. Mind like a steel trap."

"This is Solara," Faisal said. Lady Gao tucked his arm into hers and drew him into the house. The foyer had a two-story ceiling studded with skylights. Their panes of colored glass bathed the foyer in red and blue jewel tones.

"Solara," Lady Gao repeated. "That's a queen's name."

Solara perked up. "Is it?"

"Ten seconds in and you've given her a big head," Faisal scolded. To Solara he said, "Lady Gao is a historian. She knows the names of kings and queens of foreign lands since the beginning of time."

Lady Gao gave him a knowing look. "She doesn't sound like you."

"Why would she?" Faisal said.

She led them farther into the house, to a well-furnished sitting room where a tea tray waited. "She doesn't sound like those mindless dolls other people keep, either."

They both had their backs to Solara, and Faisal's shoulders grew tight beneath the smooth fabric of his jacket. He was thinking of Aliss.

"What queen?" Solara asked. If she was pretending to be a lady, she was allowed to ask questions. "Where does my name come from?"

Lady Gao released Faisal and settled onto a couch, gesturing for Solara to join her. Solara sat beside her. Lady Gao smelled of black tea and something stale. "Solara Benwerrin was queen of a desert nation. When strangers invaded her lands, she strapped a knife to each thigh and assassinated all twelve of their leaders in a single night."

"Don't tell her these morbid stories," Faisal said.

Lady Gao looked intently into Solara's eyes. "Are you a killer, Solara?"

Her heart thumped, traitorous beast. But Lady Gao couldn't possibly know any of Faisal's plans. She was merely taunting her. Solara said, "Solara Benwerrin sounds like a hero, not a killer."

The old woman laughed, gaze flicking to Faisal. "Oh, I like her."

"I thought you might," he said. He hadn't anticipated that answer. He went to the empty fireplace, absently studying the forest painting hung above the mantelpiece.

"Tell me about yourself, Solara," Lady Gao said.

Tell the truth. Enough of it, Faisal told Solara.

So, Solara spun her tale of a toiling life in a dress shop, her mental duel with Faisal, and then his offer to care for her brother in return for her becoming his Second. Perhaps she had warmed too much to her role, but the story felt as if it had happened to another person.

Lady Gao lapped up the details, one hand pressed to Solara's arm. "You must feel so fortunate," she said at the end. In their head, Faisal laughed, and Solara threw him the image of her middle finger. Lady Gao's expression turned sly. "What a mind to share thoughts with, eh?"

"Mostly he bosses me around," Solara said honestly, and Lady Gao chuckled. "And I understand it takes time for the bond to settle."

"When things have settled, you must tell me what it's like," Lady Gao said. Her keen gaze turned to Faisal once more. "I like to know how strong minds work, and I have always been curious about this one."

"Don't give her any ideas," Faisal said sternly. Solara didn't know which one of them he was talking to. "Go and study your grandson. That should satisfy your curiosity for years."

Lady Gao made a dismissive gesture. "Tessan scares me," she said. Solara went rigid, and Lady Gao felt it. Her sly smile returned as she stroked Solara's hands, her fingers running over Faisal's diamond ring. "I heard a deliciously naughty story about you and my grandson, young lady."

Help, Solara pleaded.

Faisal was silent.

"Deliciously naughty?" Solara said, her voice faint. "I've only been here a few days." Was that why Lady Gao was so silent? According to some theories, it was the strongest gifts that bred stone minds.

"Tess only needs a moment to latch onto something," Lady Gao said. She kept looking between her and Faisal. "He used to collect stray animals. One look and he was attached."

"He had quite the menagerie," Faisal said softly. There was, oddly enough, a hint of sadness in his tone, that Solara understood a moment later.

"Nikara broke into his kennel one day and skinned them all alive," Lady Gao explained. Solara's stomach lurched. "She made a coat out of the skins and wore it around for days. Nikara has always enjoyed punishing Tess for loving things. It's a game they play."

"Lady Gao," Faisal said, suddenly brisk. "You're going to scare her."

Solara was most certainly scared.

"If the stories are to be believed, you've experienced some of that, already." Lady Gao chucked Solara's chin, and Solara flinched. "But there's nothing to be afraid of. Be a good girl and I'm sure your Master will protect you."

"I don't know what you mean," Solara said. Her voice squeaked.

But Lady Gao was done with her. She fixed a stern gaze on Faisal. "Don't taunt my grandson, Lord Faisal. No need to stir the hornet's nest."

It sounded like Nikara was capable of stirring the hornet's nest all on her own. Was that why Tessan had become so terrifying? To stand up to his sister? Solara wasn't sure she blamed him.

As soon as she had the thought, she cringed, expecting the curious glance that Faisal sent her way. "Solara is my Second," he said to Lady Gao, not looking away from Solara. "All I require is her loyalty. The rest of her can do as it wishes."

All of her, loyalty included, wanted to bolt out of this mess as fast as her legs could take her. All she could see was a kennel full of mutilated animals, and the thought made her nauseous. Faisal glanced at her, his gaze a warning, although Lady Gao scrutinized it and did not seem to come to the same conclusion. The woman had warned Faisal not to antagonize Tessan, but Solara had no doubt Lady Gao was merely waiting for them to leave before she started spreading tales.

"Tell me," Faisal said. He was still perturbed by Solara's thought, and she wished she hadn't had it. "Why did Nikara stop wearing that awful coat? I can't recall."

"Oh." Lady Gao smiled. "Tessan tried to hang her with it."

The blood drained out of Solara's face.

"Ah," Faisal said, very deliberately. "Well, I came here to see if you'd simply forgotten to send along my birthday gift, Lady Gao. You disappoint me." He came over to the couch and reached down for Solara's hand, lifting her up. "So now I'm taking away your amusement."

"Don't be petty!" Lady Gao scolded.

"No. It's too late. Come along, Solara." He tucked her arm into his, and she gripped him to steady her uncertain legs, although it was only fueling Lady Gao's suspicions.

"Don't you come to me asking for any favors later," Lady Gao warned.

"I wouldn't dream of it." Faisal bent over and kissed her cheek. "Have a wonderful afternoon, my love. We'll come and visit you again soon."

CHAPTER NINE

They made three more stops before the morning was over, all in the second ring. It was a who's who of influential figures, and Solara's role varied from home to home. In two, she was a silent watcher. She was not invited to sit while Faisal discussed business with a grim-faced group of men and women. In the third, two older women with loose thoughts welcomed them in, doted on her, and coated Faisal's cheeks in kisses. One of them had a Second of her own, a vibrant young girl with her hair in wild pigtails. The girl winked at Solara when she offered her a cup of flavored ice.

As well as Solara could understand it, Faisal was integrating her into this well-established society, letting important figures grow accustomed to her face, her presence. It was all strategic, and she played her part as well as she could.

By the time they returned to the house she was exhausted and thinking lovingly of her bed, but Faisal said, "Follow me," and started up toward the glass office.

Must I?

Yes.

She grumbled inaudibly and followed, resisting the urge to stick her tongue out at his back – although, of course, he knew exactly what she wanted to do. The bond between them had its own ebb and flow. When he was engrossed in his business meetings, it had lagged. He was on his guard, his thoughts orderly and controlled. Now, as he took the stairs three at a time, and she followed at a more sedate pace, holding up her skirt with one hand, their thoughts were relaxed and entwined. He was thinking of lunch and how poorly this was going to go and whether he had remembered to feed her breakfast.

"No," she said, slightly out of breath at the top of the stairs. "You didn't. Are you fattening me up for a sacrifice?"

"I'm fattening you up to make you strong," he said. He unlocked the office door with a gold key on a chain around his neck and went inside. She followed, closing the door behind them. There was a box laid on the table, cherry wood polished to sheen. She could see her face in it.

"What latest torture is this?" she asked.

"Open it."

She lifted the lid. Inside the box, nestled in black velvet, were two knives. The blades were two-edged and the handles of molded topaz. She looked at him uncertainly.

"Pick one up."

Her courage lagged. But she reached into the box and picked up a knife. The stone was cool in her palm. *Am I supposed to plunge this into the heart of Roga Manfalon?*

Guard your thoughts.

That was not the negative answer she was hoping for. She turned the weapon over in her hand, feeling the weight of the hilt, how it balanced against the weight of the blade. She felt a strange sort of wonder. She'd never held a weapon, certainly not one as fine as this. After a moment, she looked up at Faisal.

"I'm going to teach you to defend yourself," he said.

"Why?"

"Because I would like to promise you that throughout your work for me, Lord Tessan will never lay a hand on you, but that is not a promise I can make." He read her expression carefully for three seconds. "But I can show you how to make him pay dearly for it."

Lady Rankin and her daughter Maliah arrived for lunch in the garden just after two. Lunaro, up to his eyeballs in books in the library, opted not to join, but Mage appeared in a flurry of white lace, because she would not miss this opportunity to harass Maliah. Maliah was a plain girl, with massive eyes and her dark hair in an outrageous bun nearly as large as her entire head.

Lunch was set up on a wrought iron table beneath a flowering tree. Servants stood at attention with pitchers of juice and trays of fruit. One of them was Gaius, Solara couldn't help noticing, although Lady Rankin quickly took her attention. Buxom and bombastic, the woman took up an entire side of the table with her flamboyant arm gestures.

Solara hung back, unsure of her latest role, but Faisal gestured to the chair beside him. Mage looked annoyed as she sat at the head of the table, and Solara wasn't sure if Faisal didn't notice, didn't care, or was intentionally pissing her off.

"Thank you very much for having us, Lord Faisal," Maliah murmured in the direction of the stones underfoot.

"It's our pleasure," Mage said. Her voice was disgustingly saccharine, and Maliah looked up, flushed, and looked away. Mage despised her, and she didn't try to hide it. Her thoughts were so poisonous it made Solara squirm. Mage was their mental superior in every way, but in the eyes of Lady Rankin, she was nothing but street refuse, and she would never be anything more.

Mage hated Lady Rankin for that belief. Street refuse was disposable, and what Mage feared more than anything was being disposable. Solara couldn't help sensing that, and it made the ugly sneer on the girl's face look like an inadequate mask.

Lady Rankin, meanwhile, studied Solara. "What a delicious creature you found, Faisal. Is she useful at all? I want Maliah to take a Second, but her father doubts she can hold the bond."

"Oh, really?" Mage said.

Maliah's cheeks burned brighter red.

"I find her extraordinarily useful, although she has much to learn," Faisal said. He gestured for the servants to begin serving. "She's from the fourth ring, and they can be quite common there."

Bastard.

Bide your time, Solara. And fix your face.

"I just have to take her out in public often enough that she can put on a farce of manners," he said. "Maliah, aren't you hungry? You've barely touched your food."

Do you always obsess over how much people eat?

Her mother barely lets her eat at home.

Solara's irritation vanished. Yes, upon closer inspection of Maliah, she could see the wear marks of a poor diet in the girl's sallow skin and bony elbows. Her hands hovered nervously near her plate, but she had yet to touch anything, and Solara doubted she would, as Lady Rankin shot her a warning glare.

"I heard you were in Miss Cara's hunting party last week," Mage said, suddenly leaning toward Maliah. "And you took a tumble?"

"My horse spooked at a ditch and wall," Maliah mumbled.

"That must have bruised your backside."

"Mage," Faisal warned. "You'll put your sleeve in your plate."

"Whenever I would have a fall I bruised magnificently," Mage went on. "Although of course I haven't fallen off a horse since I don't even know when."

"You're fortunate to have found a generous home that allows you to ride," Lady Rankin said, a faint sneer in her voice. Mage ground her teeth, and Solara almost felt sorry for her.

"I've always found Miss Cara's hunting parties to be an exercise in feral behavior," Faisal said. "I might throw myself off my horse to end it sooner, too." Maliah giggled. "Perhaps," he went on, speaking over Mage as she began what was undoubtedly another bitchy comment, "we ought to organize a hunt here. What do you think, Lady Rankin?"

The woman's face lit up. "Oh, that's a splendid idea!"

"I'll have to speak with Nikara about it," Faisal said. "I heard she was organizing something in the Center, and there's no point in both of us hosting one."

Lady Rankin's eyes twinkled. "Well, I suppose we'd better ask her."

"And as you are one of her favorite ladies," Faisal said with a knowing wink. "I find myself in the company of the perfect woman to make the request."

"Oh, you are conniving!" She flushed, pleased. "Is that why you had us here?"

"Lady Rankin, you wound me," Faisal said. Mage took a long, long drink from her wine glass. "But I promise if you help me make it happen, I shall personally escort Maliah through the entire course and be sure she makes it through unscathed."

Both Rankin women glowed.

Later, after they had waved off their guests, Mage spat in the grass. "She disgusts me. And you disgust me, the way you patronize her. Do you have any self-respect at all?"

"I'm sorry you find manners so appalling," Faisal said.

"Manners?" Mage shot back. "Is that what you call that? You're her *backup plan*. Rankin is desperate to marry Maliah off to Tessan."

Had he utterly given up setting boundaries for Mage? The child was out of control.

"I'm not letting that sweet girl get foisted on Tessan," Faisal said. "He'll eat her alive. Do you have a shred of empathy in your body?"

Solara took advantage of their distraction to fade back into the house. She'd barely had a moment to herself since she'd arrived at the river house, and so long as Faisal was distracted with his viper of a ward, Solara would make the most of it. She hiked up her skirt and sprinted through the house and out the back to the stable.

A groom prepared a horse for her without asking any questions and assisted her up into the saddle when she asked. Her backside was actually a bit sore from her first day of riding, but she rode confidently toward the city.

People made room for her on the main road, giving way to the clearly expensive horse and trappings. Solara felt odd, almost sacrilegious, but she kept her eyes up and gave no indication that she noticed anyone. She wasn't entirely sure where she was going, only that she wanted to see the village again, be surrounded by the nameless faces that had been the backdrop of her entire life.

She went through the tailor's district, although she was careful to steer clear of Bjorn's. Her disappearance would have put Bjorn in a tight spot, and Solara doubted the woman would have any sympathy for her even if she knew what'd happened. Bjorn had always thought Solara was careless, drawing too much attention to herself.

Solara wandered through the baker's district next, where the air was heavy with the scent of sugar. She hadn't seen a cent of the money she was earning or the stipend Lunaro was to get. The moment that money touched her hand, she was going to buy two dozen glazed pastries and they were going to eat themselves sick.

She'd hesitated for longer than she'd realized outside of the pastry shop, because its owner came to the door, a hopeful smile on her face. "Hello, my lady," she said dutifully. "Can I help you with something?"

The opened door let a waft of sweet air into the street, and although Solara had just eaten lunch, her stomach rumbled. "I was just admiring your storefront," Solara said. She almost apologized for having bothered her, but that wasn't what a fine lady would do, was it? And that was what she was masquerading as in this dress, although her free-flowing hair said otherwise. Any noble female over the age of twelve would have her hair up. It was the common folk who didn't care. Solara nudged the mare onward and continued wandering the streets, toward the printer's district.

The inky scent there always reminded her of Tessan, so she normally would have avoided it at all costs, but she felt safe, high up on her borrowed horse.

I don't recall giving you permission to leave the grounds.

She grinned but made her voice mockingly subdued. *I didn't want to interrupt your discussion with your dearest Mage.*

Faisal sounded only mildly irritated and said nothing else, so Solara focused on her escapade. She wished again for disposable income as she made her way through rows and rows of book shops, newspaper buildings, and art galleries. The Diadem was renowned for its printed word. Every inch of wall space was plastered with bills and broadsides advertising everything imaginable, from book debuts to playhouses to scribing services.

She loitered for a moment outside of a printing house with a glass front, where the printers could be seen whirring away, sheaves of warm paper piling out of the end. A boy in a smock and cap glanced up, waved at her, and continued his work.

A print shop was one of the first places she'd looked for employment those years ago, so fond of the ink and the smell of paper and binding glue. It was what her father had done. He'd owned half a shop with a friend, a man who died shortly before he did. She and Lunaro had never seen any profit from the store. She wasn't entirely sure what had happened to it, the equipment, the work contracts. All of it gone in an instant.

Someone on her far side cleared his throat, and she tore her gaze away from the shop to look down at the man standing at her knee. To her surprise, it was Gaius. He didn't say anything, merely smiled at her.

"Hello, Gaius," she said. He nodded. "What are you doing out here?" What she meant, although she wasn't sure it was all right to ask, was if he still had the mental capacity to be out and about on his own, or if he'd wandered off without anyone noticing.

Gaius just patted her knee and walked away, quickly disappearing into the crowd. There must have been something of him left if he'd been able to recognize her. She stared after him, remembering Mage's casual pronouncement about how he'd ended up like that. Solara couldn't believe Faisal had let it happen.

She nudged the mare forward absently, nearly toppling a man with an armful of books. She muttered an apology half under her breath but kept going. She wove her way back the way she'd come, thoughts divided, and it was pure instinct that led her to the familiar street, so she passed directly across from Bjorn's. She realized belatedly where she was and glanced at the store front to see Bjorn on the front walk cleaning windows, her shoulders tight, her gaze low in the familiar hunch of the seamstress. It had been such a point of vanity for Solara, to defy that workwoman's crouch, to sit up straight and proud at every second, with her shoulders thrown back and her head lifted. People would tease her that she walked like a lady.

Now, looking at Bjorn, she wondered if it hadn't been pride, but shame. Because nothing, no one, had ever looked so wretched, as that woman hunched over in front of her store, slowly wiping down the glass.

The worst part was, Solara felt utterly divorced from it, high up on her fancy horse in her fancy dress. How many times had she wiped down that front window, not even bothering to look up as rich men and women went by with their horses and carriages? Now, on the other side of the picture, she almost hadn't bothered to look down.

CHAPTER TEN

For the next two weeks, Solara didn't leave the house. Each morning she and her brother rose, had breakfast together, and went about their work. He went to the library, to write and read and organize; she went to the glass office, either to practice with her lovely knife, or to read newspapers of the goings-on of the Diadem.

She read about the mysterious death of one of Nikara's political rivals, Tessan's military battalion winning awards in war games, and the young Manfalon girls wreaking social havoc. She was absorbing names, faces, and places at an exorbitant rate, but she didn't dare gloss over anything, because every night she had dinner with Faisal, and he quizzed her.

To the outside eye, they merely sat in silence, because these conversations took place entirely through the bond, which had begun to settle into something with rules and regulations that Solara could follow, thus allowing her to hide some of her more vindictive thoughts about her situation, particularly about Mage who continued to grate on Solara's last nerve.

She would see the girl wandering the halls, sometimes with Gaius in tow, and the mere sight of them sickened Solara. But a single misplaced, disgusted thought, and Solara could feel Faisal snarling in her head, warning her off. So, she tried her best to keep it all in check, and as time went on, ignoring her feelings got easier.

Faisal was not the worst companion to keep. That irritated Solara as well, that she could even admit that. He had a deceptively placid sense of humor, and his dry commentary on his fellow noblemen often snuck a laugh out of her. He was surprisingly patient in their knife lessons, although he expected excellence, and Solara stopped dreading their interactions, if not looking forward to them.

The twins were having a late breakfast in the garden one lazy morning when Faisal strode out of nowhere. He nodded curtly at Lunaro and told Solara, "Get dressed. We're going hunting."

"Hunting?" Lunaro echoed.

"A steeplechase," Solara clarified. "Am I a good enough rider for that?"

"Doubtful," Faisal said. "But we'll see."

"Please don't die," Lunaro said.

Solara stuffed her last bite of breakfast into her mouth, kissed her brother, and said, "Let's not make any rash promises." He swatted at her as she quickly backed away and went into the house to change. Her riding outfit had been laid out, and she changed and was back downstairs to meet Faisal in the front hall in less than ten minutes.

He looked her up and down, nodded his approval, and then they went out to the carriage. He offered no further information as they sat on opposite benches and got on their way.

The thought of galloping over open territory and jumping giant fences made her feel distinctly ill, but she chose to believe he wouldn't let her do something that would kill her.

"You're far too valuable to kill for Nikara's amusement," Faisal said.

Ah. So, this was Nikara's hunt. She'd read about it in the newspaper the other day. The invitations were exclusive, and Solara hadn't expected to be dragged along.

"You're attending at Tessan's request," Faisal said. "He has a notable lack of dignity when it comes to you and does not seem to care." He considered. "Or seems to believe that making his interest obvious will stop me from being too careless with your life."

His interest. Inwardly, Solara bristled, but she kept her face neutral – another skill she had been working on nonstop. At dinners, Faisal would intentionally bait her, and she would do her best not to react. Tessan was her obvious trigger. The thought of seeing him again, especially before so many pairs of eyes, made her stomach clench. She didn't want to draw attention to herself, even knowing that that was exactly why Faisal was bringing her. She especially didn't want to draw the attention of Nikara. She didn't know if the veritable princess even remembered the altercation of a year ago, or if she'd gotten bored and moved on, but Solara was sure Nikara would make time to torment her brother further given the opportunity.

"If I fall off," she said. Rephrased. "How fast are we going to go?"

"Very," he said. "Don't fall off."

"Is there not some other, less terrifying option? Can't I ride along in a carriage? Be a hilltopper?" She had read about hilltoppers in the newspapers. They were regarded with scorn unless well over the age of seventy – or below the age of ten – and she didn't care.

"No," he said. End of story.

"Why does it matter?" A hint of whine crept into her voice, and he frowned. "Never mind."

They arrived fifteen minutes later. Nikara's personal estate was small but lavish, although she spent most of her time in her father's palace. They went quickly past the house and out to the stables, which were as large as the house, and already surrounded by carriages and riders on horseback. Some wore their house colors or a coat of arms, and all of it flew by so fast Solara barely had a chance to absorb it before Faisal was out of the carriage and striding into the barn for a horse. She practically had to skip to keep up, the two of them invisible in the melee.

In the stable, dozens of saddled horses lined the aisle. Faisal walked swiftly down the aisle, his gaze skating over the options. His attention landed on a solidly built draft mare, and he nodded his chin at it. "That's yours."

The mare was massive, and Solara quailed. Walking and trotting around had been easy enough for her, but her body had given her several reminders that access to Faisal's knowledge did not equal perfect execution, and no matter what her thoughts might convince her of, she had barely been riding for two weeks.

"Don't be a coward," he said and dragged her over to the horse.

"I don't–"

He lifted her leg, put her foot in the stirrup, and then she was on the horse, all of it so fast she wasn't entirely sure how it happened.

I don't care for you very much, she thought.

Nor I for you. He walked away, but before her terror could consume her entirely, he'd picked a horse and come back to her. Grooms moved around, adjusting tack and answering questions, as more riders came into the barn and picked out their mounts. The sheer amount of fine horseflesh was overwhelming. Everything was overwhelming.

"Relax," Faisal admonished. "You'll be less likely to fall off." He swung onto his horse, and they went out into the sunshine.

Riders had begun organizing into groups, merry chatter and laughter filling the air. This time, she and Faisal caught more attention. The combined thoughts were almost too much to absorb. *Faisal's Second. The common girl. Hair loose like a whore. This is what they're fighting over? Tessan's little distraction. They'll tear her in half like a wishbone.*

It was a quick, jabbing reminder of how much she did not belong in this world.

Solara, Faisal warned. She forced a fake smile onto her face, but that wasn't his point. *Relax. You're pissing off your horse.*

She willed her muscles to soften. The mare was indeed beginning to jig in place, excited for the hunt, feeding off Solara's anxiety.

"Lord Faisal!" Lady Rankin wove her draft horse through the crowd. Maliah trailed after her on an awkwardly put together pony. The woman beamed. "Good afternoon, my lord."

"Lady Rankin," he said. "Maliah. Well-met."

"Don't you forget your promise!" Lady Rankin beckoned Maliah closer. The girl looked as ill as Solara felt. "Watch over my treasure."

"I shall guard her with my life," he promised. *Guard* me *with your life*, Solara though. He held back a smile.

A horn blew, and the horses began prancing in place. Maliah gave a little yelp, and Faisal steered closer to her, leaning down to say a reassuring word as the crowd cheered in anticipation. Solara tried to relax, but her body was as unyielding as iron, and the mare hated it. The herd of horses moved anxiously toward the forest, and Solara cursed a thousand times, none of it audible above the noise.

In the crush, Faisal and Maliah were being pushed away from Solara, and she dug her fingers into the mare's mane and prayed that she would survive this.

The horn sounded again, and they were off. Nothing had prepared Solara for the speed with which they took off. Her head snapped back, shooting pain down her spine, and if she hadn't had a death grip on the mare's mane, she would have fallen off immediately. But the reprieve was enough for her to get her bearings, to rise into the half seat like the other riders, drop her weight into her heels, and settle into her jumping position.

A hundred horses swept down the grassy knoll and plunged into the forest. It was dark, close, and extremely loud. Solara didn't have to steer, thank heavens, because she couldn't have. Horses to her left, to her right, gaining on her ass and inches in front of her mare's face. It was a seething mass of horseflesh and Solara could barely make out faces through her sheer terror. This was it. This was how she died.

The first jump loomed ahead, and she whimpered. It was a massive hedge which would have towered over her head if she were on the ground. Solara grabbed mane, closed her eyes, and prayed.

The mare leaped, and they were airborne. They hit the ground with a jolt like a punch through Solara's ankles and off they went again, hooves pounding into the turf, Solara's blood pounding in her ears, and tears gathering beneath her pinched eyelids.

Faisal and Maliah were long gone, and she hadn't a prayer of finding them. She was entirely at the mercy of this equine mob and had never been more terrified in her life.

Eventually, they settled into a rhythm of galloping, jumping, and galloping on. People whooped and cheered. One woman's horse hit a jump chest-first and flipped wildly over it. Solara surged past too quickly to see what happened, if the woman was trampled or if anyone stopped to help her, but it left her with no fantasies as to the mercy of this group. They didn't care who fell, who was stepped on. And Faisal had tossed her into the middle of it without so much as a 'good luck.'

As the pack mowed toward the finish line, it began to thin out. Tired, unfit horses fell behind, and the remaining riders spread out to have room to take the jumps properly. Solara's legs shook. There was sweat in her eyes and her mouth. Her hair had been whipped into a frenzy and flew wildly about her face, sticking in her sweat and tears, because she had cried at least two different times throughout the course.

But there was the final jump. She locked her gaze on it, squared her shoulders, and told herself she'd make it. That on the other side of this massive ditch and wall was the stable, a delicious meal, and a chair for her to sit in, and she was going to make it out alive.

Slow down. Faisal, for the first time in the entire race. *You're not going to make it at that speed.*

She couldn't see him anywhere around her and was terrified to take her gaze off the fence.

Slower. Good. Hold the rein. Sit back. Sit up. Eyes up.

The mare leapt. The ditch loomed beneath them, and they burst through the brush atop the wall and came down with all the grace of a herd of elephants. But Solara was there, she was on, and the mare thudded down the backstretch with the others. She was foaming at the mouth, raring to go, but Solara sat back hard and whipped her in a tight circle to stop her.

Reluctantly the mare halted. Solara sat there gasping, the taste of her own sweat curdling in her mouth.

Well done, common girl.

She flipped her slick hair back from her face, chest heaving. A groom walked up with a canister of water and took her reins. Solara blinked the sweat out of her eyes and recognized him. Gaius again. Today, he had a diamond earring in his left ear.

"Thank," she gasped. "You."

He grinned as he began to walk the mare back and forth. Solara hadn't seen Gaius apart from Mage since the day she went into the third ring, but Mage had been forced to stay home today, to the girl's rage.

Solara took her loose hair, coiled it into a bun at the nape of her neck, and tried to look less terrified and exhausted than she was. She felt silly, not because of how much the run had taken out of her, but because Gaius was waiting on her so kindly.

She was the same as he was, and the only reason she was on a horse, and he was on the ground, was because Faisal willed it. And she couldn't help feeling embarrassed – ashamed – about being pandered to like all the nobles around her.

Gaius gestured at her water, and she lifted it to her mouth to drink, but then he stopped short, and the water sloshed down the front of her shirt. She almost fell off, too, she was that shaky. Their way was blocked by a sweat-soaked black mare and her rider. Tessan.

Please, she begged Faisal. *I'm so tired. I can't play these games today.*

He didn't respond, as she knew he wouldn't. He was determined to make her suffer on her own. "Lord Tessan," she said. Her voice was raspy.

"Well ridden," Tessan said. Of course, he'd noticed her, and she'd had no idea he was there.

She nodded. "Thank you. Please excuse us. My mare should walk."

Tessan turned and walked beside her, close enough that their sweaty thighs occasionally brushed. Solara feigned interest in her surroundings, taking in details of the stable yard that she had been too petrified to notice before the chase. In the riders' absence, servants had set up tables laden with food and drink. Grooms took exhausted horses, and riders – most of them remarkably well-composed after such a grueling run – ate and drank. They watched and were watched.

Some people tried to be discreet, although their thoughts screamed otherwise, but many openly stared at Tessan and at her. She spotted Lady Gao and the two chatty women that she and Faisal had visited weeks ago. Dozens of faces she recognized from the newspapers' extensively detailed and illustrated gossip columns. Members of the commerce council. Some Scarlet Guard.

"Had you ever jumped before today?" Tessan asked. Their knees bumped.

"No." She pointedly did not look at him.

"Impressive, although I suppose being Faisal's Second makes that necessary. He's one of the best horsemen I know."

"He was remarkably unhelpful," Solara snapped. "I did that on my own."

Tessan's eyebrows rose at her spiteful tone, and she thought Gaius snickered. When she glanced at him, his face was blank. "I stand corrected," Tessan said. Then, his own tone slightly testy, he added, "As suicidal as it might have been, you certainly seemed game."

"One does not say no to Lord Faisal," she said and watched the anger snap in his eyes. Every reminder that she "belonged" to Faisal was a reminder that she was not, in any way, bound to Tessan. And she thought he could do with several of those reminders every day for the rest of their lives.

"You can go," Tessan told Gaius. Gaius looked up at Solara, his expression somehow managing to be empty and sympathetic, and then he vanished. Solara's mare happily followed after Tessan's.

They had wandered farther from the stable yard. Far away enough to be out of earshot, especially with the noise, but still well within eyeshot. Faisal wasn't paying her any attention, which Solara hoped meant she wasn't doing anything to harm their plans and not that he had simply lost track of her. Or, worse, stopped caring about her wellbeing. Ahead of them, the forest was eerie in the dimming light.

"Solara," Tessan said.

She pretended to examine something in the trees. "Yes, Lord Tessan?" A reminder of his position. What he stood to lose if he weren't discreet.

"Look at me."

"You're going to make a scene," she said. "There are a hundred people watching."

"If I was afraid of these people, I wouldn't turn my back on them," he said, with a dark edge to his voice that made her swallow hard. "Now look at me."

She wondered if he was aware of how frightening he was when he used that tone of voice. Slowly, she turned her head and looked him in the eye. It had always unnerved her, the idea of stone minds. There wasn't supposed to be such a thing as a mind she couldn't read. She wondered how much of her complicated fear was because of that silence.

He studied her face, gaze tracing the planes of her cheeks, the curve of her mouth, in the intimate way he always had. "Has he hurt you?" he asked.

"If I said yes, what would you do about it?" she retorted.

Tessan's lips pursed. "Answer me."

It must have had something to do with the horse, how high up she was, that made her feel bolder. As if she could possibly outrun his wrath, when she inevitably kindled the ember to full flame. "You told me nothing breaks this bond but him," she said. "I know that. Not without shredding my mind apart. So, don't make him angry."

Murder flashed through his eyes. "Solara, if he lays a hand on you–"

She wanted to laugh. To slap the stupidity out of him. Part of her wished she could simply explain. Seeing him conjured memories she'd rather forget but couldn't. And although all of her memory of that night wasn't intact, as long as she lived, she was never going to forget the way she felt when she kissed him, and it taunted her, because it wasn't real.

A throat cleared. Gaius. Tessan seared him with a glare, but Gaius just inclined his head, then looked at Solara and tapped his earring.

"Faisal is looking for me," Solara said. Tessan made no attempt to follow as Gaius took her reins and led her away, back into the stable yard, where Faisal waited. Maliah stood beside him, clinging to his arm to hold herself upright, legs shaking beneath her impractical skirt. Solara didn't know how she was going to get down and stand on her own legs without some sort of assistance, assistance which Faisal did not look inclined to offer.

But her horse was halted, and she slithered down and gave a little mew of pain when her feet hit the ground.

"I always get so sore, too," Maliah offered shyly.

Faisal hid a smile. "If the two of you link arms, are you more or less likely to fall over?"

Maliah giggled, and Solara made a face at him. "Less, I think," Maliah said. She held out her free arm to Solara, and Solara sort of lurched from saddle to Maliah, eyes watering at the horrendous pain.

"Find a shaded spot," Faisal said. "Eat. Drink. I'll be back shortly." He bowed deeply to Maliah. "My lady." Then he excused himself, and Gaius took the mare away.

CHAPTER
ELEVEN

Maliah and Solara hobbled to a pair of chairs beneath an awning and collapsed into them. Maliah managed to politely cross her ankles, but Solara let her legs hang. A liveried servant brought them glasses of lemonade, and Maliah ordered him to bring them plates of food. "Is this your first steeplechase?" she asked, when they were alone.

"My first anything proper on horseback," Solara admitted. "I'd never ridden a horse before becoming Lord Faisal's Second, and the learning curve has been steep."

Maliah leaned her dark head close. Gone was her ridiculous bun. She wore her hair in an elegant, braided crown studded with pearl pins. She had come out of the ride still remarkably well put together but for the shaking legs and shine of sweat. "Don't think little of me for gossiping," she said. "But people were betting that you'd fall and be injured."

Solara studied the girl. "I imagine they took a few bets on you, as well, my lady."

Maliah shrugged. "They always do. I fall off most of the time. Lord Faisal was very kind to ride alongside me and help me through it. Mother wants me to be a horsewoman but–" She stopped, blushing again. "I'm sorry. I don't mean to complain."

"Complain away," Solara said. The servant returned with laden plates, and they held them balanced on their damp laps. Sweat had soaked through everything, and Solara felt ready to pass out. "As you can see, I'm not much of a horsewoman, either. And I'm a little sulky that Faisal made me do it."

Maliah cocked her head. "Are you very close with Lord Faisal? I mean, I understand the nature of the bond. But... are you friendly?"

Solara doubted Maliah was fishing for gossip. From the looks of the girl, she had no friends in this crowd. But still, Solara needed to be careful. The Rankins, after all, were close with Nikara. "I'm his employee," she said. "That fact defines the relationship above all else."

"I just..." Maliah gestured to the ring on Solara's finger.

She had grown so accustomed to her ring that she'd forgotten its existence. "He gives those to everyone remotely high ranking," she said.

"Yes," Maliah said. "But it's normally an earring."

Her tone was wary. Solara lifted her gaze to the picnicking aristocrats before her. They'd lost interest in her now that she wasn't beside a lord. In fact, only one person was looking at her. Blatantly. Utterly ignoring the person speaking beside him. Faisal.

Maliah followed her glance. "He seems fond of you," she said cautiously.

It surprised Solara, her first thought. *Don't hurt this girl with your stupid game.*

Maliah has no interest in me, he sent back. *Except to hope I offer to marry her before her mother succeeds in pawning her off on Manfalon. If her heart is to be broken, it will be if you reject her friendship.* A pause. *I told her you were kind.*

Solara looked at Maliah, who was only pushing around the food on her plate. She looked at the girl's knobby elbows – undisguisable, even in her pretty floral shirtsleeves – the hollows in her neck and cheeks. "You should eat," she said. Maliah looked surprised, then embarrassed. "After all of that," Solara said, gesturing at the track they'd demolished through the forest, "we need recovery." She took a massive bite of her own food to punctuate her point, and Maliah hesitantly followed suit. After she'd swallowed, Solara said, "I believe the ring is simply to snub Tessan."

Maliah nodded. "It must be uncomfortable."

Solara didn't know what to possibly say. But she appreciated the sympathy in Maliah's voice. She gestured to their plates and they each took another bite. It pained Maliah to swallow, and Solara felt a flash of anger, that the girl's mother was torturing her like this, trying to force a marriage to a man Maliah cared nothing for.

That is the nature of the game.

If you had a shred of decency, you would marry her and get her out of this hell. She glanced at Faisal again, found him still watching her. It had been going on long enough that people were noticing, and his companion glowered at being ignored. *Do you intend to infuriate Tessan into kidnapping me by making him believe you're using me like a prostitute?*

Faisal laughed aloud, drawing still more attention to their staring contest. *You started it.*

Solara turned away, both embarrassed and annoyed, and said to Maliah, "If you wish to preserve your sanity, don't let your mother force you into having a Second. Having another person's thoughts in your head is *infuriating*."

Maliah laughed. Not her nervous giggle, but an unrestrained, explosive laugh. She immediately seemed self-conscious and shushed herself, but Solara grinned.

"You're going to have to be my ally in all of this," she said. She didn't think of the possible consequences, deadly or otherwise, of drawing this poor girl in close. "I think we're both going to need a friend who can make us laugh."

"Deal," Maliah said. She offered one dainty gloved hand, and they shook.

Faisal had to carry Solara back to the carriage, which the gossipy masses found very entertaining. Fortunately, Tessan had already left by then.

When they arrived at the river house, Solara ran a hot bath and soaked in it for an hour. She still had to do her normal tasks, but Faisal was going out for dinner and her presence was not required.

He found her in the library before he left, her with her aching legs propped up and a book folded over her belly. Lunaro was deeper in the stacks. She could hear him talking to himself as he worked.

Take your feet off my table.

I can't move them.

Faisal fought a smirk and held out a small rectangle of expensive paper. Her name was written on it with an impeccable hand. "It seems you made quite an impression on our Maliah," he said.

Back in the stacks, Lunaro started at the sound of Faisal's voice.

"Don't make fun of her," Solara said, and held out her hand for the letter.

Faisal had already broken the seal, which didn't surprise her although it still irritated her. He handed it over, and she unfolded it.

Friend,

I had such a lovely afternoon with you today. I thought perhaps our next venture could be you joining me for a light riding lesson in three days. I look forward to your reply.

Maliah.

Solara closed her eyes, wondering if she'd made a horrible mistake.

Lady Rankin, for no logical reason at all, is close with Nikara, Faisal said. *It's a position of leverage. This friendship could prove invaluable.*

Maliah means nothing to her mother, Solara countered. *She'll mean less than nothing to Nikara. What's the point?*

Maliah needs a friend.

Why do you even care? she shot back.

"Solara?" Lunaro called. He was coming closer, although the well-oiled wheels didn't make a sound on the smooth hardwood floors.

"I can do whatever I wish," Faisal said. "And I've already taken the liberty of confirming the appointment, with your well wishes."

Lunaro came around the corner, frowning. "Lord Faisal."

"I was just leaving," Faisal said. As if to say *don't bother being annoyed.* "You should walk as much as you can, Solara, or you won't be able to walk at all tomorrow." He left.

"What did he want?" Lunaro asked.

Solara had already regaled her brother with all the tales of the day, and he had not been as sympathetic to her death sprint steeplechase as she would have liked. In fact, he'd about fallen out of his chair laughing. She held up the letter. "Lady Maliah invited me for a riding lesson next week. Apparently, I've already replied with best wishes."

Lunaro's nose wrinkled delicately. "I didn't realize you were allowed friends."

"It all has an end game, I'm sure," Solara said. Again, that stab of guilt at her not-quite-lie. How many more of those would she tell before this was over? To Lunaro? To Maliah? To other people who didn't deserve it? "But I doubt that was the last death sprint I'll be dragged on, so I'd rather be prepared for the next one."

She was, without realizing it, twisting the ring on her finger. It grated gently against her brass band, and Lunaro looked down at her nervous movement.

"You don't think that's odd?" he said.

"What?"

"That it looks like an engagement ring."

The thought had never crossed her mind, even after Maliah had pointed out the ring's oddity earlier that day. The symbolism wasn't out of place, not given her knowledge of Faisal's machinations, but of course her brother didn't know that, and couldn't. It was rare that Lunaro put his foot down, but he'd put his foot down on this. "It's just–"

"Don't start lying to me, Sol," Lunaro said.

Her half-formed lie halted on her lips. She lifted her book off her belly and folded it and placed it on the table. Her legs screamed in pain as she lifted them off the table and set her feet on the floor. There was a cramp in the left arch that had been stubbornly jammed since the moment she slid down from her horse.

"Solara," Lunaro said. "What did you agree to?"

"Exactly what I told you," she said softly. "I'm not hiding anything from you. It's only… I can't explain what it's like, to share his mind. I think it makes me slightly different?"

"Is that what it does?"

He thought it made her a liar. She should have known she couldn't pull this off. Not with him. "I'm still myself," she said. "I will always be myself."

"All right," he said, but he knew she was lying.

With difficulty, she stood.

"Where are you going?"

"To walk," she said. She left him, knowing full well that the conversation was not finished between them. She spent the next hour walking around the house and garden, stretching out the muscle cramps in her legs and arms, then went up to bed.

She slept fitfully, waking hour after hour. Faisal, too, was restless. She could sense him moving about the halls, tracing the steps she'd taken during her stretching. They dropped off together near dawn and woke simultaneously barely three minutes later.

Solara got out of bed. She threw a house coat over her nightgown and left the apartment. Something drew her up a flight of stairs to the third floor, through a conservatory, and out onto an expansive balcony that overlooked the garden. Faisal stood at the railing, his folded arms resting along the sleek gold top.

Solara stayed in the doorway, waiting.

"This is fascinating," Faisal said. With one hand, without turning around, he gestured between them. "Tell me, Solara. What compelled you to come find me? Or were you compelled to this place, as I was? And if so, who received the summons first?"

"One would assume it was you, since you were here first."

"My bedroom is closer."

"How long have you been waiting?" she asked practically.

"Not two minutes." He turned around. He, too, had simply tossed a robe over his nightclothes.

Their sleep-deprived mind felt particularly in-tune in that moment. She saw him, and she felt herself and she saw herself as he saw her, and she felt as he felt. It was a panoramic of them. She moved closer to the railing and leaned against it. She couldn't have explained why it felt important to be there, only that it was necessary for her to watch sunlight spill over the grounds and brighten the day.

"This was Aliss's favorite place," Faisal said.

He let her see the memories. Aliss, her long hair pinned back and covered with a handkerchief. She would sit in the large black chair beside the potted palm tree and read, or she would putter about watering and shearing the rose bushes.

"We would come here to watch the sunrise," he went on, and these memories, too, filled her head. Aliss standing at the rail, bathed in sunlight as the sun lifted above the garden wall. A precious memory.

Faisal straightened, became brisk. "Your brother is troubling you."

"I knew lying to him wouldn't be easy," she said.

"I didn't give you a choice."

"I had choices." She did blame him, but she wasn't exonerating herself, either. She'd chosen to lie to her brother, and she was still choosing to. If she told him now that Faisal had threatened his life, she wasn't sure what he'd do. Solara squinted at the sunrise as it warmed her cheeks. "I didn't see any of Tessan's sisters yesterday."

"Some were there. Aliss wasn't. She was an excellent horsewoman... before."

"Better than you?" She couldn't resist.

"Magnificent," he said. A fact. "Aliss was good at whatever she did. She's always been superior in that way."

"Sisters generally are."

Faisal smiled faintly. "I was more adept than Aliss solely in the strength of my mind, and that, at the end of the day, is why Roga chose this method to target her. Because I mocked her. Because this is the only way in which she can be my psychic superior."

He spoke of it so pragmatically, but their thoughts were too close, too conjoined. She could feel how much it hurt him. Taking control of those eight assassins had been a massive effort, and he'd almost broken himself. He did it as a show of strength that was supposed to stop Roga in her tracks. Instead, it only infuriated her.

Occasionally, Mage's fury reminded him of Roga.

He dismissed the thought immediately, but it still made Solara's heart patter uncertainly.

"Don't," he said.

She didn't, if only to spare him a moment of discomfort. He'd latched onto Mage desperately, and there were so many things that Solara wanted to say. Mage wasn't Aliss. Aliss couldn't possibly be as perfect as he remembered. Grief and guilt had compromised him. But she didn't say any of those things.

He'd threatened her life, and he'd threatened her brother's life, and this bond would not allow her to hate him.

Solara hugged him, laying her cheek against his chest, as Aliss had done ten thousand times. He started to brush her off, like he had the first time that she'd clumsily offered comfort. But then he sighed and hugged her back.

CHAPTER TWELVE

The first of the week, Faisal and Solara took the carriage to the Rankin estate in the third ring. It was a modestly luxurious home, although Solara felt that a sort of pallor hung over it, as if Lady Rankin starved the house, as well. They rang the bell, and a liveryman showed them in. Lady Rankin was out, but Maliah waited in the foyer, already dressed in her riding clothes. The pale hostess greeted them with a sweeping curtsy. "It's so good to see you again. Lord Faisal. Miss Solara."

"Thank you for having me," Solara said. Maliah's riding clothes were a smart split skirt and light jacket, but Solara wore her standard black breeches and white sleeveless, so she merely bobbed in place.

"There's coffee in the library if you're able to stay, my lord," Maliah said.

Faisal smiled. "I apologize if it makes you uncomfortable, but I have every intention of watching my Second flounder through this lesson."

Solara scowled at him.

"You've already seen me ride my worst," Maliah said cheerfully. "It's this way." She took Solara's arm and led them through the house and out to the stables. It was a more modest stable than Solara was used to seeing at this point, although still much grander than any house Solara's family had ever been able to afford. Two horses stood tied to a post, and one frazzled looking groom moved to help them mount.

They were smaller horses than everything else Solara had been subjected to, so she was grateful for that, at the very least. She was still sore from the steeplechase, and nothing had been able to coax her onto a horse since that day.

"Master Hannes is an excellent horseman," Maliah explained as they walked out to an arena. Faisal trailed behind. Solara could feel him smirking at her back. "I am apparently the only one he's unable to perform miracles with."

"You're hard on yourself," Solara said.

Maliah shook her head. "I enjoy riding, and I don't mind being bad at it, but I'm not made for this sort of thing. I wish Mother would accept that."

Master Hannes was waiting, a crop in one hand, a scowl already in place on his bewhiskered face. "Maliah," he said. "And you must be the Solara of whom I've heard so much."

"So much?" Solara said. Maliah cringed.

"One would think you led a charge of centaurs to hear Maliah go on," Master Hannes said, apparently unfazed by mortifying his pupil. He had a keen mind, but his thoughts were still readily available. There were few thoughts that weren't these days, and Solara had begun to wonder if the combination of her and Faisal had made a nigh unstoppable psychic weapon. Master Hannes was concerned Maliah had found another snobbish brat to attempt to befriend, and he was not eager to see his favorite student hurt again. Like flipping through a deck of cards, Solara could see the amount of times Maliah had been shunned by her peers. It made her heart heavy.

"She's too generous," Solara said. "I'm a shitty rider."

"With a common mouth, as well," Master Hannes said. He grinned. "Very well. Lady. Guttersnipe. Let's begin."

The lesson was as excruciating as she'd anticipated. Her behind was still sore, and the sitting trot exercises nearly had her crying. Master Hanes was relentless, and Faisal, though he kept his biting commentary to a psychic level, was equally merciless. Twice during the lesson, she twisted around to flip him off, which delighted Master Hannes and Maliah.

Afterward, Maliah insisted they stay for tea, to which Solara agreed so long as nobody judged her for lying face down on a couch instead of subjecting her ass to further torment.

That was how they were – Solara lying on her belly while balancing a teacup in one palm, Maliah a gracious but sweaty and winded hostess, and Faisal uncharacteristically talkative – when Lady Rankin returned.

A maid came to Maliah's private sitting room to announce, "Your mother has returned, Lady Maliah, and she's brought Lady Nikara."

Faisal's smile vanished.

Solara bolted upright, spilling her tea with a curse.

Maliah looked confused by their reactions, but said, "Thank you, Sara. We'll be right down." The maid bobbed and left, and Maliah looked between her guests, unsure. "Is everything all right?"

Solara looked at Faisal. She knew her panic was all over her face, and for the first time ever, Faisal looked sympathetic. "Maliah," he said, setting down his tea. "I need to ask you for a favor."

"Anything," she said.

"Don't tell your mother we were here." He took Solara's hand. "Nikara and I have some unfinished business I'd rather not finish right now."

"Of course, Lord Faisal," Maliah said, still looking confused. "You can take the back stairs out. Solara, are you all right?"

"I'm very sorry," Solara stammered. "I spilled tea everywhere. That was clumsy."

Maliah waved her off. "Don't worry about it. I'm glad you could come. Perhaps I'll see you again next week?"

Faisal promised that she would, then he tugged Solara out of the room and strode for the back stairs. Solara couldn't make her heart stop pounding. Right now, right below them, Nikara Manfalon was here.

Keep your head, Solara, Faisal said. *This is the only time I'm letting you run from her.*

They made it outside undetected, and Solara huddled in a corner of the carriage with her knees pulled to her chest. Faisal watched her. "What?" she said sullenly.

"Why are you so afraid of her?" he said. "She can't control you. Not anymore."

"If you don't understand already, you're not going to," she said. It didn't matter if she was strong enough to resist Nikara now. Back then, she hadn't been.

They rode in silence for a little while. Faisal spoke as they were entering the second ring. "I need you to see Tessan."

Only weeks of practice kept her from grimacing. "How exciting. What's the occasion?"

Faisal considered. *There is an event. An… opportunity. The invitations are very exclusive, and I need him to invite you to it.*

What event?

He hesitated too long to answer. *Just do what I say.*

Solara scowled. *And how am I supposed to broker this meeting?*

I know where he'll be. He looked away. *I don't fault you for keeping him at arm's length, Solara. But he needs to believe he is getting through to you. You need to let him believe that.*

He was telling her to play nice, but even he didn't have the shamelessness to say it in so many words. *Promise me something.*

What?

If I tell you I'm scared, you'll come for me.

Faisal was immobile.

Please, Faisal.

Perhaps it was the desperation in her tone, but this time, he didn't hesitate. *I promise.*

She returned to the apartment to find Lunaro belly-down on the floor, scribbling into a large notebook, his thin legs splayed behind him. She kicked off her boots and lay down beside him, taking his arm and pulling it around her.

"What's wrong?" he said.

"I almost ran into Nikara."

His scribbling stopped.

"Almost," she said. "That's all. I don't want to talk about it. What're you writing?"

Lunaro kissed the top of her head and turned back to his work. "Transcribing notes." He referenced another notebook besides the first. "There was a series of studies done on the bond and how it works. Some interesting stuff here."

"Oh?"

"Back before the Scarlet Guard, soldiers used to take the bond with each other in order to make them better in combat, only there was no Master and no Second. It was an equal partnership." His handwriting was as precise as his stitching. "Since no one had to control anyone else, the bond could link as many soldiers together as were strong enough to hold it."

"Interesting," Solara said.

"Don't be an ass." He could tell she wasn't interested.

She didn't know how any of this information, as fascinating as it might have been to him, was useful in any way. The Diadem had never fought in a war, and the army was for controlling citizens, not enemies. But Lunaro had always been interested in this sort of reading, while Solara preferred her mythical heroes.

"Are you sure you don't want to talk about it?" he asked.

"Yes," she said. She was silent for a few seconds. "I hate her."

"So do I."

Solara shook her head, scattering her thoughts. "You see Kaia again tomorrow? How's that going?"

Lunaro nodded. "The third treatment. Supposedly I should begin having feeling in my toes any day now." He didn't sound like he believed it, and Solara didn't blame him. Despite the exercises and treatments that he'd received so far, there was no change in his paralysis, not even the hint of one. Lunaro was growing bored of it all.

"Any day now, huh?" she repeated. "Well, we can go out into the garden tomorrow. See if you feel the grass under your feet." She didn't know if she was mocking Kaia's promises or trying to cheer him up.

Judging from his expression, he didn't know, either. He sighed and leaned over his work again. "We'll see."

They spent the rest of the evening lying there on the floor. Solara amused herself with a book, deciding to shirk her usual duties. She supposed this would become their new needlework, something to fill their evenings. She was dozing off over her novel when a polite tap came at the door. She stirred drowsily as Lunaro called out for the person to enter.

A maid pushed the door open and dipped a curtsy. "You're wanted, miss."

Solara rolled over, flung one arm over Lunaro in a hug, then pushed herself to her feet. "Don't wait up."

"I will."

She followed the servant out. The girl took her to a bath, scrubbed her clean, and laid out clothes for her. Solara, wrapped in a towel, gave her evening wear a dubious look. She had made a few outfits like this when she worked in Bjorn's. It was one of her specialties. It was styled after a gladiatorial uniform, with a bruised leather bodice and a short scarlet skirt that hit mid-thigh. Hers was to be worn over shiny black breeches, but the scandalous effect was much the same.

Solara dressed slowly, expecting to be told a mistake had been made. The maid returned to pull her hair up into a ponytail, which she then braided halfway down and tied with scarlet thread. Next, the maid added makeup. She smudged dirt on Solara's face and smeared red and purple paint across her mouth like a bruise. Skilled fingers unwavering, the maid created a bruise on Solara's arm and another high on her collar.

So, it was a costume party. Solara was intrigued. She felt half silly, half fierce when she stood before the mirror, surveying the maid's handiwork.

The dressing room door banged open, and Mage came in. She was already in her nightclothes and slippers, so she was not joining them. Faisal entered behind her, looking exasperated at her rudeness.

"The prize pony prancing out for the second time today," Mage said snidely.

"Mage," Faisal said. "Don't be a pain." He hadn't bothered to dress in costume. Unsurprising. He wasn't the prized pony. Lord and ward scrutinized Solara, and she glared back at them, feeling more and more like livestock at a fair.

"Satisfied?" Solara snapped.

"Better not let her drink," Mage said. "She already looks like she'll do anything in those clothes."

Control that wretch, or I am going to hit her, Solara warned Faisal.

He frowned at her. "It's a costume party, Mage. I don't make the rules. It's past your bedtime. You saw the clothes. Now, go to bed."

It was petty, but Solara smirked.

Mage sneered. "Fine. I'd rather not be around when Tessan mauls her in that whore's outfit."

Enough. Solara lunged at her. Faisal intercepted, hauling Solara clear off her feet as Mage leaped backward, the ugly sneer on her face suddenly morphing into fear. "Get a hold of yourself, Solara," Faisal snarled.

Mage quickly composed herself.

Solara was still struggling against Faisal's grip. *Be still,* he said. It wasn't an order, but she still stopped fighting. Did Mage have an ounce of empathy in her body? The spoiled bitch had gotten so comfortable in her new life that she probably didn't remember being concerned for her own safety.

Faisal gingerly let Solara go. She'd had her fingernails in his arm without realizing it. She drew back to herself, her mouth tight.

"Mage," Faisal said. "Get out."

A hurt look flashed through the girl's eyes, but she just spat on the floor, whirled, and stormed out.

Solara turned back to the mirror, swallowing the emotion that threatened to choke her. On a purely analytical level, she could understand why Mage was so vicious. But that didn't make her words any easier to dismiss. Because wasn't that exactly what she was doing? She'd sold herself, mind and body.

"Solara," Faisal said.

She wasn't trying to keep her thoughts from him. She couldn't have, even if she'd wanted to.

He took her by the shoulder and turned her to face him. "You are not a whore," he said. "That isn't what I've asked of you, and it is not what you are." She looked away, but he gently lifted her chin. "You are Solara Barthelme," he said. "Named for a warrior queen."

She'd forgotten about that story, even as much as it had captivated her. She smiled faintly.

"Now." He stepped back, slipping into his distant, disinterested persona as easily as changing an article of clothing. "Even queens shouldn't be late."

CHAPTER THIRTEEN

Solara and Faisal didn't speak in the carriage. He was troubled by the viciousness of his beloved ward, and Solara was amazed that he was so blind to her jealousy.

Their destination was a house in the fourth ring, massive but ramshackle. Raucous music and light poured from every window, and patrons spilled from the three doorways along the front of the building. Solara didn't know if she was looking at a pub, a brothel, or a combination. But she shook herself out of her own sulk enough to needle Faisal a little bit.

You're slumming it tonight, is that it? she asked him.

Behave yourself. He dismounted from the carriage and helped her down.

Solara had to roll her eyes at the scene. She'd been to many parties in the fourth ring, and she wondered how often she'd rubbed elbows with nobles without realizing it. Some of them were painfully obvious in their expensive fabrics, but others had mastered the art of innocuity.

"This should be fun," Solara said.

Faisal was tense, but he nodded. This was not his normal scene. He had made an exception in order to dangle her in front of Tessan. Solara couldn't imagine the hulking Manfalon son here. He would be as out of place as Faisal. The front walk smelled faintly of urine, but all other smells were overwhelmed by the sharp scent of inexpensive liquor.

Solara still had her hand on Faisal's arm, and she let go of it now, flashing him a bright smile, fighting the dread working through her stomach. This night, after all, was not about him, or her, or Mage's many issues. She'd come to find Tessan, so that one day soon they could save Aliss. "Shall we?" she said. Without waiting for an answer, she plunged into the crowd. It had been a while since she'd been to a bar or house party. Every once in a while, she wanted a decent drink and a little exercise, and so she would find her way into a fairly respectable establishment, have a drink, have a few dances, and swiftly make her exit. But this particular atmosphere was one she had never experienced.

It was partly the outfits. The patrons were dressed as all sorts of characters and creatures. Some were heinous monsters. Solara saw werewolves and sirens and indistinguishable beasts. Others wore overtly sexual costumes that bordered on obscene. A few had gone for taste and detail, and Solara's gladiatorial outfit fit best into that category. She was growing fond of the blood-red skirt and how it swished as she moved.

Faisal was off in her right peripheral, but he hung back, although she could feel his eye on her. She made her way to the bar, and the rushed bartender brought her the three shots of whiskey she requested.

Is that wise? Faisal said.

Are you going to let that child of yours dictate my behavior? Solara retorted, and he had the good sense to leave her be. She downed them one after the other, dulling the roar of the crowd. The musicians were invisible in the crush. Sweaty bodies pushed against hers, and despite the heat she was relieved for the protection of her leather and breeches.

Another rowdy song began, and the crowd lurched into some disorganized dance that she, for all her bar dances, had never seen in her life.

Like liquor sodden forest creatures, Faisal murmured. *What a unique class of human being.*

These are your people.

I am to these people as falcons are to chickens.

Solara laughed. A man in a grisly beast costume shoved past her toward the bar, knocking her into a dainty fairy. She apologized – inaudible in the crush – and stumbled back against a medieval king, who winked and planted a wet kiss on her cheek before she could retreat. She rolled her eyes and moved away, pressing toward the relative stability of the bar.

I'll never find him in this.

He'll find you.

How do you know? This is madness.

Just wait. Don't you dare get another drink.

Solara grinned. She had lost sight of Faisal and didn't know if he could see her, but she kept moving toward the bar just to tease him. She recognized a group of young men that she had seen at the hunt, and one glanced over, then did a double take and zeroed in on her. It was Cote, from the golfing green, looking far more at his ease here than he had in the luxurious lodge. Solara deliberately lifted her hand to adjust her hair, flashing her diamond ring. If she was here to attract attention, she might as well play the part well.

Cote nudged his companions, and like a well-coordinated pack of wolves they moved on her, the obvious leader in the front. She'd never learned this one's name, although his jet hair, shaved to skin on either side of his head, was unique, to say the least. Someone had painted a crown of roses on his forehead in brilliant blue.

Not the attention we want, Solara.

She ignored Faisal as the man slid up close to her and leaned to yell in her ear, "Where's your Master, young lady?"

"Tonight, I don't have one!" she shouted back.

Solara Barthelme. Faisal sounded mortified.

Rose Crown laughed, one hand moving to the small of her back. "Tell me, little warrior, do you like to dance?"

"Little queen," Solara corrected. He couldn't hear and had to lean closer so that her lips brushed his ear. "I'm named after a queen."

Stop flirting this instant.

"A queen, yeah?" The man leaned closer still. And then something past her shoulder caught his eye, and he swiftly withdrew his hand and took a large step backward. Solara knew without looking that her quarry had arrived, but still she feigned confusion and turned her head to spot Tessan making his way through the crowd towards her.

"Gotta run," she said lightly and booked it in the opposite direction. *Slow down. You'll lose him.*

Your job is to rescue me if this goes poorly, not micromanage my every move. Still, she was grateful for Faisal's voice in her head. A reminder that she was not on her own. She made it out the back door, and she slowed as she descended a pair of steps into an ill-kempt courtyard. Her strappy sandals smacked against the broken path tiles.

There were more people in the courtyard than she'd expected. Three men lay sprawled on the ground in a drunken heap. A couple stood in one corner, and a girl emptied the contents of her stomach in a different corner. Solara hadn't wanted this much of an audience.

The door slammed behind her for a second time, and she spun around. Tessan, bearing down on her, drew up short.

He had put exactly as much effort into his costume as Faisal had, which was none at all. He was still ridiculously beautiful. It must have been the alcohol that let her admit that. "What are you supposed to be?" she asked, politely. "You and Lord Faisal appear to be sporting the same costume."

Tessan looked her over, then his gaze settled on her face, his mouth hard. "Are you drunk?"

"Yes," she said unapologetically.

Her dismissal seemed to irritate him. "You shouldn't be here."

"Shall I go home to my Master?" she said. He inhaled sharply, and the girl who'd been sick in the corner squeaked in fear. Solara wished she'd picked a better place for this confrontation, but she hadn't had a lot of choice. *I am myself, and only myself.* How true that was, she didn't know. Nikara's careless order had wound deep into Solara's thoughts.

"Do you remember the day you met me?" she asked Tessan.

Tessan nodded once. "Of course."

"All of it?" she pressed. "You remember it that well?"

"Yes," he said. "You don't?"

"You've never had your mind overtaken, Lord Tessan," she said, and he looked defensive. "It's common for things to be a bit fuzzy afterward," she explained. "A lot of people forget everything altogether."

Tessan's face was blank, and of course she couldn't sense his thoughts. It didn't stop her from trying, instinctively. It was like reaching out for a mirage. There was simply nothing there.

"I won't apologize for my sister," he said. "Nikara's crimes are her own. She'll pay for them one day."

"Are you so sure?" Solara said.

Tessan nodded once. He would see that Nikara paid for it. Of that, Solara had no doubts. She'd heard gossip in the dress shop that he could snap a grown man's neck in half a second. Nikara's petite body would not be a challenge.

He stepped closer to her, and Solara had to tilt her head back to see his face. "What do you remember?" he asked. His words were hesitant, as if he were... but no, Tessan couldn't possibly be afraid of anything, certainly not anything Solara could say.

She let the memory surface, like something dead floating to the top of water. "People with minds like yours... nothing in, nothing out... nothing tangled up. You are always you, and only you. But me? The rest of us?" She shook her head. "Every thought snarled. You hear so many voices you don't even know which is yours. You don't know what's driving you until suddenly... suddenly, you're yourself again, in a place you shouldn't be, with people you don't know." It was an inadequate explanation. She could tell it didn't help him understand. What on earth was it like to have a mind like his, where psychic manipulation was unfathomable?

They had never spoken of any of this in his visits to the dress shop. People had stared enough as it was, just at him being there. Intimate conversation was not an option, and Solara had gone to great lengths to be sure they were never in a situation where it was.

She wrapped her arms around herself and tried to recall the details. "I'd been making deliveries with Bjorn that day," she said. "We went into the second ring, and it was so quiet and beautiful. On the way back, I remember two riders passing us on the cart." Something flickered through his eyes. She couldn't read it. "You kicked up a lot of dust and Bjorn was in a coughing fit."

Tessan stared at her for a moment. Then he laughed. It was surprisingly quiet. "We were racing, Nik and I. I lost. I saw you and I looked back, and it was enough for her to get ahead."

It was over. It was all over. But still, unease tightened Solara's stomach as she guessed, "So you told her why you lost."

"She'd sensed you already," Tessan said defensively.

"And I was just a servant, a nobody," she said. "Barely a human being. What could be the harm in a little bit of fun?"

Tessan looked away.

Solara gestured to the house, to the waves of music and laughter. "If being in your world has taught me anything, it's that none of you are afraid to take what you want from me."

She couldn't understand the emotion on his face. But she waited, her pulse throbbing in her throat. It had never occurred to her until this very moment that her gift was a crutch, that she leaned on it so heavily she'd crippled her ability to understand anyone without it.

The harsh line of Tessan's shoulders softened. "I am not Nikara," he said. "I couldn't be, even if I wanted to."

"I'm still afraid of you."

"Why?" he snapped.

"They say you're going to murder your sister," she said.

"I am."

The courtyard was dead silent. It was almost absurd, so many people holding their breath, hanging on his every word. Solara had the insane urge to laugh. It was like being in a play. "And you ask me why I'm afraid?"

"You're not my sister." A bitter smile twisted Tessan's mouth. "I'm sure Lord Faisal has a long list of people he wishes dead, and I wouldn't be surprised if Nikara was on it."

"Faisal is no killer." Solara said it woodenly, and Tessan breathed a laugh.

"Was that your thought or his?"

Solara shook her head. "I try not to question it."

She could tell her complacency rankled him. He stepped closer to her, and Solara's temperature rose. "You're too good for that, Solara," he said.

She hadn't meant to let him get quite so close, and she could hear Mage's nasty accusation in the back of her head. "Don't you doubt yourself?" she said. "If you look at me and feel anything but disinterest, do you not wonder if those feelings are your own?"

He smiled faintly. "I've felt uncertainty about many things, Solara, but never that."

She envied him that certainty. She would have given almost anything to be certain of the origin of the emotion she felt right now.

Tessan lifted his hand and put it on her cheek, thumb covering the fake bruise in the corner of her lips. His gaze settled her mouth.

She whispered, "If I told you I was more afraid of him, would you save me?"

He leaned in, the other hand moving to cup her face.

Solara felt the snarl down her spine like a chill an instant before Faisal said wryly, "Please don't kiss her, Tessan. I feel most of what she feels, and I don't think I could bear that."

Tessan went still.

"Come along, Solara," Faisal said. "Be a good girl."

"She is not a dog, Faisal," Tessan said. He didn't let her go. In fact, his fingers tensed a little, and Solara wondered if he could snap her neck, holding her head like this.

"Isn't she?" Faisal's eyebrows rose mockingly, even though Tessan couldn't see him. "She sits, stays, and rolls over." Tessan let go of her and whirled around. Faisal put his hands up and took a step backward, still smiling, but with a harsh look in his eyes. "I'm only teasing," he said. "I value my Second for all of her skills, whatever they happen to be." The amusement left his voice. "Solara. Come."

"Let her go," Tessan said. Quiet, but deadly all the same.

"I will. When I'm done with her." Faisal's vicious smile returned. "You can have what's left afterwards."

"Do not–"

Solara ducked around Tessan and went to Faisal's side. Tessan's next threat, whatever it was, stalled. "Goodnight, Lord Tessan," she said. She dipped a curtsy and went into the house, leaving Faisal to finish the discussion. She didn't want to hear any more of them arguing about which of them she belonged to.

Inside, the party had grown still wilder, and for a moment the rush on her senses deafened her. Then someone cried out, and a cluster of men and women dressed as gladiators drew her into their circle.

She had never seen any of them before, and none of them knew who she was, so she let them pull her into their midst, downed the cup of whatever was handed to her, and danced until the only thing left in her head was the music.

CHAPTER FOURTEEN

How Faisal found her in the human flood was a mystery, but at some point, he swept her off her drunken feet and carried her into the night. He laid her on one of the carriage benches and crossed her arms over her chest.

I'd be annoyed with you, but you did the work.

Solara moaned and pressed one hand to her head. "Don't do that."

"If you're going to be sick, warn me and I'll put your head out the window," he said. She nodded, curled into a ball, and slept. When she woke the next morning, she was splayed in her bed, boots kicked off, hair coming undone, her head pounding. She gingerly sat up. Lunaro sat by the window, a book laid on the sill, sunlight spilling over him as he made notations.

"So, you're not dead after all," he said.

"Don't taunt me." Her mouth felt full of cotton, and the sunlight made her eyes water. Her brother gestured to the tray on her bedside table, where two glasses – one of water, one of some foul-looking yellow concoction – waited for her. She downed one after the other without questioning the yellow liquid.

"Is that how you drank last night?" Lunaro said. "It's a miracle you walked in on your own two feet."

"I don't think I did."

"Oh, you did. Stumbling over furniture and cursing and singing some war song that I suppose you picked up last night. It was very dignified."

Solara lay back again. "It hurts to think."

Faisal's entirely unwelcome voice filled her head. *I imagine it does.*

She moaned.

Get up and get about your day. You have all your lessons as normal. A pause. *I would suggest you avoid Mage.*

It was as close as he'd come to admitting his beloved ward was in a rage. She stood up, and the sudden movement sent her stumbling to the bathroom in case she was sick.

If I'd realized you drank so much, I would have stopped you, Faisal said, apologetic.

She'd needed that liquid courage. She wished she'd drank more and erased the entire night from her memory. When her stomach was settled, Solara began running a bath.

"Are you going to live?" Lunaro called.

"I think so," she called back. She heard him wheel away, content that she had survived. *If he'd kissed me, would you really have felt it?*

Faisal was silent, but he was still there.

Well? she demanded.

The tub had nearly filled before he responded. *You didn't call for help.*

I wasn't scared. Was that true? It frustrated her that she was uncertain. Doubly irritated now, she stripped off her clothes and sank under the water. She lay there until the act of holding her breath hurt more than the thoughts hurtling through her head, and she sat up and gasped for air.

Be careful not to drown yourself, Faisal said, amused. *That would be a waste.*

He must have been able to feel her lungs burning. Remarkable. Also, unnerving, how deep the connection ran. She dunked her head into the water and soaped her hair, taking time to run her fingers through the sweaty tangles. It had been months since she'd danced, even longer since she'd danced with partners, of which she'd had no shortage last night.

Before Lunaro became wheelchair bound, Solara had danced often, creeping out of the house after he'd gone to work or gone to sleep, because he wouldn't approve. She tried not to remember too keenly – lest Faisal get a mental show – the number of tables she'd danced on as a wild teenager.

Solara climbed out of the tub, dried off, and dressed. Today's outfit was a demure black skirt with the normal white blouse, the better to at least pretend propriety. She tried not to smirk as she braided back her hair. It was unlikely that Mage would be soothed.

Solara settled into the library with a stack of newspapers and a cup of tea and began to read, grateful for the quiet and dimness. Here in the library, the hum of the river was at its deepest. She could feel it through her rib cage.

Whatever the day's tasks were, she was content to leave them for later. The newspaper held its usual plethora of inane details, but one caught her attention. Lady Maliah Rankin had taken her first Second.

Solara couldn't help feeling disappointed. From what she'd sensed of Maliah's mind, the girl wasn't strong enough to hold a Second. But maybe Lady Rankin had been smart enough to choose someone with a very weak psychic gift. Then Solara felt guilty for wishing that on someone, even for Maliah's sake.

Your moral compass is spinning, Solara.

Mind your own business. She turned to the next story in the newspaper and was surprised again. No. Shocked. There was a sketch of a face, well done and quite descriptive. It was the man she'd flirted with at the bar last night, the one with the rose crown. He had been found that morning with his neck broken, having apparently fallen down a flight of stairs in the fourth ring on his way back from the party. She'd read about many deaths in the papers, but she felt this one sharply. Of course, she hadn't really known him, but just the fact that she'd seen him in person – especially now, when she had become so isolated from everyone she'd ever known – made it different.

She became aware, then, of how silent Faisal had gone. *What is it?*

He tried, unsuccessfully, to hide it from her, but the trend of his thoughts made her tense. He remembered how swiftly the rose crown man had backed away from her when he saw Tessan coming. And he was trying to remember the exact moment Tessan had left the party, when and who with, and whether the rose crown man had left first or after.

Faisal. She felt sick.

My conversation with Tessan grew rather heated last night after you went back inside. He's more taken with you than I realized, and his jealousy has earned him a reputation.

But I didn't... I just talked to the man for a minute. It was nothing. She had never considered the possibility she was endangering his life.

My suspicions may be extreme. He didn't think they were. *But I've known Tessan for a long time. Nikara may have taught him to be wary of caring for things, but her crimes did not go unpunished.*

Solara recalled, unwillingly, Nikara's coat of animal skins and his attempt to hang her with it. She read the man's name. Asher Brannam. Twenty-three. Survived by his mother and two young brothers.

She folded the paper, leaned her head back, and closed her eyes. Tessan had said he'd kill his sister. Murder didn't faze him. *I'm sorry.*

I know you are.

Part of her had never believed the wild stories. They'd dosed her with fear, but not enough. She should have been more careful. She never should have dragged anyone else into this mess. *If Tessan killed Asher for thirty seconds of flirting, what is he going to do to you, after everything he thinks you've done to me?*

Tessan wouldn't dare lay a hand on me.

Are you sure?

Are you worried?

Footsteps sounded through the stacks, and Solara ignored Faisal's tease to greet the newcomer, but her greeting died on her lips. It was Mage. Her pleasant resting expression turned aggravated when she saw Solara. "It's amazing you got out of bed this morning," she said. "I saw Faisal carry you in from the carriage." She jerked her chin at the newspaper. "Reviewing your handiwork? Have you shed a tear for Asher?"

Solara's throat tightened. "I didn't know."

"You didn't know what?" Mage bit out. "That Tessan is an animal? That anything you do might set him off? That prancing around with Faisal is the best way to get him exactly the sort of attention we *don't* need? I swear if anything happens–"

"Nothing will happen," Solara said.

Mage breathed a laugh. "Are you in control of this situation? Asher would say otherwise."

She was right. Solara stood to leave, but Mage snatched her arm, and only the memory of the fear in her eyes last night when Solara had turned on her kept Solara from lashing out.

"Look here, you bitch," Mage hissed. "I'll kill you. I'll tear you apart if you get Faisal hurt. Do you hear me?"

Solara could hear the girl's thoughts so easily. Mage was terrified something would happen to Faisal, and Mage would be alone.

"Let go of me," Solara said between her teeth.

Mage shoved her away. "Get out of my sight."

Solara wandered through the house for over an hour, stewing in her wretched thoughts. Asher. A sweet name. She had no ideas as to his character or personality and didn't presume to imagine them, but he certainly hadn't deserved to die.

Her absent footsteps brought her to a set of double doors, each one as large as her bed, made of heavy, shiny wood. Their copper hinges were damp with condensation. Two guards stood watch side by side.

"You can't be here, miss," one said. He didn't look at her, just stared into the distance.

"I'm sorry. I don't know where I am."

The other glanced down at her, at the ring on her hand. "This is the entrance to the river, Miss Solara. No one is allowed down here unless they have special permission from Lord Casarriba."

"Oh." She turned to go, realizing now that that was the origin of the rushing sound that she'd heard for the past ten minutes. The river. Just beyond those doors.

Brisk footsteps interrupted her retreat. "Open the doors."

She lifted her head, stirring out of her morose thoughts, to see Faisal coming up the hall. The two guards came to attention, grasped the handles of the massive doors, and pulled them open. The smell of water overwhelmed her.

You wanted to see it, didn't you?

Solara nodded, still slightly dazed as she climbed out of her own head and followed Faisal through the doors. On the other side, the ground was paved with cobblestones, all of it slick with spray. Thirty feet ahead of them was a wrought iron railing. Faisal walked right up to it, and she followed hesitantly, her steps unsteady on the damp stones.

At the rail, her breath caught. Thirty feet below was the river, a massive, writhing dark beast over a hundred feet across. It pounded against its rocky banks, shooting sprays of frothy white water straight up into the black air, dampening their faces and soaking her clothes. She gripped the rail and leaned over, fear forgotten so swiftly that Faisal put a hand on her shirt, prepared to catch her if she leaned too far.

The sound was thunderous. It enveloped her head to toe. She closed her eyes and leaned farther, as if it could swallow her up.

Are you determined to drown today? Faisal's grip on her shirt tightened.

She had never seen a river, had only seen thin trickles of filthy streams, and ponds of foul standing water in the fourth ring. Nothing like this. Nothing remotely like this.

Slowly, the euphoria quieted. She opened her eyes, now adjusted to the dark, and tried to take it in. The rocky banks were jagged enough to slice flesh and break bone. Across the river, on platforms nearly obliterated in the dark, men in slick wetsuits wearing safety harnesses moved about. She couldn't tell what they were doing. Farther downstream, the water disappeared through a tall, narrow tunnel.

My father brought me and Aliss here when we were young. They tied us to harnesses so we wouldn't slip and fall in.

It's both beautiful and terrifying.

Solara leaned her belly against the rail, and Faisal knotted his hand in the material of her shirt.

I've put a lot of effort into you, Solara. I can't have you dying on me.

Nothing that went into that rushing river came out again.

That's enough. He tugged her away from the rail, and she halfheartedly struggled. There was something mesmerizing about looking over the edge. She wondered if the men working on the other side ever had the inexplicable urge to leap. To fling their bodies over the railing and be swept away in the blink of an eye. *And that is why you don't stare for too long*, Faisal said.

He dragged her out the doors. The house felt gaudily bright in comparison. The guards drew the doors shut. The roar of the river faded away.

Faisal smiled. "Everything you hoped for?"

"That was amazing," she said. Her hair was soaked, her shirt drenched, her skirt heavy with water. *A river.* She had seen a river. Not just any river, but the river that had sustained her life since the day she was born. Every glass of water she'd ever drank had come from here.

"Come along," Faisal said. He gave her a nudge back towards the stairs. She was still dazed, and he kept his hand there, a comforting pressure at the small of her back, as they ascended into the sunlight.

CHAPTER FIFTEEN

Asher's death wore at Solara. She tried to hide it, but Lunaro knew her too well, and Faisal could read her mind. They both insisted, separately, that the best way to combat the guilt was to stay busy. So, she read, she practiced with her knife, she took riding lessons with Maliah, and she mended uniforms with the staff seamstresses.

She'd thought the worst possible guilt she could ever carry was from watching Lunaro lose the use of his legs, but this left that in the dust. She had been responsible for death. *Death*.

Lunaro told her Tessan was the only one responsible. Faisal told her she needed to focus on her work. Only Mage, with her acidic comments and cold stare, seemed to understand how Solara felt, and only because she was not shy in vocalizing that Solara should feel exactly that terrible and worse.

They sent flowers to Asher's family but didn't attend the funeral. Faisal said it would only complicate matters.

Weeks passed, and Faisal kept her in the house, saying Tessan's temper needed time to cool. She wasn't even allowed to accompany Lunaro to his sessions with Kaia, which infuriated her to no end.

She was considering staging a coup when Mage stalked into the apartment one afternoon and said, "You have a visitor."

Solara eyed the girl over the top of her book. "Who?"

"Do I look like your maid?" Mage snapped. "She's in the sitting room."

Maliah, Solara supposed. Mage stalked off in a huff, as she always did whenever she had to suffer the indignity of looking at Solara. Solara went downstairs. She'd become too comfortable in this house. Too safe. She realized that the moment she walked into the sitting room and saw Roga.

Her step faltered.

Aliss's tormenter stood examining the portraits on the walls, particularly the one of Faisal and Aliss as fat-cheeked children, a pleased grin on her face.

If Solara had been on her guard, she would have heard Roga's thoughts. She could have prepared herself.

But she was woefully unprepared as Roga faced her. She wore a delicate pink dress that Solara recognized as her own handiwork. "Solara," Roga said.

Solara curtsied clumsily. "Lady Roga."

Before Solara could straighten, Roga said, "Kneel."

Solara lifted her head, confused.

"Kneel," Roga repeated, slowly, as if Solara was stupid. "You must be very talented on your knees to have my brother in such a tizzy. I just thought I'd see the sight for myself."

All the practice in the world could not have kept the snarl from Solara's face.

Roga laughed. "Nikara told me you had a little fight in you, but you've done an impressive job of playing nice. You've gotten Tessan all worked up, desperate to rescue his imprisoned damsel."

"I don't need to be rescued," Solara said coldly. "Lord Faisal is very kind to me."

Roga crossed her arms, studying Solara. Solara tried very hard not to hear Roga's thoughts, but it was becoming more difficult. Roga had chosen to visit today because she knew Faisal was out of the house, attending a city planning meeting. She wasn't sure how much of a hold Faisal had on Solara, based on Nikara's report of Solara's resistance.

"Was there something else you needed?" Solara said in the same wooden voice.

Roga stepped forward, bringing her and Solara nose to nose. She smelled of delicate perfume, but the malice in her thoughts was staggering, as vile as any odor. There was something off about her, something broken and twisted in her mind.

An image. Roga conjured it in such detail that she must have wanted Solara to see it. Asher Brannam, dead at the bottom of the stairs. Roga had done it. She'd pushed him.

Solara recoiled.

Roga grabbed her by the throat, slamming her into the wall. "You're hiding something, you conniving little bitch," she hissed.

Solara whimpered.

"Tell me what you're hiding." Roga tried to make it a command, tried to cram it into Solara's head, but it battered weakly against Solara's defenses. Roga wasn't strong enough. Not nearly.

Her hand around Solara's throat, however, was very strong. Solara coughed, trying to pull oxygen into her lungs, but she was afraid to raise a hand against the sneering Roga, and Roga knew it.

"Do you think I'm afraid of Faisal?" Roga said. "I'll slaughter you right here in his own house. Answer me." She closed her fist tighter, and Solara's vision darkened.

Someone was coming.

Roga let her go, and Solara slumped to the floor, gasping for breath. Lunaro had wheeled into the room.

Roga's gaze skated between them, and a grin cocked her lips.

Don't, Lunaro warned Solara. She'd sat up, ready to throw her mental barrier around her brother, too, to protect him from that wicked gleam in Roga's eyes.

"Faisal is back," Lunaro said, never taking his eyes off Roga. "You can profess to be unafraid of him all you'd like, but you are. You should go."

"Who the hell do you think you are?" Roga said.

"I'm her brother," Lunaro said. "I will kill you without a second's hesitation, and I don't care who your family is." He gestured to the door. "Have a lovely afternoon, Roga."

Roga sized him up, and just like Mage had at the dinner table weeks ago, she hesitated at what she saw. But Faisal *was* back. Solara could sense him coming, and so could Roga. She swept out of the room without another word. Lunaro came to Solara.

"Are you all right?" he said.

She nodded, her eyes stinging. Her throat burned. "She killed him," she said hoarsely. "She killed Asher. She thought it would be funny."

Lunaro took her hand. "Come on. Get up."

Faisal had realized something was wrong. He was coming to find out exactly what. Solara rubbed her eyes and let Lunaro pull her to her feet.

"That's going to bruise," Lunaro said, his eyes on her throat.

"Don't tell him what happened," Solara said. Her twin knew who she was talking about. She flipped up the collar of her shirt, hiding the evidence. "He's not going to react well."

"Why do you care?" Lunaro said. He already knew the answer. She still tried to lie.

"The more trouble he gets into, the more trouble we get into," she said. Lunaro stared at her. "What?" she hissed.

"Could we please stop this stupid game?" he hissed back at her. "Or if you're going to lie to me, could you at least put some effort into it?"

"Is the truth going to make you feel any better?" She forgot to keep her voice down. "Fine. If he finds out Roga came here and hurt me, he's going to feel guilty, and I don't want him to."

Lunaro breathed a sarcastic laugh. "Even if you don't tell me anything, I've pieced enough together. You're trying to save his sister. Noble cause. I get that, Sol. I really do. But you are way too attached to each other. You know this bond isn't normal."

Solara tried to speak.

"And he is dangling you like bait in front of people who wouldn't think twice about killing you," he said. "What about that is acceptable to you?"

Faisal stepped into the doorway. He'd heard the last accusation, at least. "Solara," he said warily.

"This has nothing to do with you," Lunaro said. "These are common people problems."

Please go, Solara asked Faisal. He gave her brother a testy look, but he nodded. They listened to his footsteps recede. Only when the hall had fallen silent did Lunaro look at Solara.

"You are losing yourself, Sol," he said. "And you can't even see it." Then he wheeled out of the room.

When Solara was young, her father explained to her what a Second was. She'd been suspicious of the practice, even then. He told her that it had begun as a blood oath between partners – soldiers, politicians, lovers – so that there would be complete honesty between them. Total trust. But evil men had turned it to their advantage, discovering that the mentally fitter partner could overwhelm the other, thus making the weaker partner into their slave.

We must always be careful, Sol, to whom we bind ourselves, he'd said.

She'd responded rather smartly that Lu was her only bond, and nobody had better *ever* try to make her into a slave.

Was that what she was now? Faisal's slave? He had been honest and mostly courteous with her since she'd arrived, and he'd honored his promises in caring for her brother. He had yet to put her in a situation where she genuinely feared for her life, which was a pathetic standard for trust, but their interactions felt something like friendship. Was it wrong that she was fond of him? That she wanted to help him? Would pre-bond Solara find that affection inconceivable?

Solara went out to the garden. It was a cool evening, a gentle reprieve from the hot days, and she found a stone bench beneath a rose arbor to sit with her thoughts.

She ran her hands over her face, massaging her aching temples, and when she lowered them, Gaius was there. He smiled at her, as he always did now.

"Hello," she said.

Gaius nodded.

After everything that had happened with Aliss, it still appalled Solara that Faisal allowed Mage to treat Gaius the way she did. But she'd been less upset about it lately. A side effect of the bond? Was her own sense of morality fading? Solara gestured to the seat beside her, and Gaius sat down, his hands in his lap.

"I'm sorry you're here," Solara said. "I know I'm not the one who did it, but being here in the house, it feels like I'm a part of it."

They sat in silence.

"I think we're all going to die," she said. "I think Tessan is going to kill Faisal and then kidnap me, and unless I'm everything he imagines me to be, he'll kill me for disappointing him. Someone will kill Mage because she's an asshole. Roga will kill Lu out of spite."

Gaius' smile faded.

Solara exhaled heavily and tilted her head back. "I'm so tired."

Gaius took her hand. She gave him a questioning look. He pointed at his earring, then at her.

"Is Faisal looking for me?"

Gaius shook his head. He pointed at his earring, her ring, then at her. It was the most complicated conversation she'd had with him to date.

"I don't understand."

Gaius squeezed her hand. He held up two fingers and pointed at her.

"I'm a Second," she guessed. He nodded. He pointed at himself. "You're also a Second?"

He shook his head, held up two fingers, and pointed at her again, more insistently. She nodded, and he pointed at himself, held up two fingers, and pointed at her.

"We're both Seconds," Solara said. Weakly. Because she understood what he was asking. Gaius stared at her. She pulled her hand free. "I don't think that will help you, Gaius."

He caught her arm and squeezed it.

"I can't see your thoughts," she said. "I don't know what Mage did to you, but I don't think I can undo it. I'm sure Faisal tried–" But she knew, even before Gaius shook his head, that Faisal probably had not. He'd probably had no idea how to begin. This was the man who was prepared to put his sister out of her misery because he saw no alternative. His belief in the bond was absolute, no matter how skewed that bond.

"What if I hurt you worse?" Solara whispered.

He took her other hand and held them both.

"What if–?"

Gaius squeezed her hands again, a little harshly, then closed his eyes and waited.

He didn't care what happened to him, so long as he'd tried. Solara swallowed. If he was coherent enough to ask her for help, he was coherent enough to be suffering. Perhaps even Aliss was, behind that dead façade, and Solara was risking a lot to help her.

She owed this to Gaius. Because she'd stood by and done nothing for weeks. Because she was supposed to have a better sense of right and wrong than the aloof elites of the inner rings who used people like furniture.

Solara slipped her hands free from his and held his face, laying her forehead against his. She didn't know what she was doing. She searched for his thoughts through the fog that coated him.

This was how it would have felt to dive into the river.

Blackness swept her up, making her gasp, and then she was gone, headfirst into churning chaos. It was frigid and blinding and terrifying.

Gaius. Reach back. Follow me.

He wasn't there to answer, or if he was, his answer was lost in the howling black water. Solara dug deeper, clawing through the current. It sent her tumbling head over heels, gagging and drowning, but still she surged onward.

I am here. I will lead you out. A rash promise.

But there, deep in the black, a voice called out to her, and in the physical world, Gaius gripped her arm.

I'm here, she said.

So am I.

In the apartment, Lunaro moved his legs in his daily exercises, looking bored and exhausted.

"Lu," Solara said.

"Sol." He didn't pause, and he didn't look up.

"You were right," she said. He still wouldn't look at her. "I am attached to Faisal, and he is attached to me, and it's made me complacent, but it hasn't changed me."

"It's made you into one hell of a liar," he said. "Or have you always been that?"

Solara chewed on her thumbnail. She could tell him the truth. The whole truth. She didn't know that that would make this any better. If anything, it would just make him even angrier with Faisal, and how would that help? "I wish you would trust me."

Lunaro slowly turned to look at her. His expression was incredulous. "I don't have a choice, do I? My life is in your hands. And you've put it in *his* hands."

She didn't know what to say, so she just left the room.

CHAPTER SIXTEEN

The apartment was stifling that night. Solara had never really fought with her brother before, but this one had been a long time coming, ever since she closed him out of her mind. She was beginning to think that she, sans the gift, was incapable of getting along with anyone.

The next morning, something pulled her from bed. She and Faisal met on the same balcony as the last time. They leaned against the rail side by side, staring into the hint of light on the horizon. "How many mornings do you come here?" she said.

He shook his head. "Not often. Till now."

The sun drew higher, spilling sunlight over their faces. Solara wore a high-necked nightgown to hide the bruises on her neck, and though Faisal knew she was being furtive, he'd assumed it had to do with her argument with Lunaro. That, even more than Roga, was consuming her thoughts.

"No desire to fling yourself off this balcony?" Faisal said mock seriously.

"Are you going to hold me back?"

"Should I?" He put his hand on her back, fingers curling through the silky folds of her nightgown. "I doubt this material will hold you up."

She leaned over until his grip went taut. The ground was two stories below, the cobbles bright in the sun. She could smell the flowers.

"This thing I need to be invited to," she began. She wanted to tell him about Gaius and her new, wild hope that maybe it was enough. Maybe she could help him save Aliss without killing anyone.

He didn't want to talk about any of it. It felt wrong to bring such matters here, in this place that meant so much to him because of his sister. So, she let it go for now and leaned farther out until he cursed and grabbed another handful of material.

"Don't you dare fall off this balcony, Solara."

She laughed.

Eventually, he dragged her away from the balcony, and she wandered around the conservatory looking at the plants, most of them exotic, many of them worth more money than she and Lunaro had made in both their careers combined. Faisal explained psychically that his father, grandfather, and great grandmother had all been avid gardeners, each building upon the collection of the other.

"The servants take care of them now. Even when Aliss was here, she loved them but wasn't very good at caring for them." He paused. "I don't find it a particularly hard skillset to learn, if you're interested."

Solara shook her head. "I couldn't."

"Everything in this house has sentimental value of some sort," Faisal said dismissively. "The apartment you and your brother share once belonged to my sister and I. Things take on new duties, and people do, as well." By which he meant to say that he, at least, would not be affronted by her even wishing to care for his family's flowers.

"Nothing's sacred to you, is it?" she said.

"They're just things," he said. "Perhaps because I have always had so many things, they hold little importance for me."

"What *does* hold value to you?"

"My sister," he said without hesitation. "Preserving the dignity of her life." The answers seemed automatic, but after a moment he said, "Apart from Aliss and Mage, nothing. Except, perhaps... perhaps you."

He'd heard more of her conversation with Lu than she'd thought.

"I'm sorry about your brother, Solara," Faisal said.

Solara shrugged. "You scare him."

Faisal sighed heavily. "I don't want to be a man who scares good people. I think I was a good man once. A good brother, anyway. Even if Aliss never sees me again, truly sees me, I would like to be the man she remembers."

He sounded so tired. He was not what Solara would have called a good man. A loyal one, capable of kindness. But not a good one. "I don't want to be like you, Faisal," Solara said.

Faisal just nodded.

They walked back to her room in silence. She'd been gone for several hours, and Lunaro had woken and left; he had another appointment with the physician. At her door, they halted.

I love my sister more than anything else on this earth, Faisal said. His thoughts were full of Aliss, the number of times they'd raced in and out of this door, harassing each other, laughing. *As soon as this ends, one way or another, I'll let you go. You have my word.*

She trusted his word. Once he decided to do something, he did it. It was just... *You should have set Gaius free,* she thought, and his hackles went up. *You've watched your sister be tormented, but you let Mage do it to Gaius, and you did it to me, and that's why my brother hates you. If you're not careful, Aliss will hate you for it, too.*

She didn't say it to wound him, but it did, and she wasn't sorry. Solara went into her room and nudged the door shut. She flopped face down on what had once been Faisal's bed or Aliss's, and she tried to imagine the impossible scenario where they rescued his sister.

It didn't matter what the law said. Overwhelming someone's mind like that was a heinous crime. Somehow, Solara had been able to keep herself intact, but in the beginning, Faisal hadn't cared if he'd consumed her will or not. She was a source of power, and he'd planned to use her like an object.

Solara's throat still hurt, and the reminder of Roga hardened her resolve. She had to save Aliss. Not put her out of her misery. Save her. She pushed herself up on her elbows.

A hand went over her mouth and nose. For a moment she was so shocked she couldn't react. Then she fought, kicking and thrashing, but whoever held her was much stronger. They forced her face back down into the blanket. Solara flailed and flailed, but she couldn't get a breath, and the world went dark.

Solara woke with a raging headache on the floor of a rattling carriage. She jerked upward, and Roga, seated above her, said, "Calm down, pretty thing. You've only been kidnapped."

Solara lurched backward, scrambling as far away from Roga as she could in the cramped space. Roga smiled at her.

"What am I doing here?" Solara said.

"Is that any way to greet your savior, Miss Barthelme?" Roga said. "I've rescued you from that brute Casarriba, and I'm taking you to my brother."

Solara's heart sank.

"Apparently a servant saw me attempt to strangle you, and the word got back to Tessan," Roga said. "Things have been strained between us since then. What better way to smooth things over than to bring him the thing he wants most?"

"I am not a thing."

Roga studied her with animal intent, and Solara shrank back. There was nowhere to go. Her back was to the literal wall. "I look forward to having you as part of our household, Miss Barthelme."

"You can't keep me." Her voice cracked.

Roga's eyebrows rose. "Will Lord Faisal come charging in here to save you?"

Would he? *Should* he?

"Besides." Roga gave her a knowing smile. "It's my understanding you wanted my brother to rescue you."

Solara controlled her face.

"You're dancing a fine line, Miss Barthelme," Roga said. "Be careful not to trip yourself up."

She needed to get out of this carriage. If Roga was taking her to Tessan, then they were on their way to the Center, and the ride wasn't far. She didn't have much time.

Roga sat back, crossing her arms. "There are all sorts of stories about Tessan," she said. "None of them kind. I helped spread them. I won't lie. But it has painted him in a certain light, and the world in general fears him. He knows it. For the most part, he doesn't care. But you, you pretty little thing. For whatever the reason, he cares what *you* think." Roga peered into Solara's face. "And I will not have my brother mocked by the likes of you."

It took every lesson Solara had ever had to keep her face neutral.

"I don't believe you truly hate him," Roga went on. "That's reserved for Nikara, isn't it?"

Solara swallowed hard.

Roga leaned closer. "I could give you to Nikara, instead."

"Get away from me," Solara whispered.

"She told me what she saw in your head a year ago. Such delusions of grandeur. Such pride." Roga reached out and tapped Solara's cheek with one painted fingernail, making Solara shudder and turn away. "You were vain. You were naïve." Roga said each word softly, but each was a slap to the face. "And you thought you were important. And for those reasons, she chose to remind you how very little power you actually held."

Roga grabbed Solara's face, forcing her to look at her as Solara's eyes welled with tears. "If you wish to make it through this, then you will listen very carefully to what I say next." Solara's tears spilled over, and Roga smiled. "Nod, if you understand."

Solara nodded furiously.

"You're going to stand by my brother's side. As his friend. As his lover, if that's what he wishes." Roga's fingers cut into Solara's skin, grinding against her jawbone. "You will fight Faisal's hold on you like your life depends on it, because it does."

Solara tried to speak.

"Your brother," Roga went on, her voice growing harsher.

Solara's pain was instantly forgotten. "Where is my brother?" she snarled.

"Mage refused to break her master's promises," Roga said.

Solara's mind went blank. *Mage had sold her.*

Roga laughed. "I've kept an eye on Faisal's little prodigy for some time. Nothing that insecure can be trusted for long." Roga's lip curled with distaste. "But she refused to hand your brother over, having promised she'd care for him." Her gaze bored into Solara. "I have no power over your brother's life. But before you dismiss the value of your own life too glibly, I might remind you of the pain your death would cause. To your brother. To Faisal." Her smile was cruel. "He guards you jealously for a man who claims not to care."

Welts were forming beneath Roga's nails, with tiny drops of blood beading. "When we step out of this carriage, I suggest you guard your thoughts with care, Miss Barthelme. I would hate for your brother or Faisal to come storming the palace with delusions about how it would turn out for them."

The carriage slowed. They were arriving at the palace right now.

Roga let Solara go and straightened, dusting imaginary grime from her neatly pressed shirt. "If you have no other questions." The carriage halted, and Roga opened the door. "Welcome to the Center."

Shit.

Roga dragged Solara by the arm through the palace, unconcerned with who saw the debacle.

From one brute to another, a small servant girl thought as she hurried past them.

They're going to break Lord Casarriba's bond and kill her, another thought, rife with pity. *Poor wretch.*

Roga could hear them, but her stride didn't break as she pulled Solara through the pristine halls. The palace at the center of the Center. Solara had not expected to lay eyes on it, not even as Faisal's Second. But here she was, being paraded through the glistening gold hallways in her bare feet and nightgown, the collar of which had fallen open to reveal the remaining bruises from her last encounter with Roga.

Solara locked her gaze on the back of Roga's head and wished her dead a thousand times over.

Solara?

Faisal. Her mouth dried out, and her heart started to pound. He could sense her fear, and alarm rumbled through the bond. *Wait,* she thought. *Please wait.*

Where are you?

She locked down her thoughts and thought desperately of a blank wall. It was the simplest trick in a psychic's arsenal, and it wouldn't work for long. They ascended a flight of steps. She couldn't pay attention to where they were going, not while keeping her thoughts empty. A few steps behind Roga, she passed through a set of hand-carved doors, each one made of solid gold – the sheer weight of them should have bent the walls – and into a courtyard filled with palm trees.

"Oh, dear brother," Roga called.

Blank wall. Blank wall. Think only of a blank wall.

Roga disappeared around a cluster of flowering bushes, and Solara thought of bolting, tearing back the way she'd come through the hall of mirrors, and it created such a vibrant image in her mind that Faisal knew instantly where she was, and she had never felt such immense, black rage as what spewed down the bond between them.

He was tearing out of the river house before she could formulate a thought, and for an instant she wanted it. She wanted him to burst into the palace and save her. Save Aliss. She didn't care what happened in the process. She just wanted *out*.

But if he could take the palace by brute force, he would have done it long ago and made Roga pay for what she'd done to his sister. He couldn't do it.

Faisal, **stop**. She threw every ounce of her strength into the command, and far away on the river house lawn, Faisal went dead still.

Around the corner, Roga was speaking, but Solara focused on this. On Faisal. ***You will not come for me.***

Solara...

No matter what you hear, no matter what you see, you will not come for me, and you will not let my brother come for me. Her hands shook at her sides as she tried to refute the truth of what she was doing. She had shifted the bond. Faisal told her eventually one of them would triumph, take control of the other. Her mouth tasted like ash.

Footsteps sounded on the shining marble tiles, and Tessan came around the corner. She stared at him, loathing threatening to overwhelm her. This was his fault.

"Solara." Tessan sounded stunned. His gaze swept her head to toe, taking in her disheveled and battered appearance. "What did he do to you?"

Roga waited, beaming, to see how Solara would play this. Roga knew she was a liar. That she had manipulated Tessan under Faisal's direction. But clearly, Roga did not understand the depth of the deception. Solara tried to speak. Couldn't.

Tessan drew closer, gently turning her face to take in the damage.

This was not the agreement, Solara, Faisal shouted at her. *I never asked this of you. You cannot stay there. I cannot protect you if he keeps you.*

He never could have protected her anyway, and they'd been naïve to believe otherwise. Roga had won. Again. Solara's eyes welled up again, and as Tessan drew her into his arms, she started to cry.

CHAPTER SEVENTEEN

Tessan gave her a simple bedroom in what was once the family nursery, as she was least likely to be disturbed there, he explained, and left her in the care of a hastily appointed maid, Catarina.

Solara sat huddled in the bed. She ate the meal Catarina brought, refused the new clothes, and tried her best to project an air of calm, but inwardly she was pure panic.

She was a prisoner. It didn't matter what Tessan thought she was. After the effort Roga had made to kidnap her, Solara doubted she'd allow her to walk out the front doors, even if Tessan would let her.

It took her a long time to fall asleep that night.

She woke to Catarina's thoughts. *It's a miracle she can sleep while he watches her like that.*

Solara jerked upward, and Catarina, arranging a breakfast tray, gasped.

Tessan sat in front of the empty fireplace, arms and legs crossed in a way that would have looked like sulking on anyone else. Solara, heart hammering, stared at them both. Lord and servant stared back at her.

"Leave us," Tessan said.

Catarina bobbed. "Yes, my lord." *Whatever he's going to do to her, I'd rather not see.* She fled.

"Good morning," Tessan said.

Solara glanced at the window to confirm. Yes. The sun was up, but barely. She pulled the blanket around her shoulders like a shield. She had never been as wary of him as she was now. They were in his territory, with a tightly closed door and no one around for miles who would dare interfere.

"How did you sleep?" Tessan asked.

She had to say something, but all words had fled her mind. She knew she looked a ragged mess. She looked feral in the morning even on her best days. Tessan, in contrast, looked well rested, although slightly nervous. His fingers drummed against his bicep, silent on the expensive material of his white shirt.

"I've sent for the physician," Tessan began.

"No." Her voice, unused since yesterday morning, was hoarse. "I don't want to be touched."

Tessan's jaw locked, and Solara remembered belatedly that Faisal had half the city convinced she was his personal prostitute. "Agathe is very kind," Tessan said. "She's been my physician since I was a child."

"No."

"You're hurt," Tessan said evenly.

Solara lifted one hand to the welts on her cheeks. "It's nothing."

Tessan uncrossed his legs and leaned forward, resting his elbows on his knees. "Solara, please–"

"I'll scream," she said. "I'll fight you."

He sighed. "All right. We'll wait."

"Never. No one is ever touching me, ever again." She'd have to perpetuate the lie now. As vile as it was, it might be enough to keep anyone, him included, from touching her.

"You should eat some breakfast." He brought the breakfast tray to her bed and set it on the silken coverlet. Solara's stomach rumbled, but she didn't move.

"Sol," Tessan said. "You have to eat."

Solara lifted her gaze from the blanket. "Are you going to make me?" she challenged.

"Yes."

Don't make him angry, Solara.

Faisal. His fear was greater than her own. He regretted everything. Meeting her. Bonding her. Dangling her before Tessan. He should have known he couldn't control the situation. He should have known Roga would beat him once more.

"I'm not hungry," Solara said, her defiance faint.

Tessan picked up a slice of apple and said resignedly, "Open your mouth."

She didn't need to read his mind to know he'd force the food down her throat. He'd take twisted care of her despite her wishes. Everything he did was despite her wishes. Faisal chafed at her order, infuriated. But no one was angrier than she was. She snatched a piece of toast from the plate and took a ferocious bite.

"Thank you," Tessan said.

Fuck you, she thought at him.

"I know this is difficult," he said. "But you're safe here. Faisal can't get to you in the palace. No one can."

The thought only made her despair more, and her hands slumped into her lap.

For a moment, they were silent.

Tessan sat down on the edge of the bed. She gave him a wary look, but he simply moved her plate closer. She obeyed the silent order and resumed eating.

"We're going to have to get along, Solara," he said.

"Or else?" she said. "You'll give me back?"

"That isn't funny," he snapped. She jumped at his tone, flinging crumbs everywhere. There was none of Faisal's indulgence here. "I won't hurt you," he said, gentling his voice.

She ate the last piece of fruit on her plate. The plate would make for a decent weapon, but she could think of no nonchalant way to pick it up and wield it. Besides, Tessan didn't look inclined to attack her. His body language was nonthreatening, as if he were approaching a startled animal.

You don't have to do this, Solara, Faisal said.

Was there any way out of it? "Can I go for a walk?"

Tessan nodded. She rolled off the far side of the bed and left the room. He followed two steps behind, like a cat stalking. She only dimly remembered the route he had carried her on yesterday, but she made it back to the courtyard with only one wrong turn. The sun was rosy gold, and she could hear servants moving about in the house.

She climbed into a wicker chair stuffed with cushions, pulled her knees to her chest, and tilted her head back to watch the sun's rising.

Tessan paced. She had not been able to stop thinking of Faisal's cryptic phrase, of how Nikara's crimes hadn't gone unpunished. Tessan looked angry. Tension in his jaw and hands. Furrowed brow. She'd have to learn to read these signs. Who was he planning to punish?

She said quietly, "Can you please stop pacing?"

Tessan halted. Beneath the golden dawn light, he glowed like a painting of a hero in an expensive book. That's what he thought he was. Her hero. It eked a small, bitter smile from her.

"What is it?" he asked.

She wanted to choose her words carefully. Be thoughtful and precise. She said the first thing that came to mind. "I never saw this coming."

Tessan folded his hands behind his back, lowering his gaze to the floor. "I would have taken you from him sooner. But you seemed... conflicted."

"Did I wear servitude well?" She made no effort to control her sarcasm.

Tessan narrowed his eyes.

Solara tried to cool her temper. "You know what my life was like before. He just came and... and took me." She pushed her loose hair back from her face. "I only practiced my gift because of what Nikara did to me, and because I told myself never again would someone take control of me. But it seems to have done more harm than good."

"You don't have to be afraid of Nikara," Tessan said. She scoffed, and he frowned.

"You didn't stop her before," she said. "Is everything so different now?"

"You don't think I can control my sister?"

Nikara was uncontrollable. But Solara couldn't say that, not when she could see the beginning of true irritation on his face. It was almost tiring, having to watch his expressions so carefully. "I don't want to fight," she said.

"Don't you?" he said. Solara glanced at him, and his rigid posture relaxed. "It's going to take some getting used to," he said. "For both of us."

Solara nodded slowly. "What is… what is my role here exactly?"

Tessan's expression hardened. "I am not Faisal," he said.

Yes. That's what she was afraid of.

"You are my guest here," he said. "And regardless of what you think me capable, I will protect you from anyone who wishes you harm. If Faisal himself comes to drag you back, I will protect you. Understood?"

She couldn't tell if he was threatening her or attempting to reassure her, and her confusion must have been obvious on her face.

Tessan sighed. "You don't need to be afraid, Solara. No one is going to hurt you, especially not me."

"Do you swear it?"

"I swear it."

She believed he believed he meant it. But he had already proven that he'd ignore her wishes if they were inconvenient for him. She could only nod.

"When you're ready, you'll be moved to one of the guest rooms adjacent to my apartment," he said.

Just like that, her tentative confidence evaporated.

"It'll be safer for you there," he said.

"Safer?"

Tessan's expression remained blank. "Even I cannot protect you from Nikara if she catches you unawares."

Dread washed over Solara, and she put her hands over her face. She didn't want to be subjected to any more of Nikara's torment. "I'm ready," she said. "Move me." Better Tessan than his sadistic sister.

Her bedroom in Tessan's apartment was beautifully decorated in scarlet and gold, and Solara had to wonder how long it had been waiting for her. Tessan and servants alike left her alone for most of the day, but as the evening unwound, Catarina returned. Solara traded her nightgown for a skirt and blouse, and she sat down to an extravagant dinner with Tessan, Roga, and a third sibling, Petra, who eyed Solara with interest.

Petra looked to be barely sixteen. She was gangly, but with the potential for the same beauty as her siblings. Her portion of the gift was pitiful in comparison with Roga. The moment she walked into the room her thoughts were everywhere.

Faisal certainly left his mark on her. I cannot believe my brother wants something so used. Tess better hope she's not diseased.

Solara locked her attention on her plate.

Shut up, Petra, Roga thought lazily. *She can hear you.*

Can she? Petra didn't filter a single thought as her gaze swept Solara head to toe. *Tell me, pretty little thing, what am I thinking right now?*

Blood rushed to Solara's face, and she reared out of her chair, but Tessan grabbed her arm before she launched herself across the table.

"Petra," Tessan warned. He couldn't hear any of it, of course, but he must have known his little sister well enough.

"Let her go," Roga said, rubbing her hands together. "She'll tear Petra's face off, and I'd pay good money to see that."

Petra grinned. "I was just testing her skill, brother, since you can't."

Tessan tugged Solara back into her seat. "You're only going to goad her on by reacting," he said. "Although I have half a mind to thank her. That's the most life I've ever seen in you."

Solara scowled at the younger sister but said nothing. She doubted Tessan would allow either of his sisters to lay a hand on her, but as he'd already pointed out, he couldn't be beside her all the time.

"Good for you," Petra said. "Faisal didn't ride all the fire out of you."

Roga cringed, and Tessan said, "Petra, learn to watch your mouth, or I am going to rip your tongue out."

Solara blanched, and Petra's grin faltered. Servants brought plates to the table, their thoughts shaky with fear, as well. A trembling boy served Solara her plate, and his only coherent thought was *please don't look at me* as he set the plate into its charger.

"Thank you," she said. All three siblings looked at her in surprise, and the boy turned pale, his eyes widening in alarm.

"You... you're welcome," he stammered. His gaze flicked to Tessan.

Solara remembered Asher. Tessan may not have been the one to take his life, but Asher had been terrified of him for a reason. She looked at Tessan, who eyed the servant boy.

The servant boy's thoughts were in a panic. *Catarina said not to draw attention to myself, and here I go.*

Roga smirked, lapping up the boy's terror. "I do think that servant boy is bothering her," she said.

"No, he's not!" Solara yelled it, and the boy nearly collapsed, his thoughts just a blubber of fear. Tessan's vicious expression was horrifying, and Solara *couldn't think.* "Please don't hurt him," she whispered. The boy's eyes were wet. The other three servants stood frozen, trying not to attract attention.

"I'm not going to hurt anyone, Solara," Tessan said. "Calm down."

She hadn't realized how hard she was shaking. And still, the boy's thoughts. *He's lying so she'll stop caring. The moment her back is turned he'll do whatever he wants.*

Roga and Petra soaked it all in, Roga not even trying to hide her grin. Solara glanced at the boy again, even as inwardly he screamed *don't look at me!*

Tessan took Solara's arm, drawing her out of her chair. "I think dinner might have been a bit much for you," he said. She tried to protest, but he propelled her toward the door. "I'll have a tray sent to your room."

"I'm fine–"

"Don't. Argue." He led her out of the room, and Petra laughed at their backs.

"Please don't," she whispered. "Tessan, *please*. If you–"

"Enough, Solara," he snapped. She hadn't expected kindness from him, but the harshness made her flinch. He took her shoulders and looked her in the eye. "This has clearly upset you," he said. "You should eat something and lie down."

"Please don't." Despair made her voice a whisper.

"I'll see you in the morning." He put his hand on the back of her head and kissed her forehead. "Sleep well."

He made sure of it, sending a servant with sleeping medication.

In the morning, as Catarina brushed Solara's hair and dressed her, the maid's thoughts were pure poison. *She'll have half of us dead or fired before the end of a month, and that's if she doesn't run her mouth and get herself killed first. Stupid bitch. She's unleashed a monster.*

Faisal? Solara sat up to her chin in steaming bathwater, her arms wrapped around herself, her eyes pressed closed. *Please. I need you.*

Silence. But not a dead silence. A smoldering, infuriated silence. For the first time in days, he spoke. *Are you all right?*

No. Not even close to all right. She was terrified and overwhelmed. *I think he killed a boy. A servant boy. He wasn't even twelve. Just because I thanked him. Maybe he didn't kill him. Maybe he was just dismissed. I don't know and I'm afraid to ask.*

I'm sorry. Words alone couldn't express how sorry he was, but she could feel it. *Revoke your command, Solara.*

I can't. He'll kill you. He already wants to. You can't provoke him.

You can't stay there.

Solara wanted to laugh at the inadequacy of his statement. That morning, she'd had a long talk with herself, and she'd come to a decision. She was not allowed to cry anymore. Not for Asher. Not for the servant boy, whatever had happened to him. Not for anything. *Tessan won't let me go. We both know that. I told you I would help you save Aliss, and now I'm in the palace with her.*

Faisal's silence was shocked. He hadn't realized that Solara cared about his sister.

Tessan doesn't know I was brought here against my will, but even if I told him I wanted to leave, he'd think it was you manipulating me, and he's determined to save me from you. That means I'm going to be here for a while. But he and Roga are close. It won't be hard for me to get to Aliss.

Solara, whether you can get to her or not, it doesn't matter. You don't have an escape route. There's no way out.

Solara refrained from mentioning he had never cared about that before. *I haven't thought that part out yet. But listen.* She told him about Gaius, about how she'd plumbed his confused thoughts and found him. *If I can get her conscious, she can walk out the front doors before Roga or Nikara can get to her.*

And what about you? Faisal's frustration was palpable. *Revoke your order, Solara.*

No, I won't. He's hurt people for much smaller crimes than the ones he believes you've committed. Solara couldn't let Faisal be hurt on her account. She didn't care whether he was a good man or not.

His tone became pleading. *Tessan is in love with some fantasy version of you he's created in his head. And when he realizes that person doesn't exist, all that anger turns on you. If you don't revoke your order, I can't help you. I can't disobey you until you're dead.*

She sank deeper into the hot bathwater. *You had a plan for me to take out Roga. The event you wanted Tessan to invite me to. Tell me about it.*

No.

Tell me.

He fought it, but her will had clearly usurped his. *Once a year, Roon hosts war games between his children. It's supposed to train them to rule, and it's a chance for younger siblings to vie for control. The Scarlet Guard doesn't participate. The only ones involved are the family.*

She didn't have the energy to be annoyed, but she still had to say, *You were trying to goad Tessan into marrying me.*

By law, it's the only bond that trumps mine as Master. It was the only legal way to take you from me. He didn't say he was sorry, but his thoughts screamed it. *I can attempt to involve the law to get you back,* he began.

No. Leave it be. The time for lawfulness was long, long past. Roga would probably kill her before she let someone take her. Tessan might, too, if he thought it was the only way to keep her from Faisal. If the war games were the only time each family member wasn't heavily guarded, it was probably going to be her only opportunity. *When does the game take place?*

Solara, I was an idiot. An over ambitious idiot. It can't be done.

Answer me. She wished it didn't come so easily, overpowering his will.

Six weeks. Maybe two months. Maybe less. The exact date is unclear. Roon likes to catch them off guard.

Six weeks. She put her head underwater and let the heat scald her cheeks, as if it could burn emotion out of her. When the urge to cry was in check, she lifted her head. She could do it. She could bear Tessan and his wretched sisters for a month and a half.

You're not making any sense.

Solara pinched her nose hard enough that the pain cleared her head. *I need Nikara distracted to free Aliss. I can destroy Roga easily. Once Aliss is out of the palace, she's safe. But the only way Tessan doesn't come after me is if he can't.*

Solara, no.

What would you have me do? Attempt to escape? There isn't a place in this city where I could hide if he were truly determined to find me. And he would be. He blames you already for the fact that I resist him. He wouldn't let it go. And anyone who attempted to help me would be annihilated. I can't carry that many lives on my conscience, and I can say all day long that it's not my fault but that doesn't make me feel any less guilty. With each word, she grew more determined. *Don't misunderstand me. I'm terrified. But I think I can do it. I know I can.*

You never finished your knife training. Every member of that family can overpower you on their own. Together, they'll be unstoppable.

I don't need to kill them all. That word was so flat. So final. She was going to kill Tessan. *I only need* him *dead and in such a way that it looks like one of his siblings did it.* In the ensuing chaos, she could simply disappear. Someone tapped on the door, and she dug her fingers into her calves. *How's Lunaro?* He must hate her more than ever.

Besides himself. If you won't come home when I ask, maybe you'll do it for him.

Tell him I'm sorry. She certainly couldn't open the link to her brother now, not without risking Roga finding a way past Solara's defenses. Roga kept trying, no matter how futile it had proven for her. Solara couldn't let her guard down for an instant.

Another tap at the door. "Solara?"

Tessan. She lurched upward out of the tub and grabbed her clothes, yanking them onto her still soaked body.

Faisal felt her heartbeat speed up, and his dread matched her own.

She clamped down her fear and refused to let his overwhelm her. Trying to calm her heart, she leaned over the tub and began wringing out her hair. Tessan opened the door, and she looked up, forcing her face to be blank. "I didn't hear you come in."

"I knocked twice."

Solara straightened, detangling her hair with her fingers.

Revoke the order, Solara Barthelme.

Shut up, Faisal.

Her former master despised her for her glib orders. He despised himself for how easily she had taken control of him. She looked at Tessan across the steaming tub. "Did you need something?" She had barely been able to look him in the eye since the poorly executed dinner two days ago. She made herself do it now.

"I came to ask if you'd like to go for a ride, get some fresh air."

"I would like that," she said. He kept watching her. She gripped the edge of the tub. "Is something wrong?"

"Was he talking to you?"

Her heart, somehow, sped up further. It would have been ridiculous to play stupid. "Faisal?"

Tessan nodded. In the steam rising off the bathtub, it was hard to read his face clearly.

"He tries." The room seemed to grow several degrees hotter. "I try to ignore him."

"I keep hounding Father's psychics for a way around this, but everyone tells me the bond is impossible to break," he said.

"Not without breaking me."

Again, even slower, he nodded. "Come out when you're ready." He left, closing the door with a sharp click. Solara exhaled softly and sank into a crouch, gripping the edge of the tub to hold herself up.

CHAPTER EIGHTEEN

Solara and Tessan rode side by side through acres upon acres of cultivated forest. Her mount followed his black mare closely, so Solara let the reins hang loose and feigned interest in her surroundings, which *were* beautiful, just not interesting enough to stir her worry-laden thoughts. Three Scarlet Guard officers accompanied them, following just out of earshot.

They had ridden well away from the palace before either of them spoke. "Do you think you could see him again?" Tessan asked.

"Who?" She watched a bluebird flit over the path. "Faisal?"

"Yes, Faisal."

She glanced at him. "Why?"

"Nikara is hosting a garden party. He'll be there. I don't see the point in hiding you away as if I'd committed a crime in taking you."

Technically, he *had* committed a crime in taking her, but that was irrelevant. "Nikara?" she said pointedly.

Tessan nodded.

The thought of seeing Nikara made Solara's chest constrict. But she'd attended the heiress's steeplechase without ever laying eyes on her, so perhaps the garden party would go as luckily? Somehow, Solara doubted it. "If you stay with me," she said. "Don't leave me alone."

"I will be at your side the entire time," he said.

She was so reassured. A hysterical laugh started up her throat and she turned away, fighting it back. "If you want me to go."

"Show him that you're not afraid of him."

The hysterical laughter threatened again. He wouldn't know what to do with her if she smiled, let alone laughed. "I am afraid of him."

"You don't have to be anymore."

Solara wished the ride were over. But she'd agreed to come because it was time to be brave. To be cunning. "After we formed the bond, and Faisal knew everything about me, he told me that you would never get to me. That no one could take me from him."

Tessan's grip on his reins tightened. His horse tossed its head in irritation.

Solara gave him a careful sideways glance. "But here I am. And now you're promising me the same thing."

"My promise is backed by the Scarlet Guard."

The Scarlet Guard that would slaughter her if they ever caught wind of her intentions. "All right." She pretended to look at the foliage once more, but it wasn't long before he spoke again.

"You're still worried."

"By law, he can come and take me from you," she began.

"I don't give a damn about the law," he snapped.

Solara cringed. "I'm sorry."

"Don't be." He bit off the words.

Solara wondered if he took any pleasure in being around her, when, evidently, she irritated him so much. That encouraged her, that she was herself enough to be annoyed with his impatience. *You brought this on yourself,* she thought. Simply because she could. Because he had no way of hearing her.

"I thought Nikara wasn't supposed to see me," she said, as they went left at a fork in the path.

"I told you," Tessan said. "You only need to be concerned if she catches you unawares. Nikara has always enjoyed taking things that I care for. It began with pets, but it has extended to people. I tell you this only to be wary," he said. "She knows one day I'm going to decimate her, and she wants to inflict as much pain as she can before she goes."

Solara wrapped one arm around herself. "If she knows you want her dead, why doesn't she do something to stop you?"

"She can't," he said.

"How can you be so sure?" she insisted.

"Inevitability," he said, shrugging. "My father says she is the storm, and I am the rock. One subsides. The other subsists."

"That's both poetic and horrible," she said.

Tessan smiled. "I think my father would like you."

Solara couldn't even think about another deadly Manfalon right now. "No one really does," she said. "I don't say that to be pathetic. They all have certain ideas about me. I was just a novelty at best; at worst, his spy or his wh–"

"*Don't* say that," he snarled.

Swallowing hard, Solara said, "I only meant that it might be hard for anyone to see me as anything other than… that."

You aren't supposed to be this good a liar, Solara. Faisal sounded both offended and proud.

Don't distract me.

"Then we'll need to convince them of the errors of their vision," Tessan said.

She nodded. A little calmer now, Solara could acknowledge that this wasn't entirely unpleasant. It was a beautiful day, and Tessan, in the rare moments he wasn't scowling, at least made for an attractive view. Any hope she'd ever had for his potential for goodness had been stripped away, but she could feign it. "You mentioned your father. Mine died when my brother and I were thirteen," she said. "I wish I remembered him better."

"My siblings and I would have been better off if our father died," he said flatly. "Or perhaps we would have all butchered each other by now."

Solara cringed.

He shook his head. "Hold no delusions as to the nature of my family, Solara. I love two of them and trust none of them. Petra would murder me in my sleep if she had the balls, but even if she was successful, Roga would celebrate with her, then kill her for it. We've been trained in weaponry since we could make a fist, and one day this family will end in a bloodbath."

"May I please be far, far away when that happens?" she said. "You can bring me back after you've won."

Tessan glanced at her swiftly, and then, tentatively, he smiled. "I'll do that."

Solara sighed. "I suppose I was lucky to be born the daughter of nobody. We're forged of different metal."

"You're stronger than you think," he said.

"If my brother wished me dead, I'd die of a broken heart before he lifted a finger to kill me," she said honestly. "I need people. I need people that love me." A pause, in which she violently regretted mentioning the L-word. "Lu is all I really need. As long as I have him–"

"I love you, Solara," Tessan said matter-of-factly.

She cursed herself for creating the opening.

"I suppose I haven't made that clear." He indicated the next path they would take. "You've been through enough. I have no expectations of you. But my feelings are what they are."

The pragmatic confession left her unsettled. "I've never loved anyone," she said. "Not like that."

"Neither have I." He played with the polished buckle that linked his reins. "You asked me about the day we met. But that wasn't the first time I saw you."

"What do you mean?"

"Before that night with Nikara, I saw you in a bar in the fourth ring."

Solara knew exactly where this was going, and she turned away to mouth a curse. Damn her wild behavior.

"It was the summer solstice, and you were wearing a yellow dress with white ribbons in the sleeves. Your hair was down, and you were wearing a flower crown."

She remembered the dress well. She'd borrowed it from the tailor's shop. She'd felt beautiful that night, and she'd spun on the dance floor until strange hands had lifted her up onto a tabletop. She had been drunk on the music, the light, the heat. She had felt every eye in the place on her and not cared.

"I tried to talk to you that night," Tessan went on. "But you left too fast."

Her friend had dragged her off the table and sent her home, threatening to tell Lu if she kept being wild.

"I have always thought you were the most beautiful girl I've ever seen."

Faisal.

Solara.

Tell me to control my face.

Faisal did not. "I had no idea," she said. "I remember that night. I was supposed to be at home sleeping. I had school the next day."

"I'm glad you weren't," Tessan said. "I never expected to see you again, but two years later, there you were, on that ridiculous ox cart."

I suppose this explains a lot, Faisal said. *He's been obsessing over you for a very long time.*

That's not helpful, Lord Faisal.

They left the trees and entered a cleared field, vibrant grass replacing pine needles before the horses' hooves, and her mare dove for a mouthful. The sudden yank on the reins whipped Solara forward, and she flew over the mare's neck with a shriek and landed in the grass.

Tessan laughed.

Flushed, Solara sat up, and her horse sniffed her face. "That was very rude," she said sternly.

"Are you all right?" Tessan asked, grinning.

"Fine." She stood, but Tessan still dismounted, picking up her dropped reins. She reached for them, and he folded them into her fingers, then held her hand for a moment. She kept her gaze down.

"Give it time," Tessan said. The guards were coming around the bend, and he kept his voice soft. "I will prove to you that you do not have to be afraid of me."

He sounded so sincere she almost believed him.

Solara's bedroom was close enough to Tessan's that when he was restless, she could hear him moving about. Like tonight. He kept pacing. It was driving her to distraction.

Faisal?

I don't recall seeing any memories of you dancing on tabletops when we bonded.

Solara's cheeks warmed. *You've kept plenty to yourself, as well.*

True. Although I suppose you could always command me to be honest.

She sighed. *I'm sorry that I've had to order you around.*

Had to?

Your sense of decency has had a tremendous shift since you're no longer the one in control, she said curtly. His indignation flared, then subsided. He was far too intelligent not to realize she was right. *I'm doing this to protect you, Faisal, and I don't care if you don't like it. I can deal with Tessan, but I can't have you interfering, planting doubts in his head about where my loyalties lie.*

Where do *your loyalties lie, Solara?*

With my brother, she snapped, but Faisal knew that was only part of the truth. It was a discussion she didn't care to have. *Even with my common background, Tessan's stubborn enough to do whatever he wants, no matter what anyone thinks. He'll marry me.*

The only way I considered this plan was if you remained under my roof, where I could keep him at arm's length, Faisal told her. *You are at his mercy and I'm afraid you've forgotten what that means.*

She remembered all too well the manner of man she was dealing with. *Listen to me, Faisal.* She sat up in bed, the better to argue her point, but then a knock came at her door. She had stopped listening for Tessan's pacing, but it had stopped, and only he would be bothering her at this hour.

Solara, Faisal said, and the anxiety in his voice made her feel terrible.

Trust me. Carefully, so as not to make the mattress creak, Solara lay back down, closed her eyes, and drew her hair over her face. No sooner had she laid her hands down at her side then the door opened slowly, silent on the well-oiled hinges.

"Solara?" Tessan whispered.

She timed her inhales and exhales, made them slumbering-slow. His footsteps echoed into the room. She pressed her eyes closed and thought of calming things. Perfect stitches down a length of fabric. Pearls she'd once embroidered onto a shawl.

"Solara." Tessan put his hand on her shoulder.

Solara screamed. She lurched upward, crying out and flinging herself backward so violently she fell off the bed. "Master, please don't!"

It didn't matter that he was a stone mind. She could feel the fury that swept over him.

She scrambled backward on hands and knees until her back hit the wall and she huddled there, sobbing.

"Solara," Tessan said. He tried to sound calm. "It's me. It's Tessan."

Still, she sobbed.

He came around the bed, and she huddled into a tighter ball. "Please don't touch me."

"I won't," Tessan said. "I'm not... It's me, Solara. I won't hurt you."

She let her breath even out. She lifted her head and met his eyes in the dimness. He looked hurt. And for a moment she wondered if she'd gone too far. But only for a moment. He deserved it. He deserved every ounce of pain she could inflict. "You scared me," she said hoarsely.

"I'm sorry."

She leaned her head against the wall. He sat back on his heels, his hands resting on his thighs. They sat. And sat. And sat. Her bottom grew tired of the unforgiving tiles, but still she sat there, until the sun rose over the horizon and her head bobbed, too exhausted to hold itself up.

He reached to catch her head, and she jerked backward so fast it cracked her skull against the wall, and she swore, her eyes welling with tears.

Tessan looked frustrated. "Get back in the bed, Solara, please."

"Why?" she said, and the suspicion in her voice broke him.

He stood up and went to the door. "Go back to sleep," he said. "I'll tell Catarina not to disturb you." He went out and closed the door.

She laid her aching head against the wall. *See, Faisal? I won.*

Faisal was relieved but also angry. *This time, Solara. But he is not going to keep taking no for an answer.*

It's the only answer he's getting.

CHAPTER NINETEEN

A few days later, Solara was fitted for a dress she was meant to wear to Nikara's garden party. Alone in her bedroom with the seamstress, even stripped down to her underclothes, Solara felt more at home than she had in weeks.

After the girl had gone, Solara ventured into the anteroom. Tessan waited for her on the lounge beneath the windows. A tray had been set for tea. She obeyed the unspoken summons and sat beside him, as far away as the intimate piece of furniture would allow. The expansive skirt of her pale blue dress still spilled over his knees.

"You wanted to talk to me?" she said.

Tessan gestured at her hands. "You haven't taken it off."

She looked down at her hands, momentarily confused. Faisal's ring. She had gotten so used to it that she'd forgotten its significance. But Tessan had not forgotten. She slid it off her hand and dropped it on the tea tray with a clatter.

"I would have thought you'd rip it off your hand the moment you were free."

It had clearly bothered him for some time. "They gave it to me with my first set of Second's clothes. I didn't even think about it." The lie was weak. It rang hollow in her ears.

He looked at the ring. "Do you feel like you betrayed him?" Tessan sounded calm, but there was a ripple in him, like the hint of a current beneath the surface.

"Sometimes," she said slowly. "There's a tug at my thoughts. I guess that's the bond, or... or him asserting his dominance through it." She curled her shoulders. "Sometimes I wake up in a panic and feel like I need to get back, no matter what. I can feel him calling me."

Tessan shifted.

Solara made her voice very small. "I didn't tell you because I didn't want you to think–"

"I don't think anything." He took the ring off the tray and calmly threw it. It clanged off the wall and rolled beneath a chair. Then he reached into his pocket and produced a small velvet box. He opened the lid. The ring inside was delicate, the band half as wide as her father's copper ring. It bore a trio of rubies.

Lunaro would say it looked like an engagement ring. Homesickness sliced through her. Focus, Solara, she told herself. If any of her lies were real, how would she react to this?

"It's beautiful," she said cautiously.

Tessan took her hand and slid the ring onto her finger. It settled against her father's band, the metals a perfect match. "It's yours," he said. He held her hand as if he was afraid that she'd snatch it back. "And in case you were wondering, this ring is a mark of your status, not your servitude."

How dare he, Faisal said.

Solara burst out laughing. She clapped her free hand over her mouth, horrified, but the damage was done.

Tessan's face lit up. "I've never heard you properly laugh before."

"I'm so sorry," she said. *Shut up, Faisal!*

"Don't be sorry," Tessan said. "I wasn't trying to be funny, but I'm glad you thought it was."

Solara knew her cheeks were scarlet, but she couldn't even pinpoint exactly why she was so embarrassed. "I'm sorry. I just... that was terrible of me. I'm so sorry. Thank you. For the ring. It's beautiful."

Tessan's smile was tentative. "You're welcome." He leaned forward and kissed her forehead. He had done it before, although always in a semi-condescending way, before sending her off to bed. This was different. The intent was different.

"I thought you would be happier," he said. "Here. Away from Faisal."

With him, was what Tessan did not say. Faisal very much wanted to make another snide comment, but he didn't dare, for fear of making her laugh again in this precarious moment. "I'm trying," Solara said quietly.

"I know it's difficult," Tessan said, but he sounded bewildered. He couldn't have had much practice comforting someone. He searched her face, waiting for... what? An explanation of why she was unhappy?

Had anyone ever loved him? Did he have any idea of what it looked like? She doubted it. How did you learn to be trusting and kind with people when you were waiting for your family to implode in a massacre?

Now is not the time to be sentimental, Solara, Faisal said.

She'd stared too long.

Tessan kissed her.

She recoiled immediately, before her body had even fully registered the heat of his lips.

"Please don't," she croaked. She couldn't breathe. "I can't."

"I'm sorry," Tessan said softly. There was a deep sorrow in his eyes. For her. For everything he thought she'd endured. He sighed heavily and reached for a plate of cookies on the tea tray. "You should eat. You've lost weight."

He sounded as if she'd wounded him for the second time, and she wished she felt triumphant about it.

The day of the garden party dawned bright pink and with a singular focus. Today, Solara would seek out Aliss. She had seen her in passing a few times now, but since the disastrous first dinner, Tessan barely let anyone near Solara.

The two of them had breakfast on the rooftop. They made civil conversation about a book she was reading, mostly Tessan prompting her with questions. Her silence seemed to trouble him.

At the end of breakfast, Tessan kissed the top of her head – the only physical contact he dared broach now – and said he'd see her at the party. When he was gone, she went to the roof's edge and looked down the four stories into the garden below.

Am I expected to be civil today? Faisal asked.

Solara's mouth quirked. *Yes, you are.*

You have high expectations of me, Miss Barthelme.

It had been nearly a month since the day she last laid eyes on him in the conservatory. Even with his voice in her head, she missed him.

I'm flattered.

Don't be rude. She leaned against the railing, watching servants mill about below, setting up tables and trimming bushes. She and Faisal were trying not to think of what this day meant. He had not seen Aliss for even longer than he and Solara had been apart. *I need to give you something,* she told him.

He read her thoughts and saw how she had gotten down on her hands and knees to retrieve her diamond ring from beneath the chair. *I didn't expect that to hold such sentimental value for you.*

It's pretty.

You don't prefer rubies?

It wouldn't break character for me to slap you when I see you.

Faisal's laughter seemed to dance down her spine. *I'll take it home and keep it safe for you, although I would much rather be taking you home.*

When had she begun to consider the river house her home? When had he? She pushed away from the railing and started for the stairs. *Roga will be watching today. We need to be careful.*

I am nothing but careful.

His flippancy did not reassure her, even if it did make her smile. She spent the morning immersed in her book, barraged by the thoughts of the maids cleaning the apartment. They were still angry about Tolly. One thought she was weak for bending to Tessan's will. The other thought she should keep on keeping her head down and her mouth shut so that no one else had to suffer. It took an iron will not to react to their harsh words.

About noon, Catarina dressed her for the party. It was her first time seeing her dress. The snug bodice had a demure sweetheart neckline trimmed in gold braid, and the finest lace formed decorative sleeves.

The skirt was sheets and sheets of white tulle, belted with a moonstone-encrusted gold chain. The dress went well beyond practical beauty. Its sole purpose was to showcase how much money had been spent on the person wearing it.

The girls worked Solara's hair up into an elaborate braided up-do, and then set a massive gold chain around her throat. Solara didn't look like she'd ever been a seamstress, Second, or captive. She looked like a queen.

She sat in the window seat and waited to be collected, her back straight and her expression as empty as she could make it, even as her thoughts swirled. Today was another performance, perhaps the most excruciating yet. She was going back into the public eye, and everyone would be watching. There would be no avoiding a confrontation with Faisal and no avoiding Nikara.

Terror threatened to drown her, and she twisted her rings around her finger. More than anything, she wanted her brother. Faisal had offered to bring Lu to the party incognito, but Roga had already seen him, and anyone with eyes would know they were twins. As much as Solara wanted to see her brother, she couldn't risk drawing him into this maelstrom. "This is for Lunaro," she whispered. "So that you can go home to Lunaro."

The garden party was already in full swing – she could feel the swell of human consciousness – when Tessan came for her. He stopped in the apartment doorway and stared.

"How do I look?" she asked.

He came into the room, took her hand, and lifted her to her feet. "You are extraordinary," he said softly.

I'll be the judge of that.

Faisal's quip brought a genuine smile to her lips. "Thank you." *You're being very immature, Lord Faisal.* She let Tessan slide her arm through his, and they left the apartment. She stayed close to his side, and he squeezed her hand.

"Never let them see that they scare you," he said.

"You're much braver than I am."

Tessan chuckled. "You might be surprised."

It was hard to fathom Tessan being afraid of anything. They took the rear staircase to the ground floor, and it let them out into the back hall. A series of mirrored doors opened into the garden, which was flooded with guests. The servants had worked themselves ragged in preparing the space. Elegantly dressed tables held artfully arranged food and flowers. Rose petals spilled along the walks. The guests themselves looked like trappings, neatly outfitted in every color of summer and spring.

Thoughts surged over Solara like water, and she tried to close her mind to the wall of noise, but it was impossible. She walked close beside Tessan as he picked his way through the veritable mob. He deigned to greet only a few people, and they stumbled over themselves in bowing and posturing before him.

It wasn't just Solara that they hated. They had choice thoughts for Tessan, too.

Arrogant bastard. Murderer. Cursed.

Someplace she couldn't see, a string quartet played a lovely melody. Solara tried to focus on that, instead, as Tessan stopped at a tall table. A pitcher of pink lemonade and a collection of cut crystal glasses sat on the surface, and a servant appeared from nowhere to pour them each a glass. He was there and gone swift as a ghost, and Solara systematically ignored him, as had become her norm.

"What do you think?" Tessan said, his hand grazing the small of her back. "Too much to bear?"

"No. It's... I'm fine." She touched one of the pink roses in the woven basket set between the glasses. "It's good to be around people again."

Whore. Usurper. Spy. Traitor. Bitch. Common.

The thought noise was exhausting, and Solara chugged her lemonade and wished for something stronger. Two older women across a fountain glared at her, clutching their daughters at their sides.

"Ignore them," Tessan said. She glanced at him. "Your expression never changes, but you fixate on what's upsetting you."

Solara smiled a little sadly. "I'm a terrible liar."

"Is that such a bad thing?" he countered. In an ordinary world, he would be right. But not here in the palace. Lying had quickly become a survival skill.

My compliments to your seamstress. That dress is something.

She came to attention and searched for Faisal, then realized her mistake.

"Is he here?" Tessan said flatly.

That hairstyle looks painful. It's going to rip your braids out of your scalp.

A grin tugged at her mouth. She forced herself to be still, to be calm, and looked at Tessan. "I'm sorry. I'm supposed to be trying to be normal."

"He needs to apologize, not you," he said.

Act startled.

"Hello, Solara."

CHAPTER TWENTY

She jumped, no acting required. Faisal materialized beside her, and he took her glass from her hand and sipped it. "Tessan. You look grim, even for you."

Tessan took Solara's arm and pulled her to his other side, placing his substantial bulk between them. "A bold move, Faisal. Even for you."

Faisal shrugged one shoulder. He wore his usual nondescript attire, but his necktie was studded with diamonds. His features were arranged in an expression of detached arrogance, which did nothing to dissuade the surge of fondness Solara felt when she looked at him. She had missed everything about him, even the feral curl of his lip as he said, "I heard you were going to trot her out for inspection, and I couldn't resist." He grinned at Solara. "How are you, Sol? Has he been good to you?"

"Don't make a scene," Tessan said between his teeth.

"You're the one creating a spectacle," Faisal retorted. "She looks like a cake."

"Even if that were the case, it would still be a step up from how you dressed her," Tessan said coldly.

Faisal, don't you dare.

Faisal met her eyes, his own sparkling with humor and anger. "I don't know," he said to Tessan with studied casualness. "I preferred undressing her."

Solara grabbed Tessan's arm, although she didn't think for an instant that she could hold him back. Tessan lunged at Faisal, but Faisal nimbly stepped out of his grasp.

"Don't be bitter, Tessan," he said. "You've got her none the worse for wear." *Faisal, shut up.* She didn't put enough force behind the command because it didn't stop him. "I was finished with her and now you can have the pieces, just as I promised."

"Tessan, please," Solara said, a pitiful mew.

Everyone was watching this awkward show: Faisal, still prepared for a hasty getaway; Tessan, prepared to erupt; and Solara, holding onto him like an inept anchor.

"Don't beg, Solara," Faisal said. "He's beneath you."

"Fuck off," Tessan snarled. Solara tugged on him again, and he glanced down at her death grip on his forearm, and then up into her eyes, as if he'd forgotten she was there. She thought he would end it there.

But then Faisal muttered, "Bitch." He chose the expletive specifically to insult them both, and Solara let go as Tessan's eyes flashed fire. She didn't stay to see how it unraveled, just spun and walked briskly in the opposite direction, sweeping up her skirt in one hand. Neither Tessan nor Faisal noticed her exit.

Assholes, she flung back in their general direction. Avoiding eye contact with everyone, Solara wound farther into the garden, until she could no longer hear Tessan's voice.

Deeper into the garden was a shining pool, so still it looked like a giant mirror. Lush water plants grew along the perimeter, heavy with velveteen orange and red flowers. A few tables had been set up around the pool. It was strictly women here in this small paradise, hidden from the rest of the party by more towering floral arrangements.

"Solara!"

She turned toward the familiar voice. Maliah waved to her from a table on the outskirts, attempting to be discreet now, though her shout had made that impossible. Solara smiled and made her way over. "Lady Maliah."

"You look beautiful," Maliah said, a little wistfully. She tucked their arms together, drawing Solara close to the table. The other occupant stopped Solara in her tracks. Aliss. She looked exhausted, almost ghostly in a white sheath with a plunging neckline. Her ribs were hyper apparent, and there were six dermal piercings across her collarbones, each one an obscenely large ruby, destined to fall out and leave scars behind.

"This is Aliss," Maliah said from far away. "She's Faisal's..." But she stopped, as if she couldn't bear to say it. Or couldn't dare.

Solara's blood rushed in her ears. She came closer to the table, shaking Maliah off, and reached for Aliss's hand. The girl's skin was frigid and dry. "Hello, Aliss," Solara said.

Aliss merely blinked.

In that moment, a cool stillness fell over the garden. Aliss cringed. Maliah lowered her head. All around them, the women curled up like flowers shivering in a cold front.

Solara turned around.

Nikara had joined them poolside. She looked particularly regal today in a red sheath dress. Strapped to either hip was an ancient-looking dagger, their blades naked. Her hair was piled atop her head in an intricate braided knot, held in place with a ruby pin.

Surrounding Nikara were her six Seconds. Each of the women was blank faced with hair like jet, dressed identically in gladiator costumes much like the one Solara had worn so long ago. Each of them was trained to defend their mistress to the death.

Nikara surveyed her garden of subjects, and Solara resisted the urge to bolt. She could feel Nikara's psychic presence like humidity in the air. It was mere seconds before Nikara's gaze snapped to Solara. She drifted across the cobblestones until she stood before her.

"My lady," Solara said. Her voice trembled as she dipped her head and curtsied, suddenly feeling handicapped by the heft of her skirts.

"Solara Barthelme," Nikara said. Her voice made Solara tremble, but not with fear. She remembered the sweet confidence she'd felt when

Nikara took control of her, and for a horrifying moment, she thought how easy it would be to be taken over once more. "You look exquisite," Nikara said.

"Thank you, my lady." Solara kept her gaze on the ground.

"Don't be shy," Nikara said. She lifted Solara's chin. "If the rumors are to be believed, you and I will be sisters very soon." Maliah gave a little squeak, and Nikara said, "Maliah, **go away**. You're bothering me."

Maliah turned and ran. Her hasty exit knocked the table, spilling a lemonade glass. Someone across the pool yelped as the glass shattered on the ground.

"I didn't say you had to run," Nikara called after her. She laughed. "It fascinates me, how people interpret my commands. Don't you find it interesting, Solara?"

Nikara's grip changed, her slender fingers moving to encase Solara's throat. Behind them, Aliss stirred. Everyone around them was silent as death. Nikara had made no attempt to touch Solara's mind. Yet. But Solara could feel it coming, like something creeping up on her in the dark. And with swiftly mounting dread, she knew she couldn't stop her.

Yes, you can. Faisal. Finished with his ridiculous spat at last. *You're more than strong enough.*

Solara swallowed, her pulse pounding against Nikara's fingertips. *I know I am. But she can't know that.* No one could start asking questions about how a psychic powerful enough to stop Nikara was somehow subservient to Faisal. Subservient to *anyone*. The city needed to believe she was not a threat.

You have no idea what she'll do to you.

"The interpretation can vary immensely," Nikara went on. "I have to remember to be more specific. Like..." Her gaze darted to the broken glass on the ground. "**Pick up that glass and eat it, Solara.**"

Someone made a sound of protest. It sounded like Aliss, like that sweet voice Solara had heard in Faisal's memory. She knelt in front of the broken glass.

Solara, no.

She swept up the shards with one hand. It sliced her palm to ribbons, and everyone stared at her, horrified, as Solara lifted the handful to her lips.

"**Stop**," Nikara said.

Solara froze. The glass glistened in her palm, inches from her opened mouth. Blood filled the palm of Solara's hand and ran over the edges, dripping onto the skirt of her dress.

"What a good girl," Nikara said softly. "**Eat it**." Her voice grew harsher. "**Chew it and swallow it**."

Solara closed her eyes, tipped her head back, and poured the glass into her mouth.

"Nikara!" Tessan.

Someone grabbed her by the face, forcing her jaw open before she could bite down. Glass spilled onto the ground, and the man said, "Spit it out."

She spat. She didn't care who it was or if it was believable that he could override Nikara's command. She turned to see her tormentor. Nikara was on her knees, her neck craned backward in deference to the iron grip Tessan had on her hair.

"Don't scold," Nikara said, her voice raspy from the strain on her throat. "I was only teasing her."

"Touch her again," Tessan said. "I will tear your throat out." Then he shoved her. She caught herself on her hands before her face hit the pavement, her mouth a twisted knot of anger. But her Seconds held back, and when Nikara lifted her head once more, she was smiling.

"Violo," Tessan said. The man still gripping Solara by the face tipped his head in acknowledgement. "Take her inside."

Violo lifted Solara to her feet. Her mouth was bleeding. Her bleeding hand had ruined her dress. "By your leave, my lady," Violo said, and he picked her up and carried her into the house. She twisted to look over his shoulder, and she saw Aliss kneeling, her face blank once more. Tears ran down her face.

Violo carried Solara into the house, but they only made it as far as the second floor before they were intercepted. Faisal, following them swiftly up the stairs said, "Violo, **put her down**."

Solara had never heard him give a command before. Did she sound that soulless when she did it to him? Did it make everyone resemble a monster?

Violo stopped. He set Solara on her feet.

"Thank you," Faisal said. "**Go to her room and wait there for her**."

Violo left.

Shaking, Solara turned to Faisal. His jaw worked furiously as he took in the blood on her. *I'm going to kill her*, he thought.

Solara spat blood on the floor. *I thought we couldn't massacre the entire family.*

This has gone too far.

It doesn't hurt that much. She lifted her hand to inspect the damage, and Faisal hissed. Her skin was in ribbons. Moving swiftly, he ripped the lace off her sleeve and bound her hand in it. He had to pull it snug to stop the bleeding, and Solara closed her eyes and grit her teeth at the pain. She inspected her mouth with her tongue and found only minor cuts. Violo had saved her from a far worse fate.

Footsteps sounded in an adjoining hall, and simultaneously they moved to the nearest door. It led into a small, windowless sitting room. Faisal took a straight back chair and propped it beneath the door handle, then they stood there and looked at each other.

End this, Solara.

I can't. They had had this argument a thousand times. She was sick of it.

"You act as if you want to stay here," Faisal said aloud. She jumped at his actual voice, and she glanced nervously at the door.

Of course I don't want to.

"Are you sure about that?" he said. He was speaking audibly on purpose, the better to accuse her. She took in his face, void of pretense now. It had been different when he was a voice in her head, each of them putting on a mask of courage, even when it was almost impossible to lie to each other.

Now, she had to look him dead in the eye and see the truth written there.

"When Nikara ordered you–"

"Faisal," Solara said. "Please." She didn't dare order him to stop, not now, when everything between them felt delicate enough to snap in an instant. They were combing her memory, re-analyzing everything from a year ago.

Kiss my brother goodbye.

Think of him often.

"Solara," Faisal said. "That order is wound so deep in your head that you cannot stop obeying it, even now. You can't protect yourself from Tessan. You don't even want to."

She dug her fingers into her skirt. When she spoke, her voice was broken. "I can't stop. I can't disobey that order. But it doesn't mean anything. I'm myself. And only myself."

Seconds ticked by, and Faisal struggled with whether to attempt to comfort her.

"I know," she whispered. It was a tricky business, giving orders. Intent mattered. Interpretation mattered. What had Nikara really meant, and how had Solara, dazed and confused, interpreted it? She couldn't remember. She couldn't remember any of it clearly.

Faisal took her by the shoulders. *I knew from the day at Lady Gao's that your loyalty was split away from yourself, and I should have stopped it there. That man is a threat to your wellbeing. Can you even see that?*

If I can or I can't – and I can – what does that change? She still couldn't leave. Short of faking her own death, she couldn't imagine convincing Tessan to let her go. And even then, he might cling to her corpse. The thought made her smile a little hysterically. *Nothing has happened to suggest I'm incapable of protecting my own interests.*

How much longer do you think he'll be patient with you? Faisal challenged.

She gritted her teeth. *I have no idea, but maybe you should stop baiting him.*

This is my fault, now?

Solara slapped his hands away from her. *Don't twist my words, Faisal Casarriba. Help me or don't but stop fighting me every step of the way. It's your fault I'm here.*

Faisal's expression darkened, and Solara glared at him. It was his fault. His and Mage's, although she didn't know if he'd acknowledged that fact, or ever would.

"I know I'm the reason you're here," Faisal said finally. "Why do you think I'm trying so hard to get you out?"

Solara shook her head. "I haven't forgotten the casualties, Faisal. And I won't have you be another one." If anyone else had to pay the price for Tessan's obsession, it would be her, and her alone. *Don't mistake this for martyrdom. I intend to win this.* She reached into the front of her dress and removed her diamond ring and held it out to him. Faisal's shoulders slumped as he took it. *Did you see Aliss?*

Guilt slammed him. He hadn't tried to see his sister. He'd immediately come after Solara. She put her hand on his arm. *For a moment, she was aware. I know she was. If I'd had another second to–*

Aliss is gone. He said it harshly. *No amount of wishing will change that. Gaius was different. Mage botched the job; he was only half a prisoner. Aliss has been gone for a long time.*

It would be easier to believe that than deal with the reality that beneath that empty mask, his sister was crying out for him to save her. It suddenly infuriated Solara, that he couldn't face that fact. So instead, he'd latched onto Mage. And now he'd latched onto her. And no matter how many surrogates he tried to save it was never going to make him feel any better.

It didn't matter. Her plan did not require his assistance. She'd save Aliss on her own, and she'd save her own ass, too.

Solara patted the hand that held her ring. *Take this back to my room. I'll join it soon. Now go.* She removed the chair, and he looked out into the hall to check that the coast was clear. Then, without looking back, she ran all the way to the apartment.

CHAPTER
TWENTY-ONE

Poor Violo waited at the front doors, as ordered. She dismissed him, and she tried to dismiss the vague discomfort she'd felt when Faisal had ordered Violo about. The command hadn't hurt him, and it had been necessary, not cruel.

She went to her room, stripped off her bloodied dress, and threw on her nightclothes, although it was still early in the day.

This is the last time I'm leaving this house without you, Faisal promised. She could sense him moving away, the chasm between them widening.

Don't make rash promises.

She lay on her bed and held her injured hand on her chest, and that was where Tessan found her half an hour later, as he blew into the apartment like a summer storm, bellowing at a pale-faced guard that if Nikara came within a hundred yards of this apartment, he was to be informed immediately so he could personally shred her to pieces.

His tirade stopped abruptly as he saw her open bedroom door, as she was not in the habit of leaving it open. She sat up. "Is it over?"

Tessan's aggressive posture softened, and the guard wilted with relief. "Are you all right?" he asked, coming to the doorway. The guard took advantage of his distraction to make a hasty getaway.

Solara glanced at her discarded dress, and Tessan's temper seemed to rekindle as he saw the blood. What had he felt when he saw her at his sister's mercy once more? Had it scared him? "I'm fine," she said. She lifted her hand. "It's not bad."

He hesitated in the doorway.

Solara...

Hush, Faisal. She scooted so her back rested against the wall and gestured to the vacated foot of her bed. Tessan came into the room and carefully sat down, his gaze on the floor.

"I promised I wouldn't leave you," he said. "And I broke that promise. I'm sorry."

The apology was wooden, as if he'd practiced it. He probably didn't apologize often. Solara almost laughed. "Things got out of hand," she said, gently.

Tessan's eyes flashed. "I despise that man."

You see? she told Faisal in a weak attempt at humor. *It's all your fault.*

"He torments you for his amusement, and I won't stand for it." Tessan turned to face her. "He's going to pay for what he did to you."

"You don't have to do that for me," she said. "It's enough that I'm out."

"It's not enough for me," he said.

Tread carefully, Solara, Faisal cautioned. *Don't piss him off on my account.*

"They're all going to use me to try to hurt you," she said. His eyebrows rose. "Thank you for rescuing me," she said, and his expression gentled once more, until her next words. "But if you keep proving that hurting me upsets you this much, your siblings, Faisal, anyone – are only going to get more aggressive."

"Would you rather have choked on that glass?" Tessan snapped.

She almost snapped back, but she kept it in check. Just. "Of course not. But Nikara made a spectacle out of us both. The common girl, on her knees, signing her own death warrant." And Tessan, cruel and merciless.

Tessan stood up.

The conversation was over.

"I've sent for the physician for your hand," he said. "Try to get some rest."

He was so stubborn. "Thank you," she said.

Tessan looked back over his shoulder at her. "I'll think on what you said," he said.

She nodded, and he went out and closed the door. She had only been lying down for a few minutes before she heard him begin pacing. There was her answer. Seeing her at his sister's mercy had terrified him.

They were having breakfast in the apartment a few days later when Tessan, handing her a plum-flavored jam, said, "Is it the act of sex itself that you find repugnant, or can you not stand me?"

Solara immediately began choking on her biscuit and had to grab her glass of water and down the contents before she could breathe again.

"I'm being this blunt for a reason," Tessan went on. "I love you, Solara. I hope I've made that clear." He gestured for the servant to refill her glass.

The servant crept forward, his thoughts loud enough for everyone in the building to hear. *He's going to propose over biscuits and jam? Does he truly not see how terrified she is of him?*

"However, if you can't provide me with an heir to the Manfalon empire, then I can't marry you."

Clutching her glass, Solara stared at him. He had been quiet for the past few days, and she'd been hoping – apparently naively – that he was considering her admonitions about his behavior.

Tessan stared back at her, unintimidated. There were probably very few things on the face of the earth that *could* intimidate him, and discussing sex at the breakfast table with a six-servant audience was apparently not one of them. After a moment, he smiled at her confounded face. "Did you expect me to hide you away in the apartment for the rest of your life?"

Still dumbfounded, Solara shook her head.

"You've been through hell," he said. "And life as the Lady Manfalon would bring you in more contact with the devil than I'm sure you'd like. But as my wife, you'd be untouchable. I can't force Faisal to break that bond, but if he dared try to take you back, I'd be within my rights to kill him where he stood."

Solara picked up her napkin and dabbed her lips slowly, so she would have more time to come up with a response. This was what she'd wanted. Everything she'd done had been driving to this point. She hadn't expected this caveat so soon. In fact, she hadn't expected it at all. Tessan had an abnormal amount of temper, but if nothing else, he'd respected her boundaries. Solara kept her expression serious, twisting the linen of her napkin around one finger. "Is this an ultimatum?" she said finally. "Sleep with you or leave?"

"Of course not!"

She jumped at his volume. She could see him check himself, trying to be gentler. He had to do that a lot, and he was getting better at it. "Of course not, Solara. I love you. I *want* to marry you."

"Won't that go poorly for you?" she said. "I'm no one. I'm nothing. Your family would never accept me."

"I don't care what my family has to say on the matter, as most of them are not long for this world," he said. The servants standing at the wall paled, but as far as Tessan was concerned, they didn't exist. "The survivors will know not to invoke my temper."

Yes. They most certainly would.

Tessan rested his elbows on the tabletop with a sigh. "As much as I care for you, Solara, I have an obligation to my family name and to the empire my family built," he said. "If you don't believe you can bear that burden, I'm not going to throw you out. You will always have a place in my home, regardless of who I marry, and I will defend you to the day you die, no matter the legal consequences."

She wouldn't do it. Not for the world. But, just for a moment, Solara tried to imagine that she could sleep with Tessan and think of it as nothing more than a means to an end. She had never been very intimate with anyone, as much as she enjoyed flirting in bars. Tessan was hands-down the most attractive man she'd ever known, and if they had met in a different time and place, Solara suspected this story would have unfolded very differently. She had morals, but she also had eyes.

But he was her captor. The man she planned to murder.

"You seem troubled," Tessan said.

Solara.

I was beginning to wonder if you would chime in. Give me your wisdom, Lord Faisal.

Don't attempt to string him along. Don't question yourself. Give it up. It doesn't matter anymore. It's over. I will find another way to get to Aliss. This isn't your burden.

Faisal's insistence on believing she could simply waltz out of the palace a free woman irritated her. He had no idea what they were dealing with.

"Do I have to give you an answer right now?" she said.

Why are you so stubborn?

Tessan hesitated. Was it her imagination, or had he begun to form the word, *yes*? "No," he said. A sigh, as if he'd resolved something himself. "No, you don't."

She could feel Faisal's disapproval. But she nodded and picked up her fork. Tessan resumed eating his eggs. The tension ebbed out of the room, and the servants breathed again.

Tessan's responsibilities to his father's businesses meant Solara was normally left to her own devices until evening, but after breakfast, when she collected a stack of books and a blanket and headed into the garden, he joined her. She picked a comfortable spot in the shade of an oak tree. Tessan helped her spread the blanket, the two of them working in silence, her struggling to hold the four books under one arm. Tessan smiled at her difficulty but didn't offer to help.

When everything was settled, she sat on one side, and he spread out on the other, his arms folded behind his head. "Are you going to follow me around until I give you an answer?" she said.

"I've been holding my breath since breakfast," he said without opening his eyes.

Solara bit her bottom lip so she wouldn't smile. She propped her book against her knees and read casually, not paying much attention to the story. The days had begun to cool, but a warm breeze blew, stirring her loose hair and the folds of Tessan's navy shirt. She felt peaceful. The moment she realized it, she felt guilty, as if she needed to deny herself every happiness until she'd finished her business here.

No, that wasn't quite it. She felt as if she wasn't allowed to be happy so long as she was near Tessan.

She glanced down to find him watching her. "What is it?" she said, immediately self-conscious.

"You smile when you read," he said. "I don't get to see you smile that often."

She looked back at her book, now doubly conscious. She knew he wasn't trying to guilt her. Tessan was many things, but manipulative was not one of them. He was worried about her because she'd lost weight, because she was quieter, because he'd seen her cringe under the hateful barrage of servants' and siblings' thoughts. She'd spent a lot of time perfecting her façade, and he'd spent a lot of time seeing through it.

Voices sounded somewhere nearby, and Solara's hands tightened on her book. Petra and Roga.

"Those two won't hurt you," Tessan said.

Solara turned a page. "That doesn't make them any more pleasant to be around."

Petra and Roga appeared around a hedge. They were at their ease, discussing the merits of a man they'd seen at a bar last night. As delighted as they were in their obscene conversation, they lit up when they saw Solara. And then Solara lit up, because on their heels was Aliss.

"It's our little sun," Petra said. "Tess had you hidden so well I started to think you were a beautiful dream."

"Leave her alone," Tessan said. His eyes were closed, his body relaxed, but Solara wondered if he was privately as threatened by his siblings as she was, and simply more used to hiding it.

Petra and Roga leaned against each other, looking for the world like mischievous little girls, as they switched their teasing from audible to psychic.

What a sweet picture, Roga said. *Our brother looks almost human.*

Almost, Petra said. *Don't be too hasty. We'll have to see if she lasts.*

She doesn't look particularly well-wearing. I think I could snap those pretty arms like sticks. What do you think, Solara?

Solara didn't acknowledge them. Aliss stood a few steps behind them, looking ridiculous in a frothy pink dress. Her dermal piercings had fallen out, leaving her chest a scarred mess that the sisters always took care to showcase. She gazed into the distance with her hands folded in front of her.

Aliss's mind was locked down. Not one, not two, but three walls surrounded her thoughts, whatever was left of them. One wall was solid ruby. Roga. The second was black stone, and the one after that granite. Nikara.

"Are the two of you going to keep hovering?" Tessan said.

"Why, were we interrupting something?" Roga said suggestively.

Unperturbed, Petra sat facing Solara. Her booted feet left smudges of dirt on the blanket. She noticed Solara's severe glance but just smiled and shrugged. "I'm a little sister," she said. "What can you expect?"

"She can expect you to act your age," Tessan warned.

Petra leaned forward and rested her chin on Solara's knees. She moved so fast it caught Solara off guard, and she dropped her book.

Tessan's eyes opened, and Petra's smirk faded. "Do not touch her," Tessan said.

"No need to be so defensive," Petra muttered, but she backed away. Quickly.

"She's not breakable, Tess," Roga said. "Just startles easy, apparently." She grinned at Solara. "I would hate to see one of my siblings really go at you. You might die of fright."

Solara hated them. She was sick of being their means of torment for their brother. She checked on Aliss once more, but she couldn't look long. Roga was always watching. Solara closed her book and stood. "I'm going for a walk."

"I'll come with you," Petra said.

"Follow her and I'll break your legs," Tessan said. "Sit down."

"You are obsessed with that girl," Roga said. Solara stepped over Petra's folded legs and began walking away. She heard Tessan rise, and Petra thought, *Look at the well-trained doggy heel for his mistress.*

Let him alone, Roga said mildly. *You should be happy for your brother. He finally has someone who can't run from him.*

She'll find a way, or he'll break her. It'll be a shame because I find her so entertaining. At least you have Aliss.

Solara's steps hadn't faltered. She hadn't felt the least bit sorry. Not until that last comment. She whirled around. "Enough."

CHAPTER TWENTY-TWO

Tessan was close behind her and he stopped, confused. She stormed toward his sisters, and he put out a cautioning hand, saying, "Sol."

She flew around him and tackled Petra. They slammed into the pavement, Solara's knee in her midsection.

"You bitch!" Petra shoved her, and before Solara could go back at her, Tessan snatched her up around the waist.

"Be thankful that's all you got," Tessan snapped. Roga was red faced, but she didn't move. Petra glared at them from the ground, her mouth twisted into an ugly sneer. Aliss hadn't reacted. Those walls were thick. Solara had been right. It would require Nikara's broken concentration to get to her. The elder sister was clearly doing the bulk of the work.

"Put me down," Solara said with as much dignity as she could muster.

Tessan had her feet dangling a foot off the ground. He set her down, and she turned and stalked away with her nose in the air. She threw out one final probe, running her hands down the ruby walls. Strong, but she could take it down. It'd have to be all three at once. It would have to be so fast, so furious, that no one had time to retaliate. *I'm coming, Aliss.*

None of the siblings said a word, psychic or otherwise, as she left. She turned a corner and smoothed her skirt and finger-brushed her hair, as if it could tidy her mentally as well as physically.

"Petra always gets an impressive rise out of you," Tessan said.

She'd forgotten he was there. He'd learned his lesson about letting her walk off alone. "She's an arrogant little prat," she said curtly. "If I was stronger, I'd beat the attitude out of her."

Tessan snorted. "You're lucky you attacked the sister who failed her combat training. Repeatedly."

They'd left his sisters far enough behind that they could no longer hear each other, so Solara turned around, still trying to cool her temper. Tessan looked comparably quite calm. "Do they not make you want to tear your hair out?" she said, genuinely curious. "You have to know they're muttering about you in their heads."

He studied her for a moment. Then he said, "Were you happy?"

She gaped at him.

"A moment ago, when it was just the two of us. You seemed happy."

Every one of the Manfalon offspring made her want to rip her hair straight out of her skull. She almost demanded to know how in the world that mattered. But his sisters had undoubtedly been harassing him for most of his life. Solara might have been a new means to do it, but the torment wasn't new.

"Were you?" he asked.

Solara sighed. Her temper was inconsequential. She was here for him. To manipulate and murder him so she could save Aliss and save herself. The thought gave her a little burst of panic, even as she calmly said, "The word I picked was peaceful."

Tessan's expression softened. "Good."

"Good?" she echoed.

"You smile sometimes, but not often," he said. "I don't remember the last time I saw you truly happy, except–"

"Please don't mention me dancing on the table," Solara said, and Tessan threw his head back and laughed. Her face warmed. "I'm glad you find that so funny," she said. It was silly to think his sisters mattered to him.

"Will you promise me something?" Tessan said, struggling to stop laughing.

"Probably not," she said. His laughter, so rare, was infectious. "But you can ask."

"One day, I'm going to put you on a table, and you have to dance," he said.

Her face flushed again, and it mortified her. "I make no such promises," she said haughtily, but it only made him grin wider. Solara turned and kept walking. Damn her and her wild years.

Tessan followed, and even his footfall seemed to be laughing at her. "You act very prim and proper, but I know otherwise," he said.

"You're as bad as your sisters," she fired back, and he chuckled again. "Go away."

"I cleared my entire day to spend time with you," he said, and she resisted the urge to turn back. Tolly. Asher. She reminded herself of their names. Of the price they'd paid for her. "Don't be mad," he said.

"I am mad."

He caught her wrist to halt her, and she stared at the ground. He put two fingers under her chin, coaxing her face up. "You're very stubborn," he said.

"And you aren't?" she retorted.

She didn't mean it harshly, but his hand tensed against her cheek. "I know I'm not the easiest person to get along with," he said stiffly.

Solara started to roll her eyes.

"Your friend Maliah has been worried for you."

Instantly, Solara's irritation was replaced with concern. She looked up at him, her stomach tightening.

"Perhaps it's the strength of your acting," he said. She'd pissed him off. "But Maliah seems convinced you were happier before, with Faisal."

Oh, Maliah. It wasn't fair to be frustrated with her friend for her inability to keep her thoughts to herself. She couldn't help it. But Solara didn't know where else to direct her frustration. "Maliah was kind to me when I had no other allies," she said. What could she have let slip? She hadn't *seen* anything. Had anyone? Did Violo remember seeing her with Faisal?

"She's weak-minded," Tessan said. "But she isn't stupid." He sounded like one of his sisters. Which of them had heard Maliah's thoughts and gleefully tattled?

How could she salvage this? Solara was scrambling, but before she could hit proper panic, a single thought steadied her. If she had thought farther ahead at the costume party, she wouldn't have made the mistake of involving Asher. If she had stayed calm at the dinner table all those weeks ago, Tolly wouldn't have met his murky fate.

Today, it was her head on the chopping block, and even if she survived it, next it would be someone else. If she didn't learn to manage Tessan, then she couldn't do this. She might as well give up.

"Do you doubt me?" she said. Tessan's eyebrows rose. "Do you think I enjoyed being bought like a piece of furniture, then paraded about in pretty clothes, being told to sit and stay and roll over?"

The reminder of Faisal's taunt made Tessan's mouth purse. Faisal had chosen his barbs well.

"And if I enjoyed that humiliation so damn much," she went on, and Tessan flinched. "Then why would I be here? *You* came for *me*, because *you* knew I needed help." And then, steeling herself, she slapped his hand away from her face. He blinked, stunned, and Solara swallowed hard but stood firm. "Do you want me to recount every day I spent in that house? What I did? What was done to me?" She was ready, a thousand lies on the tip of her tongue.

But Tessan said, "Stop."

"Why should I?" she fired at him. "You seem determined to make me relive it every single time someone suggests I'm lying."

He took her shoulders in his hands. "I know you're not lying." He said each word firmly, and she went silent. His grip on her was tight, almost scared. She made herself look him in the eye without wavering. "I've never cared for anyone the way I care for you, Solara," he said. "And if I need reassurance, it's because you seem like you're very far away."

Why did her conscience prick at her like that? This was ludicrous. She owed him nothing, certainly not her honesty.

"You've said before that a stone mind like me can't begin to imagine what it's like for the rest of you. But it's…" Tessan worried his bottom lip with his teeth. He started in the corner and dragged his teeth across it in a way that looked incredibly painful. He had never looked so human. "I'm the only stone mind in this house," he said. "In the Center. There's a whole, vast world of conversation taking place inside everyone's head but my own. And I worry." He stopped himself. His throat throbbed as he swallowed. "I'm afraid that I'm missing something important. I'm afraid just out of my hearing, everyone is laughing at me."

Solara stared at him, and again, her conscience cut her deep. He'd taken such care to learn to read past her façade of indifference, and she'd never attempted to see past his.

Tessan laughed nervously. "Say something, Solara."

"I'm sorry." And she had never meant anything so much in her life. The silence around Faisal had scared her before she'd broken through. What would it be like to have that silence all around? Knowing that to everyone else, it was a forest of thoughts and wishes and secrets? Secrets that everyone knew but you.

"I don't need you to be sorry," he said. "I just want you to understand. You are the only good thing in my life. I want you on my side. I need you on my side."

Wouldn't it be worse if she felt nothing in this moment? These past months of bizarre, frightening life hadn't hardened her heart. Better to be too kind than too harsh, even to someone like him. She laid her hand over his on her shoulder, and that ruby ring gleamed.

"If this is too much," Tessan began. Solara shook her head, unable to form a coherent sentence. He moved his hands from her shoulders to cup her neck and jaw. "Then may I kiss you?"

"Yes," Solara whispered. When Tessan's lips met hers, Solara's single remaining thought, *he's never asked before*, fled her mind. He was so gentle; she didn't know why she'd ever thought he might hurt her. The touch sent a delightful tremor down her spine, and she gripped a handful of his shirt without meaning to.

"You are the loveliest woman I have ever laid eyes on," he murmured. She leaned into him, her eyes closed. "Marry me," he said.

Yes, of course yes. The part of her brain still functioning had a prompt and tidy response. But he kissed her again, and the rational part of her instantly gave up controlling the situation.

When he let her breathe, she said, "Yes." Breathless. Partly faked. But not entirely.

Solara sat at her dressing table later that evening while her maids braided her hair, trying to steel her nerve to speak to Faisal, when Roga walked into her room. The maids immediately ducked their heads and backed away.

So, you're to marry my brother.

Solara picked up the discarded comb and started parting her own hair. "Don't bother me, Roga."

Roga stood behind her, meeting her cold gaze in the mirror. "You'll make a lovely bride."

"You don't intend to let me live to see the wedding," she said. Roga smiled almost sheepishly. "Are you not afraid of what your brother will do to you if you hurt me?"

Roga leaned over her, resting a hand on the table on either side of her, so her chest pushed Solara's body forward and her mouth was on her ear. *My brother doesn't scare me, you naive little thing.*

Roga wanted Solara to respond psychically and show a chink in her impenetrable defense. Solara kept braiding her hair. She would not show her any fear. But she was scared. Roga didn't need superior psychic ability to break every bone in Solara's body. "Leave me alone."

Roga smacked the comb out of her hand, and it clattered to the floor. The maids flinched. "Watch your tone, Second. You overstep your bounds."

Solara's hand tightened into a fist, but she calmly reached down to retrieve her comb. As she did, Roga grabbed the back of her neck and slammed her face-down into the table. Solara cried out in pain and surprise. Blood blossomed in her nose and ran down her mouth as Roga crushed her face into the unforgiving surface.

"Do you think you've won something?" she snarled. "You are a whore. And a well-used one, at that."

The taste of her own blood burned Solara's tongue. "Let. Me. Go."

Shall I? Roga ground her face into the tabletop, her grip radiating pain down Solara's neck and spine. *Will you call for your master to come save you if I don't? Will he come for you?*

Rage ripped through Solara. She had no master. But she didn't have the breath to say all that. "Fuck you," she gasped.

Roga lifted her head and slammed it down a second time. Solara tried to get her hands up to protect her face, but she wasn't quick enough.

You will not win this. Do you understand me? I will string you up before I allow you to bear my family's name.

"Let me go!" Solara flung her head back, cracking her skull against Roga's chin and giving her a bloody nose to match her own. The moment she saw the look in Roga's eyes, she knew this ended one way. Roga had been toying with the idea of murdering Solara when she walked in the door. But she'd just made up her mind.

Solara bolted, but Roga caught her arm and flung her into the table. It hit her in the midsection and put her on her knees, gasping for breath that whistled through her aching rib cage.

The servants were frozen. Perhaps for the first time, their thoughts were full of genuine concern for her. They wanted to help. But they were too afraid. An absent Tessan was not as terrifying as the present Roga.

"Shall we keep going?" Roga said, looming over her.

Solara's breath made a whistling sound. "Fuck. You."

Roga dug her fingers into Solara's hair and yanked her to her feet. Tears blurred Solara's eyes and blood ran down her chin. *You've forgotten who I am, you impudent little bitch.*

Roga wanted her to break, to cry out for help. Solara would rather die. Roga shoved Solara to her knees and tipped her head back, wrapping her forearm into Solara's neck until it cut off her air. "I am going to choke the life out of you," she whispered. Solara gagged, scrabbling at Roga's hands with her fingernails. "And this time, no one is coming for you."

"Roga, take your hands off her."

Roga's grip went soft, then tightened again, harder than before. Solara's vision dimmed. All she knew was the arm cutting into her throat.

"She's toying with you, brother," Roga said. "I'm doing you a favor."

Tessan's voice stayed soft, almost patient. "In three seconds, if you have not let her go, I am going to snap your neck in two."

"You would threaten your family for this–"

A sickening crack and Solara was free. Her body collapsed but never hit the ground. Tessan swept her up, cradling her head against his chest. As her vision cleared, she turned, trying to see, but he held her face away. "Don't look."

CHAPTER TWENTY-THREE

It was Solara's first time seeing Tessan's bedroom, though she saw it through a film of blood and tears. He sat her on the edge of his massive bed, pulled his shirtsleeve down over his hand, and began wiping her face. She kept hearing that snap.

"Is she dead?" she whispered.

"Yes," Tessan said. He touched a spot between her eyebrows, and she sucked her breath. Roga had shredded her skin. "Violo," he called. The servant who had rescued her at the garden party stepped into the bedroom. "Get the physician," Tessan said. "And as soon as my father arrives, bring him to me."

Violo nodded. "Sir." He left the room.

Tessan put his hand on Solara's ribs, fingers splayed. "Breathe deeply," he said. She went to inhale and her eyes watered. It felt like her bones cracked. Tessan moved his hand to the other side. "Once more."

"I can't. It hurts."

"It's all right. Lie back." He laid her back on the bed. Her nose was still bleeding, and he took her right sleeve and pressed the material to her nose.

She blinked up at the ceiling. Each inhale devolved into a gasp.

Tessan squeezed her knee. "Talk to me."

"About what?" Her breath rasped.

"Tell me what you'd like to do tomorrow," he said.

She knew he was trying to distract her, and she was grateful. "I want to go on a picnic. I want to eat strawberries."

"What else?"

Solara shook her head, and that made her chest burn. A sob caught in her throat. Tessan faded away, and when he came back, he put a small pill of something bitter between her lips. It melted beneath her tongue, and the pain lessened.

"What else," he said.

Solara went through a laundry list of food items. Quail eggs. Roasted asparagus. Candied apricots. Things she had seen in store window fronts and on lords' and ladies' tables when she was a nobody seamstress. She missed that anonymity.

Tessan sat beside her and held her hand. Each time her voice lagged, he squeezed her hand and urged her on.

She didn't know how long she lay there, although it couldn't have been long before the physician arrived and made a tsking sound as he leaned over her. "I'm going to put her under," the man said, drawing a small bottle from his bag.

She shook her head furiously.

"Do it," Tessan said.

"No," she said. "No, don't." The physician filled a needle with liquid from the bottle and took her arm. "**Do not touch me.**" The order barked out of her, and the physician froze, then looked frantically at Tessan. "**Get away from me.**"

The physician backed away, his eyes wide, the needle beginning to drip its contents on the floor. "My lord?"

Tessan gazed at her, his expression thoughtful. She glanced at him, trying to read his reaction, and then back at the physician. "Solara," Tessan said. "Look at me."

"Don't let him," she said. She didn't want to be unconscious in this house.

"You are hurt," Tessan said. "He's going to do it, or I will, and you can't stop me."

Tears trickled down the sides of her face. "Please don't."

"Let him go," he said. She shook her head. "Trust me," he said. She wasn't aware of revoking the order, but when Tessan beckoned to the doctor with his free hand, the man slowly came forward. "Trust me," Tessan said again, and the needle pricked her arm.

Faisal had been calling her name. Perhaps for hours. The fear in his voice stirred the cobwebs from her drug-slowed thoughts. She lay face down in silk pillows, and when she tried to sit up, pain exploded through her midsection, and she cried out.

Faisal felt her pain. *Answer me.*

I'm here.

"I'm here," Tessan said. Warm, steady hands turned her over, and she looked up into Tessan's eyes, dark with worry. "You kept turning over in your sleep," he said. "I couldn't stop you."

What happened? Faisal demanded. He could feel the pain splitting her body, but Solara couldn't formulate an answer. She'd locked down her mind without realizing it, making it as tense and defensive as her beaten body.

"How is the pain?" Tessan asked.

Roga had done serious damage. Each tiny movement felt like it bent her bones out of shape. "Horrible," she croaked to Tessan. Then, to Faisal, *Roga attacked me. And Tessan broke her neck. He killed her.*

That shocked Faisal silent.

It was daylight. Tessan wore the same clothes from the previous day, and the luxurious bed still held the imprint of his body beside her. She closed her eyes, dizzy. *I can't stay here. I need to get out.*

I'll come for you.

Do not come for me. He will kill you. She had feared it from the beginning, but Solara knew now with sickening certainty that Tessan would slaughter anyone who tried to take her from him.

Revoke the goddamn order.

No. Stop speaking. Find out... find out if Aliss is alive.

"Do you think you can stand?" Tessan asked. Solara didn't respond. "My father wants to see you," he said. "It would be better if you could stand."

Lord Roon Manfalon, coming to see her. Solara felt ill. "Does he know?" She didn't know whether her fear was for herself or for Tessan. "What you did to Roga?"

Tessan's mouth hardened. "I gave her fair warning."

"Is that how that works?" she whispered.

She thought he would say something. Explain. Perhaps apologize, as bizarre as that would have been. But he said, "Nikara will try to use this to get rid of me. I told you this family ends in a bloodbath. This is the beginning. Your only safe place is by my side, and you can only be at my side if you're on your feet." And then he stood up and wrenched her to her feet.

Solara cursed. She tried to beat him off as the pain surged violently, but he leaned her against the bedpost. Tears spilled down her face, and she bit her tongue so the pain would distract from the nausea.

"I need you to be strong," he said. "Bear it."

"I hate you," she gasped.

Tessan grinned. "Yes. Get angry. Because you and I are going to have to fight this whole house."

He gave her something to drink that dulled the pain enough for her to think clearly, although holding her own body up was still a monumental effort. Her nose was packed with dried blood but miraculously unbroken, and her face was a maze of bruises.

She started cursing again as soon as Tessan said she needed a bath, but he gave her no choice, and no dignity, either. He picked her up and carried her to the bathtub, and although she swore at him and rained blasphemy down on the entire household, he dumped her in the water and ordered Catarina to scrub her.

When she was clean, dressed, and arranged in a chair in the sitting room, the elder Lord Manfalon came to see her. She had never seen him in person. He was a narrow, wiry man with eyes as bright as stars. He looked her up and down, taking in her bruised face and frilly dress and the way Tessan stood beside her, arms crossed.

"You murdered your favorite sister for this girl?" Roon said. He had a low, rumbly voice that was oddly pleasant. His thoughts were guarded too well to be worth the effort to worm into when Solara was already so exhausted.

"I gave her fair warning," Tessan said.

Roon's thin mouth teased into a smile. He looked at Solara. "When Tessan was nine, he told his siblings he would never kill them without fair warning. My son honors his promises."

Solara stared blankly, willing the conversation to be over so she could lie down.

"Do you understand what it means to marry this man?" Roon said, jerking his head at his son. "I've heard horrible things about you, not the least of which being you were fucking Faisal Casarriba just a few months ago."

Was she expected to respond to this?

Roon went on, addressing Tessan now. "For this to work, you'd have to depose Nikara quickly. And deal with Petra. She's young and stupid but she's strong, and she'll hurt you one day, and torture this girl for the hell of it."

"I know," Tessan said quietly.

The frankness of the conversation was horrifying, and if Solara were less drugged, she would have cared.

"You're willing to do all of this for her?" Roon said.

Tessan nodded.

Roon studied Solara again. "She's not pretty, or is that the bruises?" To Solara, he said, "I heard you ordered the physician about. You have some gifts."

If she could have mustered the effort, Solara would have made him dance.

"Does she speak?" Roon said. "Do you speak, girl?"

Perhaps it was the drugs. "Us common types are taught to keep our mouths shut," she said, her voice a sneer.

Roon laughed. And then, quick as a viper, he swung his knuckle like a mace and cracked it against her ribs. She doubled over and blacked out. When she woke again, she was back in Tessan's bed, held in place by a fortress of pillows.

She was alone, and for that small reprieve she gave thanks. *Faisal?*

His silence rippled with anger. She was hurting him, especially now, with these careless commands. Ordering him about like he was the slave she had so feared becoming. She let her shields down, fully reopening the bond between them, and he swam through her thoughts, like an offended pet reclaiming its favorite piece of furniture.

Where's Aliss? she asked.

She's alive.

And?

As best as I can find out, she's with Nikara.

Nikara can't possibly hold seven alone, Solara said. *I can break her. I know it.* It was a good thing, really, that Nikara and Roga had split the bond. It had to be what kept Aliss alive when Roga died. She felt vaguely optimistic, but Faisal's thoughts were black. *I'm going to marry Tessan.*

Solara, please.

The siblings have already turned on each other. Roon is encouraging it, and Tessan is sure it doesn't end here. I'm never going to get a better chance. I'm going into those games, and I'm going to end this. I will get Aliss out first, I swear. I'll break Nikara. I don't care how long it takes.

Faisal's horror was palpable.

Tessan isn't going to let me out of his sight. Keep an ear on this place, get me information. If any more of them are plotting against me, I need to know before it gets this far. She shoved the order into his head, and then she shut him out, stripping his presence from her mind, reinforcing her barriers. Her thoughts were so loud in his absence that they seemed to echo.

For the next three days, the physician kept Solara drugged to the point of incoherence, but the fourth night, she was conscious and alert when Tessan came to bed. The bed was monstrous, more than large enough to accommodate them comfortably with no danger of touching. Solara knew it was for her protection that this new sleeping arrangement had begun – and to be perfectly honest, she'd rather not be left alone when she was unconscious and even more incapable of defending herself – but she was still bothered by the ease with which he joined her beneath the covers.

"Are you awake?" he said. The servants, at her request, had left a single candle burning in the fireplace. It cast a few shadows but did nothing to illuminate the room.

"Yes."

He turned over. She could feel his gaze on her, but she stared at the canopy above their heads and refused to look him in the eye.

"Are you angry with me for what I did to Roga?" he said. "After everything she did to torment you?"

"Are you angry?" she countered. "Do you regret it?"

"Roga understood who I am better than anyone else on this earth. She was either very desperate or very bold to do what she did. Either way, she'd decided to stop putting on her farce of respect, and it only would have escalated if I let her live."

Solara still couldn't understand how he'd done that to his sister, or how he could show no remorse. "I think our marriage is going to be difficult."

Tessan laughed. "You haven't changed your mind?"

"Would you accept it if I had?"

"No, not without a fight." He paused. "Does that surprise you?"

"I'm not about to pick a fight with you, if that's what you're asking," she said. She wasn't afraid of Tessan, per se. Not anymore. Overwhelmed by, tired of… those were better descriptions.

"Tomorrow the city official is going to bring the paperwork," he said. "All you have to do is sign it."

"And then?"

"And then you are a piece of this family, regardless of how they feel about it. Regardless of how much longer they're around to have an opinion on it. Did you want a proper wedding?"

Solara snorted. She couldn't help herself. "I can barely walk, and if you try to stand me up again, you'll wish you hadn't."

Tessan laughed again. The candle flickered and went out. "Once we are through this, I will never again make you do anything you don't want to do. Agreed?"

She sniffed.

"That's not legally binding assent. Don't give me loopholes, Solara."

"I need my rest," she said. "You shouldn't be talking to me."

"My apologies," he said with studied seriousness. "I'll be quiet."

They lay in silence, each fully aware the other was not trying to sleep. She was furious with him for a dozen different reasons, but the nature of her anger felt off. It should have been cold and righteous. Instead, it was haphazard. Messy. Almost confused. And despite the terrifying things that had occurred in her bedroom, she wished she was there, and not in this bed with him.

Think of him often.

Every time Solara thought of the glib command, she wanted to scream. She thought of punching through Nikara's mental barriers and destroying the woman, and it was the only thing that soothed her temper.

"You can't sleep?" Tessan said.

He sounded closer, although he couldn't have moved without her hearing him. She could have reached out and touched him, although she didn't know why she would. She shouldn't even answer.

"No," she said softly. "I can't."

Tessan got up. In another moment, a flame cut the dark, and he set the relit candle on her nightstand. He sat on the edge of the bed, his back resting against the sturdy post. "Tell me a story."

"A story?" she echoed.

"Yes."

She couldn't think of a good one. Currently, the only stories in her head were of the atrocities he and Nikara had wreaked on each other. "I can't think of one."

Tessan considered. "You said you didn't remember your father very well. What about your mother?"

Was she really having this conversation with Tessan Manfalon? It surprised her how much she wanted to speak, if not to him in particular, then at least about something good. "She taught me how to read," she said. "Lu and I both. We had all these books, a huge library. Huge by our standards, anyway. My father worked in a print shop. We got all the books with mistakes in them."

Tessan smiled. "Is that why you like reading so much?"

"I suppose so," she said.

"Tell me something else."

What else was there to tell? Solara had never spent much time talking about her childhood. The two people she felt most comfortable talking to – Lunaro and Faisal – already knew everything there was to know. "When my parents died, Lu and I sold all the books," she said. "We sold everything. Except this." She held up her hand, allowing the candlelight to illuminate her father's ring and Tessan's nestled against it. "I told Lu we could sell it, but he knew how much I loved it, and he wouldn't let me."

"Your brother sounds like a good man," Tessan said.

To Solara's horror, her eyes welled up. She could remember so well the day she'd pulled the ring off her finger and tried to add it to the pile of things to sell. She'd worn it in their father's stead for years, always captivated by what, at the time, was the fanciest piece of jewelry she'd ever touched.

Lunaro had laughed at her. *Don't be stupid, Sol. Put that back on.*

It was utterly unfathomable to her brother to take something from her that she loved. They had spent their entire lives never going a day without each other, and now it had been months, and she didn't know when she would ever see him again.

"Are you all right?" Tessan asked hesitantly.

Solara nodded, sniffling. "I'm sorry. You were trying to make me feel better, and I'm making it worse."

"You don't have to apologize."

Solara was disgusted at her own emotion, and yet he seemed unbothered. She could just make out his face, and he was wearing the worried expression he often wore when he thought she wasn't looking. It made perfect sense that someone like her brother cared about her. It even made sense that Faisal, for all his faults, could care. But Tessan? She ran a knuckle across her eyes, wiping away tears that hadn't fallen. "You can put out the light."

Tessan rose and blew out the candle. His shadow vanished into darkness. "Goodnight again, Sol," he said.

He'd quickly shortened her name to its diminutive, and she wondered that it seemed so natural to him. That all of this felt so natural to him. He leaned over to kiss her forehead.

It was a split-second decision. Solara sat up on her elbows, so he missed her forehead and caught her lips. If he was surprised, he didn't show it. He kissed her slowly, as if it was his only obligation in the world.

Solara told herself to feel repulsed, so she could convince herself their euphoric kiss in the garden was a fluke. But giving her body orders was not quite so simple as commanding Faisal or the physician. Tessan released her mouth and chastely kissed her forehead.

"Sleep well, Lady Solara."

She shouldn't have been able to, but she did.

CHAPTER TWENTY-FOUR

Solara signed three sheets of paper, and at the end, she was Lady Solara Manfalon, wife of Lord Tessan Manfalon. Apart from the county official and his assistant, Tessan was the only one present. The official bowed, offered his congratulations, and he and his assistant excused themselves. Tessan took the man's vacated seat across the desk from Solara and looked at her, a little smile tugging at his mouth. Pure joy shone in his eyes.

"Should I feel different?" she said.

Tessan tipped his shoulders. "I don't know. I've never been married before."

Waking up that morning, she had felt, for the first time in a while, well-rested. Tessan had already been gone, and she lay in the luxurious bed for another hour before her maids dragged her out of it. After a breakfast of pain medication and oatmeal, she had bathed and dressed. Catarina had laid out a beautifully embroidered skirt and neat blouse, and Solara felt pretty. That she could feel such things at all had given her hope, and now she sat across from her husband and wondered if she had lost her damn mind.

What if she couldn't kill him? What if she was bound to him for the rest of their lives? What if for the rest of her life she was dodging the

Asher's and Tolly's, terrified of what her friendship or even her attention could mean for innocent passersby? What if she did kill Tessan, and it hurt her to do it?

Tessan stood up. "Come with me."

She rose carefully, and he took her hand, the one bearing his ruby ring, and kissed it. Then he led the way out of the study, moving slowly to accommodate her shuffling steps.

"Where are we going?" she asked, as they moved toward a flight of stairs.

"Would you like me to carry you?"

She shouldn't have given him any more reason to touch her, but the stairs looked like hell. "Yes."

Tessan picked her up and held her gingerly against his chest. "Does that hurt?"

Only because she was holding her breath. Solara shook her head.

He ascended the stairs easily, her weight not even an inconvenience. At the top, he set her on her feet and held her until he was sure she was steady. They were on the second floor, where she had not had much occasion to explore, and her curiosity was piqued. He led her down a sleek hallway towards a large, glass room, and Solara's steps faltered.

The glass room held a massive conference table, much like the tower in the river house, and seated around it, each impeccably dressed and looking bored, were the Manfalon family members. Roon. His dainty wife, Narcissa. Nikara. Petra. Maliq. Adhara.

Solara stopped dead in the hall.

"Don't be afraid," Tessan said. "This is irrelevant." Hence why he had not seen fit to give her any sort of forewarning at all. He drew her forward, even as she pulled backward in a futile attempt to delay their arrival. She did not want to go in there. She hadn't seen a single sister since Roga's death, and she'd been preparing herself for the moment she would have to face them. She knew they blamed her.

Tessan held the door for her, and they were in the room.

"How good of you to join us, brother," Nikara said.

He could barely be bothered to notice her. "Solara and I were having our marriage officialized."

Solara wanted to die. Six identical hazel gazes swung to her, and she shrank back, only to hit the solid barrier of Tessan's hand shoving her forward.

I hope she kills him in their bed, Petra thought. She locked gazes with Solara. *I see how you hate him. Don't hold back. Tear him apart.*

"Aren't you rushing things?" Roon gestured to the two remaining chairs. Maliq and Adhara's thoughts bombarded her. *Roga's seat. Arrogant bitch. They think she can replace her?*

Still stunned at how quickly everything had gotten out of hand, Solara sat down. Tessan stood behind her chair, surveying his family. "If anyone is going to challenge me, do it now," he said. "I'd rather we didn't drag this out."

"Are you giving us fair warning?" Petra sneered.

"You, I'll kill as an afterthought," Tessan said. Petra's cheeks burned, and Nikara chuckled softly. Tessan looked at his older sister. "You're quiet."

"I find the little thing intriguing," Nikara said. Her calculating smile made Solara shudder. "A rabbit in a lion's den, brother? Are you insane?"

Roon settled into his seat, watching his children squabble, and seemingly amused by it all. Then Narcissa spoke. Her voice was smooth and sweet, although her eyes burned like ice. "You murdered your sister, Tessan. Do you truly believe you have a seat at this table?"

Tessan looked his mother dead in the eye. "Your daughter was an idiot to cross me, and I only hope her death served as a lesson for the rest of you."

Petra stood. "Watch your mouth."

"Speak to me once more, and I'll break your legs again," Tessan said.

Again? Solara wanted to melt off her chair, slide under the table, and out of this mess. Petra backed down, and Nikara's biting little laugh echoed.

"I will not sit at a table with him," Narcissa hissed.

"You'll do as you're told," Roon said. Her face paled, and Nikara pursed her mouth. But she didn't cross Roon, either. "Tessan, sit down."

Tessan looked like he'd lash out at his father, as well. But then he yanked his chair out and sat. His shoulder bumped Solara's, and he looked at her as if she were as much an enemy as anyone else at the table. Then he forced a tight smile, his hand finding hers beneath the table where it sat clenched into a fist atop her thigh.

"I, for one, would like to hear her speak," Adhara said. She looked to be about thirteen, lovely like her sisters, but with a cruelty in her eye that negated everything else. "Solara, isn't it?"

Solara wished to be brave. She nodded and said the first thing she thought of. "I share a name with Solara Benwerrin, a desert queen."

Adhara looked startled. So did Nikara. "You've spoken with my grandmother," Tessan said.

"I met her once," Solara said. "Before. She told me the story."

"By before I suppose you mean when you were warming Faisal Casarriba's bed," Adhara sneered. Tessan did not immediately leap to threaten his little sister, although he looked irritated. "Are we all going to pretend she's in any way suitable for this position? She's little better than a prostitute, and clearly still bound to him, since her mind is intact, even if the rest of her isn't."

Silence.

"Tired of defending her already, brother?" Petra said, daring to speak again.

Tessan said mildly, "I'm waiting for her to realize that as of this morning, she's the equal of every bitch at this table, and can put them in their places on her own."

Solara was not naive enough to believe that and certainly not brazen enough to test it.

"Have a care how you reference your mother, Tessan," Roon said, when it was clear Solara was not going to speak.

"The title Lady Manfalon hasn't belonged to a decent woman until this morning," Tessan said.

Nikara rose. The rest of the siblings shrank backward, but Tessan rose, as well. Their eyes spat sparks. "Don't overstep yourself, *brother*," Nikara snarled. "You've slaughtered enough of this family, and I would hate to spill more blood."

"I would love to," Tessan said. "Shall we begin with yours?"

"Do you think your life means anything to me?" Nikara said.

Solara turned her attention away from the bristling siblings and studied the others, hoping to use the moment of distraction, but the moment she looked away, everyone noticed. Narcissa, whose face was locked in frigid disinterest, glanced at her briefly before staring blankly at something outside of the room, trying to wish her family out of existence. Adhara, upon finding herself the subject of Solara's perusal, sneered.

Only then did Solara speak. "Did you love your sister?"

Adhara hissed, "Don't speak to me unless I speak to you first."

"Seeing her handiwork..." Solara gestured to her face, the bruises still violet and yellow. "Did you think she was a good person?"

"Careful, child," Roon said dryly.

"Or did you simply choose to love her regardless?" Solara went on. "Roga was a sadist and a bully, and I think much smarter than most of you here at the table until the moment she forgot who Tessan was, and now she's paid dearly for that mistake."

Nikara warned Tessan, "If you don't shut her mouth, I will."

Adhara stood. "I will not sit at a table with this whore."

"You can sit of your own free will," Roon said. "Or I can make standing too painful for you."

Her cheeks flushed, and she glared at their father. "You know exactly what they did to Roga but you're going to pretend otherwise? Where do we draw lines? What else can we get away with under this roof?"

"Sit," Roon said. "Down."

All three siblings still standing sank slowly into their seats.

Despite the size of his children's egos, this man still held significant power over them. Tessan's deference was unwilling, but Nikara and Narcissa were genuinely afraid of Roon. Storing that away, Solara said,

"I'm not trying to replace Roga. I'm not fighting for a seat at this table. I want nothing to do with any of you."

"Except Tess, of course," Nikara said, a cunning smile on her mouth. "Because clearly you love him so."

Tessan's lip curled.

Despite herself, Solara remembered the sadness in his voice the day in the garden, as his family's thoughts turned crueler than before. Every person at the table except Tessan knew she didn't love him and never would. And Solara's heart broke. It was exactly as he feared. Beyond his hearing, everyone was laughing at him.

"The fact remains, she's bound to Faisal," Petra said. "Who's to say her actions are her own?"

"Enough," Tessan said. "Find something else to discuss. I'm sick of the topic." He sat back in his chair, the aggression in his posture instantly relaxing.

"On that note," Nikara said, brightening. "I have news." Solara's heart sank. "I want to begin brokering a marriage proposal."

Narcissa's gaze sharpened. "With whom?"

"Our dear Petra and Lord Faisal Casarriba." Nikara watched Solara keenly, but Solara had heard her thoughts, and she steeled herself just in time to keep her face blank. Tessan went rigid. "I think the best way to smooth the whole debacle over would be a wedding."

"Is that wise, Nikara?" Roon said.

Petra had not reacted physically, although her thoughts had recoiled. She was deathly afraid of the man who had taken control of eight men, mocked her beloved Roga, and done heavens knew what to Solara.

Nikara shrugged. "He rejected the last marriage offer, but now we have his beloved Sol."

"*Enough,*" Tessan snapped.

"I'm only teasing," Nikara murmured. She rested her elbow on the tabletop and cupped her chin in her hand, turning the full force of her angelic smile on Solara. "We're sisters now. We should be friendly."

"Stay away from her," Tessan said.

"Who will teach her the ways of civilized society if not me?" Nikara countered. "I don't suppose Faisal will coach you?"

Tessan sprang out of his chair and was across the table. Solara didn't even know how he got there, but he'd wrenched his sister out of her chair and flung her against the wall, his hand on her throat, grinding her skull into the glass.

Roon tensed but didn't stop him. Solara could have sworn that, for a moment, Roon looked scared.

Tessan put his mouth by Nikara's ear, his voice a snarl. "Do you remember the last time you *really* pissed me off, you insolent cunt?"

Nikara grinned at him, but her eyes were glassy with tears, her cheeks a pained red.

Solara stood up. Her heart had reacted as fast as her eyes could take in the scene; it pounded, screaming at her to escape. She turned to her father-in-law. Her hands were in fists, fingernails impaling her own flesh. She could not stay in the same room as these people any longer.

"May I be excused?" she asked the patriarch.

Roon beckoned her closer. Tessan let go of Nikara, flinging her back so her head cracked against the glass once more. Solara came close to Roon, and he turned his head and tipped up his cheek. She leaned over and kissed his well-worn skin, just as she had kissed her own father goodnight a thousand times.

"You will make a lovely daughter," Roon said. His actual daughters scoffed. "You chose well, Tessan."

She left the room, although it pained her to turn her back on the den of lions. She hadn't gotten far up the hall before Tessan caught up to her. She started to make a remark about how well it had all gone, but he swept her up, making her gasp a little in pain and surprise, and kissed her forehead.

The rest of the family could still see them, but she knew no amount of playacting on her part would ever convince any of them that she cared for him. And truly, it didn't matter. None of it did. Not so long as Tessan was determined to believe she did.

"I think they're going to kill me now," she said. His left arm was beneath her knees, the hand gently cupping her thigh. That was the hand that had attacked Nikara. That was the hand that had held Roga's shoulders still so the other could whip her chin around, snapping bone.

"Not while I live."

She rested her head against his shoulder and closed her eyes as he carried her farther and farther away from that room, where all the people she hated most sat around a table, laughing at them both.

CHAPTER
TWENTY-FIVE

Solara.

At the sound of Faisal's voice, Solara pressed her eyes closed and sank deeper into the blankets. Behind her, Tessan stirred. For someone so willfully blind, he was remarkably watchful of her every move, even in the dead of night, when they were both supposed to be asleep.

She hadn't opened her mind to Faisal since Roga died. And now, nearly two weeks later, she lay awake for yet another night, her thoughts whirling, but her body still so as not to completely wake Tessan, who slept with one arm around her, her head tucked under his chin.

Solara?

She cursed softly, very softly, but it woke Tessan. He lifted himself up on one elbow, so he could peer down at her face in the darkness. "What's wrong?"

"Nothing." She turned into the pillow. "Go back to sleep." Perhaps he'd been awake all along, the same as she.

Solara, answer me.

She cracked her thoughts open a fraction for Faisal. They were silent as they sorted each other out, Faisal absorbing what she'd allow him to see.

This is going to require more courage than I thought, Solara said. She should have treasured her one night of good sleep more than she had. With each passing day, the threat of the war game loomed closer, and the reality of what she had to do grew larger than life.

I have more information about what the games will entail, Faisal said. *Would you like to hear it?* He hoped she didn't. He hoped she was so overwhelmed that she was willing to give up. He was trying to muscle his way into her thoughts. She was so tired, she wanted to let him win. Just bare it all, every messy bit of it, and make him come up with the next step.

But something held her in check. That something was Tessan, who had settled back down and begun stroking her hair in an attempt to soothe her that shouldn't have worked, because it was him, but it did. That was something she could not let Faisal see.

"Try to sleep," Tessan said.

I want to hear it, Solara said. *Tell me everything.*

Faisal wished he could lie to her. *It's soon. Very soon. Roon plans to catch his children off guard. He'll remove their personal bodyguards. Watch for them to disappear. Nikara's Seconds, and Tessan's man, Violo. They're free to use whatever weapon they can get their hands on, so your options are limitless, though I suggest you stick to what you know, and use a knife.*

Solara tried to imagine stabbing her knife into Tessan's chest, into anyone's chest, and had to stifle a shudder.

Faisal wanted to remind her of where best to insert the blade, what would kill the fastest. He wished he had more specifics, though he'd exhausted all his sources. When he articulated his thoughts again, it took her by surprise. *You seem conflicted about him.*

Tessan stopped stroking her hair. She'd gone rigid. "What is it?" Tessan said. But he knew. A conversation was happening beyond his hearing.

I can't talk now.

Solara!

Solara shut Faisal out. Her only motivation was guilt. Tessan turned her onto her back, and she looked up at him, her heartbeat unsteady.

When Tessan was truly angry, he was at his most composed, as he was now. "What does he want?" he said.

"The same things he always does," she said. "Although he's been particularly riled up lately." She made her smile thin. "I suppose I outrank him now."

Tessan lowered his head to hers, so they were forehead to forehead. "If I could end this for you, I would."

End Faisal, he meant. "You got me out," she said. "And he can never take me back. That's enough."

"No, it's not." He lifted his head. Even in the dark, he missed nothing. And she wondered if he was as aware as everyone else that she didn't love him. If he was choosing to believe the lie. Were they double-playing each other? And if so, how long would this fake love be enough? What would he do if he discovered the depth of her deception?

The thought made her throat dry. She sat up on her own elbows, nearly knocking noses with him, and said, "Take me out tomorrow."

Tessan smiled and played along. "Take you where?"

"Take me into the third ring, to all the shops. What's the point of being your wife if I can't spend some of your money?"

He laughed. "Very well, Lady Solara. Tomorrow, I'll take you shopping, and you can buy whatever your heart desires."

"No limit?"

He kissed her. "No limit," he said. "Now get your rest."

They both lay back down, resuming their earlier positions. Solara was awake for hours, coming up with plans and discarding them, until she finally gave into the comfort of being held, and slept.

Petra was watching when they left the palace the following day. Even if Solara hadn't felt the girl's eyes on her back, she heard her thoughts. *Butcher him. Tear him apart. Make his heart bleed.*

Solara had tried her best to ignore Petra, but now she turned and spotted his sister. She had rounded the edge of the palace on horseback, and even at the great distance Solara could see the hate on Petra's face. Tessan followed her glance.

"You really broke her legs once?" she said.

"It happened in combat training," Tessan said. "It wasn't intentional. She thinks it was, and I let her think that."

Solara looked at Tessan. "How do you unintentionally break both of someone's legs?"

"My father frowns upon holding back in training."

Was she even surprised? Solara stepped into the carriage and sat down. They didn't speak as the carriage rattled along. She could hear the carriage driver's nervous thoughts – he hated being responsible for Tessan's wife – but nothing else.

She was considering breaking the stillness with something mundane when Tessan said, "You still believe I'm cruel for how I treat my siblings, even after seeing their own cruelties firsthand?"

Solara contemplated. "Even after witnessing it, I struggle to comprehend how children raised under the same roof could be like this with each other."

"Blood means nothing to them. To any of us," he said. "I'm sure Father's had conversations with the others detailing how best to subdue me should I get out of hand. The only currency in this household is power, and if they don't fear me, they'll kill me, and in the most horrible way they can imagine. You, they would torment for months, if not years."

Solara grimaced.

"Hence why I'm very motivated to keep them in line," Tessan said. "They rally behind Nikara because they think she can protect them when the time comes."

"When the time comes?"

Tessan nodded. "In a few weeks, Nikara turns twenty-five. Father deems that an acceptable age to take the reins of the empire. If he makes her the official second-in-command, then she outranks us all, and could with a lift of her hand instruct the Scarlet Guard to massacre every one of us, and still be well within her rights."

A few weeks. She wouldn't be here by then. Neither would he. Neither would Aliss. The rest of the household could implode if it wished. Solara told herself she didn't care.

"Nikara knows I won't let that happen," Tessan said. "She'll prepare, and the others will prepare, but I won't let her have any power over me. Not even for a day." There was not a hint of doubt in his voice. "She knows she's going to lose. As much as she loves lording her age over the rest of us, she isn't as strong as I am. She's been afraid of me since we were children and tries to disguise it, but we all know."

Of course Nikara was afraid of him. Everyone was afraid of him.

Tessan was watching her. "I won't let anything happen to you, Sol. You don't have to be afraid."

She smiled weakly. "I'm trying not to be."

Sound swelled around them as they passed through the gate into the third ring, and Solara sat forward to look out the window. It had been weeks since she'd encountered the outside world, and now the sensations enveloped her. The sights and sounds. The smells, both foul and delicious. She could scent the baker's district from here, as they rumbled through the weavers' district. "Let's walk," she said. The carriage was too slow, even with people flinging themselves out of the way of the distinctive scarlet vehicle.

"Very well," Tessan said with far less enthusiasm.

She hopped out before he could help her and he followed, catching her hand before she'd gotten too far. Oh, how the people stared. Solara Barthelme, a face they had known, haggled with, seen at Bjorn's. She'd dressed plainly today and worn her hair down – Tessan had made a single disapproving comment that nearly collapsed her maid, but Solara wouldn't change it – but the simple trousers and blouse only served to call attention to the heavy ring on her finger and the unmistakable man beside her.

"You've seen all of this before," Tessan protested, as she dragged him to a storefront bright with fall colors. The man who owned it rushed to the door, bowing every few steps.

"My lord," he said. "My... lady." He stuttered over it as he recognized Solara. Everyone must have heard about the new Lady Manfalon, but it was clear some had believed, and some had not. This man had been very fond of slapping Solara on the ass when she walked out his door, and he was remembering his many infractions with a trembling heart as he looked at Tessan's menacing bulk behind her.

She ignored the shopkeeper, studying the colorful scarves in the window. "What do you think?" she asked Tessan. "Orange or navy?"

"Those are far too big for you," he said.

She had come to the glass on a complete whim, drawn by the colors. Tessan's uncooperative statement made her laugh. "It's not for me. It's for you." She could see his reflection in the window and the sweet surprise that flickered over his face.

"The blue is nice," he said.

"Orange it is!" She turned to the shopkeeper. "Wrap it up."

The man bowed nearly to the ground. "Yes, my lady. Right away, my lady."

She spun to look at Tessan, knowing even before she saw him that he would be studying the shopkeeper with that predatory look in his eye. Tessan knew guilt when he saw it. "Who is that man?" Tessan asked, as the keeper pulled the scarf from the window.

Solara had no great love for him, but she wouldn't have her shopping day ruined by Tessan's savagery.

"Your wife is buying you your first gift," she said, and his gaze snapped back to her. "Pay attention to me."

Tessan seemed confused by the petulance in her voice. No one had ever genuinely flirted with this man in his entire life. She was sure of it. Sighing, she turned away from him to accept the wrapped package from the shopkeeper. Before her fingertips had brushed the white paper, Violo – who she had not realized was there – stepped up on her left and took it.

Tessan drew Solara back to his side, saying, "You're a member of the Manfalon household, Sol. You don't go anywhere unattended."

"I didn't know he was there."

"That's the point."

Solara hadn't even heard his thoughts. Violo was better than most at keeping them to himself, but still. She didn't like that she'd let her guard down. She reminded herself she was there to appease Tessan, not plot anything, so she shook off her disconcert and surged forward again. They visited nearly every shop on the street, and if Solara so much as glanced at something, Tessan gestured for the shop owner to wrap it up.

At one point she hissed at him, "I was looking at it because I thought it was ugly!"

And he said immediately, "Then you are definitely wearing it." He put the ghastly hat on her head and wouldn't hear of her taking it off.

She would never have thought in a thousand years that she would experience the city in this way, and she was so distracted by this newfound opulence that she didn't realize they were across from Bjorn's until Tessan pointed it out. Solara ground to a halt, biting her lower lip.

"Care to go inside?" he said. He'd never cared for Bjorn. He probably wanted Solara to rub her new status in Bjorn's face.

Solara shrugged. "Why bother? I heard the only good girl there left."

Tessan was delighted at her sass, and she pulled him onward. They went through the bakers' district, and she ate pastries until she thought her stomach would split at the seams, refusing to dwell on her previous plans of coming here with Lunaro. Tessan wouldn't even taste anything until she shoved an entire cream-filled donut into his mouth mid-protest. He did not appreciate her hysterical laughter when he spat it out.

He tried to be at his ease, but Solara doubted he'd ever been truly comfortable anywhere any time ever. Even now, although he gave it his best effort, he was mostly awkward beside her, more a bodyguard than a companion.

She didn't understand why he was so anxious. The Scarlet Guard were everywhere, plus Violo and two other attending servants she'd been able to pick out from the crowd. They were well guarded, not even taking Tessan's skills into consideration. Armed or not, he was more than capable of defending them.

Nevertheless, Tessan was watchful, one hand on her always. He grew still more alert as they crossed into the smithy, and the sound of bellows and forges converged around them. Bright sparks danced in the waning light. She stopped across the street from the largest establishment and watched the muscled smith pound away on a massive horseshoe.

"Are you planning to shoe your own horses?" Tessan asked. He stood behind her, both arms around her waist. She'd finally succeeded in getting the giant hat off her head and gotten rid of it by chucking it into an alley while directing his attention elsewhere. Now, Tessan rested his chin atop her bare head.

"No limit, remember?" She'd said it teasingly to him several times that day, before making her most ridiculous purchases. She'd spent more money in a single day than she'd made in her life.

"I remember."

Solara started across the street, and he took her hand as they entered the shop. The smith gestured for them to stop at a safe distance as he plunged the glowing red horseshoe into a bucket of cold water. He set down his tongs and walked over to them, wiping sweat off his forehead.

"How can I help you, sir?" he asked Tessan, although his gaze stayed on Solara. He was an attractive man, not too much older than Solara. He'd looked at her once while she stood across the street, but now he surveyed her with a more interested eye.

"How can he help you, Solara?" Tessan said with a warning chill in his voice.

"Do you know the story of Solara Benwerrin?" she asked the smith.

The man smiled. "I've heard it in passing. She had an impressive set of knives."

"That's what I want."

"Solara," Tessan said.

"They don't have to be sharp," she said quickly. "I just want them to be pretty. I'm going to hang them on my wall." She twisted to look at Tessan, but he was still eyeing the blacksmith. "You said no limit," she wheedled.

"They can be practice blades," the blacksmith said.

She made a hopeful face at Tessan, but he ignored her. He'd zeroed in on a threat, and just like that, every attempt at lightheartedness was gone. It didn't help that the blacksmith was, in fact, admiring the curve of her ass. She turned back around, frustrated. "Two practice blades, then. And I want the handles to have those little cages on them, like the Scarlet Guard swords have."

The man smiled at her description. "Hold on." He went to a shelf and removed a sheet of rumpled paper and a small pencil. He laid them on a tool-laden table and began sketching.

"My grandmother should not have told you that story," Tessan said, putting his arms around her once more.

"Nikara *wears* hers."

"Don't ever resemble Nikara."

The smith looked up at the sharpness in Tessan's words, then glanced at Solara. He knew who they were. One did not mistake Tessan. But still, as the man leaned over his work again, he sent Solara a thought. *Are you all right?*

Don't speak to me. He'll know. She hated the cowed sound of her own thoughts.

The smith's eyes were narrowed as he straightened and offered her the sheet of paper. Tessan snatched it and held it up for her perusal. Even in simple pencil form, the blades were lovely. In the hilt, he had drawn an oval-shaped gemstone, surrounded by delicate etching that made it appear like a watchful eye.

"I love it," she said softly.

"It will take a few weeks to complete," he said. "I'll send word to the palace when they're ready."

She handed back the page. This time, he made sure their hands touched. *I will make them sharp for you.*

Solara quickly withdrew her hand and made her voice light. "We should see the menagerie before we go home," she said, tugging on Tessan's arm. He let her pull him away, barely. She got him onto the street, and the moment they were out, she let go of his hand and walked away.

It snapped Tessan out of his intense focus, and he came after her. She turned down an alley, which was mercifully empty, so there were no witnesses as she whirled on him. They were both angry, but she spoke first. "Do you remember Tolly?" She didn't expect him to. But judging by the way his mouth tightened, he remembered quite well. "And Asher?" she said.

"What is your point, Solara?"

Solara laughed. He didn't like that at all. "What are you so afraid of?" she cried. "A little boy? Two strangers? I don't even *know* them."

"It has nothing to do with you," he said harshly.

"It's *about* me," she shot back. "And the fact that you don't believe I love you."

He faltered when she said that word, and maybe she was cruel for using it like a weapon, but he'd given her no choice. "It isn't about that," he said, quieter.

"Tessan," she said. "I know you're going to misunderstand me. But just listen to me. If you hurt that blacksmith, I won't let it go."

His eyes narrowed, and he took a step forward.

"And if you lay one hand on me in anger *ever*," she said, her voice catching. "I will never forgive you."

Tessan stopped. He was trying so hard to control his temper, and she didn't know if he could do it. But at last, the fire in his eyes calmed. He gently put his hands on her shoulders. "Solara," he said. "I love you."

"I know that."

"And all I need is for you to be happy and well," he said. "But don't for a moment forget that I am your lord. And you will obey me."

It took several seconds for Solara to believe that she'd heard him correctly. Then she knocked his hands off her shoulders and darted back out of range. He took a step after her, and she said, "I may not be fast, but I know this city better than you do, Lord Tessan." She spat the title. He eyed the distance between them and the distance between her and the end of the alley, calculating his chances.

"Solara, stop being difficult."

"What are you going to do if I don't obey?" she said. "Will you snap my neck, too?"

His eyes flashed. "Tread carefully."

"Will you find someone who can bend my mind to their will, even if you can't?" she said. "Perhaps you'll call Faisal in to control me?"

"Enough!"

"No!" she fired back, and he blinked at the word as if he'd never heard it before. "You don't get to make me into your slave," she said. "If you try, I'll run away. I'll leave you."

"Get back here. Now."

She shook her head wildly. "Tell me now," she said. "If I should run away from you, too."

He stood there, poised to bolt after her if she so much as flinched. "Solara," he said softly. "Come. Here."

A sound behind her. "If you make Violo grab me..." Her voice caught. *Control yourself, Solara*, she told herself. *Control your face. Control your tone.*

"Come here, and I won't have to," he said.

She didn't have a prayer of outrunning him. There was another footstep behind her, and Violo murmured into her head, *My lady, please come quietly. He's given me orders to restrain you however necessary if you attempt to run, and I have no desire to hurt you.*

Her shoulders slumped, and Violo's hand touched her back, gently, but a warning to hold still as Tessan came forward and took her by the wrist.

CHAPTER TWENTY-SIX

As soon as Solara and Tessan arrived back from the city, a messenger came to the apartment to inform them Nikara required their presence at dinner. Solara, silent and seething, said nothing when Tessan told her they were going. She said still nothing when he left her, and still nothing when he came to collect her and led her to Nikara's suite, which was extravagant and dull like everything else in the palace. Solara was so sick of it all she could barely look at it. Aliss wasn't even there, so there was nothing to interest her.

She sat at the dinner table eating woodenly, her head lowered.

"How was your shopping trip?" Nikara asked.

"Expensive," Tessan said dryly, and Nikara laughed. The last time we sat at a table together, Solara wanted to say, you threatened to kill each other. But now here we sit, laughing and eating at the table of a woman who poisoned her last rival.

"I heard you bought two daggers?" Nikara said. "Has that story gone to your head, Solara? The rest of us had better watch out."

Solara stabbed a piece of her steak and the fork clanked against the porcelain plate.

"I also heard you were running about with your hair down like a whore."

Something inside of Solara snapped. She slammed her fork down on the table and lifted her head, her eyes narrowed to slits. "Yes," she said. "My hair was down. Because I'm a woman who can do whatever she pleases and not give a damn what any of you noble bastards have to say about it. And I'm going to keep wearing my hair down because I don't give a fuck. Not a single one. Not a half a fuck. Not even a quarter.

"Call me a whore. Call me a bitch and common and whatever the hell you like. I don't care. Because when Tessan guts you, I'll dance over your fucking corpse."

She stood up so swiftly her chair flipped over, and she whirled and stormed out of the room. The servants coming in with dessert scattered out of her way and the door slammed behind her, but not before she heard Tessan explode in laughter.

She pounded down the hall and through the first promising door she saw, which led down a set of marble steps into a section of the garden. She paced through it, headed toward the distant towers of the hedge maze, footsteps staccato with the heel of her expensive slippers. Solara cursed and kicked them off. Then she cursed and tore the pin holding up half her hair and chucked it as far as she could.

"Fuck," she screamed.

"Good evening to you, as well."

She whirled around. Roon. The king of the castle sat beside a pair of rosebushes, watching her. She curtsied, mortified. "My apologies, my lord. I didn't realize you were–"

He wasn't alone. Aliss stood at attention behind him, holding a tea tray like a glorified table.

"There," Solara finished after an exaggerated pause.

"Don't apologize. That was entertaining." Roon gestured to the seat beside him.

Solara considered retrieving her shoes and hairpin, but she gave up and sat down, tucking her bare feet out of sight beneath her skirt. Aliss was pale as paper, and her dress hung off her body. There was a massive purple bruise on her neck. How much longer was she going to last in this place? Did Solara even have time to wait for a perfect opportunity? If she missed her timing, she was going to watch Aliss die.

"You've come from dinner with Nikara," Roon said. He leaned forward, cutting off her view of Aliss.

Solara came back to herself. "Oh. Yes. I told her I was going to dance over her corpse."

Roon gaped at her.

The absurdity of it struck her suddenly, and Solara grinned. "I was angry. I didn't quite think my threat through. Your son found it funny, though."

"Yes, I imagine Tess would," Roon said. He shook his head, then said, "You have quite a gift, Solara." When she looked confused, he tapped his temple. "My children have been scratching away at your defenses, and I have employed my best psychic, but no one has ever broken through your walls but my eldest. It makes me question how Faisal ever did. How he could possibly hold this bond."

Her stomach tightened. "I struck a deal with him," she said. "He didn't have to fight through the defenses. I let him in."

"Why?"

"He said he'd make sure my brother never wanted for anything ever again," she said. Roon looked unimpressed, and that irritated her. "Food and a roof over your head may not seem like much to the man who owns the city," she said. "But life is very different in the fourth ring. I would have done anything." She trailed off as Tessan came around the corner.

"My son's jealousy will be the death of him," Roon said, correctly guessing why she'd stopped talking about Faisal. "You were wise to secure your title before that happens."

"That was never my intention."

Room smiled as if she were ridiculous. "Now the only question is whether or not you can survive him," he said. Tessan paused, surveying the two of them.

"Tessan doesn't scare me," Solara said. At some point in this game, even after today, that had become the truth.

Roon chuckled. "I admire your courage, Miss Barthelme. Tess fancies himself your master, but you and I know otherwise." Roon's smile faded as Tessan started forward again. "Prioritize your enemies, child. If Tessan doesn't live long enough to fight all your battles for you, you'll find yourself in a precarious spot once he's gone."

Tessan was now within earshot, and he said, "Have the two of you come out here to sulk together?"

"One day I'm going to tear your insolent tongue out of your head," Roon said. "Or she will."

Solara looked at Tessan coldly. "I'm not going back to dinner with that cow," she said.

Both men smirked. And behind them, Aliss laughed softly. Neither man noticed, but Solara's head whipped around. Aliss continued to stare into space, but her mouth had tilted into an impudent grin.

"I wouldn't ask you to," Tessan said. Solara didn't even remember she'd spoken. He took her hand and drew her to her feet. He looked at his father. "What are you doing out here?"

"Considering," Roon said. He waved them off. "Goodnight."

Solara reached. The walls were up around Aliss, but... weaker? Had Tessan rattled his sister before coming after Solara? She wanted to keep probing, but Tessan pulled her away. "Are you going to refuse to speak to me until you get what you want?" he said, when they were safely out of earshot. "I'm far more accustomed to silence than you are, Solara."

She snatched her hand from him. "I'm sick of you."

He laughed. She quickened her step, but he kept pace. "You don't decide when I can or can't perceive someone as a threat. I do. And I'm not going to apologize. No one gives me an ultimatum, not even you."

"I didn't give you an ultimatum," she snapped. "I asked you to consider what you were putting me through every time you hurt someone because of me."

"It isn't because of you. It's because of them."

She wanted to scream. When he reached for her again, she moved away.

"Do you like the attention?" he said.

It was too much. She whirled on him, and he drew back at the look on her face. There were no words to accurately describe the utter fury coursing through her veins. She opened her mouth. Closed it. Turned and kept walking deeper into the garden. After a moment, he followed her.

They hadn't gone far when she spun around again, stopping him in his tracks. "Why are you so intimidated?" she demanded. "You are the most beautiful man I have ever laid eyes on. You have everything anyone could ever want. Do you even understand how ridiculous it is for you to feel inferior to anyone?"

Tessan endured the tongue-lashing with grace, his eyes lowered. When she finished, he tentatively looked up. She felt like she'd just screamed at a child. He looked so crestfallen.

Then he said, "You think I'm beautiful?"

And she went right back to wanting to shake him. "I'm not saying it again," she said. "Treasure that moment."

He chuckled.

She ran her hands over her face, no doubt disturbing the makeup Catarina had carefully applied that morning. Tessan put his arms around her, placing a kiss on the crown of her head. "Are you tired?"

She nodded an instant before she realized where the question was leading.

"Come to bed."

A servant was turning back the covers in the bedroom. Tessan waved a hand, and the girl curtsied and departed, her thoughts at unbearable volume. *Is she going to do it? Is she really going to sleep with him? If she does, I'll lose two gold coins I don't have.*

Solara couldn't compose her face in time; she gaped at the girl's back. The servants were *taking bets* on whether she'd let Tessan consummate the marriage?

"What?" Tessan said, following her openmouthed stare.

"Nothing," she said. She didn't have to see the flicker of annoyance over his face to understand how her obvious lie made him feel. "You'll just get angry if I tell you," she said. "And I'd rather you didn't."

He sat down on the bed and crossed his arms. "Try me."

"Do you promise not to get mad?"

Tessan scowled. "Don't patronize me."

"See? You're already mad." She shook her head, and Tessan made to rise.

"Should I go ask her myself what she thought?"

Solara's amusement vanished. "Leave her alone." A grin tugged at Tessan's mouth, and Solara went from unamused to annoyed. "That isn't funny." Not when she had to worry about him murdering someone behind her back every two seconds.

He beckoned her closer, but she stayed where she was. "I'm going to tell you something that will make you feel better," he said.

"Will it?" She didn't attempt to hide her skepticism.

"I didn't kill Asher," he said.

"I know you didn't. Roga did."

Tessan could hear her accusation. "Not at my request, Sol. Roga was there the night of the party. She saw what I saw."

"Which was what?" Perhaps she shouldn't have been riling him up when they were still in the middle of the last argument, but Solara was sick of dancing around the subject. Of dancing around *all* subjects. "Me, flirting with Asher?"

Tessan's jaw tightened.

"I was bored, and at the time you meant nothing to me," Solara said. That was too harsh. And, also, untrue. "I didn't really know you then," she amended. "And besides, I was a servant. I was nothing. Nothing I did was supposed to matter."

"Stop saying that," Tessan said. "You are not nothing. You were never nothing."

Solara had never wished so fervently that she could read his mind. She wanted to understand him, and she didn't know any other way. She went across the room and knelt in front of him, her fingers knotted in her lap. "And Tolly?"

"I let him go," Tessan said. "Harshly, but I didn't harm him. I only wanted people to believe that I had. No one gets to hurt you. They don't even get to upset you at dinner."

She started to tell him that losing a job was more devastating for common people than he realized. He had spun Tolly's life on its axis just to make an example. But what was the point? "You can't protect me from everything, Tess."

"I want to try," he said.

Solara didn't know if she believed he hadn't sanctioned Asher's death. At the very least, he wasn't condemning his sister's actions. "I want to trust you," she said. "But I'm afraid to let my guard down and have to watch you hurt someone else."

Tessan ran his finger along her temple, sliding a few loose strands of hair back from her face. "You're very brave to care for people the way you do."

That was not a luxury he'd been given. He'd been nine years old when he promised his sisters that he wouldn't kill them without warning. Nine. And already resigned to a reality that ended in the slaughter of his family. She wanted to blame it on cowardice, but she had no idea how the Manfalon children had become as twisted as they had. How good a father could Roon have been, if he were teaching them to plot against each other now? Sighing, Solara let her tense hands go slack. "Am I braver than you?"

Tessan nodded seriously. "By far."

"I suppose that makes me stronger than you, too."

Tessan pretended to consider this. "That's a rational progression, yes."

"Braver. Stronger." She ticked them off on her fingers, starting to smile. "It goes without saying I'm prettier."

"I'll stop you there," he said. "You said I was the most beautiful person you'd ever seen."

Solara scoffed. "I told you I wasn't saying it again. And I only said that to make you feel better."

"You can't go back on your word, Lady Solara," Tessan said. "It's not suitable for a lady to lie."

Solara stood up, saying haughtily, "Scold me at your own peril, Lord Tessan. No one's allowed to upset me." It was testament to how her guard had fallen that she could make a joke in that moment. It had been a terrible idea to allow him to bring her to his bedroom and get comfortable there. The level of intimacy to which she'd grown accustomed bordered on dangerous.

She stood there, one hand on his left knee where she'd used it to help her stand. She was still barefoot from her temper tantrum in the garden, and she wondered if anyone would ever find the jewel-encrusted hairpin she'd chucked into the bushes.

"What are you thinking about?" Tessan asked.

He'd made his intent very clear when he invited her back to bed. She'd had every opportunity to avoid this situation, but here she was, hesitating, trying to recall her iron-clad resolution to keep him at arm's length. Last year, in that dark alley, she'd had no choice in the matter. Nikara had taken that choice from her. But it was her decision to make now, and while she knew precisely what she wanted to do, she didn't know what she should do.

"Sol?" Tessan said.

Solara took a step back from him. It was easier to think when they weren't touching. "What is it?" She turned away, going to the dressing table in the corner. It was a different one than hers, the one Roga had slammed her face into over and over. She sat down in front of the large mirror, but she didn't reach for her comb. She could still hear Roga's neck snapping.

"You're still afraid of me," Tessan said.

"Yes."

"Solara, I will *never* hurt you."

"I thought you were going to hit me in the alley after the blacksmith's," she said. She couldn't see his reflection in the mirror, though she tried. "Sometimes in the shop, customers would get angry and threaten to hit me, but no one ever did, not until your family."

Tessan rose, came to stand behind her, and picked up her comb. They said nothing as he, beginning at the bottom, gently detangled her hair. She didn't know why she was surprised he knew how to do it correctly, given how much hair he had on his own head.

"I would never put my hands on you," Tessan said. "Not like that. But in the alley, when you acted like you were going to run, I didn't know if that was you."

Solara lifted her head to meet his gaze in the mirror.

Tessan looked defensive. "Your thoughts are linked with a man I despise, who despises my entire family. And I promised you that I would never let him take you. But every time you do something unexpected, I am *constantly* wondering who I'm dealing with, whether it's you or him."

He made an incredibly fair point. Solara lowered her eyes.

"You always pull back," Tessan said. "I think that I've gotten through to you, that you've opened up, but you draw back. And I don't know any other way to try to convince you that I'm not some flesh-eating monster."

"I know you're not a monster," Solara said. It saddened her that those twisted rumors took up any space in his thoughts. He began braiding her hair into sections for bed, and she smiled at how quick he was. "Will you do my hair for me every night forever?"

He knew she was changing the subject, but he let her. "No," he said with a faint smile. "I will not."

Solara closed her eyes, lulled by the hypnotizing rhythm. "My mother used to do this for me. After our parents were gone, before he hacked all his hair off, Lu and I would braid each other."

The braiding paused. Resumed. "Tell me about your brother."

The thought of poking at that wound made her tired. "I miss him."

"Would you like me to bring him to you?"

"No," Solara said. "Mage Casarriba swore an oath to care for him, and I know she won't break it." As much as Mage hated Solara, she'd kept her word to take care of Lunaro. "He's safer there than here."

"Is he happy?"

"Doesn't matter," Solara said. "Not for now."

"But later it will?"

When all of this was over. Then, feelings could matter again. But not before. It wasn't fair to Lunaro, especially now as everything dragged on longer and more complicated than she had ever anticipated. But she'd sworn to herself that she would not allow the Manfalons anywhere near him.

Tessan stopped braiding, but before Solara could protest, he leaned down and kissed her neck just below her ear. She shivered. "I will braid your hair for you every day that you are with me," he said. "I promise."

She needed to leave. She needed to walk out of the room right now. "Is that an ultimatum?" she said, lifting her eyebrows. "Stay with you forever or watch my hair descend into chaos?"

"Take it as you will." He tipped her chin back so he could kiss her on the mouth, and Solara's resolve broke.

She turned her head and said, "Promise me."

"I promise," he said immediately.

An irreverent grin pulled at her lips, but she scowled at him. "Swear to me you didn't hurt either one of them."

"I swear it," Tessan said.

She could have stopped there, but as he leaned in, she put her hand on his face, halting him. "Tell me you're sorry for hurting her." He knew who she meant. And she didn't even care if he meant it. She just needed to hear it once.

Tessan still held her comb. He set it down, the polished ivory clunking against the dressing table. "I am sorry that what I did hurt you," he said slowly. "But I will not be sorry for doing whatever is necessary to protect you."

She stared at him. He stared at her.

Solara stood up. He moved the chair from between them, and she kissed him. Gently, first, as if she had never kissed him before, and oh so slowly. She could feel how badly he wanted to touch her, but he didn't. She thought he would have stood there all night and let her kiss him if she wished. "Tess," she said.

"Sol," he said, an effort to make his voice normal.

"You can touch me now."

Tessan smiled, and she kissed him again, this time with abandon, because there was nothing that he could do to her that she didn't want. He leaned into her, until the back of her head hit the mirror and she gripped the table's edge to stay upright.

There was no coming back from this. Solara asked herself if she cared. If she was ready for these consequences.

Tessan must have sensed how she retreated into her head. He stroked her thigh. "Stay with me," he said.

She could read him so easily in that moment: desire and vulnerability and fear. He had learned to be careful when people destroyed the things he loved, and this was the opposite of careful. If he died tomorrow, Solara knew she would survive. She didn't know that the opposite was true. Trying to scatter those fears, Solara smiled at him. "Are we spending the night on my dressing table, Lord Tessan?"

Tessan laughed. He put her arms around his neck and lifted her up. "May I take you to bed now, Lady Solara?"

"I was getting tired of waiting."

CHAPTER
TWENTY-SEVEN

Only a few minutes remained before dawn, and Solara hadn't slept. Not for lack of trying. She was exhausted. Cocooned in Tessan's arms in the warm bed, she was perfectly comfortable. He'd fallen asleep quickly, but lightly. The slightest movement on her part would wake him, so she'd been all but holding her breath. Even asleep, he wore the faintest of smiles.

He was going to be insufferable after this.

"Are you still awake?" he murmured, his voice thick with sleep.

"No," she said. "You're dreaming."

He chuckled. She didn't think she'd ever seen him so at ease. Despite all the time they'd spent in this bed together before tonight, they'd never been truly comfortable in it. He gave her ear a gentle tug. "Talk to me."

She wanted to tell him everything. And the moment that awful realization hit her, someone screamed.

It was Catarina.

She'd not had one second to be surprised or alarmed before Tessan was moving. One second, they were in bed, she about to make the most impressive mistake of her life, and the next Tessan was across the room, opening his wardrobe. He removed a massive sword, and she sat up, heart slamming against her ribs.

Out in the hall, people were shouting, and Catarina screamed once more. The sound abruptly cut off.

"Don't be afraid," Tessan said. "Violo!"

His guard did not respond.

He'll remove their personal bodyguards. Watch for them to disappear.

Solara's mouth went dry.

Footsteps thudded in the hall, and Solara's other maid, Lesi, cried out in terror. That galvanized Solara into action. She grabbed the nightgown she'd never gotten around to putting on and wrenched it over her head, tearing out some of her hair in her haste.

"Stay here," Tessan said grimly. Then he opened the bedroom door.

Solara smelled blood.

A figure moved in the doorway, and Tessan's sword hummed through the air. Solara heard a slick sound that she knew was the blade cutting through flesh and bone, then a wet thud as the body hit the floor. Tessan went out, yanking the door closed behind him. Lesi cried out again, this time a garbled version of Solara's name. More wet thumps. Her maids did not make another sound.

The outer door slammed, and Solara moved, her steps hesitant. She opened the bedroom door and stepped into the sitting room. Dark shapes littered the floor.

Dawn broke, leaking orange light into the room. Catarina's dark hair spilled like blood over the carpet. And then actual blood, pools of it. Three men in black uniforms and masks lay felled like flies.

"Catarina?" Solara said hoarsely. "Lesi?"

She spotted her second maid's scarlet hair in the corner, and she stumbled over and knelt beside her, laying two fingers to the girl's pulse. Nothing. Her dark eyes stared up in death. Panic made Solara's fingers tremble, but she rose and walked to one of the fallen men. He had a knife in his belt. She pulled it free from its sheath.

She was unprepared, but this was happening. The war games had begun, and this was the only chance she would have to free Aliss. Faisal hadn't warned her there would be so much death and so quickly. She hadn't known her maids would be casualties.

Solara opened the outer door and stood in the doorway, listening. From somewhere far off, a man was in pain, wondering if his wound was fatal and if he had made a mistake when he chose sides in this war.

"Tess?" she whispered. No answer. A single light shone at the end of the hall, its sconce skewed. She put her back to the wall and advanced slowly, clutching her knife in cramping fingers.

Somewhere far off, shouts. And, she thought, Nikara's voice. The princess sounded angry. She sounded distracted.

Solara closed her eyes and searched. There were dozens and dozens of Seconds in the palace, but by now she knew Aliss's particular silence like she knew her own thoughts. There she was. Solara threw caution to the wind and ran. She flew down the back stairs and followed the silence towards the servants' barracks.

A handful of servants were coming out of the barracks, speaking both psychically and audibly, a cacophony of fear. This game was not like the ones they'd witnessed in previous years. Something had gone wrong.

Solara pushed into the room, where rows and rows of beds lined the walls. Aliss was at the end, a lump beneath the blankets. Solara rushed down the aisle and put her hand on Aliss's shoulder. "Aliss?"

Aliss turned her head and blinked at Solara with eyes as large as moons. Solara put her hand on the girl's cheek. She was cold to the touch. Her heartbeat was slow, erratic.

"I'm coming for you," Solara whispered. Ever so faintly, Aliss smiled.

And then the whole room went silent.

Footsteps. A thought. A sing-song voice. "Oh, dearest sister!"

Petra.

Aliss's smile vanished, and Solara's whole body went cold. Petra's thoughts were unbearably loud. She wanted everyone to know exactly what she planned to do with Solara when she found her. Petra may have failed her combat training, but she did not lack ingenuity. Aliss bore the scars to prove it.

Solara sat on the edge of the bed and tucked her knife out of sight beneath her thigh. "Don't be afraid," she said softly, taking Aliss's hand. "You're going home."

Aliss leaned into her, laying her forehead against hers as Solara had with Gaius.

I am Solara Barthelme, named for a warrior queen.

Petra's footsteps drifted closer, staggering, as if she were drunk. The servants, over thirty of them, retreated to their beds, to the walls, to the shadows, anywhere they could pretend not to see. "Don't be shy, darling!" Petra called. "I've only come because I missed you."

She was close. Solara felt nauseous from the force of Petra's twisted thoughts, but she bit down on her bottom lip until she tasted blood, then she closed her eyes and went under. Gaius's mind had been a screaming river, black and cold and strong. Aliss was a winterscape, flat, white. A dull wind stirred snow over a barren wasteland.

On the horizon, Nikara's walls rose, glimmering black and white. Solara dropped her head like a bull and charged.

I am Solara Barthelme. You are Aliss Casarriba. There is no place here for anyone else.

The walls shuddered under Solara's attack. Nikara didn't notice. Yet. Solara could hear a roar in the background.

You are yourself, and only yourself.

A plaintive cry rose over the rumble of Nikara's walls failing. And then Nikara noticed. Aliss's mind went dark. The snow swirled around Solara, growing colder, biting into her skin.

You've overstepped yourself, little girl, Nikara purred.

She attacked, and Solara's mind itself bent under the fury of Nikara's onslaught. Instantly Faisal was there, holding her up. She flew back into Nikara's face. If Nikara was cold and dark, Solara would be light and heat, burning and cleansing.

Never again.

Aliss's scream joined Solara's. Mental or physical, it didn't matter. Solara could feel herself gripping Aliss by the hair, clinging to her with her mind and her hands, trying to wrench her out of Nikara's grasp.

Petra was coming. That didn't matter. Not yet.

Fight, Aliss. Fight.

Nikara tore into Solara. Her snow ripped the skin off Solara's body. It burned her eyes and shredded her face. Solara fought back with fire. Black smoke billowed into the black sky of Aliss's mindscape, and still, the redhead screamed in utter agony.

Sol, she can't take it! Faisal shouted at her.

Solara ignored him. The ground opened beneath her to swallow her up and she moved, changing it into an earthquake that battered the black stone wall. Cracks spread across its surface, and Nikara responded with a flood of frigid water that threatened to carry Solara away.

Sol! Faisal tried to stop her.

Solara would feel bad for this. Later. She shut him out, evicting him from the single mindscape the three women now shared. At her back, Solara's battlements loomed, and beyond Aliss's prison were Nikara's own walls, spiked and black and dripping blood.

A single shriek split the air, the real air, and suddenly Solara couldn't breathe. Petra. Petra had caught her in a headlock.

Real world and mindscape were superimposed on each other. Solara couldn't fight both battles at once. She swore but refused to back down. First, Aliss. She drew up fire and wind and pounded the walls.

I am Solara Barthelme, named for a warrior queen. You are Aliss Casarriba. I don't know who you were named for, but I know it wasn't any weak bitch.

The black wall crumbled with a shriek. Solara's vision dimmed. She didn't have much longer.

My name is Aliss Casarriba.

The world darkened further. Solara clung to the mindscape as her body began to fail.

I was named by my big brother, and I am going home to him.

With a roar like the end of the world, the white wall came down.

Solara woke in Aliss's arms. Her throat burned, and her head felt fuzzy. "Hello, Aliss," she said weakly.

Aliss smiled. "Hello, Solara Barthelme."

Petra lay in a crumpled pile on the floor. Blood pooled around her head like a crown. Her thoughts flickered in and out of consciousness. Aliss had certainly taken her combat training seriously.

Solara sat up slowly, still dizzy. "You have to go," she said. "Run. Get out of here before Nikara–"

"First," Aliss began.

"No!" Solara shoved her arm. "I swore to your brother I'd get you out of here. You've got to run. Do you understand me?" Aliss looked confused. Solara gripped the girl's shoulders. "I will be fine," she said. Tessan would find her. But he was also going to find Petra, and then there was going to be a problem. "Swear to me that you'll run."

"I..." Aliss nodded unwillingly. "What about you?"

Solara's knife had fallen to the floor beneath the bed. She couldn't look at it. "Don't worry about me. Get out." *She's coming to you, Faisal.* Solara forced a grin to her mouth. Petra must have hit her in the face. Her lips were swollen. "It was nice to properly meet you."

Aliss stood, her thin limbs unsteady, and bolted out of the room. The servants had scattered. Solara was alone with Petra. The thought made her inch away from the girl, until she could lean back against the cot. The tip of her stolen knife pressed against her hip.

She should be running – towards Tessan if she were fierce and ruthless and following her own plan. Away from him, if not. But she just sat there, watching Petra for signs of life. She'd wanted to torture Solara as payment for what'd happened to Roga. Even so, Solara didn't think she could bury this knife in Petra's chest. Not even to save herself.

Footsteps sounded in the hallway. "Sol?" Tessan called.

A servant, her thoughts incomprehensible in terror, squeaked, "This way, my lord."

Solara slid the knife under the bed. A second later, Tessan came through the door. Half a dozen Scarlet Guard were at his back. Their weapons glistened with blood.

"Hello," Solara said.

Tessan's gaze locked on her neck. It was bruising. Was it only the third time one of his sisters tried to strangle her? "What happened?" he said.

"Petra and I… had a disagreement." She almost laughed. Maybe she was in shock.

Tessan strode toward Petra's limp form.

"It's all right," Solara said. "I don't think she's in any condition to–"

Tessan grabbed Petra's hair and yanked her head up, baring her fawn-brown throat to the blade in his hand.

Solara lunged across the floor and flung herself over Petra, knocking her out of Tessan's grasp.

"Solara," Tessan said, his voice hard. "Move."

Solara held Petra's head against her chest, covering the girl's throat with her arms. "No. Tessan, she is just a girl."

"She is a monster," he bit out. "And I've had enough. I'm not fighting with them every day for the rest of my life."

Petra stirred, and Solara held her tighter, lifting tear-filled eyes to Tessan's face. "Please," she whispered. She'd begged him for lenience once before and he'd ignored her, so she didn't know why she expected now to be any different.

Tessan stared at her as if she were just one more enemy in his never-ending lineup. And Solara understood. Even if she'd never hear his thoughts and she'd never feel that bone-deep perception she shared with Faisal, she understood why Tessan was so sick and tired of fighting these battles.

What may very well have been the happiest, most peaceful moment of his life had been interrupted by more battle, more blood, more chaos.

Solara willed Petra to be still and nonthreatening for just a moment more. "I know," she said softly. Tessan's grip on his knife loosened. "I know you're tired, Tess. But you can still choose not to do this."

She was a split second too late in recognizing the danger.

Petra's fragmented thoughts snapped together in consciousness, and pain burst in Solara's stomach as Petra tried to drive the hidden blade on her wrist into Solara's gut.

Tessan grabbed his sister by the ankle and yanked her backward, and she whirled on him with an enraged scream, knife held high. He neatly brought his blade across her throat. Her blood spattered the floor tiles with a gush.

Solara's hand crept up to cover her mouth, then her eyes, as she sank back against the bed. Petra's thoughts went silent.

Another set of footsteps sounded, and someone said, "My lord, Nikara and Adhara have locked themselves in the apartment with your mother. We can't find Maliq."

"Nikara was smart enough not to choose sides today," Tessan said. "Find me Maliq. If the sun is fully up before she's down, I'll take your heads instead."

The soldiers responded in unison. "Yes, sir."

Solara opened her eyes to watch them pivot and march away in search of the second youngest daughter. She and Tess were alone because Petra no longer counted.

"What. Happened." Each word felt like it clawed at her throat.

"My father's war games have only ever had one rule," Tessan said. "We cannot kill anyone. Petra and Maliq decided to change the rules." Footsteps again. Tessan said, "Violo, take my wife to the nursery. Keep her safe until I come for her."

Violo put his hand on Solara's elbow, gently tugging her to her feet. In the corner of her vision, she could see Petra's body, a side of meat in a pool of blood, and she twisted away, unable to hold in her gasp. She was sixteen years old. Crazed, murderous, and vengeful, but sixteen.

"My lady," Violo said. "Please come with me."

She made herself look back once more. Tendrils of Petra's dark hair dangled from Tessan's fingers as he stood over her body. His eyes were closed, as if he, too, couldn't believe what he'd done.

She was in the nursery until noon, when Tessan collected her. She didn't speak to him, and he was lost in his own thoughts as they walked silently back to the apartment, which had been scrubbed clean of blood, top to bottom. The only difference was that instead of Catarina or Lesi, Violo was at her heels.

She stood in the center of the sun-bathed room and stared at the place where her maids had died. "Is Maliq dead?"

"Yes," Tessan said. He went to the sideboard and poured a glass of whiskey, then drank straight from the bottle.

"How old was she?" Her voice was fainter.

Another long, hard swallow of the amber spirits. "Fourteen."

Her stomach rebelled, and she pressed one fist to it. "And your other sisters?"

"Mother's taken Adhara to my grandmother's. Nikara's too proud to go."

"This was the slaughter you promised," she said.

Tessan set the emptied bottle back on the tray and picked up the glass, which he held in one hand, staring blankly at the wall. "Father may kill me too when he sees what I've done." A pause. "Maliq was his favorite."

Solara stumbled to a chair and sat down. "Why?"

"Petra never forgave me for Roga. They were closest of my siblings. The three of us were. Before."

Before Solara.

Tessan turned the glass in his hand, as if admiring the intricate design. "She blamed you for turning me against Roga. And whatever Petra was doing, Maliq was always eager to follow."

Now they were dead. Solara ran her hands over her face. Her heart felt as if it weighed a thousand pounds. "I can't take this anymore."

"You have to," he said flatly. "Not taking it means not surviving."

"She was a child!" she shouted.

"Maliq has been skinning kittens and torturing servants for years. She would have grown up to be a twisted beast just like the rest of us." He finally drank from his glass, all in one go. "There's not a person in this family worth crying over, Solara. Don't cry over me when I'm dead, either."

She should have killed him. The thought twisted into her like a knife. "I won't."

Tessan smiled faintly. "My warrior queen." His voice shook, as if he were going to break down.

Solara stood up, although her legs still felt weak enough to break, and went to stand beside him and take the glass out of his hand. He released it unwillingly.

"If you're going to execute a quarter of your family, at least give them the dignity of facing it sober," she said.

There was a panicked look in his eye, and Solara wondered if, despite his confident declarations as a child and as an adult about how he would deal with his siblings, he had never truly expected to be in this situation. Or, perhaps, he had not expected it to be so painful.

He leaned against the sideboard, making the glasses clink. "When Maliq was twelve, she hid in my wardrobe and tried to stab me when I opened the door. Father laughed about it because she's so much smaller than me it seems absurd to think she tried to best me in a physical test, even with the element of surprise."

Tessan stared at his booted feet, his breath shallow.

"She almost killed me." He ran a thumb over the faintest of scars on his throat. "If she was half a second faster. A quarter inch taller. I would be gone, and she'd be here."

Solara was still holding his glass. She wanted to down it herself and go numb. She set it down on the glass tray and mirrored his defeated position.

"I'm tired," Tessan said quietly. "I'm so tired of this."

Violo inhaled. Solara had forgotten he was there, but a quick glance showed her the normally implacable guard looked deeply troubled for his friend.

Gently, Solara said, "There has to be something better than this."

A slow, one-two knock came at the door.

Tessan's shoulders braced, and Violo instantly moved to answer it.

Roon came in. He looked at Solara, still in her nightgown, and then at his son. "Violo, return to your barracks," Roon said. "This conversation will be private."

Violo nodded and left.

Tessan straightened. "Have you come to lecture me?" he said. He removed the stopper from a second bottle of alcohol.

"For murdering your sisters?" Roon said in the same conversational tone. "Three makes a pattern, Tessan."

"Yes, it does. You would think they'd realized by now that trying to murder my wife is a lethal mistake."

Solara shrank under Roon's second, more thoughtful glance. "They tell me you'd already incapacitated Petra by the time Tessan arrived," Roon said. "Though I wonder you didn't strike the killing blow yourself. Petra had such plans for you, had she ever gotten the chance."

Solara didn't need or want the reminders.

"You're not a fighter," Roon said.

"Yes," Solara said softly. Tessan turned around. "Yes, I am. But I am not a killer."

Did she imagine Tessan's slight flinch at the term?

Roon couldn't take his eyes off her. To Tessan, he said, "I expected you to take the opportunity to rid yourself of Nikara, but I suppose you no longer consider her a threat given the amount of varcella you've dosed her with."

Solara looked at Tessan. He avoided her eyes. "There's enough built up in her system by now," he said. "No. I'm not concerned about her."

"You poisoned her?" Solara said. She didn't know that much about varcella, only that it was used to cloud the gift, generally at the expense of the user's sanity.

"Poetic justice, no?" Roon said. He at last turned to look at his son, his expression almost rueful. "That leaves Adhara."

"Adhara is the only one of my sisters who might actually deserve to live," Tessan said. He poured a glass and downed it all once more. Even as large as he was, it had to be affecting him by now. "As long as she behaves herself, I have no issue with her."

"You underestimate how deeply she hates you," Roon said. "Especially now."

Solara must have made a sound because they both looked at her. Her voice was hoarse as she said, "You're discussing the murder of your children and siblings like the sale of bread." Blank stares. *"What is wrong with you?"*

"My dear," Roon said. "Whatever gave you the impression I would let these acts go unpunished?"

And quick as a snake, he pulled a knife from his belt and drove the blade through Tessan's chest.

CHAPTER TWENTY-EIGHT

Solara caught Tessan around the shoulders as he hit his knees, choking on the blood that immediately spilled over his lips and gushed down the front of his shirt. His deadweight was so heavy that they both crumbled.

"Are you out of your mind?" she screamed at Roon.

Tessan's father gazed impassively at her as his son suffocated on his own blood.

"Tess, no," she whispered. "Please. *Please.*" *Don't go. Don't go. Don't go. Don't leave me here alone.* Blood pooled on the ground around her, making her bare feet slip. "Please don't leave me."

His head slumped in her arms.

Solara looked up at Roon.

"That was not the reaction I expected you to have," he said matter-of-factly.

The apartment door slammed open, and Solara could only stare numbly as Violo burst into the room, his face flushed as if he had sprinted every step back from the barracks.

"Violo," Roon said. "Take care of your master's wife."

Violo stared at her, his jaw slightly hanging.

Solara's hands shook so violently that it was making Tessan's hair drift, trailing through his blood, and she scrambled away from him and vomited on the floor.

"Violo," Roon said, sharper.

Tessan's best friend strode forward and picked Solara up. Tessan's blood was on her arms and down the front of her nightgown and on her knees and her bare feet, and Solara thought she was going to faint until Violo turned her head and forced her to look away.

He carried her into Tessan's bedroom as Roon, in a voice macabre for its nonchalance, called for the guards that always stood watch in the hallway.

"He's dead," Solara said, her voice hollow. "Isn't he?"

Violo kept carrying her across the bedroom and into the bathroom. He set her down in the tub, and she didn't understand why until she looked down at her body and realized all over again that she was covered in Tessan's blood.

Violo put his hand over her eyes. "What did you have for breakfast yesterday?" he said. The faucets squeaked as he turned the water on.

"What?" Solara said.

"Tell me what you had for breakfast yesterday."

Her heart hammered against her ribs like a frightened thing trying to escape. She couldn't see the blood, but she could still feel it. It dripped down her skin.

"Lady Solara," Violo said sharply. "Tell me what you had for breakfast."

"Toast," she whispered. The warm water gushed from the faucet, splashed her feet, pooled around her, just a little cooler than Tessan's blood.

"And?" he said. He splashed the water over her legs with his free hand. "You spent an hour at the table. You ate more than toast."

"I don't know," she said hoarsely.

"Try harder."

"Peach jam," she said. "It wasn't toast. It was biscuits. Honey cinnamon biscuits, like I used to get from the bakery in the fourth ring on my birthday."

Footsteps pounded in the anteroom as the guards moved about. It must have been her imagination, but she thought she could hear their boots squelching against the blood slick floorboards.

Violo hadn't put the plug in the drain, and the water swished away from her as he briskly rubbed blood off her arms. Her nightgown had to be ruined. She'd have to look at it when he moved his hand. There was no avoiding that.

He went still.

"Is it gone?" she whispered.

"To the best of my ability."

She didn't move, and neither did he. The sounds in the anteroom continued as the guards took Tessan's body away, and the swish of water was unmistakable while someone mopped the floorboards.

It was over half an hour before the apartment was silent. By then, Solara was shivering, and Violo's hand must have ached from holding its position across her eyes.

"Are you ready?" he said.

She shook her head.

With his hand still over her eyes, he used one arm to help her stand on shaky legs and step out of the bathtub. Carefully, one uncertain step at a time, he walked her into the bedroom and sat her on the bed. "I'm going to move my hand," he said. "Keep your eyes closed."

"I will."

He let go. It felt incredibly bright without him. He pulled the blanket around her and held it there. Eyes closed, one of her senses denied, Solara noticed how unsteady his breathing was, as if he were as close to a complete come-apart as she was, and that made her open her eyes.

Violo was pale, and he stared at her as if he had never seen her before. His best friend had just died in her arms, and he'd washed his blood off her body.

Solara jerked away. "Go."

He dropped his hands to his sides and stepped backward.

"Violo, please go," she said, her voice catching.

Violo started to speak, but then he just nodded tightly. "Yes, my lady." He strode out of the bedroom, and the door slammed behind him, but not before she heard him bark, "Maid! Get your mistress some clean clothes."

Solara sank off the bed to the floor, then leaned over until she could lay flat on the rug, suddenly too tired to hold up her own body.

The bedroom door creaked open, and the new maid's thoughts announced her arrival. *What the hell happened here?*

"Get out," Solara said. "Get away from me."

The girl wavered. *You'd think she'd be happy.* "But my lady–"

"Get out!" Solara screamed, and the maid fled. Alone at last, Solara burst into tears.

Roon returned not long after his departure, this time with the chief inspector of the Scarlet Guard. Solara was sobbing too hard to give a proper statement, so Roon did all the talking. She'd sat there and she'd cried while Roon told the inspector that Tessan had gone into a fit of rage and attacked his defenseless wife, and she'd been forced to fight back to save her life.

As soon as they left, Solara had stumbled back into her own bedroom, then onto her balcony, so she could lay there on the cold tiles. Violo stood watch behind her, his hand on the hilt of his knife. She'd told him three times to leave, but he probably thought she was considering putting herself over the railing. He'd stayed silent, but he'd stayed.

Solara was all cried out now. Seven, apparently, was the number of hours you cried for the husband you'd had for six weeks. It felt like too little.

"You're going to catch a cold," Violo said quietly.

She was still in her wet nightgown, and the blanket he'd put around her earlier was damp, too.

Violo went into her bedroom and returned holding the quilt from her bed. He laid it over her prone form.

"Thank you," she whispered.

The sun slipped beyond the tree line, and as silky darkness enveloped them, a burst of emotion hit Solara so hard she gasped. It wasn't Faisal's. She scrambled to a kneeling position, trying to pinpoint its origin.

"My lady?" Violo said.

Solara no longer saw her balcony and her bodyguard. She saw a dark forest as she plunged through it, her aching legs beginning to give out. Sheer willpower kept her moving, even as exhausted tears tracked down her cheeks and her worn muscles trembled.

She was Aliss, sprinting through the trees toward the river house as fast as she could – not fast at all, so far from the athlete she'd once been – but with singular focus. Home. Faisal.

When Solara went into Aliss's mindscape, she must have left a path that remained even after her exit, and Aliss's emotions were so amplified they'd tugged Solara back.

Aliss was terrified. She kept to the tree line just to the left of the main road, for fear Scarlet Guard or Nikara's Seconds would burst from nowhere to drag her away, just as they had the first time. She'd hidden for as long as she could, trying to find the strength to move, and now the cover of darkness was the best chance she had.

"Solara." Violo shook her shoulders, but Solara paid him no mind.

She and Aliss raced through the woods until, in the distance, the river house gleamed. Markan guarded the gate. She was staggering more than running now, and he came to attention as she stumbled into the driveway.

He unsheathed his knife. "Who goes there?"

"It's me," Aliss gasped. She dropped to her knees at his feet. "Tell Faisal I'm home."

Markan gaped at her. "Aliss?"

Aliss could only nod.

He shoved his knife away and picked her up. It felt like heaven to go limp in his arms.

He shoved the gate open with his shoulder and left it swinging as he ran into the house. The servants came to investigate the noise, and Markan shouted at them to clear the way. The murmur of thought noise was almost more than Aliss's exhausted mind could take.

Markan carried her up the stairs, and the moment Markan's foot hit the third story landing, Faisal, Solara, and Aliss became aware of one another.

Faisal thought his chest would explode from the burst of relief.

Aliss shuddered back from another presence in her mind.

Solara realized that every single horrible thing that had happened in the palace was worth it.

The glass office door flew open. Aliss stumbled out of Markan's arms and threw herself into her brother's. As small as she was, the force took them both off their feet.

No one could produce any words, physically or psychically. There was just relief, and exhaustion, and love so brilliant it was like trying to stare at the sun.

Solara could feel tears on her cheeks, but she didn't know if they were Aliss's or Faisal's or her own.

"Never, ever, ever let me out of your sight," Aliss whispered.

"Never," Faisal promised. *Thank you.* He took Aliss's face in his hands and looked into her eyes. For the first time in too long, he could hear her thoughts, and her psychic voice was as brash as ever.

You should have seen me beat Petra's ass.

He smiled. "I have no doubt" – his voice caught – "you were as impressive as always."

Aliss smiled, and her bottom lip, cut and swollen from a fall on her run through the woods, began to bleed again. "Who is Solara to us and why is she in our heads?"

Sorry. Solara shook herself, slipping out of their senses like shrugging out of a coat. Violo knelt in front of her, patting her cold cheeks. She thought Faisal had been going to tell her not to go, but the siblings more than deserved their first moment of privacy in years.

"Are you all right, my lady?" Violo said.

Solara nodded once. Her head felt like it weighed a thousand pounds. She'd pushed too hard in the mindscape by holding that link. "Help me to bed."

He swept her and the blankets up all at once and carried her into the bedroom. He laid her in the bed, then closed the balcony door and went to stir the dying fire.

Solara wrapped herself in her quilt and held her head in both hands, trying to breathe away the ache growing between her temples. Using her gift had never been so painful, though her most recent uses of it were certainly unprecedented. Was that why she felt so spectacularly ill? From battling Nikara?

Finished with the fire, Violo leaned against the mantle, arms crossed, and watched her.

"Why are you still here?" Solara said.

"I was told to attend you."

"You are going above and beyond what you were told to do." Solara touched her cheek and was surprised to find it dry. She hadn't been crying; it was Aliss's tears she'd felt. Solara hadn't realized so deep a connection could exist between two people not actively sharing a mindscape. But if she poked at that little pathway, she knew she could just as effortlessly follow it back to Aliss's thoughts as she could find Faisal's.

Solara sat up in bed, and Violo straightened.

Lunaro. With a single thought, she reopened the door between her and her twin, and instantly, her brother was there.

Sol.

She imagined that tunnel, and she fortified it as she'd fortified her wall a million times, stones and bricks and guardians to protect it. She'd kept it closed for fear one of the Manfalon sisters could find a way through, but Solara was beginning to think there was not a soul in the city who could out-will her.

Aliss is home, Lunaro told her. *But you... are you all right? The things everyone's saying about what happened–*

I'm fine, she said. If it was a lie, so be it. *It's so good to hear your voice, Lu.*

Come home, he said. *If he's dead, he can't stop you. Come home, Sol, please.*

Solara's throat tightened. *I will. I promise. Just... I need some time.*

Her brother's silence was accusatory and confused. She didn't want him to understand what she felt, but she'd been lying to him for so long. Solara let her guard drop. She let him feel it all, every messy, overwhelmed, frustrated, aching bit of her heart that didn't know whether it was allowed to grieve for the man who'd died in her arms.

Lunaro didn't know what to say.

She slumped over in the bed again, and he stayed with her while she cried some more.

CHAPTER TWENTY-NINE

She dreamed she was covered in Tessan's blood. In the middle of the night, she stumbled out of bed and into the tub, and she huddled there in water so frigid it turned her fingertips purple. She felt unmade. Torn apart and then shoved back together with too many important parts in the wrong places. She stayed there until morning when someone tapped at the door.

"My lady, are you unwell?"

Violo.

"Please go away," she whispered. She splashed some water on her face and stood. She hadn't eaten anything since her few bites of dinner with Nikara, and her head spun as she staggered out of the tub. Violo knocked again. "Go away, Violo. I'm fine."

"My lady, if you're unwell, you shouldn't be alone."

"Fuck off!" She grabbed a bar of soap and threw it at the door for emphasis. He was mercifully silent while she dried her water-wrinkled body and wrapped herself in her robe. Her hair hung down her back in dripping wet tangles. It reminded her of Tessan's promise. She twisted it into a knot that it might never come out of and went into the bedroom.

Violo had fallen back to the doorway. She climbed into bed and burrowed under the blankets. After a while, she said, "If you're planning to haunt me until the end of eternity, at least sit down."

He didn't. "Your breakfast is waiting, my lady."

Solara could hear the new maid, Kylee, setting the table. "You eat it," she said. "I'm not hungry."

"You haven't eaten in days."

"Violo," she said. "Shut up or get out."

He pursed his lips and remained silent. Solara was being hateful. Violo certainly hadn't volunteered to nanny the woman who, for all he knew, killed his friend.

"Perhaps a cup of tea," Violo said.

Solara pulled the blanket over her head. He was quiet at first, but then he pulled the blanket away. She blinked rapidly in the sunlight.

He held a cup of tea. "Drink this," he said. "And then I will leave you alone. My lady."

Kylee stood back with a laden plate, prepared to come to Violo's assistance if Solara looked agreeable. She thought Solara currently looked like the most disagreeable person she'd ever known.

"My lady," Violo prompted. "Your husband would want you to take care of yourself."

Solara rolled off the other edge of the bed, bolted to the bathroom, and dry-heaved into the bathtub. Kylee squeaked in alarm, and Violo sighed. The only thing her empty stomach had to offer was bile, and it burned her tongue.

Solara, talk to me. Faisal's voice was so loud in her head.

I can't, she thought. She slumped to the floor. *Please just leave me alone.*

Violo and Kylee retreated. Kylee asked Violo in a low tone if they were just going to leave Solara there, and he said, "For now."

Solara was still lying there an hour later, but when footsteps sounded behind her once more, they weren't Violo's. Roon stood over her. He shook his head. "I expected you to handle this better, Solara."

She considered telling him off as well. Instead, she wearily sat up and faced her father-in-law.

"Leave us," Roon said. Violo, of course, was right behind him.

Violo looked to Solara, and she said quietly, "It's all right, Violo."

He nodded and left, closing the door. "I see he's taking his duties seriously," Roon said. "He and Tessan were inseparable from boyhood. Not much up here" – he tapped his temple – "but he's as loyal as the day is long. Nothing will happen to you as long as he's with you."

"Unless you decide to put a knife through my chest," Solara said.

"I don't think that will become necessary," he said.

"Why are you doing this?" Solara whispered.

"If you need to ask that question, my dear, you haven't been paying attention," Roon said.

She wasn't interested in his riddles. But what happened next if she refused to play? "Maliq was your favorite," she said.

Roon made a dismissive gesture. "Maliq was weak-willed, governed by Petra's cruel imagination. The only thing that stopped her from being as violent as her siblings was her size."

Solara told herself to read his thoughts. To pry his iron mind open like a stubborn nut husk. The mere thought made her tired.

"My children were little better than beasts," Roon said. "Different in their ways, but wicked and savage and cruel. Nikara undoubtedly deserves her current suffering."

Her current suffering? Was the varcella still taking her mind apart, even without Tessan here to keep dosing her?

"You were not the first woman she tormented," Roon said. "From the beginning, she thought it great fun to indulge her younger siblings' sadistic whims, like taking Aliss Casarriba. You're a proficient liar, Solara, but you could never hide your feelings about that."

"I had no desire to hide them," Solara said flatly. "She didn't deserve that. No one does."

Room shrugged. "I've gone numb to it. But it's possible to have a sense of right and wrong even when you've long ceased to care one way or another."

"How does this pertain to me?" Solara said wearily.

Roon's smile was strangely kind. "I doubted your judgment and your intentions when you married my son, but it has certainly propelled us all in some interesting directions. Nikara is going to die, and when she does, you will be my eldest child."

Solara couldn't keep up with the conversation. Her brain was tired. His words sank in. "I'm not your daughter."

"In the eyes of the law, yes. You are. And that makes you heir to the Diadem."

Solara couldn't marvel at the absurdity of it. Seamstress to heiress. Nobody to nobility. She couldn't feel anything.

"I've been watching my children for decades, waiting to see which could maintain what my father and his fathers before him built, and I saw nothing but rage and violence."

Where did he think that had come from? Solara almost laughed.

Roon said, "I have had my strongest psychics attempt to break into your mind and even now, when you are at your lowest point, they can't break you." He took her chin in his hand, peering intently into her eyes. "You said you were a fighter. Did he mean so much to you that you've lost your will to live?"

"We will never know," she said. She turned her head. "I don't want your empire."

"You have no choice."

"Don't I?" There was something to feel: a flicker of anger. It made Roon smile, and that further enraged her. "Your children are dead."

"A tragedy."

She'd wanted to believe this family was still capable of caring about one another. But they weren't. And Tessan had been no different than his sisters. She was willfully stupid to have kept hoping.

Roon was watching, always watching. "There was a whisper amongst my children that Nikara ordered you to love him."

"That isn't true." Solara's voice was ragged.

Roon didn't look like he believed her. "Perhaps not. They have always loved to torment Tessan, and as a child he was not so invincible."

"I don't want to hear anymore," Solara rasped.

"Our family history is an ugly one, Solara," he said.

"This isn't my family."

"You'll have your husband spinning in his grave."

Solara gripped her wrist until her fingernails broke the skin.

"And speaking of graves," Roon said. "I'm here to tell you the behavior I expect from you at the funerals, which will be held tomorrow afternoon."

"I have my story memorized," she said bitterly. "What more do you want from me?"

"I want the world from you, Solara," he said. "Do you intend to cooperate?"

She could say no. His plans for her were long-term; he might be patient enough to let her fall apart for a week. But what was the point in prolonging the inevitable? "What do you want me to do?"

The next morning, she bathed and dressed. She couldn't get the knot out of her hair, and she tried to cut it out, but Violo stopped her. She sat at her dressing table and cried while he detangled it for her. He didn't ask why the simple gesture undid her, and she didn't tell him.

The funerals were held in the gray stone chapel on the northern end of the palace grounds. There were so many people. They arrived in carriages and on horseback, a river of black fabrics. Nobody felt sorry for the slaughtered Manfalons. They'd come out of curiosity.

The three caskets sat on their biers at the front of the chapel as one speaker after another intoned how precious these lives had been and what a tragedy it had been to lose them so soon.

Solara stood beside Roon in the front row of spectators. They were the only ones there bearing the Manfalon name. Narcissa and Adhara were still at Lady Gao's. Solara didn't know what was happening with Nikara.

Roon's instruction had been simple. *You are my heir, Solara. As far as these people are concerned, you have no emotion.*

It was harder than she thought.

The chapel was extraordinarily beautiful. The red and gold glass panes in the two-story high windows glittered. Each high-backed pew was handcrafted of yellow pine, and the air smelled like the forest. Solara would give anything to be in the forest right now, far away from this place.

Roon lightly tapped her elbow with his. A reminder. A threat.

Solara slowed her panicking breath and glanced left, looking for Violo. He stood in the shadows with the other bodyguards, close enough to launch to her side if something were to happen. He met her gaze and gave her a slight, reassuring nod.

Roon tapped her again, harder.

Solara locked her eyes on the red lacquer caskets. Tessan was in there. Maliq was in there. Petra was in there. She closed her eyes. Breathe.

"Solara," Roon said very softly. "Pull. Yourself. Together."

She'd been trying and failing to pull herself together for days. Her own emotions were unbearable. But there were also the emotions of everyone around her, a shrill barrage.

Jealousy. There were many, many people who coveted her position beside Roon. Disbelief. Hatred. Disgust.

Build me a wall, Sol.

Solara was so lost she didn't know if she imagined Lunaro's voice or if her brother were truly giving her support. She closed her eyes and began to build. She had always built walls designed to keep her thoughts in. Now, she built it backward, to keep thoughts out. She built silence around herself, until the roaring thoughts of the chapel dimmed.

Solara opened her eyes, and immediately a tear escaped. She thumbed it away quickly, but Roon had seen.

The next speaker was Tessan's childhood caretaker. She talked about how picky he was about his foods and how he never ate sweets.

No wonder he'd spat that donut out so fast in the city that day.

It almost made her smile, but the tears were instant. "Roon," she whispered. "I have to go."

His mouth tightened. "Get out."

She'd taken one step before Violo came to her side. His vicious gaze sent curious eyes hurriedly turning in the other direction, and she walked out of the chapel as fast as she could, almost tripping in the massive skirt of her mourning attire. They exited the side door she'd entered through, which deposited her in the private driveway where the Manfalon carriage waited.

"My lady," Violo began.

Solara climbed into the carriage and slammed the door. She gulped in a massive breath, held it, and spewed it out so heavily she spat on herself a little bit. She was not at all the refined lady she was pretending to be. She never had been, and she was never going to be.

Faisal, she thought.

What do you need?

She let her head flop against the velvet bench. *I'm coming home.*

CHAPTER THIRTY

Solara rode in the carriage, and Violo followed on horseback. The driver was concerned when she told him psychically to take her to the river house. Mercifully, he didn't argue. Violo didn't realize where they were going until it was too late. He rode his horse up next to her window as they turned down the winding driveway towards the river house. "Driver, stop the carriage."

It came to an immediate halt.

"No," she said. "Do not speak to me."

Violo still tried. "Are you–"

"Why are you still speaking?" she said.

He was quiet for mere seconds, punctuated by his horse's nervous prancing. "Is it your own will or his that has you running back to that little lord?"

Solara's tenuous self-control snapped.

She could not stand Violo. Everything about him reminded her of Tessan. Not that he resembled Tessan in any look or manner. Violo was slender and innocuous as a shadow. But it was as if every time she turned around, there was a shoe Tessan had left behind, or a shirt, or a hat. Violo was one of Tessan's accessories, and he wouldn't leave her alone.

She couldn't hide him in a box, as she'd done with her ruby ring. He was just there, an entirely necessary evil, but not evil, because he'd literally washed his friend's blood off her body and never said a thing to accuse her. And she hated him for that, too.

Solara spat her words. "What does it matter and why should you care? Your job is to protect my body and nothing else. Now that Tessan's dead and I don't have to worry about him killing everything that moves around me, I can choose to have a friend if I wish."

The carriage didn't move, and Violo's silence was disapproving. Solara sighed. "You don't need to protect me from Faisal. Even if I wanted to, I couldn't go back. This is just a visit."

Still, they didn't move. Solara's wall of silence held. The only thoughts she heard were her own, tearing her conscience apart.

"Is that what you want?" Violo said at last. Solara covered her ears, but he kept talking, and she could still hear him. "To leave the home he made for you and go back to the man who you said controlled and abused you?"

Who you said. Violo was catching on. It was only a matter of time before her story fell apart. "Don't insinuate that I'm disloyal," she said. "I probably cared for Tessan more than anyone else in his life."

"My lady–"

"Shut up, you insufferable bastard."

He was quiet for ten seconds. She counted. "You've become quite liberal in your speech since your husband's passing."

"Driver, move this fucking carriage," Solara said, and the horses lurched into motion.

Violo didn't move until the carriage had passed him, and then he brought up the rear.

Solara hadn't laid eyes on the Casarriba house in months. It looked lovely in the dazzling light. Barely an inch of snow had fallen overnight, and only the river house, with its icy river below, still wore frost like lace.

She could feel the hum of the river the moment she stepped foot through the front doors. Faisal waited in the foyer, pacing, and their eyes met. She had kept her walls up since the moment Tessan fell, but now she couldn't hold anything back, and in a rush, Faisal saw it all, every horrible detail, and then she'd bulleted into his arms, and he held her.

It's all right, Solara. I'm not angry. Don't even think that. Just cry.

Violo froze at the display.

"I can't cry anymore. I can't anything. It hurts to breathe."

"Focus on doing that, then." Faisal held her tighter, his own eyes closed.

"My lady, this is not appropriate," Violo said, his voice as rigid as his posture.

"Be quiet," Faisal said. Violo fell silent, but his eyes raged. Faisal stroked Solara's hair, saying, "For now, just breathe. We'll straighten out the rest afterward. It's all right. You're safe."

She couldn't even do that. She sank to her knees, and he sank with her. He sorted through everything Roon had said to her, trying to pin down the next immediate danger. Solara pressed her cheek to Faisal's chest and let his heartbeat drown out everything else.

At last, Faisal pulled her to her feet and sat her on the bottom step of the staircase, then knelt in front of her. "How are you?"

"Perhaps you would best honor the dead by not making designs on his widow, Lord Faisal," Violo said.

Widow. The word shredded Solara. And the more wounds she sustained, the more she wanted to inflict some. "Violo, you're here to assist me, not aggravate me. Be quiet."

"Yes, my lady."

They sat in stilted silence.

"Do you want to come home?" Faisal asked. "And stay home?"

"She is lady of the Diadem," Violo said. "The palace is her home."

Solara shot him a vile look. "I am aware of my position, Violo. I think the whole world is. Thank you."

Violo didn't take his eyes off Faisal. "I am under no obligation to be polite to a man your husband despised."

"The only despicable one in the room is you," she snapped. She stood up, but Faisal took her hands and pulled her back onto the step. Violo didn't appreciate that, either.

"Do not overstep your bounds, Lord Faisal," he said. "I can do many things in service of my lady's protection."

"Shut up, Violo," Solara bit out.

"Solara," Faisal said, soothing.

I do, she said. *I want to come home so badly and be with Lu and with you, but Roon won't let me go. I'm a prisoner again, and this time it's worse. I can't do this, Faisal. I want to cut my own throat and end this.*

"Don't say that," Faisal said.

"If you had any decency, you would end that bond," Violo said. "You should have ended it the moment she returned to Lord Tessan."

It hurt to hear his name. She wanted to run. To tear her way out of the house and outrun every single thought inside her head. Roon had tethered her to the palace. He would announce it publicly soon, but everyone already knew what was coming. Solara. The common girl. Lady of the city. She burst into laughter, unable to contain it. It was idiocy. All of this.

"Sol," Faisal said. He squeezed her arms. "Look at me."

She looked at him, partially. Partially at Violo, who looked ready to pull out his knife at the slightest provocation. She averted her gaze. "I want to see Lu."

"Let's go."

Violo wore a permanent sneer on his face as the three of them mounted the stairs single file, but she preferred him judging Faisal than him judging her. She quickened her step as they approached the apartment, until she was almost running. She pushed past Faisal and burst through the door.

Lunaro sat in a chair by the window, scribbling rapidly in a book. He jerked when the door flew open, but then he saw her and dropped the book. He removed the blanket from his lap and stood up.

Solara's hands flew to her mouth. She screamed through them. Then she ran and tackled her brother to the floor.

"If all I had to do was learn to walk again to get you home, I would have hurried," Lunaro said, his voice shaky.

"I love you," she said, her voice muffled in Lunaro's shirt. He patted her back. "And I missed you. And I love you so much."

"I'm still your favorite sibling, then, Lady Manfalon?" he said.

"Always." She lifted her head and kissed him on both cheeks, then dove back into the hug. Here, she was safe. Death and power-hungry nobles and extravagant funerals were far, far away. "Since when?" she said.

"For weeks now," he said. "But with everything else happening... it seemed like a small thing."

He didn't say the other part: she'd never asked. She'd been so hyper-focused on everything happening around her that Lu and Faisal were often an afterthought, and the realization that the cornerstones of her life had changed so drastically was not an easy one. "I'm sorry," she whispered. "Everything was utter chaos, and if I'd let one of them get in my head–"

"It's over now," Lunaro said.

"No, it's not," Faisal said. He'd come farther into the room and sat on the arm of the couch. "Now there's Roon."

Solara burrowed deeper into Lunaro's arms as if she could escape the conversation.

"I know you didn't put that knife in Tessan's chest, Solara," Lunaro said. "Even if I couldn't see your thoughts, I know you. And I feel like I know Roon enough from the state of the children he raised."

"Failed to raise," Violo bit out.

Lunaro gave Violo a level look. "Who is that?"

"That's Violo," she said. "We come in a set now, apparently."

"I am her bodyguard and her protector," Violo said pompously. "Any threat to my lady, and I will deal with it forcefully."

Did he just threaten me? Lunaro asked her.

I think so. He's surprisingly ferocious.

"Sol," Lunaro said. "I can't breathe."

She rolled off him and sat up, and so did he, balancing himself on his arms. He'd filled out hugely since they'd been apart. She flicked the hair around his face. *Looking shaggy, brother. Your rats' nest is coming back.*

You look wretched, as well. He poked her ribs.

Don't sass me.

I'll do what I like. You have a lot of groveling to do, little sister. Lunaro looked her up and down, taking in the wear marks. *I wanted to storm into the palace as soon as they took you, but Faisal said storming is best done on your feet. So, I waited. And waited. And I kept hoping you'd come home.*

There was no accusation in his words, but Solara still felt guilty. She'd already given herself away when she shared her thoughts. Faisal and Lu knew she'd had no intention of leaving the palace. *Faisal was right. And probably motivated to save his own hide. I'd have tossed him in the river if he let anything happen to you.*

"I feel very excluded," Faisal said.

Solara turned to smile at him. "I'm so sorry, Lord Faisal. Your humble Second certainly didn't mean to offend."

"Keep running your mouth," he said. "See what happens."

Violo bristled. She couldn't take him anywhere. She leaned against Lunaro and held his hand, closing her eyes. With him, she could pretend none of this hell had ever happened.

CHAPTER
THIRTY-ONE

Lunaro said, "Come home, Sol."

"Her home is in the palace," Violo said.

"Her prison was the palace," Lunaro said. "But her jailer's gone."

Violo took two threatening steps forward, and Solara said, "Don't you dare touch my brother."

Her bodyguard looked furious. "After everything he did to protect you, this is how you allow him to be spoken of the moment he's dead?"

Solara's guilt was so loud both her brother and Faisal felt it, and Faisal said, "Violo, you are out of line."

Violo ignored him. His hot gaze bored into Solara, and she wished it couldn't make her squirm the way it did. "It doesn't matter what I want," Solara said. "Roon's claimed me as his heir. Heirs live in the palace."

"You're not his daughter," Lunaro snapped.

She squeezed her brother's hand. "Roon has been planning this for a while." It made sense now why he had watched her, questioned her. "He chose me, for whatever reason. I hate him, but I don't think I'm in any danger."

"Aren't you?" Faisal said. He didn't take his eyes off Violo. "Heir to the throne, Sol. That's no small burden."

"She is no small woman," Violo said.

"Violo's my biggest supporter," Solara said, attempting to diffuse the tension. "Roon is going to come looking for me. I didn't ask for permission before I left."

"Don't go," Lunaro said. It was a plea and an order.

"Fuck off," Violo said.

"Enough," Solara snapped. He jerked at her nasty tone. "Watch your mouth when you speak to my brother. Do you understand me?"

Rebellion burned in his eyes. His absolute obedience was only for Tessan, apparently. But he set his rigid jaw and said, "Yes, my lady."

His tone equally snide, Faisal said, "If your bodyguard will allow it, Aliss would like to see you."

It was the only thing that could have convinced Solara to let go of her brother. They left Violo fuming on the landing and went to see Aliss. She was staying in a massive suite of rooms that had belonged to their parents, and the giant curtained bed that took center stage of the bedroom could have held half a dozen people her size.

She, however, was not there.

Before Faisal could get worried, the culprit flounced through a side door. Her loose-fitted silk pants and blouse hung on her gaunt body, and she looked like a baby bird, so petite and frail. But she flashed her quirky grin, and every tense muscle in Solara's body relaxed.

"Finally, some visitors," Aliss said. "I feel like a doll in an antique cabinet in here."

"You are supposed to be in bed," Faisal said. "The doctor said–"

Aliss completely ignored him. "The great Solara Manfalon, née Barthelme," she said. She dipped a curtsy. "Scourge of the noble hordes. Freer of prisoners. Crown jewel of–" She broke off as Solara hugged her. Aliss patted her back, as awkward with affection as her brother. "I have fifteen more names I came up with for you. Don't you want to hear them?"

"No," Faisal said flatly.

Solara let her go. Yes, there was certainly still a pathway remaining between them, an innocuous door tucked between their thoughts. Aliss was aware of it, but it didn't alarm her.

"One of them is rather embarrassing for him," Aliss said in a loud whisper. He took a step toward her, and she ran to her bed, clambering into the avalanche of blankets. "I'm going. I'm going."

"Don't announce any of those names too loudly," Solara said. She leaned against one of the bedposts, unwilling to take her eyes off Aliss for even a second. It was bizarre, almost, to see her operating under her own willpower. And she had quite a bit of willpower. "I'd rather the Diadem not know exactly what I'm capable of."

"That's probably for the best." Faisal glanced at the closed door, his thoughts on Violo beyond it. It was a reminder for the two pairs of siblings to watch their words.

As angry as Violo was at her, Solara thought he was far too loyal to Tessan to let anything happen to her, especially if that 'anything' was Roon. He hated Roon much more than he hated her.

"Is it for the best?" Aliss said.

"What do you mean?" Lunaro said. He propped his chin on Solara's shoulder, like he used to when they were children.

"Solara's going to be the crown jewel of the Diadem," Aliss said. "That position comes with a target on its back, no matter who it is. Don't you think people should know exactly what she's capable of?"

Faisal looked incredulously at his sister, but Aliss had eyes only for Solara.

"The thing everyone fears the most, from the king of the castle to the poorest soul in the seventh ring, is losing their self-will," Aliss said. "They should know you can take it from them if they cross you."

Solara stared at Aliss.

The heiress shrugged one shoulder, her mischievous grin making its reappearance. "I'm not saying you should. I just think they should know. Solara Manfalon, the Dancemaster's Master."

Faisal rolled his eyes, but, for only the second time that day, Solara smiled.

"Go back to sleep." Faisal tossed a pillow at his sister's head and began ushering the twins out of the room. "Leave, before she comes up with anymore names."

Aliss laughed. "I already have a dozen more!"

"She has a good point," Lunaro said, and Faisal groaned as Aliss cackled. As soon as they were back in the hall, Violo fell into formation half a step behind Solara, his hand on his knife.

"Aliss always has a good point," Faisal said. "It's what makes her annoying."

Speaking of annoying. "Where's Mage?" Solara said as they approached the stairs.

"Hiding, if she knows what's good for her," Faisal muttered. He pivoted, making Violo tense, and looked at the twins. "I have a meeting, Sol, so I'll leave you in your brother's excellent care." He touched her shoulder. "You need me, I'm there."

Solara could only nod. She'd thought Violo was going to lunge at him when he touched her, and she didn't want to rile him up anymore.

Faisal dropped his hand, nodded at Lu, and strode away.

Solara watched him go for a moment before looking at her brother. "You two don't seem to hate each other anymore."

Lunaro shrugged a shoulder. "When we found out what Mage did, Faisal said he was going to throw her back in the streets," he said. "I have never seen that man so angry."

Mage must have been devastated. Solara felt sorry for her. "I'm sure she was the picture of repentance."

"She's not sorry," Lunaro said. "But I hope you'll forgive her anyway." He tilted his head in the direction Faisal had gone. "That man put no value on your life until it was snatched out of his grasp. But since then, he's spent a lot of time evaluating his sins."

Solara's eyebrows rose.

"That's not the same man who kidnapped me and bought you," Lunaro said. When Solara's brows rose even higher, he shrugged. "Maybe I don't hate him. Maybe I even understand the little devil, too."

That explained the amity between the two men and the compassion in Lu's thoughts for Mage.

Violo stayed in a foul mood for the rest of the visit, which wasn't long. Roon would come looking for her if she didn't reappear in a timely fashion. Lunaro didn't protest again when she left. He didn't understand what she wanted, but he didn't think she did, either. She had missed the river house, no question. But it wasn't home. Not anymore.

It had gotten dark and cold during the visit, so Violo rode in the carriage with her, and they sat in silence as they rolled back toward the Center. Her friendship with Faisal was more than Violo could stand, and it didn't paint a flattering picture of her, that she'd left her husband's funeral to come here.

"I will no sooner forget him than you will, Violo," Solara said.

"You have a far greater responsibility to his memory than I, my lady."

Solara wanted to shake him. "Have you ever been in love, Violo?" she said.

It took him a long time to answer. "Once."

"This person you loved, tell me about them."

A few more seconds of grumpy quiet. "She was extraordinary," he said.

"That's not a description, Violo."

He said, "I was nothing, and she was kind to me regardless. She cared for me as she cared for everyone else, and that was good, but... I wanted to be special to her."

"Did you tell her that?"

"Many times. It made no difference. You can't tell a person what to feel."

Solara held her hands in her lap, picking at a cracked fingernail. "I'm sorry," she said. Violo made a dismissive gesture. "Do you still love her?"

He didn't hesitate. "With every fiber of my being."

They were quiet.

"Is it hard for you to be in the palace?" Violo asked.

The question was begrudging, but she was touched that he asked. "It's the hardest thing I've ever done," Solara said. "Everything I see every day was his. There's nowhere to hide from everything that happened." Solara shook her head. "I'm supposed to be a fighter and there's nothing left inside of me that wants to fight."

"You don't have to fight right now, my lady," he said. "Right now, rest. I won't let anything happen to you."

Solara smiled wryly. "Thank you, my gallant protector."

"I thought I was despicable."

"Mostly you're a smartass," she said, and he chuckled. She leaned her head against the cushioned wall and closed her eyes. "Thank you for being on my side." She paused. "For what it's worth, I'm on your side, too. That girl is probably missing you right now."

"Thank you, my lady," he said. "That's worth more than you know."

CHAPTER THIRTY-TWO

The next few days passed quietly. The only word she had from Roon was the note he sent her along with a stack of ledgers. *Read these and be prepared to discuss them.* They were accounting books, filled with balance sheets of more money than she'd realized a single person could possess.

It felt like she was getting an assignment from Faisal, and Solara was a good student and did her homework.

Four days after the funeral, a knock came at Solara's apartment door. She was in the window seat, read. She expected Roon, but Violo opened the door to reveal an older woman in physician whites. She bowed deeply to Solara.

"My lady," she said. "I'm very sorry to disturb you. But I have a request if you'd be so kind as to entertain it."

No one had come near Solara apart from Violo and Kylee. The other servants avoided her as if she were diseased. "What is it?" Solara asked. The woman had a well-wrinkled, kind face, and she guessed. "Agathe?"

She nodded. "I've been the Manfalon's physician since Nikara was born." She paused, gauging Solara's expression. "Nikara is dying, my lady. I expect she'll pass very soon."

The mystery surrounding her sister-in-law had slipped Solara's mind, just like a thousand other things that seemed too much for her brain to hold.

"Roon has left the palace on business. Her mother and sister are still with Lady Gao." Agathe paused again. "I would rather she didn't die alone."

Ten minutes later, Solara was following Violo deep into the bowels of the palace, where there was a pair of steam baths. The water came from an underground hot spring which may or may not have technically been part of the black river, and thus they may or may not have been responsible for paying Faisal for their usage. But the Manfalons had handily neglected to ever mention them, and they were one of their better kept secrets. Violo explained it all to Solara in an undertone as they navigated the narrow, damp stairs into the granite cave.

Solara could think of a million things she'd rather do than see Nikara, including lay on a bed of nails. The only light came from a cluster of candles – each of them as thick and as tall as Solara – in an alcove. Nikara sat in the larger of the two pools. Her white linen robe floated around her on the bubbling water. She no longer resembled the woman Solara had feared. Her skin was gray and flaky, sinking against her bones like wet paper. The elegant braids were mostly gone, and in their absence her skull looked massive, her yellowed eyes monstrous in her face.

None of her Seconds were there. Her only attendant was a thin, pale-faced girl holding Nikara's glass of water.

At the sound of Solara's footsteps, Nikara blinked rapidly, trying to focus her eyes. "Sister. Come to see me off?"

Solara stayed in the doorway. Reflected candlelight glimmered on the surface of the pools and in the puddles on the floor. "Agathe told me you were dying alone," Solara said. "I felt sorry for you."

The macabre smile widened. "And your company is supposed to be better than dying alone? Come closer."

Solara didn't move.

"Is it difficult to see your dead husband's handiwork?" Nikara said.

Yes. "You don't think you deserve it?" Solara said. The attendant winced delicately.

Nikara trailed one skinny, limp hand along the water's surface. "When Tess was little, and he realized one day we'd have to kill each other, he promised he'd never make us suffer."

Violo shifted, crossing his arms over his chest.

"Varcella isn't deadly," Nikara said. "It's meant to cloud the mind. To dampen the gift."

"I know," Solara said. "It shouldn't even work on someone as strong as you. How are you dying?"

"I don't think Tessan anticipated this effect." She waved one hand at her body. "Agathe tells me I have an unprecedented allergy. My organs are failing. The varcella had so little effect on my mind that Tess just kept dosing and dosing." She smiled. "Now I die a slow, torturous death."

Solara shuddered.

"You know why he did it, don't you?" Nikara said.

Nikara's gift posed no threat to Tess. He'd done it for Solara, so Nikara would never manipulate her again. Slowly, Solara stepped into the sunken room, made her way through the puddles, and sat on the stone bench beside the pool. Even her billowing robe could not hide how Nikara had wasted away. Her belly extended in a swollen pouch, but the muscles that had defined her legs and arms had atrophied to strings.

Nikara smiled. "I still believe I was his favorite. I was more of a threat to you than Roga, but he wouldn't kill me. Not even for you."

Solara supposed that was what passed for favoritism in this family.

"Tell me something, little pretty." Nikara's voice was softer, weaker. "Did you place the knife in my brother's chest, or did Father?"

Solara looked down at her hands. "Roon."

Nikara made a wheezing sound barely recognizable as laughter. "He finally pushed him too far. Did he see it coming?"

"Enough, Nikara," Solara said.

"Did *you* see it coming?" Nikara pushed. "Were you happy when you watched your captor fall?"

Violo exhaled long and slow in a way that somehow was a warning.

"You defend her so well, Violo," Nikara said hoarsely. "Will you fulfill all of her husband's duties now that he's gone?"

"Leave him alone," Solara said.

"Do you mourn my brother, loyal dog?" Nikara said.

Violo's gaze was cold. "I honor his memory by protecting what he cared for."

"Does she honor him?" she said. "How long till she runs back to the arms of her beloved Faisal?" At Violo's growled *enough*, Nikara hacked a horrible laugh once more. "Has she already?"

"Make your accusation or shut your mouth, Nikara," Solara said. "If you have a question, then ask it, but I have no patience for your childish bullshit."

Nikara snapped, "You and Faisal planned it all, didn't you? Getting you into this house?"

Solara hadn't lied. She wasn't afraid to answer. "Mage Casarriba conspired with your sister, Roga, to drug me and smuggle me out of the river house. Roga swore me to secrecy on pain of death, and then presented me as a peace offering to Tessan."

Nikara blinked at her, startled. Despite Nikara's hold on Roga's mind, her younger sister had still managed to keep some secrets. Even Violo was silent for once.

Solara said, "Everywhere I went I was used for my worth to someone else. What did it matter if it was Faisal or Roga or Tessan? My goal was to survive, wherever I ended up." All of it true, if not all the truth.

Nikara must have decided to believe her. "Shall I tell you a secret, too, little pretty?"

"I don't think I could stop you," Solara said, uninterested.

But Nikara's face went slack, her eyes drifting closed as she slumped in the water. Solara thought she was dead, but the servant girl whispered, "She drifts in and out, my lady. She'll be back."

Was it disappointment or relief? Solara didn't know what to feel. She heaved a long sigh and leaned sideways to prop her shoulder against Violo's leg.

"You're generous to entertain her on her deathbed," Violo said, when it was clear Nikara truly was incognizant.

"It's my fault she's alone. It's my fault she's dying."

"Tessan didn't mean to kill her."

She supposed he would know. "Still. I don't know that he'd be sorry." Solara lifted her gaze to survey the servant girl, who huddled, trying to become invisible. "Don't think me too noble because I feel sorry for her," she added after a moment. "It's easier to forgive sins after death. Or at least just before."

Violo's leg was tense against her shoulder. She wasn't sure if it was because he seemed to hate her touching him or if he was unnerved by their grisly task.

"He'd be sorry," he said quietly.

Nikara jerked, inhaling a sloppy, wet breath that made Solara's chest tighten in sympathetic pain. The woman's gaze drifted aimlessly. "I have a secret for you."

"Tell me or don't. I don't care."

"Come close."

Solara resisted the urge to roll her eyes. She had promised herself she would be kind. She moved to the top of the pool's descending steps, sacrificing her pant legs to the warm water as she sat and leaned down, so her ear was beside Nikara's blistered lips.

"The night in the alley, I looked into your head."

"Yes, I know," Solara said.

Nikara's fingers picked at Solara's arm, hushing her. Her voice was failing. "Do you know you saw him first? Before he saw you. Before I saw you."

Maybe the varcella *had* compromised her mind. "Is that so?" Solara said politely.

Nikara frowned. She knew she was being dismissed. "I looked in your head, little pretty. I saw all there was to see. There was pride and love and joy. All those beautiful things good girls feel. And there was something else, too. A night with bright lights and a yellow dress, and a dance on a tabletop. A little warm feeling in your chest for a man with golden hair like a lion's mane."

Solara went rigid.

"And I thought to myself... what fun it would be to make sure my brother never knew you were his all along. To make sure you never knew that you'd wanted him first."

Solara sat back, a thousand questions on her tongue, but Nikara went still, a cruel smile distorting her swollen mouth. A bit of spittle trickled down her chin. Solara stared, her heart thudding with anger that suddenly had nowhere to go.

Nikara was dead.

CHAPTER THIRTY-THREE

Solara sent a note to Maliah, apologizing for the late hour but requesting that her dear friend be at her side as she dealt with the death of her sister-in-law. Violo muttered that it was unseemly for visits at this time of night, and he stood at his post looking sulky. Solara sat in her window seat once more with a cup of tea, staring blankly at the dark glass.

She had seen Tessan first that night of the solstice. How was that possible? She didn't remember it. Had Nikara snatched the memory of him from her head that night in the alley, leaving Solara with emotion that seemed unexplainable? And then Nikara had provided an explanation, by manipulating Solara to believe she was following an order. The woman was unhinged.

It made Tessan no less complicated a man to care for, but it meant that it had been her choice. Her own free will. And that – that changed everything.

"Do you mourn that woman?" Violo said.

Solara chucked her teaspoon at him. He caught it before it hit him, and she smiled as he brought it back to her, placing it in her teacup. "You're a good caretaker, Violo."

He returned to his post by the door. She stirred her tea absently. "Did you love Tessan?" she said.

"He was my closest friend, as I was his."

"The other day I said I cared for him more than anyone, and that wasn't fair," she said. "You knew him much longer than I did."

Violo lifted his head, his expression flat and hard. "He loved you more than anything else on this earth."

Solara looked away.

"You doubt that?" Violo said. "Still, after all this time?"

She laid her head against the window. "I'm sorry. I'm sure I'm the last one you want to talk to about him. Even if Roon was the one to commit the act, I'm the reason we ever got to that place. I understand if you hate me." She hated herself, too.

"What did Nikara say to you? When she whispered in your ear?"

"Nothing."

A loud, annoyed silence.

"Tessan didn't like it when I said that, either." Solara breathed a laugh. "Tessan didn't like a lot of things." She reached up and pulled a curl of hair free from its knot, twirling the lock around her finger. She'd tried to cut it off again. Violo had confiscated all the scissors.

Someone called out, "Lady Rankin is here to see you, my lady."

Violo opened the door, and Maliah came in. She looked like she hadn't eaten since the steeplechase. Pinched and pale, she was squeezed into a dress two cuts too small and wore an obscene diamond at her throat, reminiscent of Faisal's.

Solara crossed the room and hugged her friend. She was skin and bones.

"What can I do for you, my lady?" Maliah said.

"Don't call me that," Solara said. She released Maliah, and they studied each other. Though her body was wasting away, Maliah's eyes were sharp and missed nothing.

Solara tapped the diamond at Maliah's throat. "That's pretty."

Maliah scoffed, then flushed. It made Solara genuinely smile for the first time in days. "It's garish," Maliah said. "But since… lately, she's been trying so hard for Lord Faisal's attention."

"Since Tessan was no longer an option?" Solara said. As much as she didn't want to discuss the debacle that was her brief marriage, she could hardly pretend none of it happened. She gestured, and they sat on the couch. Maliah toed off her shoes and drew up her legs. Smiling, Solara copied her. "Tell me what I've missed," she said. "Any exciting hunts?"

"Only one dull one," Maliah said. "I fell off, but Carmina–" She faltered, but swallowed and soldiered on. "Carmina's my Second. She's just a girl, but she's a better rider than I am."

Solara didn't need to hear her thoughts to guess. The bond would not have held between them, and poor Maliah was probably desperately pretending for her mother's sake that it had. Solara changed the subject. "This is Violo, by the way. He's… well, my bodyguard, I suppose."

Violo inclined his head. Maliah looked at him coldly. "Yes, I remember him."

"He saved me from eating glass once," Solara said, oddly prodded to defend him. "He's a good man, even if he's the most annoying one I've ever known."

"My only job is to serve my lady," Violo said.

"Yes, yes." Solara rolled her eyes. Maliah giggled. Encouraged, Solara said, "Everyone else is pretending that I'm a noble, dignified lady, but Violo knows I'm an imposter and seems determined to keep me in check." He inhaled, probably to intone another platitude, and she said, "All as a part of his faultless service, of course."

He shut his mouth.

Maliah laughed. "You're terrible, Solara. I wouldn't want to be your bodyguard, either. You probably get into all sorts of trouble."

"He hasn't seen me cause trouble yet," Solara said. "But he will soon enough." She sat forward. "I have a proposition for you."

"My lady," Violo began.

"Hush, Violo. You were so quiet before. Do that disappearing thing you did like when…" Just like that, her composure broke. Like when

Tessan took me to the city, she'd been going to say. She'd formed the T of his name, but her breath caught. All she could think of was the look on his face when she'd shoved the donut in his mouth, and how she'd laughed so hard she had to lean on his arm so she wouldn't fall. Before Solara could break down, Maliah threw her arms around her and hugged her fiercely.

"What's your proposition, Lady Solara?" she said.

When Solara spoke, her voice shook. "Back when I was a common girl, I used to go to a bar in the fourth ring."

"Absolutely not!" Violo said.

She and Maliah snickered. And it was so, so wonderful. She was just Solara. Nobody's wife or heir or enemy. "Come with me," Solara said. "It'll be the most fun you ever have."

"No, my lady." Violo unwrapped their arms, shoving them back to their respective bodies. "You will do no such thing. I forbid it."

But Maliah's eyes glittered. "Yes."

"No," Violo said. "Stand up, Lady Maliah. You're going home." He held out her boots to her.

"Why are you so bossy?" Solara said. Maliah made no move to take her boots or leave.

"You two will no longer be allowed to visit if it continues to give you such wild ideas," Violo said.

"You're not in charge of me," Solara said rudely.

"Yes, I am."

They'd see about that. "You're going to have to borrow some clothes," she said to Maliah. "We have to go in disguise."

Violo set his teeth. "My lady, your sister-in-law just died. This is unseemly."

Solara cocked her head as if she was confused. "You don't really expect me to pay that woman any respect, do you?" She kissed her fingertips and lifted them skyward. "Burn in hell for what you did, sister. I'm sure the lot of us will be joining you shortly."

Maliah looked horrified but also possibly delighted.

"My lady," Violo began.

"Stop me if you dare," Solara said and started stripping off her fancy clothes. He tried to stand firm, but she started unlacing her underdress and he turned around.

"This is not in the least appropriate," he said between his teeth.

Maliah, too, had turned her back, her cheeks scarlet, but she was trying not to laugh. Solara retrieved the clothes she'd borrowed off a maid from her room, calling back, "You can change in here when I'm done."

"My lady," Violo appealed to Maliah. "I cannot guarantee either of your safety in the fourth ring if you insist on going without a set of guards."

"He's right, Solara," Maliah said.

"I've been running those streets since I learned how to walk," Solara said. "I'm not afraid." She wrapped herself in a plain skirt and shirt. To the casual observer, she was just a servant in a fine house. She brought Maliah's clothes out to her, put them in the girl's arms, and then pushed her into the bedroom. "Change. Don't be afraid. I won't let anything happen to you." She closed the door.

"My lady." Violo took her elbow.

Solara swung around and punched him in the side as hard as she could. It felt like she cracked her knuckle against his ribs, and he sucked in a breath, backing up a step. "Don't manhandle me," she said. "In fact, don't put your goddamn hands on me at all."

He rubbed his side, grimacing.

"Do we understand each other?" Solara said.

"It isn't safe," he said between his teeth.

"That is not what I asked," she snapped.

"Your rules of conduct mean nothing if it's a threat to your wellbeing," he snapped back.

Solara stepped closer, lowering her voice. "Don't mask your need for control as concern for my wellbeing. If you ever put your hands on me without my permission, I will end you. I don't care what the situation is."

In the bedroom, Maliah had gone still, holding her breath.

"I have belonged" – Solara spat the word – "to far too many people in the past six months, and you are not about to become the latest. My rules of conduct mean everything. Do you understand me?"

Violo's jaw worked furiously. She didn't know what she was going to do if he refused to back down, though she had every intention of making his disobedience painful. But at last, the fury eased from his posture. "Yes, my lady," he said dutifully.

"Good." She turned back to the bedroom. "Almost done, Maliah?" The door opened, and Maliah stepped out, looking self-conscious in her homespun. Solara's lips quirked. "You should probably take the diamond off."

"Oh." Her cheeks flushed, and she removed the gaudy necklace and set it on the tea tray. "Better?"

"Much." Solara nodded her approval. "Come along. We have havoc to wreak."

Violo was a wreck, but they made it to the fourth ring without incident. Maliah, too, was a bundle of nerves as they walked down a dark avenue flanked by ramshackle buildings. "You did this for fun?" she said.

Violo was so close behind them that he'd already stepped on Solara's heels twice, and if she hesitated for even a step, she could feel his breath on her neck. She was going to give them heart murmurs, and it was selfish of her, but she needed to pretend for just a little while that everything was normal.

"Fairly often," she said. "Poor people are not as dangerous as your mother would have you believe."

They turned a corner and came upon a man pissing on a wall. Maliah gasped, and the man grinned at her over his shoulder. Solara tucked one arm through Maliah's and reached back with her other to be sure Violo didn't overreact. "Come on," she said.

The streets grew brighter, and a swell of noise reached out to greet them. "This is a terrible idea," Violo muttered.

"I think so, too," Maliah said pathetically.

Solara kept moving toward the glow of lights. They cut through an alley – also a terrible idea, judging by Violo's naysaying – and then they were there. The row was lit bright as day, every bar stuffed to capacity and spilling into the streets. A dozen different songs played from various buildings, accompanied by drunken voices lifted in song, and Solara grinned.

"My lady, this is no place for you," Violo shouted in her ear. He was careful not to touch her.

"Shut up, Violo!" she shouted back. She looked inward, fortifying her silencing barrier to keep the thought noise at bay, and plunged into the crowd, hauling Maliah with her. Her friend looked absolutely horrified by everything she was hearing, psychically and audibly.

Solara wove through the crowd in search of her favorite spot, the Cider Jug, which was a large round building at the end of the street. She felt the pulse of its music through the street tiles, and Maliah stopped being terrified and took notice of it.

Solara thought she'd lost Violo in the crush, but there he was, tromping on her heels, saying, "My lady, please–"

She hurried forward, the better to shut out his whining. A giant man holding a club eyed them at the establishment door, and a grin tugged at his mouth. "It's my little girl!" he said.

Maliah gaped.

Solara swept a mocking curtsy. "Hello, Jonquin. You haven't gotten rich and left this life behind yet?"

"I heard you had, but here you are," he said.

Her smile was pained. "Don't believe everything you hear."

Jonquin nodded his club at Violo, a question.

"He's with me," Solara said. They went inside. The crush was as close as she remembered, torsos and hands and hips brushing and knocking and shoving. Maliah gave a little squeak and pressed closer to Solara for protection, which Solara gave by throwing an arm around her shoulders. The music pounded in her ears, a demanding invitation.

"I can't dance very well," Maliah shouted.

"You just need a drink!" Solara didn't have any money, but that had never stopped her before. She resumed her press through the crowd to the bar. They were mainly new faces behind the counter, but there was one she remembered, and who remembered her. The girl shook her head in exasperation, but held up two fingers, and Solara nodded. An instant later, the girl brought two glass thimbles of sparkling clear liquid.

"Hello, love!" she shouted.

"Hello, Maraki!" Solara shouted back. She could feel Violo judging her. "One more, please?" Maraki rolled her eyes but obliged. Solara took the first thimble and turned to Maliah, who looked grim. "You can't drink it yourself. I do it for you. Open wide."

Maliah opened her mouth and tipped back her head, and Solara upended the thimble. Maliah coughed as she swallowed.

"Good girl!" Solara picked up the second and handed it to Maliah, who had flushed dark red from the spirits and was trying to smother another cough.

Maliah turned to Violo. Violo glared at her. "Please?" Maliah wheedled. He looked like they'd asked him to tear his fingers off one by one. But he surprised Solara. He opened his mouth, and Maliah stood on her tiptoes to clumsily feed him his shot of alcohol.

Maliah cheered, grabbed the third thimble, and handed it to him. He took it and turned to Solara. "This is not appropriate," he said but poured it into her open mouth. It burned like hell going down, and she closed her eyes and gave an eloquent shudder.

"Ah. Perfect."

Another song began, one she knew, and she grabbed Maliah's arms and hauled her into the center of the dance floor. She had missed this. The freedom. The abandon. The utter lack of pretense in each body flinging itself about as if suddenly loosed from confines. Eyes closed, head back, she let the music take her. Maliah laughed as the alcohol melted her fears. Her hair whipped Solara in the face, and it didn't matter; nothing mattered.

Solara danced away the death, and the pain, and she tried to shake away that little thing inside of her that Nikara had seen and corrupted, but it wouldn't go. And as her body relaxed, her hold on her silence weakened.

Somebody nearby wondered if her face was shiny with sweat or tears.

Someone else thought they'd like to get nearer her if that terrifying man wasn't beside her.

She opened her eyes and look for Violo. He stood still amidst the chaos, glaring at everyone that glanced at her or Maliah, and Solara burst out laughing. His glare extended to include her, as well.

"Stop it!" she yelled at him, and his glare deepened. "You're impossible!" She took Violo's hand and tugged him back toward the bar. He was the most unwilling companion she'd ever had. He'd put Tessan to shame. She held up four fingers to her friend at the bar.

"Is that wise, my lady?" Violo shouted for the thousandth time.

"No, Violo," she shouted back. "It is not." Her friend lined the shots up on the bar, and Solara shot back two, then gestured at the others. "Those are for you!"

He shook his head tightly. "I cannot guard you if I'm impaired."

"Fine." She grabbed the other two. He tried to stop her, but she downed those, as well. She felt nauseous almost instantly, and Violo muttered a curse. "Better watch me carefully!" she sang and plunged back onto the dance floor.

Tessan had told her not to cry for him when he was gone. She was doing a poor job following orders. An entire family had gone to pieces around her. And here she was, holding the wreckage.

The world went dark, and she grabbed Violo to steady herself.

"My lady, it's time to go home."

"No!" She pushed him away, almost falling against another reveler, who pushed her back at him. She held onto him this time, letting the world settle, and she looked up at his face and couldn't read his expression. How he must hate her.

A whimper clawed at her throat, and she pushed away and started to spin. She spun the way she had on solstice three years ago, with her head back and her arms out. Her skirt flared around her. Colors slurred. Maliah cheered.

I am Solara Barthelme, named for a desert queen. I am myself and only myself.

This was her pain. This was her grief wracking her body. This was her heart, breaking.

CHAPTER THIRTY-FOUR

She had no recollection of leaving the bar, the trip home, or getting to bed. One minute, she was dancing, and the next she was in bed, having a half-waking dream about Tessan. He kissed her forehead with a heavy sigh, saying, "I told you not to cry for me, Sol."

Then she snapped awake, and it was just Violo tucking the blanket around her, and she started to cry. Violo cursed. "Please sleep, my lady. You'll feel better in the morning."

She cried all night, and Violo stood at the door, his shoulders slumped and his head nodding with exhaustion. When she woke the following afternoon, he had taken her dressing table seat and set it beside the door, and he slept with his head propped against the door jamb.

Solara moaned, and he jerked awake, almost falling out of the chair.

"I'm dying, Vi."

"Are you ill?" He rose, alarmed.

"Yes. It's alcohol poisoning." She rolled over, face-down in the pillows, and he came and rolled her onto her back.

"You'll smother, my lady. Here." He took a kerchief from his pocket, folded it, and laid it over her eyes.

"Better." She pulled the blankets to her chin. Her body was sore. She hadn't used it that aggressively in some time. "Go sleep, Vi. You're going to die taking care of me."

He muttered something that sounded like agreement. Between the poor sleep and hangover, she felt like death. She rubbed her belly soothingly.

"You called out his name as you slept," Violo said.

"I miss him." She sounded defensive.

The bed creaked. He'd sat down beside her. His breach of protocol would have made her laugh if she wasn't afraid it would also make her vomit.

"Tell me what you miss," Violo said.

"You don't have to do this."

"You say you cared for him. Tell me how. Why. What you miss."

She smiled again, thinner this time, grateful for the darkness his kerchief offered. "Is this a test? Are you deciding if I'm honorable enough to be worth your effort?"

He waited.

Maybe it would help to talk about it. Nothing else had. "When I was little, I always wanted to sleep alone," Solara said. "I'd try to push my brother out of our bed after he fell asleep because I wanted all the room to myself." Lunaro had been a very patient roommate.

"The first time I slept in the same bed as Tess I was mad because he didn't ask, but I got so used to it." Being near him. Having his arm around her. "It got so I could fall asleep right away, but if ever I woke up, he was already awake, and I just… I wonder if he ever slept well."

For every night she'd slept peacefully, in his bed or her own, he had probably been up, pacing, worrying, plotting to protect her, when it was his own life that he should have been afraid for.

"I don't know," Solara said. "Never mind. It's your turn. What do you miss?"

Violo was quiet for a long time. "Instead," he said. "Let me tell you something I imagine he misses about you."

Solara pulled the kerchief off her eyes.

Violo smiled faintly. It was the first time she'd ever seen him smile. "He talked about you very often, my lady. I don't think he talked about anything else from the day he saw you at the Casarriba party."

Slowly, Solara sat up. Her head swam, but she held her breath until it settled.

"He said he'd told you how difficult it was, being a stone mind. And he noticed that you only conversed audibly in his presence. With the servants. With his siblings. You didn't cut him out. And that meant a great deal to him."

She'd done it out of fear, not consideration. And the fact that he'd taken it as a kindness made her heart heavy with something that might have been guilt. She drew up her knees and wrapped her arms around them. "Tell me something else," she said. "Not something he said about me. Just... something about him."

Violo's expression grew very proper, then he said, "I understand you owe him a table dance."

Solara's face turned bright red, and she grabbed a pillow and flung it at his head. He caught it and set it back in place, grinning. "You're awful," she said. She mocked his prissy tone. "That's inappropriate."

"My apologies, my lady." He wiped the smile off his face. But she thought, just maybe, he was still teasing.

"Tell me a real story, you ass hat," she said.

But Violo stood up, saying haughtily, "I doubt your husband would appreciate your foul mouth, my lady."

"Tessan very much appreciated my mouth," she shot back, and Violo's face turned pink. Pleased that she'd had the last word, Solara lay back down and pulled the blanket over her head. "I need to rest. Don't let anyone disturb me."

"Yes, my lady."

She made herself comfortable in her nest of blankets. Her head was still pounding, and she thought it was going to split open a second later when Lunaro spoke. *I need you to come to the river house. We need to talk.*

She groaned. *Why?*

Hurry up.

Lunaro was mostly hidden behind three massive stacks of books when Solara came to the river house library looking for him. He was surrounded by desks, each one covered in notes and more books, and he sat with his legs propped on the least messy one and his current read propped on his knees.

"You look very studious," Solara said.

He held up a hand to tell her to wait as his gaze raced across the page, finishing his sentence. When he was done, he laid a silk ribbon in the book to mark his place and snapped it shut. "Solara."

"Lunaro," she said, mocking his grave tone.

He smiled. "Where's your bodyguard? Not attached to your hip?"

Violo had stopped in the doorway, and Lunaro could clearly see him. The two men gave each other sour looks.

Solara perched on the bit of desk visible between the book stacks. She'd stopped in the kitchen for a glass of Faisal's hangover cure, but her stomach was still less than pleased about the amount of alcohol she'd forced on it. "What on earth are you doing?"

"Something you should be doing, honestly," Lunaro said. He waved a hand to encompass the entire library. "Faisal's family has stockpiled books for decades, and almost anything you could ever think to ask concerning the gift is written in one of these books. The answers might not necessarily be there, but all the right questions are, and all the research and case files you could possibly read in a lifetime."

It sounded impossibly boring, but Solara nodded. "I'm not reading the entire library. What are the important parts?"

Lunaro frowned. "They're all important, Solara. That's the point. We never had access to anything like this before. Our understanding of the gift is pathetic, especially considering how much of it you possess."

"Our understanding of it was just fine when there weren't people trying to kill us," she muttered.

"And now there are people trying to kill us, so now we do better." Lunaro stood up, and Violo came to attention, making both the twins roll their eyes. Lunaro cast around for a particular book. "Twenty years ago, there was this woman, her name was Aine, and she claimed she was actually an entire other woman named Scipia. She said she'd taken her Second's body permanently and was stuck and couldn't go back."

"Really," Solara said skeptically. "You can control another body, but you can't inhabit it. It isn't soul-swapping."

"Aine said it was," Lunaro said. "Whether it was possible or not–"

"What happened to her body?" Violo interrupted.

Lunaro paused. "What do you mean?"

"Scipia," Violo said. "Why couldn't Aine, or whichever it was, go back to her body? And what happened to it?"

Solara took the book her brother had pointed to and scanned the words. She read the correct paragraph as Lunaro spoke it.

"Scipia, or whoever was in the body at the time, if you believe the story, was dead. She died in a riding accident. That's why Aine said she couldn't go back."

"So Scipia died?" Violo said.

"That's what I just said," Lunaro said.

Violo straightened, looking irritated. "No. You said Scipia's body was gone, but Scipia was using Aine's body. So, the body was gone, but what happened to Aine?"

"How would I know?" Lunaro said, not unkindly. "No one believed her. They didn't ask that many questions. Anyway." He waved a hand. "That's talking souls, and that's beyond my level of expertise."

"Or consciousness," Violo said.

"I didn't realize you were interested in any of this," Solara said.

"We came here to learn," Violo said defensively. "I'd like to understand."

"We don't have to understand every single case," Lunaro said. "We just need to understand, or at least begin to understand, the limits of what Solara can do."

"What are you planning to make me do?" Solara said, still skimming the book. No one conducting the interview of Scipia-Aine had been particularly interested in facts or specifics. It was a courtesy interview before they packed her off to a psych ward. "Just because I can do things, doesn't mean I should."

Lunaro mock-swung a book at her. "You know what I mean."

"No, I don't," Violo said. "Would you like to explain?"

Solara's twin didn't look inclined to do so, but she gave him a sideways glare. *He's trying, Lu. Be nice to him.*

As far as I'm concerned, he's Roon's watchdog, Lunaro thought. *I don't know why you like him. He's not even very nice.*

Solara grinned. "Violo's very nice to me," she said aloud. "Aren't you, Vi?"

Violo did not look amused.

"I'm not saying that we should experiment with Solara's gift," Lunaro said. "Or even that we need to test its limits. But we all know that the gift can be a weapon. And if my sister is carting around a weapon that's quite literally a part of her identity, we need to understand what could make it go off, if only so that it doesn't go off accidentally."

Slowly, Violo nodded. "You don't think this is a dangerous path to wander down?"

Solara opened her mouth to protest, but Lunaro spoke over her. "Solara isn't dangerous, so I'm not concerned with her intentions. The most heinous thing she's ever done was make me give her my half of our cake as children."

"That was an accident," Solara said, straight-faced. She knew her flippancy was annoying them. She snapped shut the book she held. "What other case files would you like me to read?"

Lunaro set his hand on the tallest stack, and Solara slumped. "I've marked the areas I'd like you to focus on," he said over her groan. "Would you take this seriously, Solara?"

Violo smirked. "You see what I have to put up with."

"Don't join up against me," Solara said. "I literally sit and study ledgers and history books for Roon for hours every single night. Don't act like I'm being lazy. I'm tired!"

Lunaro took her by the shoulders. "Solara. Look at me."

She sighed but met her brother's serious gaze. It took her back, with a sudden nostalgic jolt, to the nights in their little apartment when she was elbows-deep in homework, mouthing curses because she would never dare complain about school in front of Lunaro as he patched up his bruises from an evening in the fight cage.

Now, he said what he would always say back then. "We knew this wasn't going to be easy. But we agreed we were going to do it."

Solara looked away, ashamed.

Lunaro pulled her into a hug with a heavy sigh, propping his chin on her shoulder. "It's hard work being the gifted one."

"You would know," she whispered.

"Yes, I was definitely talking about myself," he said. She laughed, and he patted her back and released her. "So, take this stack of books home, fit it into your busy schedule at some point, and we'll talk after." He planted a kiss on her forehead. "Now, go away. The gifted one is busy."

She slid off the desk and gave her homework a dubious look. "Vi?"

"I could not possibly carry those," he said. "I need my hands free in case an assassin rushes out of nowhere."

Lunaro snorted. "Put out your arms. I'll load you up."

Solara obediently held out her arms, and Lunaro stacked the books in them. It was a good thing they'd come in the carriage. She wasn't even sure she'd make it out to the vehicle, but she gritted her teeth and told herself not to complain. She'd pitied herself enough for one day, and neither of her companions looked sympathetic, anyway.

Violo came forward, and she really hoped he was going to take pity on her, but he grabbed the book she'd held earlier – the one with Scipia and Aine – and put it atop the stack.

"To satisfy my curiosity," he said, at Lunaro's questioning look. "Come along, Solara."

CHAPTER
THIRTY-FIVE

Roon was home. Solara had no sooner dumped her armful of books on the nightstand beside her bed then Kylee informed her that Roon had summoned her.

"Where to?" Solara asked, shaking out her sore arms.

Kylee gave Violo a nervous look. "The combat room."

With all his harping about danger and protecting her body, Solara was sure this would be the thing to make Violo say no. But he merely nodded. Unbelievable.

"Let's go," he said.

The combat room was not very large. There were no windows, and the walls were covered with white quilting – in case someone was thrown headfirst into them, she assumed. She'd seen racks upon racks of weapons in the hall on their way in, but Roon stood in the center of the room empty-handed.

Violo leaned against the wall beside the door, arms crossed. He looked mildly concerned but mostly grimly resolved to watch this happen.

Slowly, Solara approached her father-in-law. She hadn't seen him since the funeral, which had surprised her. She'd expected him to come double-check her homework very quickly.

"No tears today?" Roon said. "Your eyes aren't red."

"Do you have people report to you how many tears I shed each day?" Solara said. She could hardly deny the fact that she did indeed shed tears every day.

"I have people report to me every single thing you do," Roon said. "You are my daughter and my heir." He beckoned her closer.

"Doesn't this seem too ambitious?" Solara said. "I trained with a knife for two months and never got very good at it. Hand to hand combat is well beyond my skillset."

"You don't give yourself nearly enough credit, Solara," Roon said. "Based on what my other daughters did to you, your ability to take a hit is impressive, even if you're incapable of giving one." He rolled the cuffs of his silk shirtsleeves, revealing muscled, scarred forearms. "But as much faith as I have in Violo to throw himself between you and an oncoming assault, I would prefer to have some faith in you, as well."

She had spent a lot of time feeling vulnerable the past six months, but this, somehow, was the worst. "I'm half your size."

"And this will no doubt be painful." Roon gestured again for her to join him. "But necessary."

Solara glanced at Violo. He was grinding his teeth, but he held still.

"Your mind will always be the best weapon in your arsenal," Roon said. "But that's no excuse to neglect your other options. Come. Here."

Nervous sweat trickled down Solara's chest, but she forced her bare feet to carry her forward onto the sparring mat. It was just the right amount of firm to lend stability, yet soft enough to spare someone from head trauma. Solara had never thought of Roon as tall, since she'd always had him in ratio to Tessan, but he still had a few good inches on her, and she felt small – frail, even – in comparison.

Roon smiled. "I'm not going to break any bones. I managed not to break any of my other daughters."

Not physically, anyway.

He took her wrist, almost kindly, then turned her around and put his arm around her throat. Solara's panic reflex was instant, but she made herself be still. "This is a chokehold," Roon said. "Pay attention to where my hands are because you're going to do this to Violo later. If I close my elbow angle here, it will stop the blood flow to your brain, and you will very quickly be unconscious. The Scarlet Guard is taught to subdue women this way. You won't be out for long, and there are no lasting side effects."

"What if I'm too short to reach?" Solara said in a small voice.

"You most likely will be. Our focus today is on you escaping this hold, not conducting it. Tuck your chin into your chest, now go sideways, and tuck your leg behind mine."

Solara halfheartedly obeyed. Nothing happened.

Roon gave a patient sigh. "If I slightly choke you, do you think you'll be more inclined to take this seriously?"

"Maybe," Solara said. "Right now, this feels insane."

He laughed. "Try again. Hook your leg behind my knee and pull forward. It'll knock us both backwards and give you time to get free."

They ran through three different drills over a dozen times each. The point, Roon said, wasn't to win a fight. It was to keep her conscious and focused, so she could use her gift to end things. The odds of her fighting an opponent who was her psychic superior, or a stone mind, were so slim that he wasn't concerned about it.

"Violo, come be her practice."

Her bodyguard had been remarkably quiet at his post by the door. More than once, when Roon was being particularly enthusiastic in the lesson, Violo had tensed, leaning forward just slightly as if he were about to intervene. But he'd stayed put. Now, came to stand beside them.

Solara smiled at him. He didn't smile back.

"The element of surprise is always going to be your best bet, should it come to a test of physical prowess." Roon took her hand and helped her to her feet. "You may have to jump. But for now, Vi, kneel."

Violo knelt, and Solara stepped up behind him, suddenly nervous. "I don't want to hurt him."

"Set your stance," Roon said, as if she hadn't spoken.

"Sorry," Solara murmured. She slipped her arm around his throat. Everything about it felt wrong as she loosely settled both arms into position. His body was warm and relaxed, the opposite of her nervous tension, and she wondered if he'd been forced into this role before, when he trained with Tessan.

"You're going to put him all the way down," Roon said.

"But–"

"It won't hurt," Violo said. He touched her elbow, the faintest reassurance. "You should know what it feels like."

Solara didn't know why her hands were shaking, and she dug her fingers into her arm so Roon wouldn't notice.

"You cannot afford to be lackadaisical about your safety, Solara," Roon said. He paced a circle around them, critically eyeing her form. "As the ruler of the Diadem, your portfolio of enemies is immense. We control them with pressure. With bribery. But, if it comes to it, we control them with force. Go ahead."

It was a simple task. Squeeze her arm and render him unconscious. Yet, everything in Solara balked at it, and she knew Roon could tell.

"I'm beginning to think you wish for death," he said. "You seem set on encountering it, and you don't bother to prevent it. Is that the problem, Solara? You have a death wish?"

"It's all right," Violo murmured. "Go ahead, my lady."

Solara squeezed her eyes shut and tightened her grip as hard as she could. In five seconds, Violo slumped in her arms. The weight almost took her off her feet, and she squeaked and let go. He crumbled to the mat.

"Well done," Roon said.

Solara stared at her incoherent bodyguard. "Should we wake him?"

"Leave him," Roon said. "He'll wake on his own."

It seemed unkind. Solara knelt beside his prone form and carefully arranged his splayed limbs. He was so quiet. Even now, when his guard should have been down, his thoughts were vised. Perhaps that was why he and Tessan had gotten along.

Solara looked up at her teacher to find him shrewdly watching her ministrations.

Her kindness toward Violo bothered him, although Solara wasn't entirely sure why. She cleared her throat. "In all the thousands of soldiers in the Scarlet Guard, there are no other stone minds?"

Roon went to the door where a servant had left a pitcher of water and two glasses. He poured them each one and brought hers to her. "Decades ago, stone minds weren't quite as rare. But such people made the masses uncomfortable. A group of radicals made it their mission to destroy them."

Solara had lifted her glass to drink, but at his dry pronouncement, she went still. "They were hunted?"

"Like dogs," Roon said. "Hung from trees. Impaled on gate spikes. Tessan's lucky he was born in the year he was."

Solara's stomach churned. She'd never heard of this before, even as curious as she'd become about the gift recently. "No one helped them?"

"Obviously, some survived, if the curse is even hereditary, as they say," Roon said. "Get up. This isn't a history lesson."

"So now there are barely any left," Solara said. She fought back a shudder at the thought of those mutilated corpses.

Roon crossed his arms and studied her. "The men and women who have run this city for the past three hundred years were accustomed, and are accustomed, to power. That power came from their gift. But if they had outright gone after stone minds, it might have become unsavory for them. So, instead, they stirred up the masses. Manipulated them into hating their enemy. And let that hate run its course."

The sick feeling in Solara's stomach intensified. He gestured again for her to stand, but Solara didn't move. "Is that what you did with your children?" she said.

Roon's expression didn't change, but the muscles in his crossed arms tightened. "It saved me getting my own hands bloodied, didn't it?" Roon said. "Never do yourself what you can manipulate someone else into doing for you. And Tessan was a magnificent weapon if you could point him in the right direction."

Solara looked down at Violo, willing her breath to steady.

"Don't become emotional," Roon said. "It affects your ability to remember what I just taught you."

Violo stirred.

"I won't," Solara said.

Roon knelt on the other side of Violo and lifted Solara's chin so he could look her in the eye. "I never said I wasn't a monster, my dear," he said. "That was your husband who pretended he was something he wasn't. But if this disturbs you so deeply, you should be more motivated than ever to take my crown." He let go of her and straightened. "Now. Has insipid emotion gotten the best of you, or do you clearly remember our drills?"

"I remember."

In a single fluid motion, he snatched her off the ground by the throat so fast her legs thrashed the air. She'd known it was coming, and even still, she couldn't help the debilitating panic that seized her as she tried to inhale and couldn't.

Whether she remembered the drill or not, it didn't matter. As fast as Roon moved, Violo was faster still.

He swung one leg and swept Roon's feet from under him, landing them in a heap, then drove Roon's elbow up and snatched Solara out of his grasp.

Roon, looking the most inelegant Solara had ever seen him, scrambled to his feet.

Violo stood and put himself between them.

Solara thought Roon would swing at him, but the king of the city grinned. "Barely halfway out of a stupor and your reflexes remain excellent. You know that's precisely why I sent you from the room before I murdered my son. I was quite sure you'd be quick enough to stop me, and I wouldn't have gotten a second chance."

Violo's hands clenched into fists.

"Vi, don't," Solara said. She took one of his whitened fists. Her heart hammered against her ribs, both from the sudden attack and Roon's soulless words.

Roon looked down at their clasped hands and then up at Violo's face. "You can't always be there, guard dog. These are skills she needs to learn."

"Then I'll teach her," Violo said. His voice was rigid, thick with hate. "You can go."

Roon's smile flickered over his face again. "I have every faith in you, Violo." He strode past them and left the room.

Solara and Violo didn't move.

"Did you hear what he said," she whispered. The fist tightened further. Gently, Solara turned him around. He'd closed his eyes and wouldn't look at her. She didn't know how much of Roon's monstrous monologue he'd heard, but any of it was enough to warrant the hatred in his eyes when he finally opened them and looked at her.

"He did it on purpose," he said, his voice faint. "To get rid of the monsters he made."

And Tessan had played right into his father's hands. Solara had no words. She looked down at their tightly clasped hands.

"What a hellhole this place is," Violo said.

She tried, uselessly, to come up with something to say, but he just pulled his hands free from hers and left the room.

She stared at the door as it eased closed in his wake. The sight of a room without him was odd; he never left her side. Was it loyalty to Tessan or hatred for Roon that prompted him to take up his role as her protector so fiercely? For five terrifying seconds, she'd believed he and Roon were going to come to blows, and that was a fight that would end with only one man standing. Roon would never swallow the insult of being attacked in his own home, no matter how much he deserved it.

Solara went to the door and stepped back into the main hall. Violo was ten feet away, forever watchful, but with a dull look in his eye that told her he was still trying to process what he'd heard.

She had to protect him. From himself. From Roon.

Roon's earlier taunt reverberated in her head. *You should be more motivated than ever to take my crown.*

"Very well, Lord Manfalon," she said under her breath. Violo looked up, his gaze meeting hers. "I'll take your crown."

CHAPTER THIRTY-SIX

Roon gave her one day to herself before the next lesson began. She suspected the reprieve had been to give Violo's temper time to cool, but he was still a tense cloud of rage when Roon collected the two of them after lunch and said they were going for a ride.

Her father-in-law dropped them off at a teahouse in the third ring, leaving Solara with a brief set of instructions on how he wanted her to run the meeting she was attending in his place.

Lords Canton and Blythe, although they didn't know it, were simply a test of Solara's negotiation skills. Roon wasn't interested in whether she could change their minds about which schools received their funding. He was interested in her ability to negotiate a charged situation without, at the very least, making it worse.

The two men were surprisingly amicable, and despite her first nervousness, Solara left the meeting feeling a little more capable than when she'd gone in.

Outdoors once more, the cool afternoon air immediately chilled her, and she'd barely shivered once before Violo was putting his coat over her shoulders.

"I told you to wear a real coat, and not that glorified handkerchief," he said.

"Why bother when you'll just give me yours?" She grinned and swung up onto her horse, somewhat hindered by the heavy coat.

"Did that go the way you intended?" Violo mounted his mare, and the two horses instinctively turned towards home.

"Better," Solara said. "Much better. I didn't realize there were so many politics behind school funding, and I certainly didn't realize the school I went to was funded by lords."

"They both have daughters your age," Violo said. "Canton has a bastard who goes to that school."

"How do you know all this?" Solara said curiously.

"I pay attention," he said. "In a world full of enemies, Solara, you need to know who is most dangerous and who is most negotiable. You need to keep them both close."

What a delightfully intense pair he and Tessan had made. Thinking of Tessan made Solara realize something else. Violo was riding Tessan's horse. The black mare.

"Were you there the day of the steeplechase?" she said.

"Yes," Violo said. He kept his head on the swivel, not bothering to look at her as she spoke. "If Tessan was there, I was there." He glanced at her, a tiny smile tugging at his mouth. "I remain very impressed by your riding skills."

Solara scoffed. "I survived by the skin of my teeth." She paused briefly before saying, "It seems silly that you were Tess's bodyguard when he was bigger than you and had more training."

Violo kept scanning their surroundings. "The role of a bodyguard is to die in their master's place. My job is to stop a blade from ever touching your body, even if that means my body is what stops it."

Her stomach tightened. "Did Tessan say you could have his horse if he died?" Solara said. It sounded petty.

Violo looked at her. "Does it bother you that I'm riding his horse?"

"No," Solara said. "I was just wondering."

At the palace, they found Roon waiting in the courtyard, leaned comfortably against a pillar, smoking a cigar.

"Do I have my funding?" he said, blowing a perfect smoke ring.

"You have it," Solara said. He didn't look surprised. "Is that the answer you expected?"

"You underestimate your abilities," he said. "I do not."

She studied him, a slight frown on her face. "I don't know where you find all this faith to put in me."

Roon laughed. "Solara, my dear girl, I watched you taunt, cajole, and manipulate two of the most powerful men in this city. My older daughters decimated every woman who dared step foot in this palace, and you've outlasted every one of them. You know when to push. And you know when to mime humility. It doesn't matter whether you consider yourself a leader or not. You know how to survive, and you have just enough kindness to remain fair."

His depiction of her made her sound like someone she didn't know. "All of this to protect your empire after you're gone," she said.

"The empire is nothing," he said. "My name is everything."

Violo frowned.

"I might have your name, but my children wouldn't," Solara said.

"We'll see," Roon said. He straightened, tossing his expensive cigar as if it were a bit of trash. "See to it that you spend some time in the combat room tonight, Solara. That mind won't break, but let's keep your body strong, as well." He disappeared through an archway and into the palace halls.

Violo and Solara looked at each other.

"You don't think he's crazy enough to…" Solara couldn't even say it.

"Divorce Narcissa and marry you himself?" Violo finished. "No, I don't think he's that crazy. And that would defeat the purpose of grooming you to take over. He can say what he wants about his children, but he was waiting with bated breath to dump this responsibility in someone else's lap."

"Roon never wanted to rule?" Solara said.

"He was an only child," Violo said. "He was never given a choice."

There was no sympathy in his voice, and Solara felt no sympathy for Roon, either. He'd had a million chances to be better than what he was, and he'd made his choices. At this stage in his long career of rulership, he had no one to blame but himself.

She dismounted, grimacing as her booted feet met the unforgiving cobblestones, and instantly a servant rushed forward to take her horse.

Violo had already dismounted, and he stroked the black mare's nose and spoke very softly to her. She butted her nose into his hand for another pet.

"To the combat room?" Solara said with grim determination.

Violo smiled as he relinquished the mare to another groom. "To the combat room."

If Solara had to make a preference for trainer based solely on the number of bruises she sustained, she would have chosen Roon. Psychosis aside, he had more respect for her body than Violo.

She lay on the mat gasping for breath after another tap-out while Violo stood impassively over her. "Your problem, Solara, apart from a lack of physical fitness, is that you give up too easily," he said. "I realize this is a controlled situation–"

"Is it?"

His eyes narrowed. "But I need you to train as if your life were truly in danger. If you think I'm being too rough, then imagine if I had bad intentions."

She heaved a long, annoyed sigh. "Roon said I don't need to win. I just need to stall."

"For what?" Violo snapped. "Someone to come and save you? What if no one is coming?"

"Why are you taking my weakness so personally?" Solara said.

"Get up."

He'd just drag her if she didn't, so she rolled onto her belly and pushed herself onto her hands and knees. The thick linen of her sparring uniform was making her sweat, and it seemed to her that the thick folds just made excellent handles for Violo to yank her around with. Her maids hadn't been around when they'd gone back to her room earlier, so he'd neatly and tightly braided her hair down for her.

Yes, she was perfectly capable of doing it on her own. But she was getting woefully used to being spoiled.

"I'm just saying," Solara said. Stifling another sigh, she hauled herself to her feet. Every muscle in her body hurt, and she stood, hands on hips, and surveyed her tormentor. "All the people who really wanted me dead are gone. And you never leave me."

"What if I'm asleep?" he countered.

"You don't sleep," Solara pointed out.

Violo looked exasperated. "Get in position, Solara."

"Why?" she whined. "I'm not a soldier, Vi! This is ridiculous."

He took a step toward her, and she jumped backward so quickly she tripped and fell. She smiled sheepishly at him. Violo took a deep, calming breath. "Solara, would you please explain to me what you think you're going to be doing."

She didn't understand the question, but she loved it regardless, since it gave her a brief reprieve. "What do you mean?"

Violo squatted in front of her, forearms resting on his knees. "If and when you take the reins of Roon's empire and, for all intents and purposes, are queen of the diadem – what do you think your life and responsibilities will entail?"

Solara sat up and crossed her legs. "Apart from all the boring bits?" she said mock seriously.

Violo didn't smile.

Solara considered. "I know Roon has had three attempts on his life since he was sixteen years old," she said. She'd learned that from Faisal the previous day when she was complaining to him about her training. "And he's generally considered likeable. So, I can imagine that number will be multiplied for me.

"But if I expected to rule the Diadem through fear and physical prowess, I'd hope someone would relieve me of that delusion." Solara tapped her temple. "People can say what they want about me, about how weak or how strong my mind is, or that my only strength is in doing what I'm told.

"But I'm still here." She let that statement hang, let Violo's face crinkle into an almost adorable frown. "Not because I'm strong. Not because I'm even that clever. But because I was patient, and I watched, and I used what little strength I have in a moment when it could be more than enough."

Solara gestured to the room. "I could train my body until I'm such an athlete that no one could stop me, but I think very few of my battles are going to involve fists."

Violo bit his lip, dragging his teeth across the length of it. The familiar gesture in a slightly-less-familiar face startled Solara.

"You have a point," Violo said. He stood and offered her his hand. Only when she'd grasped it did he say, "However–"

"Violo!"

He laughed, refusing to let go when she tried to yank her hand away. "Listen to me, you little brat," he said sternly. When she stopped struggling, he began again. "However, I still think you need to train, if only because you're weaker than average."

Solara wrinkled her nose.

"I've taken your words to heart," he promised. "I will ease the intensity." He pulled her to her feet and back to the center of the mat. When they were facing each other once more, Violo hesitated.

"What?" Solara said.

"None of the siblings actually wanted to rule," he said. "The point was to hold power over each other, not really anyone else." He searched her face. "Are you sure you want this, Solara?"

He sounded troubled. "And if I didn't?" Solara said. "Do you think Roon is giving me a choice?"

"If you didn't want it, I would see to it that it didn't keep you," he said with the cryptic confidence he wore like a coat.

Solara grinned. "I cannot imagine the stupid girl who didn't want to keep you, Violo." His cheeks reddened, and she laughed. "But in all seriousness," she said, settling into her stance. "Yes. With all the strings. With all the dangers. I want this."

Violo held her gaze, his cheeks still red, for a moment longer. Then he nodded. "Then we'll see to it that you keep it."

CHAPTER
THIRTY-SEVEN

It was a grueling week. She spent mornings in Roon's office, going over every report and manifest alongside him. Roon said she needed to know the deepest, inner workings of the empire to oversee it effectively.

The afternoons were Violo's territory, and he continued to terrorize her in combat lessons.

She managed two visits back to the river house, where Lunaro added to her ever-growing load by grilling her on her reading.

At the end of the week, a formal invitation to breakfast arrived from Lord and Lady Casarriba. Roon was gone on business, so Solara abandoned the stack of forms he'd left her to decipher and went to the river house.

Solara could hear Faisal and Aliss bickering like children as she approached the hothouse in the center of the garden.

"You are going to make yourself sick, Aliss," Faisal said. "Stop eating so many."

"I'm skinny! I need to eat!"

"Then eat real food!"

Solara tapped on the door, biting back a grin. "Good morning."

Aliss sat sprawled on a painted wrought iron bench, a cream-crusted donut in each hand. Faisal, looking exasperated, sat across from her with a cup of steaming coffee. Aliss waved a donut at Solara. "Good morning, warrior queen." She just wrinkled her nose at Violo.

Faisal stood to pull out her chair, but Violo beat him to it. Faisal made the exact same irritated expression as his sister.

"Did something important happen?" Solara said. There was only one donut left, and she didn't want to deprive Aliss, so she went for the biscuits, instead. "The fact that you sent a proper invitation and not a dog whistle straight into my head seems portentous. Where's Lu?"

"He promised he would be right up, from behind a giant stack of books," Aliss said. She had cream on both cheeks. When Faisal moved her napkin closer, she pretended not to see. "Not even the promise of donuts could hurry him."

Solara had seen him yesterday, but she was still offended. She poured a cup of coffee and handed it to Violo to keep his hands warm. It was just slightly chilly in the greenhouse. "Well?" she asked Faisal. "What's the occasion?"

"Maybe he missed you," Aliss said.

"Aliss," Faisal said, aggravated. "Would you please sit up and tell Solara what you told me."

It was so easy for Aliss to get under his skin that Solara, as always, found herself fighting back laughter. Aliss was eighteen, she wanted to remind Faisal. Old enough to behave better than she was, certainly, but also finally enjoying her freedom. Solara doubted she would find it within herself to worry about decorum if she were in Aliss's position.

All the same, Aliss sat up, licked the last bit off frosting off her thumb, and grew serious. "I went out yesterday–"

"And missed her appointment with the doctor," Faisal interjected.

"–to do some shopping," Aliss said. "There's a candy shop in the third ring that I used to love going to before Faisal leeched all of the fun out of my life."

Solara snorted.

"Don't encourage her," Faisal said. "Get to the point, Aliss."

"I ran into Anim, who is Markan's cousin. He works for Jane Kiery, who works in Roon's treasury. Anim overheard her talking about a massive bribe that Roon had accepted from Ahdieh Samos after his last business trip. She said Roon seemed very pleased with the situation, and that your name came up in the conversation."

"How so?" Violo said.

Solara had barely opened her mouth to ask the same question, and she gave him a sideways look.

"Anim couldn't remember the specifics," Aliss said. "His memory was too faulty to be of use, though he tried to share it. Something about proving your resilience. He only took note of the exchange because Markan had mentioned how much he liked you once."

Solara was flattered that she had a good reputation in at least one small circle.

"Mr. Samos is a wealthy landowner. He's not titled, but he's integral enough to commerce that people overlook that," Faisal said. "He owns a set of farms a mile outside the city limits."

Solara understood in theory that life existed outside of the Diadem's walls, but it was still odd to contemplate. She'd never been out of the city and didn't expect to ever leave it, despite the number of vacation homes the Manfalon family owned beyond it. "What would he be bribing Roon for that has to do with me?"

Aliss and Faisal looked at each other. Their similar, grave expressions made Solara nervous.

"Don't do that," she said.

Aliss picked up the last donut, and Faisal snatched it out of her hand. She grinned but didn't retaliate. "Lords Canton and Blythe have been spreading the word that Lady Solara Manfalon might make for a more formidable opponent than the stuffy lords and ladies previously thought." She reclined in her seat again, arms crossed. "You're a commodity, Solara. But Roon doesn't let anyone get close to you. We're probably lucky he allows you to visit."

"Ahdieh is bribing Roon to see me?" Solara said, baffled.

"He wouldn't be the first to try," Faisal said. "Although if that is the case, he's the first to be successful. Multiple other nobles have attempted to gain an audience with you, but Roon won't let them."

"And he won't," Violo said quietly. "Not until he deems her trained enough to protect his interests."

"Unless Ahdieh is more practice," Solara said.

"That's a dangerous man to practice on," Aliss said.

"He murdered his wife," Violo said. Solara's insides felt queasy. "She was infertile, and he wanted children. He didn't want to embarrass himself with a divorce."

"How do you know that?" Aliss said. "Roga said it was because he thought she was ugly."

To Solara's surprise, Faisal answered. "Tessan hated Samos. He hated most people, but he particularly hated Samos. They got into it at a city meeting once." He tapped the rim of his coffee cup. "Samos wants recognition. Respect. Tessan didn't tend to give out either. The clash was inevitable."

Solara was very confused about how murder was less embarrassing than divorce, but she had to focus on one thing at a time. "Should I be worried?"

"Maybe," Faisal said. He was still holding Aliss's confiscated donut, and she slowly reached across the table and took it back. "I doubt Roon intends to see you hurt, and I have every faith in your hardiness, but there's no point in taunting fate." He sipped his coffee.

It reminded Solara that Violo was still holding his coffee. She took it back from him now that it had cooled and added cream and sugar. "Between Violo's training and Lunaro's schooling, I'm probably the most formidable I'm ever going to be."

"That's no reason to be careless," Violo said. "Samos is no posturing fool. He's worth your respect."

"Yes, Solara has proven to be so careless in the past," Aliss said wryly. "It's a wonder she's survived with all the reckless things she does."

Solara laughed. Violo did not. "I will be very, very careful," she promised. "If that's all, I'm going to see Lu. Am I allowed to have coffee in the library?"

"You didn't eat," Faisal began.

"Faisal," Solara said slowly. He fell silent, and Aliss smirked. "Don't hover." Violo did more than enough of that.

"He misses you," Aliss said. "He can't help himself."

"I don't hover," Faisal said. "You're emaciated."

"Concern yourself with yourself, Casarriba," Violo said. "She isn't your responsibility."

Aliss grinned. She opened her mouth, undoubtedly to make the situation worse, and Solara looped her arm through Violo's and tugged him away. "Thank you for the coffee, Faisal!" She dragged Violo out of the hothouse.

They stopped in the library to say hello to Lunaro. She got two new books for her trouble, and no amount of her whining would get him to take them back. He and Violo just laughed at her.

They rode back to the palace the long way around. The scenic route took them to the northern gate into the Center, where the road was canopied with violet jacaranda trees. The horses picked their way slowly down the path, unbothered by the chill in the air. This would take them directly past Lady Gao's, and Solara wondered if Narcissa and Adhara were still there.

"What are you thinking about?" Violo said. She kept craning her neck, looking for Lady Gao's driveway.

"Tessan's grandmother."

"Why?"

Solara settled back into her saddle with a sigh. "She seemed like she genuinely liked him. I wonder if she's... how she is."

"You wonder if she misses him?" Violo said. "Lady Gao might not have been afraid of Tessan, but don't mistake it for warmth."

"You're very grim," Solara said.

Violo lifted his eyebrows. "I'm realistic, Solara."

There was Lady Gao's driveway. Solara was probably asking to have herself hurt, but she turned her mare down the driveway. Violo sighed but followed. They rode up the driveway, and by the time they reached the front door, a servant was waiting to take their horses.

"Don't expect her to be kind to you," Violo said. He dismounted, patted his horse, and handed the reins to the servant boy, who looked baffled by their appearance.

He was more adept than she'd given him credit for. That was exactly what she was looking for. Someone who was as sad as she was. Solara looked down at him for a moment, the reins twisted in her fingers. Her horse fidgeted.

Violo put his hand on her knee, his expression gentle. "We should go home."

The front door opened, and Lady Gao stepped into the doorway.

Solara dismounted, nearly landing on top of Violo as he went to catch her. She eluded his outstretched hand and went to Lady Gao. "Good morning, Lady Gao," she said.

The old woman stared at her. "Are you here to pay your respects for my grandson?"

"Yes, ma'am," Solara said.

She turned and hobbled into the house, leaving the door open for Solara to follow. It felt akin to walking into a lion's den, but Solara followed, her throat suddenly feeling quite tight. Violo followed close behind.

Lady Gao led them into the sitting room and sat in the same place she had sat when Solara came with Faisal so long ago. She was not the same mischievous, smiling woman now.

Solara stood in front of her, hands in the pockets of her coat. Violo's coat, actually. She hadn't given it back since the other day.

"You look more composed than I would expect for a woman who killed her own husband," Lady Gao said at last.

Solara could have told her that it wasn't her, but she suspected Lady Gao knew that, anyway. "Composed is a strong word," she said. She toyed with her fingers within her pockets. "I'm sorry for what happened, Lady Gao. I know that you cared about your grandson."

Lady Gao smiled faintly. "He was my favorite." Her eyes narrowed. "To hear the tales, he put you through hell. Are you sorry?"

Solara didn't know what to say.

"He was certainly a conundrum, my grandson," she said. "But if you didn't know what kind of man you were marrying, why did you marry him?"

"Leave her alone," Violo said.

Lady Gao spared him a brief glance. "If he loved you, he wouldn't have hurt you."

Her accusatory tone felt warranted, in some ways. But there was another part of Solara that felt like she didn't deserve it. That she didn't deserve anyone's judgment, including Violo's.

"You look ill," Lady Gao went on. "Is Roon feeding you? Are they poisoning you too?"

"I'm fine," Solara said.

Lady Gao pushed herself up, leaning heavily on her cane. "Are you pregnant?"

Violo must have choked on his spit. His sharp inhale sounded like a wheeze. Solara couldn't imagine the stress he'd feel if he were responsible for her and an infant. "No," she said calmly. "I'm not pregnant. I'm not ill. I'm not weak. I came here because I thought you might be sad, and alone, and that troubled me."

Lady Gao peered at her.

"But since my presence is clearly causing you discomfort, I'll leave," Solara said.

"Watch your tone." Lady Gao raised her hand.

Violo stepped forward.

"Don't touch me."

Lady Gao froze. Violo, his own hand raised to stop the strike, also froze.

Solara stared at her grandmother-in-law, her heart thumping. Using her gift, after stifling it for days, was like stretching a muscle that hadn't moved forever. She had to settle into the feeling of exerting her will. Her voice soft, Solara said, "There is not a single person in your family who will ever put their hands on me again." She released Lady Gao, and the woman stumbled backward and sat.

Violo lowered his hand.

"I'm sorry for your loss," Solara said. She inclined her head and turned to go. She swept out of the house even faster than she'd come in, and she stood on the front walk, huddled in her coat, while the harried servant ran to fetch their horses.

Her stomach felt uneasy, as it always seemed to, now. Lu said the massive effort it had taken for her to free Aliss might have aftereffects for some time, which explained why even issuing a simple command felt hard.

"I'm concerned about your health, my lady," Violo said. "I know what your brother said, but you're very weak."

"That doesn't stop you from tossing me around in combat practice," Solara said.

"That's for your own good."

The servant returned with their horses, and Violo boosted Solara up into her saddle. She waited until they were on their way down the road again, well away from listening ears, before she spoke. "You can't threaten old ladies, Violo. Even if she had tried to hit me, whatever you were about to do was going to be too drastic."

"Tessan's grandmother was the only parental figure he didn't hate," he said. "And I still would not have allowed her to strike you. I believe your husband would have been in full agreement."

Yes, he probably would have. "As we have discussed in the past, Tessan was wrong to do many of the things he did," Solara said sternly.

"Was he?" Violo said. "He loved you. It was within his rights to protect you."

"From what?" Solara said. "A slap on the cheek? She's a little old woman. At worst it would hurt my feelings."

"You were angry as well," he said. "Clearly."

The single, snide word effectively communicated how he felt about her giving Tessan's grandmother an order. "You are incredibly hypocritical," Solara said.

"We both use violence," Violo said. "Mine is physical and yours is psychic. But my version will never be mistaken for anything other than what it is."

Solara ground her teeth, incensed that she was having this conversation at all. "Three of Tessan's sisters tried to kill me," she said. "That's more than half. And I have been beaten and manhandled and condescended to, and I never fought back. I'm…" She searched for the right word. "I'm ashamed of that. And I've decided I will never allow another person to strike me. Certainly not in the face, with such contempt. That's why I got angry. And if I use psychic violence, as you like to call it, since I am physically weak, then that's the fault of the person who picked a fight with me."

She shook her head. "But Roga and Nikara and Petra were monsters, and they hurt me simply because they could. I can hardly classify what they did the same as Lady Gao. Her grandson is dead, and it's because of me."

They rode in silence for a quarter of a mile.

At last, Violo said, "Roon Manfalon murdered his son, and it had nothing to do with you. By all means, my lady, feel sorry if you must. But don't feel guilty. Even if you'd placed that knife yourself, I think he'd still be inclined to forgive you."

Solara breathed a laugh. "What do you know about it?"

Violo studied her so intently that she had to look away. "Tessan confided everything in me," he said. "Perhaps more than he should have, once he had you." He paused, formulating his words. "He said that everyone else, people who are not stone minds, becomes accustomed to a certain amount of intimacy simply because they cannot hide their thoughts. That's not something he could experience. And you were very closed off."

Perhaps guilt was a true sickness. Solara chewed on her thumb so hard she broke skin. "I didn't want to be."

"Then why?"

She looked away again, but Violo reached over and took her reins, bringing the horse to a halt. Solara dropped her hand. "Try to imagine being the object of a love that violent and tell me you wouldn't have been scared."

She'd made her thumb bleed. Just as she realized it, Violo gently took her hand. He pressed his shirtsleeve to the tiny wound and held it tight. "All I know is that he loved you," he said quietly. "Despite every dark thing he had ever done. And if any man can love even one thing, or one person, honestly, then he cannot be an entire monster."

Solara swallowed hard. "I never said he was a monster."

"No," he said. "You've been very vague."

"I want to stop talking about this now," she said. She pulled her hand free and urged her horse forward.

CHAPTER THIRTY-EIGHT

Ordering Lady Gao left Solara with a throbbing headache for the rest of the day. Despite Lu's assurances that she'd eventually return to full health after her fight with Nikara, it still had Solara unnerved.

But the following morning she felt well enough to resume her lessons. After a few hours with Roon, lost in a swirl of papers and ledgers and manifests, Solara went back to her room with homework, and Violo, who had learned alongside Tessan the inner workings of the Manfalon empire, helped her sort out the numerical mazes.

The palace was still a prison. Roon allowed her to visit the river house but nowhere else, and he warned her she had to return in a timely fashion, or she'd be collected by a team of Scarlet Guard.

On the days when Solara could stop replaying Tessan's murder in her head, even Roon seemed normal. Although it made Violo's lip curl, Solara was perfectly civil to her father-in-law. For now.

"How long do you intend to pander to that beast?" Violo asked her one day, after Roon had left them in the library.

"I'm not pandering," Solara said. She shuffled her mock city plans into a pile. "I'm trying not to get a knife in my chest."

"Are you going to continue trying not to get a knife in your chest until you turn twenty-five and you inherit the Diadem?"

"I'm not convinced Roon is going to wait that long," Solara said. It wasn't an answer, and she could feel Violo judging her, but she marched out of the library and refused to look back at him. For better or worse, they were partners now. They were the only ones who knew and cared about what Roon had done to Tessan. And now, Violo was the only one left in the palace who genuinely cared about her.

He kept two steps behind her as they walked through the palace toward her apartment. They passed two maids walking briskly down the hall, and Solara was just a few seconds too late in putting up her defenses. She heard them wondering how Solara had the gall to look morose when she would shortly own the Diadem.

Solara turned her head to look at them coldly, and they blushed and hurried on. "Sometimes, I think being a stone mind wouldn't have been so bad," she said.

"Spoken like a powerful psychic. What did they say?"

"They thought I should be grateful for my inheritance and how little I did to get it." She shook her head. "In the beginning I tried to refuse. Roon wouldn't have it. And I can hardly believe I'm saying it, but he's right." It was time for someone else to take the reins, someone who still cared one way or another about what was right.

Violo's eyebrows rose. "You consider yourself the best choice?" His tone was curious.

"That's not the point, Vi."

"The point escapes me," he said.

"Were you born here?" she asked. "In the inner rings?" She didn't wait for his answer. "I was born and raised in the fourth ring, and after my parents died, Lu and I held onto that status by the skin of our teeth. We went hungry sometimes, and some nights we were so cold we couldn't sleep. But compared to the fifth ring? Or the sixth or the seventh? We were rich. We were millionaires."

Violo frowned at her mention of being cold and hungry. Regardless of where he'd been born, he had clearly been raised here.

"It's a different world beyond the third ring. Hundreds of people die of starvation every year, or they break their bodies fighting in cages so their little sister can stay in school."

"That life is behind you," Violo said. "You don't have to worry about those things anymore."

They'd stopped walking, and she sighed and kept going. "The point is still escaping you. I might have escaped that life, but it was by pure chance. There are so many people who never will. Roon says they're collateral damage, and it doesn't matter, but..." She started over. "There's a moment in every decent person's life when they realize everyone has a life as complex and as important as their own. And once you realize that, collateral damage becomes unacceptable."

Violo said, "And what if you become the collateral damage?"

Solara pivoted, walking backward, to smile sweetly at him. "You'd never let anything happen to me."

In the apartment, Solara fell into her chair by the window, and Violo took up his post by the door, silent now. Every time she told him something that surprised him, he took a moment to absorb the information.

She kept a sketchbook by the window, and she pulled it out now, propping the book against her knees. She was a terrible artist, but she'd found drawing to be helpful when she felt particularly low. While Violo pondered, she attempted for the tenth or so time to draw him. She could never get the angles of his face right, and his body proportions always tended to look more like Tessan. More than once, she'd simply given up and drawn in Tessan's gold hair, then tossed the drawing into the fireplace before anyone saw it.

Perhaps Violo would like her more if he knew she never stopped thinking about his friend.

"It sounds like you plan to run the Diadem very differently than what people are used to," Violo said. "Do you expect to make these changes without any pushback?"

"You don't think I can push back?" She measured the distance between his eyes, and then turned back to her sketch.

"I've seen a remarkable amount of pushback from you in the last few weeks," he said. "Were you that afraid of Tessan, you couldn't even speak openly?"

Solara studied his mouth for several seconds before attempting to recreate it with her pencil strokes. "In the beginning, yes. Reading minds has always come so easy to me that I think I struggled to understand him. He might as well have spoken a different language."

"He confused you because he was ungifted," he said. "You confused him because you were."

Solara's pencil paused. "He was surrounded by gifted women. You'd think he would have understood me perfectly."

"Given the option, I don't think anyone would choose to be surrounded by Roon's daughters." Violo paused, his expression contemplative. "I told you that you need to keep your greatest enemy close. For Tess, that was Nikara. He had to keep her close. To watch her.

"Tess was six when his sister realized that he could be competition for inheritance. She locked him in one of the palace's escape tunnels and left him there, bound and gagged, to die."

Solara's hands went slack in her lap.

"He was there for four days before I found him. He was nearly dead. He said that the dark and the silence climbed into his head. That he couldn't get it out." Violo lifted his gaze. "Until that day, he believed that Nikara loved him, despite all the torment he'd endured to that point. But after, he realized that this rivalry would be a fight to the death."

Solara swallowed. That was exactly what it had become. "I don't think I would have sat with her while she died if I'd known."

Violo smiled faintly. "There was a delicate power balance they tried very hard not to upset. And nothing could have made him upset that balance, until you."

Every semblance of balance had gone out the window then, and Tessan and Nikara's rivalry had proved fatal for them both. Perhaps the story would sound very different told from Nikara's point of view, but Solara couldn't help thinking that some – only some – of Tessan's aggression was warranted.

"What are you doing?" Violo said.

"My homework." She leaned over the sketchbook, letting her hair fall like a privacy curtain. Tessan was gone. She didn't need to concern herself with the ethics of what he'd done, or the ethics of how she'd felt about him.

Violo snatched her sketch out of her hands.

"Hey!"

He had crept over while she wasn't paying attention. He frowned at her work. "You have actual homework to complete, my lady."

Solara snatched it back, flushing. "And I'll do it. Later."

"That doesn't look like me," he added haughtily.

"Yes, I know." He'd morphed into Tessan. Even colorless, his hair was unmistakable. "Go back to the door. Assassins could rush in at any moment."

"That's only funny when I say it."

Solara flipped to a clean page. "Sit down and I'll draw you properly."

He looked down his nose at her, and Solara smiled up at him. She expected him to stalk back to his post at the door, but he pulled up one of the chairs from the breakfast table and straddled it, facing her. They gazed at each other.

Solara studied his face as she began to draw. "Thank you for telling me about Tess. Thank you for every time you talk with me."

"It's my duty."

She rolled her eyes and sketched in his lashes. "Then thank you for executing your duty so well. Everything is a little less awful with you here."

"You said this is what you wanted. I will protect your place here." He paused, and she glanced up at him, committing the lines of his mouth to memory. "Whatever that entails."

"That's cryptic. Turn your head to the left. I can't see all your mouth," she said. Violo obeyed. "If you're thinking about doing anything drastic," she began.

"Define drastic."

Solara looked up from her sketch and fixed him with a cold stare. "Don't touch Roon."

"Don't tell me you've grown fond of him," Violo said. "Even your soft heart must have its limits."

"Relax. Your mouth is harder to draw when it's angry." She hid a smirk when he shot her a dirty look. He made himself relax, and Solara resumed her work. "You're the last person in this palace that I care anything about," she said. "If Roon hurts you–"

"I am more than capable of handling that man."

"I'm sure Tessan thought so, too." She wouldn't look up, even as his silence drew out. "He said Roon would kill him for Maliq, and Roon did. Well, he killed him for... everything, I guess. And Tess was Roon's own son. Roon cares less than nothing about you."

"But you do."

She sketched his shoulders, the plain black cloth over them. "Even though you're mean to me sometimes, yes."

"Why?"

She looked up to check the size of the buttons on his shirt. "You are obsessed with the ins and outs of love and loyalty."

"I find you an interesting study."

"Is that so?" She sketched the miniature coat of arms stamped on each button and carefully shaded the rumples in the cloth at the bend in his elbows.

"Did you love Faisal Casarriba?"

The question caught her off guard. Her pencil halted mid-stroke, and she looked Violo in the eye.

He didn't flinch. "When you were at your lowest, you ran to him. You laugh and talk with him, and you have never flinched away from his touch."

Not like she had from Tessan. Solara resumed sketching. "Faisal is my friend. The particulars are complicated."

A slow, one-two rap came at the door.

Solara's heart lurched, and Violo's eyes narrowed. He rose, drawing his hidden dagger from its sheath as the door swung open.

Roon paused in the doorway, taking in the scene. "I don't think I could have chosen a better bodyguard for you, Solara," he said, a smile softening his mouth. Then, to Violo, he said coolly, "Leave us. This conversation will be private."

Was he doing it on purpose? Echoing the phrases that he'd said before murdering his son in front of her eyes?

"Will you put a dagger through her heart as well the moment I leave the room?" Violo said.

"I may put one through yours," Roon said evenly. "Solara, control him."

Solara stood up and laid one hand on Violo's arm. He ignored her entirely. "Vi," she said. "Stop it."

Roon's gaze drifted between them. "Does it not intrigue you how much his mannerisms have come to resemble those of your late husband?"

Solara wasn't entirely sure what to say.

"You should be wary of any man who's so possessive," Roon went on. "No matter how primitive, men know they can't possess people – only objects. And you are far too fierce a woman to be objectified."

Violo's arm tensed under Solara's hand, and she tightened her grip on him. "I'll be fine," she said, her voice softer. "Go wait in the hall."

He took her hand and laid the weapon in it. Roon's nostrils flared, but there was no other indication of emotion in either man as Violo slowly walked out of the room. The door slammed behind him more aggressively than necessary.

Roon turned to Solara. She made herself lay the knife down atop her sketchbook. "This couldn't wait until tomorrow morning?"

"I have a task for you," he said briskly. "There's something I want to acquire, and your particular strength may be my only way of getting it."

"What does that mean?" Solara said.

"There's someone coming to ask for your hand," he said. "While I have no intention of handing you over to this man, it's in our best interest to entertain him."

Ahdieh Samos. The bribe. Solara had been waiting for this. "No," she said. "I'm not entertaining another tyrant. I don't care what you want to acquire."

"Do you think your bodyguard will object?" Roon said with an acerbic smile.

"Leave him alone," Solara said sharply.

"My, how the two of you have grown attached."

He didn't need to phrase his threat any clearer. Solara narrowed her eyes. "I'm not spending the rest of my life being threatened by you. By anyone. Half your family has been butchered around you. At what point will you realize enough is enough?"

Roon lifted a single eyebrow. "Are you rebelling, Solara?"

There was no point in attempting to play it off now. "Lay a hand on Violo, and I may cut my own throat to spite you," she said. His mouth tightened. He knew she wasn't posturing. "I am no delicate flower, Lord Manfalon." *I am Solara Barthelme, named for a desert queen.* It had become her battle cry, and it bolstered her. Not a killer, but a fighter, nonetheless. "I'm not so easily cowed."

"Aren't you?"

He caught her by the throat and held her to the wall, Violo's dagger pressed to her chest. The exquisite blade cut straight through her shirt.

She should have been afraid. She should have thought of Tessan, and the agony in his eyes when he died.

But Solara leaned forward, pushing back against the knife. "Look me in the eye," she said. "You tell me. Am I afraid?"

Roon's grip on her throat loosened. "Do you think you have nothing left to lose?" he said.

"I have everything to lose," Solara said. The dagger tip bit into her ribs. "That's why I'm fighting."

They stared each other down, Roon's face unreadable.

He let her go.

Blood stained her white shirt, and Roon wiped her blood off the knife and dropped it on the table where it clattered noisily. No words were necessary. They'd reached a truce.

"I will do what you ask," Solara said, and he looked back at her. "To a point."

"To a point," Roon agreed. He swept out of the room, and Solara darted into her bedroom. She kicked the door shut and started pulling her shirt over her head as Violo's loud footfall announced his reentry.

"My lady," he said, coming to her bedroom door.

She tossed the bloodied shirt under the bed and pulled a clean shirt from her chest of drawers. The wound was small and already crusting over. "What?"

He tried the doorknob, but she'd locked it. "Solara," he said, louder.

Violo had seen too much of this family; he knew exactly what these people were capable of. She flipped her hair out from beneath her collar and checked her reflection in the dressing table mirror. No trace of blood.

"Sol!"

"Why are you yelling at me?" she said.

"Did he hurt you?"

"Of course not." She opened the door, and he came in, eyeing her for damage. "I'm fine," she said.

Violo looked her up and down. "Why did you change your shirt?"

She had not given his attention to detail enough credit. "Because I didn't like the other one. Why do you care?" She brushed past him and returned to her seat, snatching up her sketchbook. "Sit down. I wasn't finished."

If he stared at her any harder, he was going to burn a hole in her forehead.

"Roon is right about one thing," Solara said, pointing at the chair. Violo, slowly, sat. "You're very loyal, and I'm grateful. But you're my bodyguard. You get an opinion as my friend, but you are not in charge of me."

"My lady–"

"Enough of the bullshit, Violo," Solara said. He set his jaw. "Enough," she said again, softer. She swiftly drew the stern lines of the chair, then ripped the page from her sketchbook and offered it to him. "Tell me what you think."

Violo took the offering, saying, "What did Roon want to speak to you about?"

"Does it look like you this time?"

"No, not particularly." He handed it back, and she balled it up and pitched it into the fireplace and began again. "My lady," he said. "I cannot protect you if I don't know what the threat is."

He had been easier to deal with when he just judged her silently.

Violo leaped out of his seat.

Solara jumped, almost falling out of hers.

"You're bleeding," he said.

"It's nothing," she said, one hand going to cover the offending splotch. Violo's face had turned dark red, and she dropped her drawing utensils and took his hands. "It wasn't his fault," she said.

"Don't lie to me, Sol."

"I'm not lying," she said. "It was an accident." She'd leaned into the dagger, but she doubted Violo would find that any less damning on Roon's part. "You're breaking character, Vi," she said. Something flickered through his eyes. "People might think you actually cared about me," she teased. He didn't smile, although that wasn't a surprise.

She abandoned his hands and hugged him. He went rigid. "Put your arms around me," she said, and he did it awkwardly. "I know you're angry. So am I. But not everything has to come to blades and brawls. We're playing the long game. It requires more patience, but it demands fewer casualties."

"I don't like the long game," he muttered.

Solara leaned her head back, and he looked down at her, brow furrowed. "So, trust me," she said. She hesitated over the next part. "I might not have trusted Tess, but he never trusted me, either."

Violo, to her surprise, nodded.

"I can't undo anything," she said. "And I know I'm not blameless. But we're a team, you and me. Even if you don't like me sometimes. Agreed?"

Again, Violo nodded. "Agreed."

"Good." She let him go.

"Let me see your wound."

"I'm not taking my clothes off for you, no matter how nicely you ask," Solara said. Violo looked appalled, and Solara laughed. "Are you going to tell me how my husband would not have appreciated that?" she said with a grin.

"You are far too liberal in your speech, my lady," Violo said primly.

"You're such an easy mark, I can't help it," she said.

Violo picked up his knife and resumed his post at the door. "Your grief must be less pronounced, if you can mention him and laugh," he said.

Solara shrugged as she sat and picked up her sketchbook. "Our marriage was a disaster. There's no arguing that. But I can still choose to focus on the good. He was kind to me, and we did laugh, sometimes. And for all his faults..." She paused, waiting till Violo met her eyes with a quizzical look. "He was *so pretty*," she said, and Violo rolled his eyes, but he laughed.

"That's the real reason I'm never getting married again," she said. "Everyone else would pale in comparison. I would spend all my time annoyed by how ugly they were. There's not another person on earth as pretty as Tessan."

"You are the only one on earth who thinks that," he said.

Solara grinned, and he shook his head, as if she were exasperating beyond words. She looked at her drawing and saw that she'd been drawing Tessan again. Her smile faded. No. The grief was no less pronounced. She ripped out the page, balled it up, and threw it into the fire.

CHAPTER
THIRTY-NINE

They spent the rest of the day in the apartment, reading. By midnight, Solara's eyes felt like someone had held an open flame to them. She huddled in the middle of her bed with the blanket around her shoulders, and Violo sat at her desk. They had been reading in studious silence since dinner time, and perhaps she was the only one so childish, but they might have been having a contest to see who would cave first and go to sleep.

She turned another page, blinking rapidly so her tired eyes would focus. This page held only a slightly charred, ripped page pasted into it. The scroll-laden script, written in a shaky hand, was barely legible.

"Hm," Solara said. Faisal had mentioned that part of the library caught fire decades ago, so she supposed this was a survivor.

"Anything interesting?" Violo said. He was pouring over Aine's book again.

Solara propped the book against her knees and willed her tired neck to keep holding up her head. "Do you remember how Lu said a ton of soldiers could take the bond together and all hear each other's thoughts?"

"Yes," he said, turning a page.

The communication would eventually break down over distance and number of participants, Lunaro had explained. But because no one was overpowering anyone else, it could still work between far more people than what would become the typical Master's bond.

"This is something called a relay," Solara said. She didn't dare touch the decrepit scrap of paper, so she let her finger hover above it as she read. "The Master is the center of the wheel, and the Seconds are spokes, each willingly yielding their power to increase their Master's strength. An infinity loop of power."

"I don't like the way you say power," Violo said without looking up.

"I'm reading exactly what the book says," Solara said. "I'm just saying... it's interesting." She wasn't sure how a Second could do anything willingly, but it sounded a lot like what she and Faisal did for each other. Her gift had only strengthened since their connection, and the more trust they built, the more powerful it felt.

Violo pivoted in his chair, fixing her with a curious stare. "Why would you need a relay?"

"The point is to expand my horizons, Violo," she said. "Just because I'm reading about something doesn't mean I'm going to do it. And if I had that much more power, the only thing I'd use it for would be to free more Seconds."

A smile that she might have dared call proud flashed over Violo's face. "What else does it say?"

"That's it. Just the description. It's from a book that burned, I guess." She flipped to the next page, to another charred fragment. Most of the words were illegible but for the footnote, which she read aloud. "Both the relay and the nexus theories were discarded after the disbanding of the Collective, due to their pervasive and onerous use of force."

"Shocking," Violo said dryly.

"Just because people choose to use force, doesn't mean it's necessary," Solara said. "Perhaps it would have been more effective if the spokes were actually willing."

"And perhaps it's slavery, just like everything else that has to do with psychic ability." Violo turned back to his book.

Solara made a face at his back, but she closed her book and moved onto the next one. When it came to the Diadem, Violo was right. It was just a dozen different disguises, with the same monster underneath every single one.

"Are you reading about Aine and Scipia again? The book isn't going to change because you stare at it."

"I find this story the most fascinating. Worry about your own homework." He turned a page, adding a second later, "My lady."

Solara snorted. "You can stop faking propriety with me any day now, Violo. There's no one around to tattle."

Violo snapped his book shut and stood. "It's long past your bedtime, Lady Solara." He came to the bedside and took her book out of her hands. "Go to sleep."

"No matter how many times I remind you that you're not the boss of me, you keep bossing me," Solara said.

"Goodnight." He put out the lantern on her bedside table. "Sleep well."

She slept excellently, and she woke to Roon's voice informing Violo they were going out for breakfast, and for him to bring Solara downstairs when she was ready.

Solara dressed at the speed of light but made Violo braid her hair, mainly because he looked so harassed when she came out waving her hair ribbon to ask. It was the little moments in life, like that expression on his face, that brought her the most joy every day.

She, Violo, and Roon went to a teahouse in the third ring for breakfast. The two-story building was covered in climbing ivy and roses, and all the servants were prettily dressed in pink and white like living dolls. They took the top floor's best room, which looked over a manicured water garden through a wall of tulle curtains.

Roon gestured for her to take the chair with its back to the windows. In the shower of sunlight, it was the warmest seat, which she thought was his intention until he stood back and eyed her critically.

He didn't want her to be warm. He wanted her to look attractive. They must have come to meet Ahdieh Samos.

"What, exactly, is our business with Mr. Samos?" Solara asked, as Violo checked the locks on the balcony doors.

Roon smiled. "Your powers of deduction are excellent, Solara." With a glance at Violo that almost looked like requesting permission, he adjusted a few of her wayward curls. "You're a commodity. It's always in my best interest to make you look both expensive and chaseable."

Solara resisted the urge to swat his hands away from her. "I'm impressed you think anyone would still consider me a commodity after the amount of manhandling I've supposedly been through."

Violo stopped messing with the doors.

Roon grinned. "Supposedly?"

Solara had given up maintaining her story. Roon knew she was a liar. She could see it in his face every time her history with Faisal came up, even if she never so much as poked at his thoughts.

When she didn't rise to the bait, Roon went on. "Your resiliency is exactly what makes you valuable. And it's in your best interest to be valuable to the lords and ladies of the Diadem. Your marriage offers the most strategic potential of any move you make in your lifetime. At what other point are you given the ability to choose your family? And despite what my example would suggest, your family should be your most valuable allies."

Violo scoffed.

Roon ignored him. "So, Solara, smile." He took his seat. "And look valuable."

Every cell in Solara's body rebelled at his tone. She didn't smile.

A polite tap came at the door, and one of the staff called, "Your guest is here, my lord."

"Please, bring him in."

The door swung wide, and Mr. Samos entered. He was a short, burly man with messy, sandy hair and a genial smile that made Solara want to be at her ease. He wore an emerald coat that she recognized – she'd made it – hanging open over a silk shirt that might have also been her stitching.

He swept a deep bow. "Lady Solara Manfalon. The pleasure is all mine."

"Good afternoon, Mr. Samos," she said politely. Violo was back at her shoulder, so close she could smell the pine soap used to wash all the guardsmen's clothes. "You say that as if you've been looking forward to meeting me."

Ahdieh tucked his hands into the pockets of the coat, his easy grin widening. "You're the talk of the city, my lady. I had to bribe your father into allowing this meeting."

"Is that my coat?" she said, nodding at it.

"I paid a pretty penny for it, too," he said. He took the seat across from her and crossed his legs. Everything about him exuded indulgence, which was surprising. She would have expected a man who clawed his way to power to seem less spoiled. "Clothing hand-stitched by the famous Lady Solara are all the rage now. Your former employer has made a fortune off your fame."

Even if Bjorn hadn't liked Solara all that much, she'd depended on her. Solara was glad her infamy had finally been useful.

At last, Ahdieh acknowledged Roon. "I didn't realize you'd be supervising my visit, Roon."

Roon smiled indolently. "Her bodyguard is supervising the visit. I am supervising the bodyguard."

Ahdieh's jewel-green gaze shifted to Violo, curious.

Solara cleared her throat. "I've never been outside of the city, Mr. Samos. What is it like?"

"Green," he said. "The air is a thousand times better than the filth you breathe here. From the looks of you, you could stand some fresh air."

Roon looked offended on her behalf.

Solara just smiled. "Was your intention today to come and hurt my feelings? Because that's truthfully one of the kinder things people have said about me."

Ahdieh laughed. He sat forward suddenly, making Violo move even closer to Solara, and rested his forearms on the table edge. "You must come and visit me outside the walls."

His tone was playful, but Solara wasn't an idiot. Roon wouldn't bother to consort with anyone who wasn't capable of being dangerous in some way. Her protective silence held, but the look in Ahdieh's eyes told her she wouldn't like what she heard if she let her grip slip for even a second.

"Must I?" she said. "In all the stories you've heard about me, didn't anyone mention that I don't like being told what to do?"

Ahdieh blinked, startled. Then his smile returned with a slight edge. "I heard you could sit, stay, and roll over."

The moment she heard 'sit,' Solara knew Violo was going for his throat. Out of the corner of her eye, she saw Roon wince in anticipation. She took Violo's hand. It snapped him out of it immediately, even as Ahdieh frowned at her familiarity. Solara squeezed Violo's hand once and let it go.

"What you should take away from that, Mr. Samos, is that I'm a bitch," she said. "And I'm a bitch standing above both of her former masters."

Roon laughed, and Ahdieh's mouth hardened. "Don't play word games with her, Ahdieh," Roon said, amused. "She's going to win."

"What on earth made you believe I was playing?" Ahdieh countered. He jerked his chin at Violo. "Is that not your newest master?"

His every word grated at Solara's soul. She made herself smile. "Oh, no. He sits and stays for me." And then, because this man was irking her down to the bone, she said, "I think I could make you sit and stay, too, Mr. Samos."

His face flushed with anger, and Solara steeled herself and let her shield lower.

From the moment he walked into the room, Ahdieh had thought it would be fun to make Solara cower. He didn't like the way she held her head, as if she thought she was better than him. He didn't like the deference Roon gave her – deference he'd never given Ahdieh, although their common backgrounds were similar. Solara had commanded the fear and awe he'd always wanted and never gotten.

As quickly as he'd lost his temper, Ahdieh reeled it back in. He knew it was unwise to exchange hostilities at this point in the game. He sat back. "Roon suggested I didn't know what I'd be getting myself into with you."

It gave her perverse pleasure to see him back down. Solara acknowledged that about herself. She'd played meek for so long she couldn't stomach it anymore.

This man was just the first. Noble after noble would come prodding at her, expecting to find someone they could boss, bully, and berate. She was not taking orders from these people ever again.

"No," she said. "You have no idea." She stood up, and although decorum indicated both men should stand, neither moved. "I'm done with you."

Anger flashed across his face as Solara swept out of the room, Violo ever at her heels.

Solara had received the message the day before that the daggers she'd commissioned were ready for her appraisal, and since they were in the city, she decided she'd pick them up herself. Roon didn't follow her in her exit, so she and Violo got their horses and joined the rush of traffic on the main road. The street was extra crowded today, and Violo was watchful, eyeing every person who dared brush close to Solara and her horse.

Servants rushed here and there with arms full of things and heads full of to-do lists, dodging manure, horses, and carriages. Two scruffy children were begging on the street corner, but already a pair of officers were headed in their direction to hurry them off before they could bother some noble man or woman.

Part of Solara wanted to ride past Bjorn's, just to check on her former mistress, but she curbed the urge. She was of no use to Bjorn anymore.

At the smithy, the bellows were quiet, and the smith sat at his worktable chipping away at a block of wood. He smiled when he saw her. "It's the warrior queen."

Solara nodded her greeting.

He rose, went to a lockbox, and unlocked it with a small metal key on a chain around his neck. "I'm sorry for your loss, my lady."

"Thank you."

"Should I be?"

Solara was so sick of this song and dance. "I'm sorry," she said. "You can be whatever you like."

The man laid a wooden box on the table, smoothing fine shavings of metal off its lid. "You can speak freely now that he's gone. Are you sorry for that?" He looked up as he spoke, his shrewd gaze landing on Violo. "Though you appear to have a new companion. Do you fear this one, too?"

"You are the only one who needs fear me, should you choose to keep running your mouth," Violo said flatly.

"You're a servant at the beck and call of your lady," the smith said. His gaze came back to Solara. "And regardless of who you were named for, Solara, I see nothing but kindness in your eyes."

"Enough," Solara said. "Show me my knives."

The man opened the box.

The blades gleamed, their cutting edges catching every fragment of light. Each gold and silver handle was beautifully engraved. The jeweled eyes shone up at Solara and scattered beams of emerald light across her and Violo.

"That is not a practice blade," Violo said.

Solara ignored him and lifted them both. They were heavier than she'd anticipated, but the hilts fit perfectly into her palms.

"I made them sharp for you," the man said. He smiled lazily. "May your every enemy tremble before you."

CHAPTER
FORTY

The day's economic lesson had Solara planning a wedding. She gave herself the luxury of an exasperated sigh before settling down to it. Roon sat at his desk across from her, signing papers and handing them off to a scribe, a wisp of a boy who kept stealing looks at Solara. He looked so enamored that Solara finally gave in and listened to his thoughts. His head was full of gossip and wonder, and today he was wondering if the rumors were true, and Solara had bested Nikara in a battle for Aliss Casarriba.

Solara's pencil hesitated.

The rumor had begun in the second ring. Aliss had been seen frequenting her favorite shops, free of her tormentors, nonchalantly mentioning *the Dancemaster's Master*. Everyone knew she would have died if she were still connected to one of the Manfalon daughters when they were killed, and with her tossing about a title like that, clearly it hadn't been Faisal to save her.

Roon, too, had stopped writing, although she doubted any of the boy's loud thoughts were news to him. He was watching Solara's reaction.

"Is something wrong, my lady?" Violo asked.

"Only that I'm expected to spend ten thousand gold pieces on a wedding dress." Solara lowered her head and resumed writing, although her thoughts had scattered like a flock of disturbed crows. Aliss had taken matters into her own hands where Solara's reputation was concerned.

Solara closed her left hand into a fist, as if she could feel the cool metal of her knife in it. She'd carefully balanced the box on her lap for the ride back to the palace, and Violo had stared at her disapprovingly the whole way. At one point he'd told her she didn't know how to use a pair of blades and she'd end up losing a hand, and she'd coolly responded that Faisal had taught her. That fact had him sulking, and he hadn't spoken to her since then.

She'd already decided dinner that evening would be a lecture in how grown men should behave when their feelings were hurt.

"A wedding isn't about fashion, Solara," Roon said. "It is a display of power. There are pieces the groom pays for, and pieces the bride pays for, and at the end whoever has spent more money carelessly is the winner."

"Ten thousand gold pieces could feed the sixth ring for a year," she said.

"I care about the sixth ring in theory, my dearest daughter, not in practice," he said impassively. "Those beggars create a constant source of desperate workers that the Diadem thrives on. They don't need my charity. I need their labor."

Solara's grip on her pencil tightened. Roon had said plenty of similarly cruel things in their mornings together. He simply no longer cared. Everything was a number to him. He didn't see people, families, or homes.

"You're still balking," Roon said. He set his pen down and leaned back in his chair. "Imagine that your future husband was cruel. Powerful. A true bastard of a man. Would you be prepared for him to think you weak?"

"I don't think the price of my dress would affect such poor character either way," Solara said.

Roon smiled. "No, but it would remind him of your price. And the price he would pay for harming you."

"You said you had no intention of handing me over to Samos."

Her father-in-law laughed. "My darling Solara, you have annihilated every man or woman in your way. Regardless of who I 'hand you off to' I'd be more concerned for his safety than yours." His gaze shifted to Violo. "Particularly if he has the gall to lay a finger on you in the presence of that."

"I doubt anyone would be so careless," Violo said. "Even you had the good sense to send me from the room before you touched her."

Roon's smile vanished, and Solara's stomach dropped. The poor scribe shrank. Solara wanted to close her eyes and sink through the floor.

No. Tonight's lecture would be when to keep his damn mouth shut.

Roon leaned forward, resting his arms on his desk. "Are you so smitten, little boy, that you've lost your desire to live?"

"Lay a hand on her again and you will lose your right to live," Violo said.

Solara winced.

Roon said softly, "The only reason you are alive is because your obsession has proved useful in keeping my daughter safe. But have a care those hands don't tie their own noose."

He lifted his pen, signed a final paper, and handed it to his scribe. Solara held her breath. "Have your plans finished by lunch," Roon told her. "I'll assess them then." He rose. "If I stay in this room with your watchdog any longer, I may kill him."

He left, and the scribe scampered after him. The moment the door closed Solara whirled on Violo. "Are you trying to die?" she hissed.

"You're right," Violo said. "Not everything has to come to blows. But he drew blood, and that is unacceptable."

Solara scowled, but Violo would not back down. She flicked her pencil at his head, and it bounced off his temple and clattered to the floor. Violo didn't flinch. "You're a stubborn jackass," she said.

"Yes, I am. Consider this my nonnegotiable in our agreement." He glanced at her sideways. "People don't put their goddamn hands on you."

Solara recognized her words from their disagreement the night of the fourth ring excursion, and she pursed her lips. She couldn't argue with herself.

Violo smirked. "The warrior queen struck dumb. I'm floored."

Solara grabbed her other pen to throw at him, but he caught her wrist and pinned it to the desktop.

"Let. Go."

"Behave like an adult and I'll treat you like one," he retorted. "Until then, be prepared to be punished like a child." And he grabbed her ruler and rapped her knuckles.

Solara had not been rapped on the knuckles since she was five years old, pestering her schoolteacher, and she did not appreciate it. She swung at him with her free hand, but he grabbed that wrist, too, crossing them in her lap.

"Every time I start to think you are a distinguished lady, I'm quickly reminded that you're still in large part a petulant brat," Violo said.

"Directly after your heartfelt declaration of protection, I find not one, but two uninvited hands on me." She lifted her eyebrows. "How does that work?"

"Mine don't count," he said.

Violo was proving quite the conundrum with his behavior. Solara bit back a grin he would undoubtedly call inappropriate. "You aren't quite the distinguished gentleman you pretend to be, either," she said. She leaned forward, about to tease him for breaking protocol, but Violo suddenly drew back, his face flushing, as if he'd realized the breach himself. "Do I make you uncomfortable, Violo?" she said, feigning hurt.

"No," he said too quickly.

She stood, and he backed up a step. She smirked. "See? Easy mark."

She turned to flounce off, but he caught her arm and spun her around in a smooth motion, as if they were on a dance floor.

Solara laughed. "Vi, are you a dancer? So many hidden talents."

He narrowed his eyes at her.

Solara took his free hand land laced their fingers. "What do you think Roon wants from Samos?" She took a big step forward, forcing him to move with her or trip. "The fact that he won't tell me makes me suspicious."

"As you should be." Violo put his arm around her waist, his fingertips landing in the divot of her spine. "Roon thinks you're very capable, and you are," he said. "But that means he'll expect a lot of you. This task is inherently dangerous."

"I'd be shocked if it wasn't." She smiled as he spun her. "Aren't you just the least bit curious?"

"No." Violo stopped moving, bringing their dance to an abrupt halt. For the briefest of seconds, his thumb brushed over the pale band on her ring finger, where her wedding ring once sat. Or maybe Solara imagined it.

A firm knock on the door interrupted their staring match.

"My lady, you have a visitor."

"I'm not expecting anyone," Solara said, stepping out of Violo's arms.

Faisal's voice penetrated her protective quiet, making its way through the door she kept for him. *If you bothered to listen to me when I spoke to you, you would be.*

Faisal, you sound peeved with me. Solara went back to the desk to retrieve her homework. When she turned, Violo's face was blank, his arms folded over his chest. She remembered what he'd told her about Tessan, how she hadn't spoken psychically around him, and she wondered if it alienated Violo, as well, when she was so obviously conversing outside his range of hearing.

"Faisal's here," she said, and his expression grew still stonier.

"Yes," Violo said. "Your friend, Faisal."

At some point, they were going to have a conversation about Faisal. Trust was a part of this partnership now. She owed it to him. *I'm coming.*

As they walked back to her apartment to meet Faisal, Violo said, "I feel that I have inherited a large, if fair, amount of hatred for Faisal from Tessan. The tales you told–"

"I know it was terrible," Solara cut him off. "Yes, I lied. I lied a thousand times. I'll explain it all one day." They were silent. As they crossed a mirrored hallway, Solara said, "Are you mad at me now?"

"I'll wait for your explanation," Violo said. "Then I'll decide."

She smiled faintly. "Thank you."

"For now, I'll ask just one question," Violo said.

Solara stopped, giving him her full attention.

"Do you regret it?" he said.

Solara considered. On the one hand, it could be said that the price for Aliss's freedom had been incredibly steep. But on the other hand. "Every time something bad happened, people blamed me," she said. "Whether it was Mage or Roga or Petra or even Tess. And the truth of the matter is, lies or truth, nothing I said, and nothing I did, compelled these people to commit their atrocities. Those were their choices, and I am not responsible for them." She held his gaze. "So, no. I regret nothing."

Violo's eyebrows rose, and Solara could practically see the sarcasm rising to his lips.

"And no," she said. "I do not require your approval or permission for the fact that I feel that way." She turned on her heel and walked into the apartment. He didn't follow.

Faisal sat at her table, a stack of books from Lunaro on its surface.

"Lu realizes he's going to work me to death, doesn't he?" Solara said. The stack was alarmingly tall, but at the very top he'd put something for her amusement: a gilt copy of *The Storybook of War.*

"Seems morbid," Faisal said, as she snatched up the book and settled into her window seat with it.

"My mother used to read this to me and Lunaro. I love these stories." She ran her fingers over the beautiful cover.

He stood looking over her shoulder and concluded, "This is how you built your fortress in your mind. I recognize that." He pointed at one of the hybrid beasts cavorting in a bloody river. "It's a wonder you're not more terrifying, growing up with this for a primer."

"There were lots of milder texts," Solara assured him. "But this was our favorite. It's why I went to Bjorn's in the first place. She has one of the drawings over her door."

He sat opposite her, one arm resting over the back of the furniture. The bond between them was quiet today, thoughts drifting lazily between them like dust motes on air. "Where's your bodyguard?" he said.

"Sulking in the hallway," she said.

"What happened?"

She had no desire to discuss any of it with Faisal. Instead, she said, "I met Samos this morning. He's a charmer."

"Most of your new peers are," Faisal said. He drummed his fingers against the seat cushion. "Roon has never indicated any interest in aligning himself with Ahdieh. I don't like this situation at all."

"You're hovering," Solara said.

"Ahdieh is an anarchist and a slave trader," Faisal said. "His wife? The woman he murdered? He drowned her in her bathtub and told everyone she was drunk and slid under."

"Roon doesn't want me dead," Solara said. "All he's talked about lately is making the right connections. Ahdieh seems like a dangerous ally, no matter what Roon stands to gain."

"I have no idea what his plan might be. My fear is that it goes terribly wrong." Faisal attempted not to articulate the thought, but the fact was obvious: Solara was not physically capable of defending herself from Samos, even after all her lessons. "If Violo harms the wrong person in his attempts to protect you, he'll answer for it with his life."

"When it comes to protecting me, I truly don't think Violo cares what happens to him," Solara said. That was its own problem.

Faisal rubbed his forehead between his eyebrows, frowning. He was mildly concerned that Violo's intensity would cause trouble for Solara. Like Roon, Faisal thought Violo had become more aggressive since Tessan's death.

I'll see what I can find out, Faisal thought. He lifted Solara's chin with a small smile. *Don't be afraid. You're Solara Barthelme.*

Her smile was faint as his own. *Named for a warrior queen.* Then, aloud, she said, "I'm not afraid."

The door opened and Violo entered. Faisal glanced at him dismissively, and then his head snapped back around, his eyes narrowing.

Violo stared at him coldly. "My lady, you have work to complete before lunch."

"I know," she said.

Faisal rose, his brow furrowed. *I'll let you know as soon as I have news.* He leaned over and she tilted her head to receive his parting kiss on her cheek. "That is from your brother. He told me to smack you as well, but I'd like to live."

Solara grinned, but Faisal's amusement didn't reach his eyes. He'd withdrawn from their shared thoughts, and she preferred her quiet. He left, and she turned to her homework. Perhaps it was fear that kept her out of the mindscape these days. Fear of pain. Fear of becoming soulless like Nikara or Roon. Fear of learning to enjoy that power.

"I'm sorry, Solara."

Solara looked up. "What?"

Violo was the picture of humility, his head bowed. "My duty is not protecting his memory," he said. "It is protecting you."

Solara had no words.

"When Roon told Tess to marry Lady Gaimbi, he thought maybe it was for the best. That he wasn't meant for you. But Nikara thought he liked her, and she had her killed."

Always Nikara.

"He had committed to letting you go," Violo said. That must have been why Tessan had stopped coming to Bjorn's. "And then you appeared in the last place he ever expected to see you."

"With Faisal."

Violo's mouth tightened. "Yes. With Faisal."

"They grew up together," Solara said. "Why did they come to hate each other? Was it all because of Aliss?"

For a moment, Violo looked confused. Then understanding snapped into place. "You came here for Aliss," he said. "Faisal sent you here, plotted to get you into the palace, for his sister." A thousand emotions flitted across his face. "That's why you lied to him. To get close to his sisters and break the bond."

"It was the only way I could help Aliss. Tessan was the only one who could get me into the palace." Something in his eyes had her on edge.

Does it not intrigue you how much his mannerisms have come to resemble those of your late husband's?

Roon's voice echoed in her head, and she tried to stuff down the bizarre comparison. It didn't make any sense. "What was I supposed to do, tell him the truth?" Solara said. "Tessan didn't care about Aliss. He watched her suffer and he did nothing. I begged him to be kind to Tolly and he wouldn't listen to me. He *never* listened."

Violo looked down, but it was too late.

"You don't have to pretend that you're not angry, for yourself or on his behalf," Solara said. "I don't want to fight with you, and I'm not going to waste my time defending myself to you. I did what I had to do, and I'm not sorry." She stood up, carried her things to her bedroom door, and paused there.

"What Tess and none of those other people realized is that Aliss's life was precious, and if they wouldn't give her up willingly, I had every right to use force."

Violo's lips parted but nothing came out.

"When it comes to protecting people like Aliss from people like this family, I'll keep using force. That's why I'm going to take the Diadem, and I'm going to do it a hell of a lot better than Nikara or Tess ever could."

She went into her bedroom and shut the door.

CHAPTER FORTY-ONE

Several days of sullen silence ensued. Although Violo still guarded her with the utmost care, he did not say a single word to her. She breakfasted each morning with Roon, and her father-in-law talked Solara through the dozens of machinations he always had in motion.

She worked in the library reading ledgers and consulting history texts until lunch, which she generally spent at the river house with Lu. Maliah came to visit her there, and she and Lu hit it off right away. When Aliss joined the group, usually with some teasing commentary at her brother's expense, they would end up laughing so hard they could barely breathe. Mage was never anywhere to be found on these visits. She was deathly afraid of what Solara might do to her, Lu said. And while Solara had no intention of exacting revenge, she did nothing to allay those fears.

In the evening, Solara and Violo read, still not speaking. Many of the books Lu was having her read were dull tomes of stuffy scholars pretending to understand how the gift operated. Solara preferred the firsthand accounts of normal individuals who fought battles, won wars, and protected their family with the gift.

She would read for hours if no one stopped her, but she knew it was bedtime when Violo closed his book and walked out of the room.

Other nobles came and went from the palace, having teas and lunches with Roon and Solara. When they were gone, she and Roon discussed what they'd learned from the conversation and what had been gleaned from open minds. Roon incised thoughts from people's head with surgical precision. What he lacked in raw talent, he made up for with skill.

Solara, despite her every wish, was impressed daily by Roon. He would probably still run the Diadem even if he had started out in a gutter in the seventh ring.

Three, four, then five days passed of utter silence in the apartment. It made Kylee so nervous she even breathed softer, trying not to draw Violo's attention.

Solara missed their conversations and their laughter. She thought of a thousand things a day she wanted to tell him before remembering they were feuding. She wanted to share her worries with him. She wanted them to watch each other's backs. But as much as she missed him, he didn't seem to miss her at all.

On the sixth day, the silence broke. The seamstress had been by the day before, leaving behind an army of dresses and nightgowns. Solara's favorite nightgown was sapphire blue, though the long train made it beyond impractical. Kylee helped her with the two dozen tiny buttons down the back, and as she tucked the last button into its spot, Solara felt a sharp pain in her low back, and she screeched.

"I'm so sorry, my lady!" Kylee cried.

The bedroom door slammed open as Violo came through it, knife in hand.

"It's all right!" Solara said. "Undo the button. *Undo the button.* Hurry up!" Kylee popped the last button free, and Solara sagged in relief. "She forgot a pin. That's it. It poked me. I'm fine."

Kylee and Violo both relaxed.

"I'm sorry," Solara said. "I didn't mean to scare you."

"You didn't scare me," Violo said. "You merely stopped my heart."

She smiled weakly, and they seemed to realize in the same instant that they'd spoken to each other again. He jammed his knife back into its sheath and turned to go. Solara's pride was a formidable, stubborn thing. Still, she said, "Vi."

He hesitated, his hand on the doorknob.

Kylee slipped the wayward pin out of the fabric, laid it on the dressing table, and redid the final button. "Goodnight, my lady," she murmured. She dipped a curtsy and left, slipping past Violo in the doorway.

Solara turned, flipping the train out of her way. "I know you're angry. I'm not even saying you don't have the right to be."

Slowly, Violo closed the bedroom door and turned to face Solara. "Then what are you saying, Solara?"

It was a start, even if he sounded furious. "I'm not staying in this apartment with someone who refuses to speak to me," she said. "Yes, you're angry, but I know you still care about me because you're still here. And clearly, I still care about you because I've put up with this insanity for the past week."

Violo's jaw tightened.

Does it not intrigue you how much his mannerisms have come to resemble those of your late husband?

She had to stop entertaining the thought. She strode across the room, pushed Violo's hand off the doorknob, and stood with her back to the door. "You're not leaving until we have it out."

"You've more than said your piece," Violo said coldly. "What more do you have to say?"

"Nothing," Solara said. "You do. Spit it out."

"You've already been up too late. Go to bed." He reached for the doorknob.

Solara shifted, blocking it with her body. "I won't."

"Move."

"If you want me to move, you're going to have to drag me," Solara said. "You're the only ally I have left, Vi. You don't get to abandon me."

Violo breathed a laugh. "I have been nothing but loyal to you, Solara, from the first day I laid eyes on you." His lips parted as if he would say more, but then he set his jaw. "Move."

"When did you first lay eyes on me?" she said. He looked away. It was as good as a lie. **Look at me,** Solara thought at him. **Look me in the eye**. She made it an order. She tried to force it into his thoughts as she had with Lady Gao or the doctor from weeks ago.

There was nothing there. For the first time possibly ever, Solara really listened for Violo's thoughts. There were none.

It was like reaching for a mirage.

The apartment door opened and closed as Kylee took her leave, but Solara couldn't pull her eyes from Violo, from the wrenching silence around him.

"Go to bed," Violo said. He took her by the arm and pulled her away from the door. "Goodnight."

Stop moving, Solara ordered. **Hold still**. Nothing stuck. Violo didn't even falter or acknowledge her psychic voice as he strode out of the bedroom.

Faisal. She could hear the panic in her voice.

I know, he said.

He had realized it, too. The other day when he'd come to visit, he'd been startled by something about Violo, and she knew now that he, too, had reached for Violo's thoughts and been met with the silence of a stone mind.

Solara picked up her train and went after Violo. He went straight across the anteroom towards the other bedroom without a word. She wasn't sure when he'd started sleeping in Tessan's bedroom. Probably around the same time he'd taken over Tessan's horse. Solara followed him, but only to the doorway. She didn't want to step foot in there.

"Vi," she said.

"Go to bed," he said. He lit the lamp on the dressing table and picked up the book he always read – Aine and Scipia. Two people in different bodies.

"Vi, look at me," she said.

Violo turned around and leveled her with a cold stare. "Why are you yelling across the room? Come closer if you want to speak to me."

He knew she wouldn't. "Is this your purpose in life now?" Solara said. "To punish me because I lied to him?"

"Why would you need to be punished?" he said flatly. "He's a monster and deserves to be unhappy."

"Don't say that," Solara said. He started to speak, and she cut him off. "Did Tessan love me?"

Violo's eyes narrowed. "You know he did."

"Was he happy while he was with me?"

Every muscle in his body went rigid. "Yes." He had to grind the word out between his teeth.

"Then why are you mad?" she cried. "How long do I have to be miserable before you're satisfied?" Her voice caught, and it just made her angrier. She slammed the bedroom door, stalked across the room, and back into her own bedroom, where she slammed and locked that door, too.

She was too angry to sleep, so she crawled into bed with a book. Lunaro would be thrilled. She considered speaking to her brother or Faisal to release some of the fury building inside her like a teakettle coming to full boil, but it felt like a betrayal to Vi. And to Tess.

Tess, and his stone mind.

Vi, and his stone mind.

Solara must have been losing *her* mind.

Violo knocked on the door. "Solara."

"Get away from me." She turned her back on the door and tried to focus on her book.

"I have the key to the door, and I'm just going to open it myself if you don't," he said. She didn't answer. His footsteps faded away from the door and returned a moment later. The key turned in the lock, and he opened it.

"Go away," Solara muttered.

Violo sat down on the bed behind her, and after a moment, she rolled onto her back to look at him. His expression was serious. Frustrated. At last, he sighed. "I find you a very hard woman to say no to, Lady Solara."

"What is that supposed to mean?"

"I don't want you to be miserable," he said. "I just want you to be happy. And safe."

Solara sat up, and he stiffened when it brought their faces close together. But she just looped her arms around him. "Put your arms around me."

He laughed softly and did as he was told. She relaxed in his arms, her head tucked under his chin. Maybe it didn't matter who he was. She wasn't going to care, not so long as he'd hold onto her.

Solara sat at her breakfast table the next morning, scribbling furiously through the final page of her homework. Violo sat on her right, holding her hair back with one hand and spoon-feeding her oatmeal with the other, while Kylee stood back, looking as if she didn't know whether to be charmed or disturbed.

"You should have gone to bed earlier," Violo said.

Solara would have retorted but she didn't want to end up with oatmeal on her face. Roon did not tolerate tardiness in his classroom, and she wasn't anxious to be on her father-in-law's bad side today. She needed his permission to leave the palace for more than a day, and she wanted to spend the night with Maliah.

"Last bite," Violo said, and Solara obediently gulped it down.

"Done." She slapped the last sentence into place. "Just in–"

The apartment door opened, and Violo turned around, immediately irritated that someone hadn't bothered to knock, but it was Roon.

"You're not late, Solara," he said, as she looked frantically at the clock. "We won't be having lessons this morning. I need you elsewhere."

This did not bode well for her night away. "Oh?" Solara said.

Roon smiled. "Don't look so pensive, dear. I received a very politely worded request from Mr. Samos. He would like to see you again." Violo's lip curled, and of course, Roon noticed. "I know it may seem that there's so much money in the Manfalon coffers that we shouldn't be bothered to continue growing the empire," Roon said. "It would take several careless generations to undo what this family has built. But we're aspiring to greater and greater heights. Why be satisfied being the richest family that ever lived when you could be the richest member of the richest family that ever lived?"

"Perhaps to eschew sinful amounts of greed?" Violo suggested.

Roon didn't acknowledge he'd spoken. "Samos is no match for you, Solara. None of these people are. But it isn't enough for me and you to know that. You need to make sure they know it, too."

"And entertaining Samos does this how?" Solara said in the politest tone she could manage.

"*Managing* Samos does it," Roon said. "The more powerful people you can make fall at your feet, the quicker the others will fall."

Solara opened her mouth to argue.

Roon cut her off. "Besides, he has something you want. This time, try not to be so familiar with your servants. Being your fourth paramour might be more than even Samos can stomach."

Violo stood up. "Don't speak to her like that."

Solara laughed. Violo, Kylee, and Roon all turned to look at her. She'd already given up on her night out, so she was no longer concerned with upsetting him. "What if I was sleeping with Vi?" she said. "Who's going to stop me?"

Kylee's jaw dropped. Violo looked mortified.

"What are you going to do, Roon?" she said. Her father-in-law's eyes narrowed. "Throw me back in the streets? I don't care. I know you're not going to kill me. You like me too much. I'm already locked up in here. What more do you have to punish me with?"

Roon's jaw worked furiously, as if he could barely control his anger, but Solara had learned to pay attention. He wasn't angry. He was trying not to laugh.

She gathered up her stack of homework, stood, and offered it to Roon. "Where am I meeting Samos?"

At last, Roon's grin broke free as he took the pages. "Wherever you tell him he's allowed to approach you."

"I'll let you know how it goes," Solara said.

He inclined his head. "Enjoy yourself."

When he was gone, Solara pivoted to face her appalled maid and bodyguard. "What?" she said.

Kylee sighed. "My lady, you can't be like this."

Solara shrugged. "Help me get dressed."

Violo ate his own breakfast while Kylee dressed Solara. Her favorite day dress from her new line-up was made of black silk and scarlet lace. Though its yardage was small, its dramatic lines and contrast made it every inch a battle-ready gown. Bjorn would have liked it.

Solara sat at her dressing table while Kylee wove her hair into an elegant crown. She twisted small ruby pins into the braid at intervals. When Kylee was done, Solara reached forward and took her small ring box from its place of exile and set it on the table in front of her. She remembered the day Tessan gave her this ring, how she'd laughed, and how he'd lit up at the sound of her laughter.

She slid the ring onto her finger. It was a little tighter around her finger than it had been when she last wore it.

Solara went to the nightstand by her bed, and opened her dagger box. The blades shone, and she reached into the box and gripped the handles.

Also in the box was the other thing she'd commissioned from her seamstress: a simply tooled leather belt designed to hold both daggers close to her thighs. She strapped it around her waist and then slid each dagger into its holster.

They felt good. Awkward, but necessary. Her lessons with Faisal could have happened a thousand years ago, her combat training was a mess, and she wasn't skilled enough to best any of her enemies. But it wasn't about the weapons. It was the story. The possibility of victory. *I am Solara Barthelme.*

Actually, Faisal said wryly. *You are Solara Manfalon.*

It doesn't sound as good that way. She turned away and marched out her bedroom door. Violo rose, eyebrows rising even higher as he took in the sight of her. Eight Scarlet Guard waited in the hallway to escort her. They wore their dress coats and looked very sharp in shoulder pads and ceremonial swords. They closed ranks around her, a single entity in eight parts.

Solara had never been so well guarded in her life. But the fact that Roon thought it all necessary gave her pause. She wasn't afraid; she was just aware of the danger.

Ahdieh Samos would perhaps be her most difficult lesson yet.

CHAPTER FORTY-TWO

Violo gave her the longer version of Kylee's lecture as they rode to meet Samos at the golf course. "Outright rebellion will make these people balk at some point, my lady, no matter how much money you inherit. However much it irks you, you do have to be at least on speaking terms with the nobility. At least the important ones."

"Are you telling me to act right?" Solara said. She'd mostly ignored him, and she knew he could tell. "Roon *wants* me to rebel. That was the entire point of pushing me and pushing you. He wants to know what level of aggression I'll accept before I put my foot down. Or up someone's ass."

Violo started coughing, and the two guards closest to them both quickly looked away to hide their laughter.

She'd meant every word she'd said earlier that morning, but she was doing this for the shock value now. It was too satisfying to make Violo laugh when he was trying so hard not to, and the guards' amusement was a bonus.

When Violo had composed himself, he gave her a stern look, but she smiled, and he started laughing again. "I can't stand you, Solara," he said.

"You're the one who needs to behave yourself, anyway," she said. They were arriving at the clubhouse. It felt like a lifetime ago that she'd been here with Faisal. "Is Mr. Samos here yet?" she asked the young groom who took her mare.

"Yes, my lady," she said. "He's waiting for you in the library."

The Scarlet Guard officers led the way into the building, taking in every shadow, nook, and cranny as they went, no trace of their smiles anymore. Violo walked beside her, less obvious in his perusal of the space but no less watchful. Solara could hardly be surprised people were suggesting she was sleeping with her bodyguard; Violo was certainly no normal guard. And perhaps she was fonder of him than she should have been.

Despite his disapproval and haughty righteousness, she'd immediately felt at home with him. She felt safe with him. And safety was the most precious commodity she had right now.

Ahdieh waited for her at one of the bookshelves, leafing through a pocket-sized book of antique weapon illustrations. He snapped it closed when she came in, his gaze immediately drawn to her weaponry. "Solara."

"Ahdieh," she said. "I hope you weren't waiting very long."

"You're only fifteen minutes late," he said. "More than acceptable for a woman of your social stature. And how could I be upset when you took such care to dress for me?" Ahdieh gestured to the table in the corner, where a bottle of wine and two glasses sat.

"You are not drinking that," Violo said under his breath.

Solara didn't know if he was concerned about poison or her sobriety. She was concerned about neither. Ahdieh pulled out her chair for her, and she sat down, arranging her skirt across her lap.

Ahdieh sat across from her and poured the glasses. "I believe your eldest sister-in-law would approve of your clothing today."

"Nikara was always impeccably dressed, insanity aside," Solara said. "You're not wearing my clothes today. Did you give up impressing me or has Bjorn run out?" She took the glass he offered her, despite Violo's side eye.

"Neither," Ahdieh said with a satisfied smile. "And I am wearing your clothes, just not any that you can see." He looked deliberately at Violo. "I much prefer having your handiwork on my skin."

Solara desperately wanted to laugh. Not because Ahdieh was funny – he wasn't – but because she could imagine how pissed off Violo was and how much effort it took him to be still.

She handed her glass to Violo. "Are you going to taste that for me?"

Ahdieh met her gaze. "Do you expect me to be stupid enough to poison you?"

Violo inhaled over the glass, sipped it, and then handed it back.

"Maybe," Solara said. "Violo knows the taste of thirty-three types of poisons. Isn't that impressive?" She downed the glass in one go and held it out to Ahdieh to refill.

He filled it to the rim, and one of the Scarlet Guard made a sound of disapproval.

"You're far more valuable as a warm body," Ahdieh said. Violo's hand closed into a fist. "Do you understand the vastness of what you stand to inherit if Roon truly gives you control of his empire?"

Solara bit back her irritation and kept her tone playful. "They do teach us how to count in the fourth ring, Ahdieh. I understand the concept of money."

"I'm not sure anyone understands the concept of that much money," Ahdieh said seriously. "And I am speaking very plainly because I think you and I understand each other." He tipped his glass at her, and they both sipped. "The highborn lords and ladies feign politeness and whisper business behind their fans because it's impolite to be straightforward, but you and I weren't raised under such nonsensical standards."

"I doubt our childhoods were as similar as you think," Solara said. She downed her glass again, mostly for the incredulous look Violo gave her. When Ahdieh offered the bottle, she held her glass back. "And you forget, my introduction to high society was with the Manfalon daughters. There was no pretense there."

Ahdieh smiled crookedly. "Very true. Should I speak even more plainly?" He leaned forward. "I know six men off the top of my head who are simply waiting for what they deem the right time to make your father-in-law a marriage offer for you. One of them is desperately broke and even more desperately trying to hide it. Two of them are murderers, though you don't seem to mind that."

Solara willed herself not to break Ahdieh's cool stare, to give no hint of how that comment had wounded her. Her morals certainly had taken a beating under Tessan's watch.

"One of them has thirteen children from three mistresses, each with her own house, and his coffers are caving under the strain. The others..." He made a dismissive gesture. "I'll forego the particulars, as I think even your iron constitution would quaver under them."

Solara mimicked his posture against the table. "That's your offer? That you're the best of my options? If that's what we're going to call them."

Annoyance flickered over his features, but he quickly hid it. "The only way you hold onto that crown, Solara, is if Roon stands your ground for you, or you align yourself with someone people are afraid to cross."

The sheer nerve of this man was flooring. Solara wanted to laugh in his face, but she was too annoyed. She leaned forward even further. "You realize you're a playful kitten compared to Tessan, don't you?"

Ahdieh's eyes narrowed.

"And despite your delusions of grandeur, Mr. Samos, you are holding onto your crown because nobody can be bothered to leave the Diadem and take it from you." Solara sat back, if only so she was out of slapping range as Ahdieh's hands clenched into fists. "I don't need you to glower behind me and lend power to my words. You need me because that would mean the world saw you gain Roon's stamp of approval, but I have no interest in being an accessory to the likes of you."

She stood up, and Ahdieh stood up quickly, prompting her guards to move forward. "You don't have a choice," he said.

Violo breathed a laugh and pulled his knife halfway from its sheath.

"What on earth makes you think you can force me to do a single thing I don't want to do?" Solara said. As the words left her mouth, she recalled Roon's admonishment. *He has something you want.*

Ahdieh held up his hands in a defenseless gesture for the guards' sake. "You can be hard to read at times, Solara," he said. "But there was a moment when your guard was down, and anyone with eyes could know precisely what you were feeling."

Solara couldn't name the dread that welled up in her.

"At Tessan's funeral," Ahdieh said. His expression was solemn, but the amusement in his eyes made Solara's heart sink. "That was not the grief of a woman who survived an attack," he said. "That was the grief of a woman who'd lost her husband."

"What does that have to do with anything?" Solara said. Her voice squeaked.

Look and see.

Even with her protective wall of silence, Samos' purposefully directed voice registered, and the smug purr in her head made her shudder.

Violo watched her, knife at the ready, no doubt prepared to sweep her out of the situation if she looked even a touch more uncomfortable.

Ahdieh's invitation tremored between them, and Solara, despite the unwillingness of every sinew of her body, answered the summons and looked into Ahdieh's thoughts. Everything in his head was rigid and tidy, numbers and figures and business deals, and he swept her past all of it and to a single moment.

Deep in the lower levels of his tower home on the plain beyond the final wall of the Diadem, there was a sick room. The white walls were bare. The tiled floor scrubbed spotless. The patient lay on a massive bed pushed to one wall, and a nurse spooned broth into his unconscious lips, then massaged his throat to prompt him to swallow.

Solara's hand crept up to her mouth, her breath so shallow that it was little more than a succession of gasps.

It was Tessan.

The doctors say his condition is most likely irreversible, Ahdieh continued psychically from what seemed like a thousand miles away.

Solara sank into her chair, rooted in that moment that played over and over between them. Tessan was pale, and thin, but that golden hair was unmistakable.

Which I imagine is why Roon has thus far been unwilling to cross me for him. My cooperation is worth more than what might still become a corpse.

Solara's gaze snapped to Ahdieh's. That bastard. Roon had watched her cry herself sick, knowing full well his son wasn't dead.

Ahdieh smiled. *The physical trauma he sustained at your hand was catastrophic, Solara. He drooled blood for days. I imagine you feel quite guilty about what happened.*

When had she started crying? There were tears on her face.

"Solara," Violo said quietly. He put his hand on her shoulder. "We should go."

"And now we come to the question, Lady Manfalon, that I'm dying to ask you," Ahdieh said aloud. He sipped his wine. "How much did you love your husband, and what are you willing to do for him?"

She couldn't speak.

"I'll give you time to think about it." He smiled and bowed deeply. "I'll await your attention." He swept out of the room, brushing rudely past the soldiers, and was gone.

CHAPTER FORTY-THREE

It took every ounce of Solara's self-control to keep her face blank and her mouth shut until later that afternoon, when Roon agreed to see her in his private office. It was a room she had not yet been in, and she found it comfortably cozy with books and armchairs. He sat on the edge of his desk, waiting for her, a wry smile on his face as she burst into the room and snapped at Violo to shut the door.

"You seem incensed, my dear," Roon said.

"Why didn't you tell me?" She bit out every word. Her blood roared through her body, making her skin hot. "How long have you known?"

"I confess, I was careless with my son's body," Roon said. "I thought he was dead, and corpse stealers are no concern of mine. I doubted it would matter. I was hardly going to inform you at his funeral that you were distraught over an empty coffin."

Solara took a step toward him, but Violo was right on her heels. It was his presence alone that stopped her from slapping Roon – or at least attempting to. She had no doubt her father-in-law would hit her back, and the odds of her containing Violo after that infraction were none. "How long have you known?" she repeated, harsher.

"What good would it have done you to know?" he said. "I didn't know. I had my suspicions, but I didn't *know*, not until today, when I sent my best negotiator to confirm." His gaze flicked to Violo behind her, and his smile turned cruel. "Do you hear that, hound dog? Your master still lives."

She wanted to turn around and see Violo's face. But she was also terrified to know what he was thinking. "You murdered your son," she said. "Why would you want him back?"

"Because I regretted it," Roon said. "Possibly. Possibly because I can still see some use for him. But your behavior since his death has made it very clear to anyone with eyes that you truly cared for my son, and that's why Ahdieh is choosing this method to manipulate you."

"My apologies," she said coldly. "I should not have shown my weakness."

"Is that what my son is to you?" Roon said, lifting his eyebrows. "A weakness?" Solara didn't answer. Roon went on. "He's been unconscious for weeks. Even if we can reclaim him, there is no guarantee that he'll ever wake. And even if he does, I intend this throne for you. He never considered you capable of doing anything but being his pet. Can you defend this city from him?"

Solara ground her teeth, fighting to keep her voice even. "How do you expect me to take Tessan from Samos without walking up to the altar? Samos is no idiot. He won't give up his leverage until my name and his are on a legally binding sheet of paper."

"Yes, I agree," Roon said. "But he knows he can't kill him, not when you could pry his skull open like a melon." She flinched at the description, and Roon shook his head. "You cower back from your gift as if it were something wicked. Did besting my eldest take so much of your spirit from you?"

"I have spirit to spare," Solara said, and Roon grinned. "Samos has too many men for me to control. My gift is useless."

"My lady," Violo said. His face was grim, his eyes hard. "Tessan would not want you to risk your safety for his corpse."

"How noble of you," Roon murmured.

Violo's gaze hardened still more. "Ahdieh is a sadist and a monster. How dare you dangle her in front of him like a trophy?"

"Some people said the same about her last husband," Roon said. "We mustn't judge people by the rumors."

"Vi," Solara said. She could practically feel his anger smolder. "Don't."

"My lady–"

"I said enough!" she snapped. Violo's eyes flashed, and Roon chuckled. But both men remained silent. Stifling her anger, Solara turned back to Roon. "What use have you decided you have for Tess? And how do I know you won't decide two days later that you preferred him dead?"

"My dear," Roon said. "I took drastic measures to teach my son a lesson. He was, and remains, unfit to rule my empire, not so long as his morals remain as flimsy as my own. However." He leaned forward. "If you convince me that you can keep him and his homicidal tendencies in check, then I am content to leave him be."

They stared at each other.

Roon said softly, "I lament none of my children's deaths, Solara. None. But I acknowledge the brutality of my son's actions, and he paid the price for it."

His words made her stomach hurt. This man truly had not cared for a single one of his children. "The Scarlet Guard have no jurisdiction outside the city walls," she said. "And Ahdieh is clever. He won't fold easily."

"You will simply have to be cleverer than he is," Roon said. He came forward, and Violo moved closer. She could feel his breath on her neck. "But I have every faith in you, my dear," Roon said. "Whatever you need, it's yours. The Diadem is at your disposal." He turned to go, and she caught his sleeve, halting him.

"When I bring Tessan home, you don't touch him," she said. "You don't speak to him. And you certainly will not use him."

Roon studied her face, then gave a gentle shake of his head. "I watched him brought into this world, Solara, and I loved him only until Nikara twisted him into little better than a beast. How on earth did you come to care for him?"

"I'm not asking," she said. "I'm telling you what's going to happen."

Roon looked down at her hand gripping his sleeve, then back up at her face. "I hope one day he appreciates how hard you fought for him." He patted her hand, removed it from his arm, and left the room.

He left the door open, and she could see into the hall where her Scarlet Guard waited for her, their faces blank and their hands folded behind their backs. It was quite the entourage. She was never going to get used to it.

"It's just a body, Solara," Violo said. "Tessan is dead. No one could survive what Roon did to him. No one."

"I watched him breathe," she said.

"A body can cling to life long after its soul has left it."

Solara opened her mouth to argue and found she had no words. Her legs gave out, and Violo scooped her up and carried her to one of the giant leather chairs and laid her in it.

"I watched him breathe," she said again, and her voice cracked. Tessan was *alive*. Violo could say what he wanted about corpses and souls, but Solara knew. Beyond a shadow of a doubt, she knew Tessan was alive, and he was waiting for her to come retrieve him. As of yet, she had no idea how that was going to work, but she would figure something out.

"Solara," Violo said. "You can't. I forbid it."

"You can't forbid me from doing anything," she said, dazed. "You loved Tess, Violo. Why are you balking? I would think you would leap at the chance to see him again."

"That's exactly what it is, Solara. A chance. Not a certainty. Not even good odds." He took her face in one hand, turning her so she had to look him in the eyes. "Listen to me."

Solara shook her head, dislodging him. "It isn't that simple, Violo, and you know it." Even if it was a corpse, Solara knew she would still go get it. It wasn't just a body. It was Tessan.

In her mind's eye she saw his chest rise and fall with each breath. He was alive. He was *alive*. She still had time. She could look him in the eye. They could talk. Maybe she'd apologize; maybe she'd demand an apology. It didn't matter. None of those particulars mattered quite yet.

"Solara!" Violo shook her shoulders so hard her teeth rattled. "Listen to me!"

"Get off me!" She slapped his hands off her. Out in the hall, her guard rustled closer. Solara's legs were still shaking, and she gripped one knee, her painted fingernails cutting into the material. On her finger, her ring gleamed. A dead man had no claim to her. But a living one did. Ahdieh didn't expect Tess to ever wake, because the moment he did, Ahdieh and Solara's marriage would be thrown out. He was counting on Solara to be so blinded by emotion that she would give up everything just to make sure that almost-corpse kept breathing.

"I will not let you die," Violo said, his voice grim.

Solara smiled faintly. "You'd be hard pressed to explain that to Tess, wouldn't you?" She set her feet on the ground. *Faisal, I need to see you. I need you, Lu, Aliss, and Mage. I'll explain when I get there.* Faisal didn't respond, but he'd heard. Dread and resignation wavered through the bond.

"Why do you care?" Violo said softly. "You don't have to take this risk."

"Yes, I do."

Solara strode into the glass office, and her gathered friends looked up expectantly, their expressions ranging from sullenness to confusion. The redheaded siblings sat close together, Faisal with his arm around Aliss and her worrying a piece of hard candy.

"Everything I'm about to say is going to sound insane," Solara said, gesturing for Violo to close the door. "Hear me out."

"I'm on the edge of my seat," Mage said. She was all sullenness, not bitterness, which was a pleasant change. Solara could deal with a brat, just not a malicious one.

She stood at the head of the table and surveyed their faces. Lunaro had dark circles under his eyes because he'd been up late reading every night for weeks on end, and even now, he had a book on the table in front of him with half a dozen trailing ribbons marking his places between the pages.

Mage, while well-rested, was all glower and glare. Her excellent health lent her gift another edge, and she seemed to crackle with it, like lightning glimpsed at a distance. Similar in strength, Aliss, too, had a mental gleam to her that Solara suspected would grow more impressive as her health returned.

Faisal, as always, was a brick of silence, although at the back of both of their minds there was a tether, like hands clasped behind backs, always gently entwined.

It felt like it had been forever since she allowed everyone's thoughts and feelings to flow over her. Here in this room, surrounded by people she cared about, it was safe. Almost a comfort.

"Tessan's alive," Solara said.

Lu, tipping on the back legs of his chair, let it fall with a bang.

Everyone thought that Solara had finally lost it.

"Hear me out," Solara said. "I saw him. Not with my own eyes, but in Samos' mind. He's alive. Barely. He's unconscious. The doctor isn't optimistic. But he's breathing. And no, I'm not being tricked. You know no one can lie to me."

"Why on earth would Samos have your husband's comatose body?" Lunaro said in the most practical tone he could muster. After his initial moment of disbelief, he couldn't help thinking that this was the worst possible thing that could happen. He knew Solara was troubled by Tessan's death, but he still thought she was better off.

Solara knew no one was going to jump for joy at the thought of Tessan coming back into their lives, and she didn't have the gall to defend him to their faces. Not with what she was about to ask.

"Samos has spies in the palace," Violo said quietly. "As I'm sure you do as well, Casarriba. Roon is not sentimental in any way. Tessan's body would not have been watched very carefully after he was pronounced dead."

"Yes," Faisal said. "Pronounced dead. By very capable doctors, I assume. You expect me to believe he was revived from a stabbing?"

"I don't know how it happened," Solara said. "And I don't care."

"What do you expect us to do about this?" Lunaro said. "Samos is trying to marry you. What purpose does it serve him if your husband is still alive?"

"He doesn't think Tessan's going to wake up," Solara said. "The doctors said as much. His continued good care, or lack thereof, is the leverage."

Aliss took her lollipop out of her mouth. "He expects you to sacrifice the rest of your life and your happiness for Tessan's body," she said, staring hard into Solara's eyes. "And you've already agreed."

If Solara had an ounce more of shame, she would have lowered her eyes from Aliss's hard stare. But if she had to look at Faisal or Lunaro, she'd probably feel worse.

"You are insane," Mage said, and stood up.

"Mage, sit down," Faisal said. She glared at him. "You are the only one in the room who has sold a human being like cattle," he said, and she dropped her gaze. "That makes you insane. Sit down and hush."

She sank back into her chair.

"The child makes a point," Violo said in an even quieter tone.

"I'm not a child," Mage snapped.

"Technically, Samos has committed kidnapping," Solara went on. "A crime he'd be severely punished for if he's caught. Meaning that if I involve the authorities, he's going to get rid of the evidence as quickly as he can. I know that, and he knows I know it. Roon isn't willing to go to war over this."

"You're going to marry Samos?" Mage said, unable to keep the disdain out of her tone. She didn't try very hard, either.

"Of course not," Lunaro said with a sigh. "We're going to have to take him."

Solara was so grateful he said "we." She let her crossed arms slide free. "I know it's not fair to ask," she said.

"Tessan certainly never did any of us any favors," Faisal said in a surprisingly mild tone.

"Samos is taking a big risk, showing his hand that blatantly," Lunaro pointed out.

"Hardly," Aliss said. "I'm sure you tried your best to be stoic at the funeral, Sol, but it was very obvious how much his death ate at you." When everyone turned to look at her, she smiled. "I was there, just in disguise. I wouldn't have missed Petra's funeral for the world. I told her I'd gloat over her corpse one day, and I'm a woman of my word."

It was hard to believe that Solara had tried to save Petra's life. It felt disrespectful.

"What is your plan, exactly?" Mage said. "And why do you think Faisal is going to make me help you?"

Faisal wanted to laugh but he didn't dare encourage her.

Solara looked at Violo. He stood right beside the door as if he were considering escaping, arms crossed, his chin slightly lowered into his chest. She'd never seen him look so uncomfortable. "The gift has always had its limits," she said, pivoting to face her friends again. "Even Faisal, the strongest psychic anyone knows, can only coerce so many people at once. Numbers will always prevail."

"I think we can all agree you're significantly stronger than Faisal," Aliss said, just to elicit the dirty sideways look her brother gave her.

"You've given plenty of orders, but you've never truly taken control of anyone," Lunaro said. "Those aren't the same, Sol."

"The number of guards and servants in Samos' house is going to be more than either one of us, possibly even both of us, can control," Faisal said. "This liberation needs to be perfect. We can't leave any trace of what we've done."

Solara took a deep breath and braced for resistance. "I want to use the relay."

CHAPTER FORTY-FOUR

Faisal's tone lowered warningly. "With. Who."

"What's a relay?" Mage said.

Solara scrambled to explain. "The relay in theory uses force, but I don't think I'll need to. I think I can be stronger without it."

"I told her it was a bad idea," Violo muttered.

"You want to use an experimental technique when lives are at stake?" Lunaro said.

"What is a relay?" Mage said, louder.

Aliss, with a loud sigh, said, "Mage, stop acting like a toddler."

Mage's cheeks flushed, but she knew she'd upset Faisal if she backtalked to his sister. "Would someone please explain this experimental technique?" she said between her teeth.

"In a nutshell, Solara takes your power," Lunaro said, still studying Solara's face. "Rather, you lend the strength of your gift to her."

Mage scoffed. "No."

"You don't have much to spare," Aliss agreed. "Faisal and I would be far more useful."

Mage was instantly offended, although she knew Aliss was needling her on purpose.

"Actually," Solara said. "I think the most useful ones would be the people who are already linked. Me. You. Mage. And Gaius."

Faisal was also instantly offended, and then annoyed because it was childish, and he knew Solara had felt it. "Mage and Gaius?"

Mage's cheeks reddened again.

Solara was exposing the little brat, but she'd ask forgiveness later. "There's a bond between friends that is amicable and equal. Mage and Gaius have it." Lunaro looked curiously at Mage, who sank into her chair, and Solara kept going. "The relay in the text depended on the nexus having an equal hold on everyone involved. But I want to create a cascading effect instead. I pull from Aliss, and Aliss pulls from Mage, and Mage pulls from Gaius."

"This may surprise my brother, but I have no concerns about linking minds with you," Aliss said. "You moved heaven and earth to save me. But I'm not agreeing to do this because I feel guilty or grateful. I just like you."

Solara smiled. "I like you, too, Aliss."

"Why would you not skip to the most powerful one?" Lu said, jerking his head at Faisal.

Now came the other part they were going to balk at. "I have to get close to my targets to put them down. There's no way Samos lets Faisal in the house with me. But if it's just me and my attendants–"

"But you think he'll let Violo in?" Faisal said.

Solara heard her bodyguard straighten. "Violo can't come either," she said.

"No," Violo said. "And I am not repeating myself."

"For the first time ever, I agree with the asshole behind you," Lunaro said. "What if it's more people than you can handle? Samos might not be a lord, but you will get in trouble for manipulating someone at his social standing if there's anyone to witness it."

"Your brother's right," Faisal said.

"I'm more than capable of protecting Solara from the likes of Samos," Aliss scoffed.

Violo stepped forward, putting himself in Solara's line of sight. "I am not letting you walk into a position where your only physical protection is that wraith of a girl."

"Violo, shut up," Faisal said.

"You don't give me orders, Casarriba," Violo said disdainfully. He turned to Lunaro. "Are you going to sit there and encourage your sister to potentially throw her life away for the corpse of a man you hate?"

"Nobody is doing this because they liked Tessan," Aliss said. "We're doing it because we like Solara. And even if I think Tessan was a coward with the moral rigidity of a strawberry, I still think Solara should have what she wants."

Mage laughed.

Violo's mouth opened, then closed.

While Faisal tried to puzzle out what the moral rigidity of a strawberry was, Lunaro said, "I don't love the idea of any of this plan, but you're not getting the final say regardless. Now, step back, so I can see my sister."

If Solara were a better friend, she'd tell them to give Violo a break. She took his arm and pulled him back. "Anyway," she said. "I haven't even said the craziest part yet."

"There's more?" Faisal said with another heavy sigh.

Solara smiled. "I think I can wake Tessan up."

Most of the next hour was spent arguing back and forth about the logistics of the relay and whether Solara could wake Tessan with the same method she'd used to help Aliss and Gaius. She knew they'd balk at her claim; no amount of gift should be able to puncture a stone mind. And Solara wouldn't tell them the entirety of why she believed she could.

Once they were all argued out and everyone had insisted that they weren't going to help her, whilst privately admitting to themselves that they would, the group dispersed, and Solara cornered Mage in the kitchen.

The blue-haired girl sat at one of the prep tables, picking at a plate of cookies, when Solara came and sat beside her.

"Get away from me," Mage said.

Solara picked a cookie. "You realize we're going to be in each other's vicinity for the rest of our lives, don't you? Are you planning on skulking away every time I show up?"

"I'm hoping the novelty of you wears off, and Faisal can't be bothered anymore." Mage cast Violo a baleful look. His expression assured Mage their distaste was mutual.

"That isn't going to happen," Solara said. She was *almost* amused. Almost. Mage had more than proven what her bad attitude was capable of. Solara took a bite of her cookie and spoke around the crumbs. "Even if Faisal pissed me off every day from now until eternity, I'd still want to see him, and hear his voice, and watch him smile.

"I know you hate me because you think I took your place, but what I feel for Faisal and what you feel for Faisal are two entirely different things, and the same goes for him. Love is far more complicated than people give it credit for."

Mage made a face. "I thought you were here to scream at me, but your lecture is worse."

Solara laughed. "I think Aliss will be giving you most of your lectures in the foreseeable future."

Mage felt the faintest, slightest something that might have been warmth. Not for Solara, of course. For Aliss. That somebody besides Faisal would be bothered enough to hound Mage about her behavior.

"So?" Solara prompted. "Are you going to skulk or are we going to be civil?"

Mage eyed Solara. She was a little suspicious that Solara could forgive her so easily. But she also wanted this to be over. She didn't want to run and hide every time she heard Solara coming. She'd rather be able to inform Solara guiltlessly to her face how much she disliked her, and that was only partly because of Faisal.

"We don't have to like each other," Solara said. "I don't like you. I think you have the ugliest temperament of anyone I've ever known."

Mage grinned.

The knot of worry in Solara's chest loosened. "We can agree to hate each other without being enemies," she said. "For Faisal's sake, if nothing else."

"We'll see," Mage said. But the nervousness in her chest, too, had loosened. "There's only so much I'm willing to do, even for Faisal."

Solara stood up. "Good enough." She took two more cookies off the plate. "Vi, let's go."

"Yes, goodbye, Vi," Mage said in a sickly-sweet voice.

He flipped her off, and Solara swatted his hand as she pushed him out of the kitchen ahead of her. "Don't trade insults with a child, Violo. That's embarrassing. Here." She offered him one of her cookies, and he literally turned up his nose.

"No, thank you. I don't trust anything–" he began haughtily. Solara crammed the cookie in his mouth and took off running. He choked on the crumbs, cursing. "Solara!"

She booked it down the hall laughing the whole way. He'd catch her as soon as he stopped choking, but that didn't matter. She was halfway down the glass corridor towards the front entryway when he caught up. He snagged her around the waist and whipped her around. There were still cookie crumbs on his mouth, and she started to laugh again.

"First of all," he said.

"I'm telling Tess," Solara said with a straight face.

His eyebrows crinkled.

"I'm telling him you put your hands on his wife while he was gone. Multiple times." She did her absolute best to keep a straight face, but the slightest of smiles tugged at the corner of his mouth.

"They were extenuating circumstances," Violo said.

"Is that the story we're going with?" she said. She wished she had some greater power than the gift, that she could fully understand every tiny line and crease on his face. *Who are you?* Had she entirely lost her mind? Had grief or guilt shifted her thoughts so completely that she could look in Violo's somber dark brown eyes and still feel that it was Tessan looking back at her?

Violo cleared his throat and let her go. "I don't like sweets," he said with great dignity. "I'll thank you to keep them out of my mouth."

"Maybe," Solara said. She'd dropped her own cookie somewhere in her sprint. She dusted off her arms, trying to brush away the sensation of his arms around her.

CHAPTER
FORTY-FIVE

Solara had dinner with Violo in the apartment. Once Kylee had cleared the dishes away and left them alone, Solara said, "I need something."

"Yes, I could see it burning a hole in your tongue all evening," Violo said. "I don't suppose it's an early bedtime and a good night's rest?"

"I want to go into the fourth ring." She expected an immediate no. "It has the densest population numbers, and I need to be inundated with thought."

"To prepare you for the relay," he said.

Solara nodded. "All this time in the Center, I've been building denser and denser walls in the mindscape to keep my thoughts separate. I'm out of practice. I need practice. But we need to go quietly. Without the Scarlet Guard."

Violo drummed his fingertips against the tabletop, considering.

"You said yourself there wasn't as much of a target on my back as Roon said," Solara said.

"That was before," he said. "Now we have Ahdieh as an enemy. That changes everything. You may be of more use to him as a warm body for now, but that can change at any moment."

"Will you take me?" she said.

His mouth curved into a smile. "I don't know how to say no to you."

Solara scoffed. "You did just this morning."

They changed clothes. Solara still had the dress she'd borrowed off one of the maids, and Violo forewent his guardsman uniform in favor of some of Tessan's more nondescript clothes. They were much too big for him, but a belt and a few cuff rolls made it serviceable. He also brought Tessan's sword, though he wrapped it in a dark scarf to hide the Manfalon crest on the hilt before he strapped it to his back.

They reconvened in the anteroom, and Violo gave Solara a stern look. "What I am about to show you is knowledge that you will never, and I mean *ever*, employ without my presence. Do you understand me?"

"Yes, sir," Solara said. He knew she was mocking his intensity.

They went into her bedroom, and he opened the balcony doors. Snow-filled clouds hung heavy on the horizon, obscuring starlight. Violo, easy as you please, stepped up onto the balcony railing. It enabled him to reach the gable above, and he pulled himself up and over, then turned back for her.

Solara gaped at him.

Violo grinned. "When Roon said not to go out and we wanted to go out, we went this way. Careful."

Very wary, Solara stepped onto the railing. It was slick with dew, but Violo quickly grasped her upstretched hand.

"Brace your legs against the wall and climb."

He made it sound simple, but climbing on rooftops was not Solara's area of expertise. She braced her booted feet against the smooth marble slabs, and he helped her scramble her way up onto the roof.

It was a long, long way down. She leaned back from the edge, heart hammering. "I didn't realize Roon had curfew for anyone but me."

Violo stood up and offered his hand to her. "Come along."

He was entirely too comfortable navigating the slick rooftop for Solara's taste. She slipped several times and would have fallen if he hadn't been holding her hand. "How often were you and Tess scampering across rooftops like squirrels?" Solara said.

"Summer solstice, three years ago, for one," he said.

That made Solara smile. "If Tess were a law-abiding citizen, he never would have seen me dancing on the table."

"And what a tragedy that would have been."

They came to the edge of their gable. It was a six-foot drop to another rooftop, and from there, they could drop to the relatively soft landing of a tulip bed. Violo had to lower her over both edges because she was too scared to jump. He left her waiting in one of the gateways while he went into the stable, and he returned shortly thereafter with Tessan's black mare.

"You really like that horse, don't you?" she whispered.

"She's faithful," he said. "She never leaves her rider."

They walked her out of the stable yard, going slowly to keep her hoofbeats soft on the cobblestones, and when they'd reached the quiet of the trees, Violo mounted and then pulled Solara up behind him. He didn't point the mare at the gate in the wall. Instead, they meandered through the forest. Solara wasn't quite sure where they were going, but she trusted he knew what he was doing.

Almost thirty minutes later they arrived at the wall. Its sleek marble surface was spotless and looked as slick as water. Solara wasn't sure how Violo expected to get through without a gate.

He swung down from the mare and then pulled Solara down, making sure she was steady on her feet before releasing his hold on her waist. She waited beside the mare while Violo went to the wall. He laid his hand on it and began walking. He hadn't gone six paces before he stopped, then dropped to one knee, and began rustling around in the turf beneath their feet. She heard a click, and a section of ground rose. A trap door.

"The wall is impenetrable," Violo said, as her mouth fell open. "But there's half a dozen of these tunnels around the Center." He gestured for her to join him at the tunnel mouth. "Rats don't like to be cornered."

She stood at the mouth, peering down into the black. "Vi?"

"Yes?"

"You said Nikara locked Tess in an escape tunnel."

He propped the door open with a mechanism at the hinge. "There's no light. Don't be afraid."

"Is this the one?"

Violo took her hand and laced their fingers. "This darkness is different. Don't let go of me." He led them down. When the trap door clanged shut overhead, Solara immediately stumbled, and if Violo hadn't held onto her, she would have tripped down the narrow stairs.

Yes, this darkness was different.

It was smothering. She didn't know where her body was. She didn't know if there was ground beneath her. She could be floating in the black of the heavens for all she knew. Her breath quickened.

"It takes some getting used to," Violo said. His voice echoed.

She couldn't breathe. The dark clotted her breath.

"Sol," Violo said. He took her other hand. "Breathe deeply."

She *couldn't*. She was choking.

Violo pulled her into a hug. He crushed her face into his shirt, enveloping her tighter than the darkness. "The dark only scares us because we don't know what it hides," he said. "You can't see, but you can hear, and you can feel. Tell me what your other senses know."

Solara took a shuddery breath.

"Tell me," he prodded.

How could he stand this darkness? "Your shirt," she whispered. "It's… it's made of cotton, and it smells like peppermint soap." Tessan's soap, because it was Tessan's shirt.

"Good," he said. "What else?"

She'd wrapped both of her arms around him. She could feel her own elbow under one hand. His ribs pressed to her cheek. She could hear his heart beating. She could hear him breathing, steady and unafraid. He was real. Though the darkness claimed nothing else existed, Violo was real.

"What else, Sol?"

She shifted her hand, laying it on the hilt of Tessan's sword beneath its cloth disguise. Here was Tessan's belt and its metal buckle. Violo's knife at the back of the belt. She listed each thing, and her panic subsided.

"Are you ready?" he said. Solara nodded, her head bumping against his chin. He took her hand once more. "Walk slowly. Trust me."

She did. She listened for his footfall in the dark. It was just a whisper, his steps sure and near silent.

"What's the first thing you're going to say to Tessan when you have him back?" Violo said.

"I'm not going to say anything," Solara said. "I'm going to kick him in his shins."

Violo chuckled. "A small price to pay, I'm sure."

"You?"

"I don't know," he said. Solara didn't press him. She stumbled, her other hand shooting out to grab something to steady herself. She stepped on Violo's heel and fell against him. "Would you like me to carry you?" he said, when she was steady.

"I'm not a child," she said.

"We'll go faster."

Her cheeks warmed. "Fine."

He picked her up. It was odd, being lifted by arms she couldn't see. They were instantly moving more quickly, as best as she could tell with nothing to orient herself by.

"How often have you been in these tunnels?" she said.

"After finding Tess?" He breathed a laugh. "Many times. We hated it, both of us. But we had to prove we weren't afraid. That Nikara hadn't won."

"I never want to come here again."

"It's the only way to leave the Center undetected," he said. "You'll get used to it, as I did."

They began ascending. A moment later, he set her down and lifted another trap door. The faint starlight that had seemed inconsequential before now felt like daylight as it spilled over them, and Solara scrambled up the remaining steps and out into the open air.

Violo lowered the door, and it disappeared into the grass. "You'll get used to it," he said again.

"No. Don't you ever take me down there again." She sank into the grass. They were pressed for time, but she just wanted to drink in the sight of… well, *sight*. Nikara had been pure evil to do that to her brother. Solara couldn't believe Tess had survived four days there as a child.

Violo crouched in front of her. "Just a minute," he said. Solara nodded. In forty seconds, he pulled her to her feet, and they kept going. Getting past the first wall anonymously was the hardest part of their journey. Passing from the second ring to the third was as simple as Violo flashing his crest, the crest of a Scarlet Guard captain, at the guards. Leaving the third ring and going into the fourth was simpler still. Anyone could leave; the guards' true job was keeping lower ring riffraff from trying to enter after work hours. As they passed through the rings, Violo kept closer and closer to Solara, until they were pressed shoulder to shoulder.

The farther into the fourth ring they went, the louder the thought noise became. It didn't matter that the streets were growing quiet for the night as people hurried home. There were so many people: crushed into apartment homes, packed in inns, closing their street merchant stalls. The noise washed over Solara like water.

She'd forgotten how bad everything smelled. The snow from days before still sat piled in some dark corners, filthy gray and sometimes yellow. Muck filled the street drains so deep they no longer drained, and water stood in puddles between the street tiles.

Violo had one hand on his knife and one hand on Solara's back, his palm a faint pressure through her thick woolen coat.

Solara turned down a side street she never would have trekked alone. A handful of beggars sat huddled together beside some discarded shipping barrels, their reek worse than the clogged streets.

"Have you got a penny for me, pretty girl?" one, an old woman said. She was eighty years old, and she'd lost her sister a week ago. She had no one left in the world now.

"I'm sorry," Solara said softly. She had access to most of the money in the Diadem and not a penny of it on her.

Here, in this alley, she could hear the tired, resigned thoughts of the dozens of people preparing for bed in the apartment building whose wall made up the right side of the alley. Some of them were as young as nine or ten. They'd worked a full day. They had a half-full belly at best. It made Solara feel hungry. Feel tired.

It had been a long time since she last felt hungry. Truly hungry.

She passed through the alley and kept going. Instinct guided her steps. It was second nature to head for the basement apartment she and Lunaro had shared for so many years. Some part of her brain still thought it was home, and that if she went there, everything would go back to normal.

But Solara kept trudging onward, and Violo sighed deeply when he realized where she was headed.

The Cider Jug was an entirely different setting on a workday. There was no need for Jonquin to guard the doorway. The dance floor was covered with tables, and families sat eating their dinners before heading home.

The volume of thought was staggering. Solara literally staggered, and Violo slipped his arm around her waist to hold her up.

He took her to a table in the corner of the room and sat her down. "Catch your breath," he said softly.

"I am so out of practice," she whispered. She had been hiding for a long time. Now, there was no hiding from the two brothers to her right. Both had lost their wives. One had a son who'd run off. They didn't know how to speak to each other anymore because they were trying so hard not to fall apart.

Ahead of her, a weary family scraped soup from their bowls, already dreading their early rise the following morning to work their laundry business. The daughter's hands were so burnt from harsh soap that they bled every night.

A server came to the table. "What'll it be?" she asked, plunking two wooden cups in front of them. The tepid water they held sloshed over their rims.

"Honey cinnamon biscuits," Violo said. "And something warm for her to drink."

She nodded and left.

Solara felt woozy from the stimuli she was trying to process. Another group of patrons came in, their harried thoughts adding to her overwhelm. Builders, all five of them. They were working a repair job in the third ring and were relieved to be back in the fourth after a long day's work keeping their heads bowed to cocky noble overseers.

Violo touched Solara's knee. "Sol, how are you doing?"

"Wonderful," she said faintly. There had to be a hundred people in the room, never mind the amount of noise still bleeding in from outdoors.

That's her. Roon's little pet whore.

Solara hadn't been aware of closing her eyes. She opened them now, the caustic thought like a hot knife through her confusion. She didn't see the culprit in the room. Most of the occupants were busy with their meal and had no concern for anything else.

"What is it?" Violo said.

Solara scanned the room, searching, and her attention settled on the cloak-clad man at the counter paying for his meal. He and his companion were both well-muscled, burly men armed with multiple blades.

I know a dozen people who would pay for her head on a platter, his companion thought to him. *Are you sure that's her?*

That's Violo with her. Tessan's man. He never leaves her side.

"We have to go," Solara said.

Violo followed her gaze and assessed the two men at the counter. "Street enforcers," he said dismissively. "They're no threat to you. I could kill them both one-handed."

"I would rather you didn't," she said.

The server came back to their table and set a plate of steaming biscuits between them. "Something warm for you, love." She handed Solara a mug of whisky and tea. "Drink it slow. It's fresh hot."

The two men finished at the counter and made their way towards Solara. Violo's confidence assured her somewhat, but she still felt nervous. She picked up a biscuit and took a bite. It was both sweet and spicy, exactly how she loved them.

The men stopped at the table. "Solara Manfalon," the first one said.

"Move along," Violo said coldly. "Or everything that comes next will be unfortunate for you."

The second one chuckled. "There's a nobleman who's willing to pay a hundred gold crowns for her tongue. Just her tongue. I won't even have to bother with the rest of the body."

Violo stood up. Everyone in the building registered alarm. "I'm going to nail your tongue to the door the next time you even hint at such disrespect."

The man grinned. "I haven't had a good fight in ages. Don't threaten me with a good time."

Violo drew his knife. On the other side of the room, the patrons panicked. Footsteps stampeded toward the door, and the woman behind the counter swore, worried about how the dining room would fare in the fight.

Solara surveyed the room. The occupancy had dropped abruptly from a hundred to ten. *Faisal.*

Yes.

Talk me through this.

Taking control of someone's mind doesn't have to be any more difficult than giving an order. Their bodies are like suits of clothes. Put them on.

She thought it would be hard, so she put every bit of her strength into it. She didn't whisper a thought into their ears. She didn't nudge a thought into their heads.

She evicted their minds from their bodies and took their bodies for her own. Solara felt their fingers, warmed from mugs of tea and hot chocolate; their toes, chilled in cheap and falling apart boots; noses red and running, cold necks and snug coats and the weight of muscle fatigue and sleep deprivation. She saw herself through their eyes, a young woman sitting up proudly with a vicious look in her eyes, teeth bared in concentration.

It was an odd feeling. She didn't know how many bodies she held, but she laid them on the filthy floor, so all she could see was the wooden ceiling.

Sleep, she thought. *When you wake, this will have been a strange dream you will never speak of. It was a normal evening. You go home, and you rest well.*

Her mind felt a thousand miles larger, spilling over tundra and spring fields and black forests, more mindscapes than she could fathom at once. They bent to her will like grass in the wind, swept up in the sheer force of her thoughts.

"That's good, Sol," Violo said from far away. His cold hands cupped her cheeks. "Let go now. Gently."

She retreated to her own body, and it was like running into a wall. Her knees hit the ground, and blood spilled from her nose like a dam burst, dripping over her lips and to the sticky floor.

"Shit," Violo said. He lifted her up, and she vomited, her stomach wrenching itself into horrible knots with such violent pain that she started to sob.

"Hold onto me, Sol," Violo said.

She couldn't make her limbs work.

Sol, what happened?

She mewed in agony at Faisal's voice in her head. She dry-heaved, and foul-smelling bile spilled down the front of her shirt. She could smell her own blood as it clogged her nose.

"It's all right," Violo said. "I'm going to get you help."

"Lu," she croaked. "I need Lu."

CHAPTER
FORTY-SIX

Solara blacked out on the ride back to the palace. Fortunately, it meant she missed the trek back through the tunnel under the first wall, and she woke in her own bed, clutching her stomach and vomiting.

Violo was instantly at her side. He tucked a basin under her face and pulled back her hair. "This is becoming a bad habit, my lady," he said.

She fell back into her pillows, curling into a ball. "I'm going to die."

"I certainly hope not." He laid a cool towel over her forehead and took the basin out of the room. He returned a moment later with a clean pail and a glass of water.

"Why does this happen to me?" She sounded pathetic.

Violo offered her the glass of water, but she made no move to take it. "Lu said it would be different. Harder. And I told you that your body is weaker than average."

She ran one hand over her face. "He was right. It's not easy."

"Solara," he said. "Your ability–" But he seemed incapable of forming a sentence, and he just pushed the water glass into her hand and lifted her head so she could drink.

The water made her nauseous, and she lay back, buried her face in her pillows, and sighed. She was going to be useless to Tessan if she got this sick every time that she attempted to control someone. And if she couldn't make them stand down peacefully, it meant Violo would have to do it. Much less peacefully. She moaned, curling into a ball.

Violo turned her head. "You're going to vomit on your pillow."

His hand was frigid, his fingers reddish-purple from the cold night. "Caring for me is turning out to be much more work than you thought, isn't it?" she said with a weak smile.

Violo shook his head. "No, you are exactly as difficult as I anticipated."

Solara responded by vomiting again. He wasn't quick enough with the pail, and it went all over her pillows and silk quilt. She started to cry. "I'm sorry."

"No one cares about the blankets, Sol," he said. "Come here." He picked her up, gently enough not to spur another expectoration, and carried her out of her room. He marched across the anteroom, and she shook her head.

"No. Put me down."

"You're being a coward." He nudged open the door to Tessan's bedroom.

"I'm not sleeping in here." She sounded tiny and defiant.

"Yes, you are." With one hand, Violo flipped back the comforter and then laid her on the cool sheets. Just the thought of climbing back out of the monstrous bed made Solara feel worse, so she glared feebly at him as he tucked the blanket around her.

A quiet tap came at the antechamber door, and Violo went to answer it. It was the dead of night, so Solara assumed it could only be Lu or Faisal, having realized she was falling apart. Whoever it was, she couldn't hear them coming, and not because of her silent shield. Her mind was an eerie wasteland. She couldn't hear her own thoughts.

A moment later, the bedroom door opened, and it was Lunaro who came through it. Her shoulders slumped, and her lips trembled. "Lu."

"Sol." He climbed into the bed and wrapped his arms around her. "Vi just told me a wild story."

"Oh?" she said.

He smoothed her hair beneath his cheek. "He tells me you took control of a lot of people."

"There were only a few people left in the bar."

"No," Violo said from the doorway. "There weren't."

Her gaze flitted between the two of them, confused.

"There were eleven people in the bar, not including you and I. But there were four women in the kitchen. And there were three unconscious on the front walk when I carried you out."

If it were anyone but Violo telling her this, Solara wouldn't have believed them. But he wasn't one to exaggerate, and he certainly didn't joke. Her head ached so much she didn't want to do the math. She curled into a tighter ball, pressing her fisted hands into her aching belly.

"The human body isn't meant to take that much strain," Lunaro went on, stroking her hair. "That's why you got sick and weak after fighting Nikara, and it's why you're sick now."

"I didn't mean to," she whispered.

"I don't think you have to mean it for it to happen. Not when you're as strong as you are." He kissed her forehead, then looked her in the eye. "Did you read the books I sent you?"

"Yes."

"The one about Sara Cabal?"

Solara wracked her aching mind. Sara Cabal had written half a dozen volumes about the mindscape and how to help it recover from strain. "Yes, I remember."

"Good," he said. They closed their eyes, and her mindscape rose around them. The forest waned, the trees limp and their branches brown with disease. Her wall held firm, as it always did, but spiked vines covered its surface like a malevolent creature, searching for weaknesses in the marble. Solara's physical body trembled with the effort to hold herself and Lunaro there. He stood beside her and took in their surroundings.

"I love what you've done with the place," he said. His voice echoed in the stillness.

"Shut up, Lu," she said matter-of-factly.

He grinned, and it steadied her. "It's sheer willpower," he said. "Once the mindscape recovers, the body can begin to recover, as well. But it begins here."

Solara was certain she'd used up all the willpower she had. Her bones ached, and her brother tightened his grip on her hand. She'd told Faisal once that Lunaro's strength lay in the twin bond, and that strength seemed to flow between their clasped hands.

Slowly, the trees straightened. Their leaves changed from sickly to vibrant, the brown giving way to a rich green. A carpet of emerald turf studded with white flowers unrolled at their feet.

"You're really very extraordinary," Lunaro said thoughtfully. He turned away, scanning, and said, "That's Faisal?" He pointed into the distance, where the twisted spires of Faisal's glass palace rose against the horizon.

"Mhm," she said.

He kept turning. "Then who is that?"

Solara pivoted to follow his accusatory finger. There was another horizon. A third end of her mindscape earth. It was smothered in low, black clouds. The moment her eyes locked on them she felt a crushing weight on her chest that almost put her on her knees. She thought the clouds were heavy with rain, but no. It was simply darkness. A heavy, utter darkness, reminiscent of the horrible tunnel Violo had carried her through.

"Sol?" Lunaro said.

She shook her head. "I don't know."

Solara didn't think she had so much slept as just blacked out in the wee hours of the night. She woke to the sounds of Kylee setting the breakfast tray in the anteroom. Violo sat in a chair at her bedside, his head nodding as he tried not to doze off.

"You have to sleep sometime, Vi," Solara said.

He jerked upright. "I'm not tired," he said. He sounded ridiculous. Carefully, Solara rolled to the edge of the bed, leaned over, and ran her hand over his face, forcing him to close his eyes and tilt his head back.

"Sleep," she said.

"Is that an order?" he said, his voice slightly nasal under the pressure of her hand.

"It is a request," she said. He smiled tiredly. "I don't want to answer to Tessan if you drop dead of exhaustion."

"I'm sure I'll be very low on his list of priorities when he lays eyes on you, my lady," Violo said dutifully.

Solara rolled her eyes and lay back.

A polite tap came at the door. "My lady?" Kylee called softly. "Breakfast is ready. And Lord Roon will join you."

Solara cursed and pushed herself up on aching arms. Violo rose, but he wavered, his eyes unfocused and his limbs trembling with effort. He hadn't slept more than a few hours in almost three days. He'd pushed himself past the point of exhaustion in his unerring service to her, and Solara felt guilty. "Violo," she said. "**Go to bed**. Please." She tried to force the order into his head, more from idle curiosity than anything else.

She meant with no resistance. It was as if she'd tossed something into open air. Where his thoughts, his mind, should have been, there was nothing. Just silence.

"I'll go to bed when I'm tired," he said. "You can barely sit up. Tell Roon you're not well."

He'd spoken to her psychically once before, so she knew he hadn't been born silent. Was it possible to abruptly lose psychic ability? She didn't think so. "No, I won't," she said. "And you are tired. **Sleep now**." She threw every ounce of her strength into the order – not insubstantial, no matter how weary she was.

But Violo simply shook his head. "You can't help Tessan if you drop dead of exhaustion, either."

He wasn't quiet. She wasn't weak. He was a stone mind. There was no other explanation. "Vi," she began.

Her bedroom door banged open, and Solara fell silent, but she couldn't pull her eyes from Violo.

"Still abed at this hour, daughter?" Roon said.

"She isn't well," Violo said. There was a haughty sneer in his voice whenever he spoke to Roon, and now Solara's baffled mind realized that it was identical to how Tessan had addressed his father.

"Again?" Roon said, studying her.

"I'm fine." She stammered it. "I'll come to breakfast. I'll be right there."

"You look terrible." Roon approached the bed and reached to lay his hand on Solara's forehead, but Violo grabbed his wrist.

"Don't touch her," he snarled.

Roon was a blur, and then he held Violo in a choke hold, Violo's face turning scarlet. "Lay a hand on me again," Roon said patiently, while Violo struggled. "I will pop your skull like an overripe berry."

"Let him go," Solara said.

Roon ignored her. "Should you really test my temper, not even that child can save you. Do you understand me?"

"**Let him go.**"

Roon released Violo. Solara wasn't sure if it was of his own will or hers. Violo slumped to the ground, gasping for breath. "I will tell you this one time, Solara," Roon said. "Control him." Then he swept out of the room.

Solara fell out of bed and knelt before Violo. "Are you all right?"

He leaned his head against the side of the bed, as if he couldn't hold up its weight. "I'm going to kill him."

Everything in Solara rebelled at the thought of another death. She dismissed it and focused on Violo. Violo and his stone mind. If she had never heard the story of Aine and Scipia, if she hadn't watched him obsess over that story for weeks, Solara would never have thought it.

Tessan.

She thought his name in a whisper, and Violo opened his eyes. They were full of exhaustion and hate and, at the same time, tenderness.

"You don't have to protect me from everything," Solara said softly. That was why Tessan was where he was, like a slab of meat on a table.

Was that where he was?

Or was he here, before her, looking at her through the eyes of someone else?

Violo closed his eyes once more, but not before a solitary tear slid down his cheek, leaving a glistening trail. "I am so tired." He barely breathed the words.

She wanted to tell him to rest, let her be his protector, just this once. But every word trembled on her tongue, uncertain. *Tessan.* It was a desperate prayer. A violent wish. The force of it could have put the black river to shame. She leaned forward and pressed a kiss to his forehead, and her guardian slept.

At morning lessons, Roon acted as if nothing had happened, but Solara couldn't keep the hate out of her eyes when she looked at her father-in-law.

She'd become accustomed to that phrase – father-in-law – and though in the beginning she'd vehemently denied any attachment to him, legal or otherwise, Solara still felt the oddest regard for him. If he was being honest with her, and she mostly believed he was, he wanted a better future for the Diadem, and he was staking everything on his belief in her ability to make it happen.

But what he'd done to his family was unforgivable.

At the lunch hour, Roon came over to her desk and gave her a list of assignments. "Complete them when you have time," he said. In other words, he knew she would be otherwise occupied for a while.

"I don't understand why you hate him," she said.

Roon shrugged. "I think Violo was the only person who loved Tessan. They were playmates, then classmates. They graduated military school together. Violo saved his life once when they were both just boys."

Solara shook her head, confused.

Roon smiled emotionlessly. "He's much testier since he became responsible for you, but he's a good man, and his loyalty is faultless. To be honest, I find it annoying. It makes me feel inferior."

Solara looked down at her pages, struggling to comprehend. To organize. Violo. Tessan. The black silence.

Does it not intrigue you how much his mannerisms have come to resemble those of your late husband?

She was mad. She had gone absolutely insane.

Roon put his hand on her shoulder. "Tessan loved you with everything his black heart could muster," he said. "But should he come back to you I would be cautious."

He didn't have to say more. There were a thousand reasons to be cautious. Solara nodded. He had a look in his eye that she recognized. Her father had often worn that expression.

Love and regret.

He patted her shoulder and left the room, and Solara, her heart heavy enough to make her steps drag, went back to the apartment to change clothes.

Before she'd begun her time in the library, she'd sent a message to Ahdieh Samos, inviting him to join her for an early dinner at the golf course clubhouse. It was time to give him her answer.

She arrived at the apartment to find Kylee tiptoeing about so as not to disturb Violo, whose snores could have roused a mountain. Despite everything, Solara smiled.

Kylee dressed and braided Solara in complete silence, communicating psychically only. She was gifted at her work, and Solara emerged on the other end of it a delicate beauty in blue silk, her hair bound in an exquisite bun at the nape of her neck and held with a ruby pin to match her ruby ring. Altogether, it created the effect she wanted: that of a tender-eyed, easily managed target.

Violo slumbered on, and Solara forced herself to set aside her worries and questions and focus on the single straightforward task she had – dealing with Ahdieh.

She stepped into the hallway and surveyed the pair of Scarlet Guard soldiers flanking the door. "I need four guards to go with me today, since Violo is resting," she said. "I need two of them to be women in plain clothes."

Both guards looked baffled. "I'm sorry?" one said.

"I need four guards," she began again.

"We understand, my lady," the other interrupted. She cut her eyes at her companion.

Thirty minutes later, Solara left the palace with her four guards. Two of them were the biggest men the Guard had to offer, and their combined bulk drew the eye like a magnet. The other two, the women she'd requested, were approximately Mage and Aliss's sizes. They made good time on horseback, and when they arrived at the clubhouse, the dinner rush was just beginning.

It was Solara's first time seeing the place occupied, and it was a perfect opportunity to stress her mindscape a little. She let her silence barrier disintegrate as she dismounted and handed off her horse.

There were probably a dozen patrons on the front patio, sipping pre-dinner drinks and shamelessly watching her approach. The group of teenage girls and their harried chaperone wondered if Solara was here to eat alone. The couple who hurriedly turned away from her had been discussing her before her arrival, whether she'd survive long enough to inherit from Roon.

The man in the farthest corner of the patio had been the one to offer a hundred gold crowns if someone brought him her tongue.

Solara deliberately and mockingly licked her lips as she passed him, and his eyes narrowed.

This was why she preferred silence.

Solara lifted her chin, relaxed her shoulders, and marched across the patio. A few people murmured a greeting in her direction, and she ignored them all.

Inside, the crowd was denser. There were several groups of ten or more clustered around the dining tables, chatting, drinking, and laughing, though the cheer covered darker intentions.

There were two murderers here.

Seven unfaithful spouses.

Eighteen individuals currently engaging in crooked business deals.

Solara breathed through the barrage of information and kept moving, barely aware of her guards in their aggressive formation around her. The library was blessedly empty but for Ahdieh, who was already two glasses deep into a bottle of wine. His gaze settled on her. *Like a lost fawn in the forest*, he thought.

Just loud enough for him to hear, Solara thought, *Don't be afraid.*

Ahdieh smiled as he stood to pull out her chair. "I hope this meeting is about to go the way I want it to, Lady Solara."

Solara sat and held her hands in her lap, knotting her fingers together with nervousness she didn't feel.

Ahdieh took his seat. "Where's your fanatic bodyguard?"

He was probably enjoying the deepest sleep of his life. "He was going to drop dead if he didn't sleep, so I made him," she said. "Of course, I had to promise I wouldn't come see you without him."

Her fake-Aliss thought, *Ah, that's why she was so particular about her guards.*

Ahdieh smiled crookedly. "You don't take orders very well, do you?"

"I could potentially be a very difficult wife for you," she said. "Are you sure you want to make this arrangement?"

I think you care about Tess too much to be too difficult, he thought. He poured her a glass of wine, and she took the glass and inhaled over it. "Still worried I'm going to poison you?" he said.

"Someone offered a hundred gold crowns to whoever cut out my tongue," Solara said flatly. "Forgive me if I'm wary."

His crooked smile widened. *I think we'll have no problem dealing with each other, Solara.* He was relieved that she was being so docile. He'd doubted how much she cared for Tessan after seeing her with Violo, but his plan was going to work. He would be the richest man in or out of the Diadem.

Despite what she'd thought first walking into the building, now Solara didn't know why she'd cloaked herself in silence for so long. The riches she stood to inherit from Roon were nothing compared to the portion of the gift she'd been allotted. She knew every thought this man had, from the too-tight button on his right boot to his distracted wondering if he'd remembered to put a letter on the pile for the post.

"I do have some stipulations," Solara said.

"You'll want to see him first," he said.

She nodded.

"No," Samos said confidently, as she'd known he would. "You'll have to take my word for your surety." He smiled. "You're not as helpless as you pretend to be. I'll trust you when our signatures are dry on the marriage contract."

Solara took a shaky breath and picked anxiously at a fingernail. *The day of the wedding, then. You'll let me see him. You'll let me see him whenever I ask.*

Ahdieh nodded once. *You can sleep beside his body every night if you're so inclined.*

And if he wakes… you won't hurt him.

Ahdieh considered lying, since he thought she was desperate enough to believe him. If Tessan woke, of course he had to kill him. There was no other way to keep his alliance with Solara legal. "We'll discuss that if and when the times comes," Ahdieh said aloud. "Your interest should be in the undeniable present, not a possible future."

His dismissal irritated her, even if her question was feigned. She would have belabored her point, but deep in her mindscape, the dark cloudbank rumbled. It was like a murmur of thunder in the distance, but swiftly approaching.

Ahdieh's gaze shifted past her as he said, "I'm quite impressed with your loyalty to your husband, Lady Solara."

Solara twisted around.

Violo stood in the doorway. He still looked tired, though in no danger of dropping dead. He wore his clothes from that morning, rumpled and entirely inappropriate for the venue, but Solara was quite sure he'd woken up, realized she was gone, and immediately come after her.

"I'll discuss the rest of the specifics with your father," Ahdieh went on. "I'm sure I can count on your acquiescence to my requirements."

Solara turned back to him. "I'm not finished."

"I'm finished with you," Ahdieh said. He stood up, a saccharine smile on his face.

Every fiber of Solara's being wanted her to retort. *Do it for Tess*, she thought. Loud enough for Ahdieh to hear. Soft enough he wouldn't know it was intentional.

He came around the table and stopped in front of her, his eyes on her hands in her lap. Not her hands. Her ring. "Stop wearing that," he said.

Solara let her voice ever-so-slightly tremble. "I don't want to."

Ahdieh breathed a laugh. Very slowly, because he knew a sudden movement would set off her guards, he took her hand and slid the ring off. It thumped softly on the table as he set it down. "Count on this, Lady Solara. You'll be much better at taking orders when we're through."

Fake-Mage could not believe Solara allowed him to speak to her like that.

Solara sat still, head bowed, as Ahdieh moved away. Violo, silent as stone, simply stepped out of the doorway and gestured to it with a sarcastic flourish. Ahdieh hated Violo even more than Roon did, and he made no attempt to temper that hatred in his thoughts as he brushed past the bodyguard and walked away, content in the knowledge that Solara would do as she was told.

As soon as Ahdieh's footsteps were swallowed in the general murmur of noise in the main room, Solara lifted her head and glared at Violo. His expression was unreadable. "You're supposed to be sleeping," she said.

"I've slept enough," he said.

She studied him in silence for several seconds, wondering what he was thinking about as he studied her back.

He came forward, picked up her ring off the table, and offered it to her.

Solara bit back a smile as she slipped it on. "Take me home."

CHAPTER FORTY-SEVEN

At breakfast the next morning, Roon said, "Ahdieh wants to meet with me."

"Good," Solara said. He gave her a long, measuring look. "Take your time discussing the particulars," she said.

Roon nodded. "How long?"

"Two days will be enough."

For the next two days, Solara ate, and she slept. It was Solara's body that gave out on her when she fought Nikara and took control of the people in the Cider Jug. She wasn't going to improve her physical stamina in two days, so her best bet was to be as well fed and well rested as possible. She wandered out of her apartment only twice, to sit in a stairwell and listen to the cacophony of servants' thoughts.

The night she was going to get Tessan back, Solara woke because she thought she heard thunder. Her half-asleep mind panicked at the thought of a torrential downpour, and Violo touched her shoulder.

"It was just a dream, Sol," he said.

She was sitting halfway up in bed, so twisted in her heavy blankets she couldn't move her legs. He'd lit the collection of candles on her nightstand, and they illuminated his serious face and the chair he'd pulled up to the bedside. "You were supposed to be resting," she said. "How long have you been sitting here?"

"Five minutes," he said.

"Liar."

He was already dressed head to toe in black for the excursion, complete with knives. Tessan's sword and scabbard lay on her dressing table. "Ten minutes, then," Violo said with the hint of a smile. "You were tossing and turning. I came to make sure you didn't fall out of this very small bed."

"My bed is built for normal sized people," Solara said. She let her gaze roam over her little room and tried to remember how uncomfortable she had first been in it. "Did Tessan make this room for me?" she said, turning back to Violo.

Violo looked down at his hands. "Yes."

"When?"

He hesitated for a second longer. "The day after Faisal's birthday party. Just in case you wanted... needed... a place of your own. A safe place."

Solara gently detangled her legs from her blankets, then slid off the edge of the bed and hugged Violo. For once, he didn't jerk away. He didn't hug her back, but he relaxed into her arms. "This room isn't a safe place for me," she said softly. "But you are."

She pushed him back, and, before she could doubt herself, planted a loud kiss on his forehead. Even in the dim light, she could see his cheeks flushed pink.

"Let's go get Tess."

By the time they reached the river house, Solara had begun to shiver from nerves. Her coconspirators waited in the stables. Aliss, Mage, and Gaius stood huddled together for warmth, all three of them in nondescript serving gear. Lunaro paced, but Faisal stood still, his implacable exterior suggesting he didn't have a care in the world. When Solara and Violo entered, Faisal said, "Is it too late for me to forbid you from going?"

"We're well past that," Solara said.

"You could probably marry anyone in the Diadem if you wanted to," Aliss said through chattering teeth. "Are you sure you want him?"

"I'm sure," Solara said.

No one was surprised at her answer. Mage was still in a little disbelief, and Gaius was generally confused by everything, but all the siblings had known from the moment she spoke in the glass office that she wouldn't back down.

Lunaro took Solara by the shoulders. "I will literally burn that place to the ground if you don't walk out of it," he said. *Show them what a fourth ringer can do.*

I will. Solara turned to Faisal. *I'm the most extraordinary psychic you've ever known. Don't look so worried.*

"I'm worried about my sister and my child, not you," Faisal said. He laid his hand on her cheek, his lips parting to say something else, but words failed him. "Be careful," he said.

"I'm always careful," Solara said.

They brought out the horses. Mage and Gaius rode double since Gaius wasn't used to riding. Aliss, once mounted, flipped up the hem of her skirt to check the knives strapped to both ankles. Faisal swatted her knee. "Last resort, Aliss Casarriba," he said. "Don't start swinging unless you're told."

She made a face. "Solara's in charge of me, not you."

"Have I already mentioned I hate this?" Lunaro muttered.

"You're making it worse," Violo said. The gravity in his tone quieted them all.

Everything felt portentous. If Solara failed, if she couldn't work the relay... if she couldn't wake Tess... if he was out of her reach forever... A lump rose in her throat, and without another word, she nudged her mare forward.

Ahdieh Samos' tower on the plain was a two-hour trek, even taking the high road. The cobbled, arching bridge began in the third ring and deposited its occupants just before the final wall. Solara had always looked up at it as a child, marveling at the architectural feat. She'd never expected to ride on it.

Lunaro, Faisal, and Violo were riding straight through the city. The high road toll documented every person who went in and out. If the excursion became violent and they left bodies in their wake, there couldn't be any record of the inevitably guilty parties. Everyone radiated anxiety; except Violo, of course. Every time Solara checked on her bodyguard, he watched her with a conflicted, worried expression. He returned none of her smiles. They rode straight to the toll bridge, and the three men split off shortly before. Solara could tell how badly they wanted to give parting admonitions, but her grim silence kept them in check.

The man at the toll booth looked at her through sleepy eyes, noted the Manfalon crest on her coat pin, took the toll, and promptly went back to sleep in the booth.

"Excellent security," Mage quipped, as they began their ascent. She'd never been on the bridge, either. Faisal could never be bothered.

"Solara's face is the security," Aliss said. "Roon has all of the Scarlet Guard memorize his family's faces."

Their horses' hooves clip-clopped on the dew damp cobblestones. The ascent was steep at first but then leveled as they traversed the open air between the fourth and fifth walls. Solara's stomach tightened as she realized she was afraid of heights.

Mage, too, realized she didn't like it, and she started chattering questions at Aliss to distract herself. Gaius alone seemed unperturbed. He gazed up at the glorious night sky.

Are you looking at the stars? Solara asked Faisal. He felt very far away. Depending on which ring he was in, this might very well be the farthest apart they'd physically been since taking the bond.

My sole interest is in successfully pulling off this crime, Faisal retorted.

He was criminal first.

Yes, that would be an excellent defense in a court of law in a city where nobody likes you to begin with.

Solara smiled. The cold was setting in, numbing her fingertips. She sank lower against her horse and tried to relax her mind. It took everything she had not to doze as they crossed over each ring. She didn't dare look down. She already felt queasy. But before long, they began their descent. Mage's nervous chatter settled. Aliss took out one of her knives and began twirling it.

The bridge ended in a courtyard just before the seventh wall. The final wall of the Diadem came in two parts. The first layer was twenty feet high and made of clay brick, slowly crumbling under the weight of time, with a series of wooden doors that led into a narrow garrison before the final fortification. Built entirely of granite blocks, the wall rose forty feet into the night sky, its veins of pink and charcoal glimmering like tiny rivers.

They had to dismount and lead their horses through a narrow walkway to make it to the wooden doors, and there a heavily armed guard stopped them. "State your business."

Solara said coolly, "My name is Solara Manfalon. My business is my own."

He eyed her up and down, taking in the expensive clothing and crest. He thought it very odd she was traveling outside the city without her father-in-law, or at least a more impressive guard than the three ragtag attendants with her.

"I'm not repeating myself," Solara said.

"It's not safe for a lady to be–"

Solara sighed loud and long, and the guard rushed to open the door. She swept haughtily through. In the garrison, a pair of soldiers manned the gate. They looked inexhaustible despite the late hour, shoulders squared and chins high.

Ahead of them was the final gate, which was built of solid iron. A complicated pulley system would muscle them open, and seven men manned the mechanisms, waiting for orders, which Solara, a thin smile on her face, gave. "Open the gate."

Violo, Faisal, and Lunaro were waiting. They'd made better time galloping through the rings and taking the sub-wall tunnels – a secret Violo had been loath to share. For the first time in her entire life, Solara was outside of the seven walls of the Diadem. She didn't know what she had been expecting, but it was more of the same landscape as the Center. Dense foliage. A hardpacked dirt road. Nightbirds flitted in the trees.

"You seem disappointed, Sol," Faisal said. He led the way on his gray mare side by side with Lunaro, whose backside was aching from the amount of riding he'd done tonight.

Solara, riding beside Violo, shrugged. "I thought it would be more exciting than this."

"Boring is best," Violo said.

Faisal nodded. "In combat training in the military, they bring you out here to practice maneuvers. I had never been beyond the wall without my parents and my nanny. I was disappointed, too."

"I've never been outside the wall till today, either," Gaius said. He wasn't sure he was allowed to join the conversation. "It's very spacious."

It made Mage feel exposed.

"It's funny, the comfort the walls provide," Aliss said. "Even a cage can be comfortable once it's familiar."

Solara twisted to look back at Aliss, and the heiress winked at her.

They rode for a solid twenty-five minutes. Solara, despite her two days of mostly sleeping, had dozed off, her chin resting on her chest, when her horse halted. She sat up and took stock. They'd come to the end of the forest, and past the tree line were the plains she'd only read about, vast fields of tall sawgrass as far as the eye could see. Rising out of the grass to the south was Samos' tower, an accusatory finger pointed at the sky.

Impressed yet? Faisal asked. Aloud, he said, "This is where we'll leave you. Once you're in the house, and he's confident you're alone, we'll approach on foot."

Mage said, "Approach fast."

Faisal smiled thinly at his ward. "There's not a fight on this earth you can't win, little tiger. Have some faith."

Lunaro opened his mouth to remind Solara for the thousandth time to be careful, but she nudged her horse into a canter and left without looking back. Mage cursed, but Aliss just laughed and followed.

The house was as lovely a structure as Solara had seen in Samos' head, but as their horses approached, there were other things to see. It was enclosed with a barbed wire fence, and turquoise-clad soldiers patrolled the perimeter, weapons at the ready. A deep moat separated the tower from the plain. There was no water in its depths; instead, pikes and barbed wire waited to impale a trespasser.

Solara drew her horse up at the gate. The guard stared at her without recognition. "Tell Ahdieh his future wife is here to see him," she said.

Beyond the fence, one of the other guards ran into the house to relay her message.

"It's a cold, dark night to be out alone, my lady," the guard said. He eyed their ragtag band and judged Aliss the greatest threat. She'd put her knives away, and she was the scrawniest one in the group, but he didn't like the look in her eyes.

The door opened again, spilling light over the damp ground, and Ahdieh emerged, still tugging on the sleeves of his coat. "What the hell are you doing here?" he demanded. He'd tossed the coat on over his nightclothes, and he didn't even look at her. His gaze scanned the plain, searching for Scarlet Guard, or worse, Violo.

Solara dismounted. "I want to see Tess."

"You are outside of your mind, little girl," Ahdieh said. He wasn't sure if he should be relieved or more concerned that Solara appeared to be lacking any of her ferocious guardians.

"No one knows I came," Solara said. "No one has to know I've been here at all. But I need to see him. I don't trust you."

He laughed incredulously. "You rode all this way in the middle of the night?"

"It was the only way no one stopped me," Solara said. She softened her voice, let her shoulders sag. "Please."

Her obsession with him is an illness, Ahdieh thought.

I couldn't agree more, Mage said.

Solara almost shot the girl a dirty look. "Please," she said again.

Ahdieh had no intention of letting her anywhere near Tessan. He jerked his chin at the guard. "Let her in."

The guard thought it was a terrible idea, but he moved to open the gate.

"The guard stays outside," Ahdieh said, his eyes on Gaius.

Gaius, as rehearsed, began to protest.

"Stay," Solara said. She handed him her reins. "He won't do anything to me. I'm too valuable to him."

Aliss and Mage flanked Solara. *Try to look less likely to kill a man, Aliss,* Solara admonished.

Ahdieh, without another word, turned and walked back into the house. Solara took it as her invitation to follow. The entryway of the tower home was surprisingly sparse, and the unsealed flagstones bore dark marks, as if blood had spilled there. In the middle of the space was a round couch, and Ahdieh sat on it, crossed his arms, and looked at her expectantly. "Make your case, Solara, before I tell you no."

He's so charming, Aliss thought. *Are you sure you don't want me to stab him?*

Focus, Faisal said. *Let Solara focus.*

"What difference is it to you if I see him now or weeks from now?" Solara said. "There's no reason to keep him from me unless you're hiding something."

"Yes," Ahdieh said. "My crime, Solara. I'm concealing my crime. He's alive enough for it to be considered kidnapping, and Roon would love the opportunity to sue me for damages."

Solara looked down at her hands, eyes closed. She needed just a moment to drift into the mindscape and become aware of the people in the house. Four guards on the grounds. Ahdieh. Probably a dozen different members of staff on the first floor alone. She opened her eyes. This was going to hurt.

Ahdieh watched her, waiting.

"You've already won," she said softly. "Why do you have to be cruel, as well?"

He stood up, and Aliss and Mage crowded close. Mage didn't want to touch her, but they both slipped an arm into the crook of Solara's elbows. The steady pressure was like anchors as Solara let the doors between their minds drift open. Aliss's winterscape. Mage's mind was a grassy meadow that bled seamlessly into Gaius's waterscape. Even without physical touch, she could find him because he was bound so tight with Mage.

"Save your tears, Solara," Ahdieh said. She didn't hear the rest.

She, Aliss, Gaius, and Mage stood in the forest of her mindscape like shadows. Two powerful psychics. Two former psychic slaves. Energy crackled between them like lightning. It made Solara's nerves sing. The world felt vaster than it ever had, particularly with Faisal approaching; and, of course, Lunaro, the first mind to which she'd ever linked her own.

Ahdieh grabbed Solara by the throat. "Are you listening to me?"

Solara reached out. Mage, Aliss, and Gaius were there, power spitting between the three of them like sparks. It was like seizing fire. She grabbed hold of that power. Thunder cracked in the mindscape. White fog and black water rushed through her and around her, almost more than she could hold.

But she held it.

Ahdieh said something else, his fingers biting into her throat.

The power built and built. It was going to rip her skull open.

Ahdieh let go of her. "What's wrong with you?"

Solara found the thoughts of the guards outside and all those people on the first floor, organized and occupied, mildly concerned with who had arrived in the middle of the night. Then she let her consciousness widen, spilling over mindscapes like ink, until it was stretched to its absolute limit. Lastly, she found Samos, and she directed that crackling power and let go.

You're so tired, she thought. *Utterly exhausted. Sleep.*

You're so tired, she thought. *Utterly exhausted. Sleep.*

CHAPTER FORTY-EIGHT

amos collapsed.

Solara hit her knees. Her vision blurred, both from tears and dizziness. Voices swam around her, and a pair of arms – Aliss – went around her, holding her up. "Mage, let the boys in!" she ordered, and Mage ran to obey.

Sol, are you there? Aliss demanded.

Sol. Faisal.

Solara! Lu.

My lady? Poor Gaius.

They all called her name like a mad chant, but Solara was awash in fog and black river and meadow and forest, all four mindscapes converging in a tsunami of elements and staggering power. Faisal's palace of glass and mirrors was far away; her own fortress was out of her reach.

Thunder cracked in the cloudbank, and Solara stumbled toward it, out of the tsunami and windstorm. The dark enveloped her, and it was every bit as horrible as she'd feared. She was once more in the tunnel under the wall, struggling to breathe.

I'm here.

A hand closed around hers, and the touch wrenched Solara from the mindscape and back into the physical world. Her bile-burned throat hurt so badly she couldn't speak. Lunaro held her on one side and Violo held her on the other. "Oh," she said faintly. "You got here so fast."

"There are six guards on the next floor," Faisal said. He stood with eyes closed, listening. "But you took them out, too. If we're quiet, we might not attract the attention of the third floor."

"This needs to be the fastest smash and grab in the world," Aliss said. "Places, everyone!" She beamed at Solara. "Save your strength."

The group split, Aliss and Gaius headed up the stairs and Lu and Mage headed down, to whatever dark bowels of the house were below ground level.

"I can get up," Solara said.

"Don't," Violo said. He stood, sweeping her off her feet. On the ground, Ahdieh moaned.

"We don't know how long they'll stay down," Faisal said. "That was a heavy hit, Solara. We almost went down, too. You'll have to learn how to point it better."

Downstairs. Now.

Solara really didn't know if it was Lu or Mage ordering them about, but Faisal had heard, and when he made for the basement stairs, Violo followed. The sudden movement made her head ache, and Solara curled into Violo's arms.

I cannot believe you talked me into this, Faisal thought.

For shame, Mage said.

Shut up, Mage, Solara said matter-of-factly. She could feel the girl's exhaustion. The merge had not been easy for her, and it had been worse for Gaius. He was still shaking.

Lu and Mage were at a heavy, dark door at the bottom of the stairs. Mage knelt beside the doorknob, fiddling the lock with her hairpin. The mechanism clicked, and she pushed the door open to pitch black. Everything in Solara almost gave up at the thought that Tessan had been abandoned in darkness again. Violo gripped her tighter.

"Guard the door," Violo said. Faisal bristled, but he nodded, and he grabbed his ward's arm before she could attempt to lead the way.

"You're staying with me," he said.

Violo set Solara on her feet, relinquishing her into Lunaro's grasp. Without a moment's hesitation, he descended into the dark, and the basement swallowed him up. Lunaro waited ten seconds, and then he and Solara started after Violo. She hoped that they wouldn't need to leave in a hurry, because she could barely stand, even with Lunaro's help.

The flight of stairs was so long Solara could almost believe she was descending into the pits of hell. "Vi?" she whispered. Her voice echoed. The silence stretched out so long she was about to get worried when he spoke.

"I'm here."

A spark flashed and then grew into the dim light of a lantern, illuminating Violo where he stood beside an empty sick bed.

Tessan wasn't there.

"Well, that's not ideal," Lunaro whispered.

At the same time, Faisal hissed down the stairs, "We've got company."

Why wasn't he here? This was not supposed to happen. Solara's panic burgeoned. This was a huge building. They didn't have time to search every room on every floor, not before people started to wake. She didn't know how long they would stay down, and she didn't know how long till the guards on the upper floors grew suspicious of the silence below. She couldn't take down that many people twice.

"Now what?" Lunaro said.

Solara, we don't have time, Faisal warned. Up above, a guard came around the corner, and Faisal ordered the woman to sleep. Mage caught her before she hit the ground. Faisal tried to search Samos's slumbering mind, but he couldn't penetrate the fog of disorientation. *Decide now. We cannot get caught.*

Violo turned his grim expression on her. "Time to go."

Solara remained still, but her mind raced. She had only casually drifted through Samos's mind herself, but what had she learned? Samos was pretentious. Easily offended. Tessan was more than just a bargaining piece to him; he was a prize. He would have kept him somewhere he could gloat over him.

Aliss, Gaius, what's upstairs? Solara demanded.

Lunaro hurried Solara toward the stairs, and Violo was right at their heels, probably about to pick her up and carry her.

The main suites, I think, Aliss said. *Bedrooms. Servants' quarters. Second floor. Lefthand hallway.*

We are leaving, Faisal bit out.

Sol, you've got to move faster, Lunaro urged.

Incoming, Mage said. At the top of the stairs, someone shouted in alarm, and Faisal swore. Solara heaved every ounce of strength into her legs to jog up the remaining steps. Two soldiers came around the corner one right after the other, and Faisal silenced them swiftly but not fast enough. Footsteps pounded down the hall, punctuated by the ring of metal.

She'd gotten them into a horrible mess.

You're here now, so focus, Gaius said. *Don't let this be for nothing.*

"Mage," Solara said. The reinforcements were right around the corner. *Help me.*

Mage grabbed her arm. Violo snatched for her, but Mage and Solara booked it back down the hall. Faisal swore but also missed as Mage and Solara sprinted up the stairs. A guard waited at the top, and Mage spun and kicked, battering him into the wall like a rag doll.

You're very impressive, Solara thought.

For the first time ever, Mage's voice lacked its customary derision. *Aliss has been teaching me.*

They charged down the second story hall, boots pounding on the slick floor tiles. Aliss and Gaius were there, flinging open doors with abandon, stealth no longer an option.

Aliss halted at a large, polished door and grabbed the handle. Locked. Entwined thoughts moving them in perfect sync, the four of them threw their combined weight at the door. It flew open, and the momentum propelled them into the room in a heap of limbs.

Tessan lay in a bed beneath a window, arms folded atop the crisp white sheet pulled over his body. "Found you," Aliss said.

Solara crawled across the room to the bed and pulled herself to her feet. His chest rose and fell beneath the sheet, and warm breath spilled over her fingers when she held them to his nose.

"It's now or never, Sol," Aliss said, still lying on the floor. Mage was panting for breath, and Gaius lay sprawled as if dead. "Wake him up."

Solara's eyes were wet. She wasn't sure when she'd started crying, but now, she wasn't sure she'd ever truly stopped from the moment Roon buried his dagger in Tessan's chest. The day she sat on her apartment floor holding his bloody body in her arms felt a thousand lifetimes removed.

Your current lifetime will be removed if you don't get your shit together, Mage snapped. *Wake him up before everyone gets slaughtered.*

As infuriating as every breath out of her lungs was, Mage was correct. Solara climbed onto the bed, lay her forehead against Tessan's, and went into the mindscape. It was still a tsunami-sundered catastrophe. Mage, Aliss, Gaius, and Solara were so violently entwined that they had lost all limits. She turned away from the mess and looked toward the dark.

The third horizon was no more welcoming, no less terrifying. Solara drew strength from the madness around her and walked into the clouds. It consumed each one of her senses, silencing them, until she didn't know what was up, down, in, or out. Still, she walked, letting it surround her, until her balance was so skewed that she was afraid to move. Only then did she go still.

You called out to me. Somehow, through the silence, you came to me, and now I've come to bring you back. I would stand in this darkness until the end of everything, but we don't have that much time.

Her words didn't even echo. That was how deep the silence ran. It was like a living thing in her veins.

Tessan. Saying his name released something in her. She'd doubted herself. Every time she looked at Violo and questioned... even after seeing Tessan's body in Samos's mind... she hadn't truly believed he was alive. That his mind was intact. Not until now.

Tessan, wherever you are, I need you. **Wake up.**

"Sol!"

Someone hauled her off him, and she fought halfheartedly, unsure what was real, until Lunaro bellowed in her ear, "Stop fighting me, you stupid girl! Run!"

The room came into sharp focus, too bright and loud after the dark. Gaius and Mage were up, and someone else lay unconscious on the floor – she thought it was Violo – but somewhere else in the house a fallen guard was screaming their pain psychically at such unbearable volume she couldn't focus on anything else. She twisted to look back for Tessan.

I've got him, Faisal said. *I promise. Run.*

She let Lunaro haul her out of the room, and they stampeded towards the stairs. More guards were rushing up and she ordered, weakly, "Sleep," but only a few stumbled and the rest didn't even falter.

It didn't matter.

Aliss charged into their midst like a screaming firecracker, ploughing a way through, and Lunaro beat off the stragglers. She could sense Faisal close by, but her nose and her ears were bleeding, and it was all she could do to keep her eyes open, gaze locked on Lunaro's back, and run.

They considered stopping at the river house, but Faisal vetoed it. *If there are repercussions, we need the fortress of the palace.*

That was the last thing Solara could remember of the feverish rendezvous once they were in the limited cover of the trees. She was sick the whole ride back, desperately trying to hold her aching head together. When they clattered into the palace courtyard, Roon was there. Everyone was arguing and cursing, and then the next thing she knew was Roon carrying her up to her room. Kylee washed her face and put her in a nightgown and put her to bed.

Her mind had so completely overburdened itself that she couldn't even hear her maid's thoughts as she worked, and Solara thought she was already dreaming when Kylee tucked the blanket up to her chin and whispered, "I'm so glad you're safe, my lady."

That little kindness undid her. She slipped into a black, dreamless sleep. She woke what seemed like seconds later to find Kylee braiding her hair and another maid, Nyssa, fluffing her pillows, saying, "I know personality isn't supposed to be a part of it, but Lunaro Barthelme is the sweetest man in the palace, and honestly, I think he's more attractive than Lord Faisal, anyway."

"He'll be thrilled to hear that," Solara murmured.

"My lady!" Nyssa flushed. "I'll get the doctor." She bolted out of the room.

"They'll be so glad to see you're awake, my lady," Kylee said. She tied off Solara's braid and laid it over her shoulder. "We've been worried." At Solara's blank look, she said, "You've been asleep for four days."

"Oh," Solara said. She felt suspiciously well-rested. "Where's my brother?"

She hadn't gotten the words out before he burst into the room. Solara grinned, and he came over and fell on top of her, wrapping both arms around her neck in what was either a hug or an attempt to strangle her. "I can't take the stress of being related to you anymore," he mumbled.

"What happened?" she said. Her mind was quiet. Black river and white fog had retreated, leaving her once more in sole possession of the mindscape, minus Faisal's ever-present spires. And there was the black cloudbank looming.

"I'll wait in the hall," Kylee said, dipping a curtsy. She excused herself.

Lunaro lifted his head and looked Solara in the eye. "Your husband's alive," he said. "He's alive and he's asked to see you. No, demanded to see you, repeatedly."

"Roon wouldn't let him?" Solara said.

Lunaro nodded. "He's chained to a bed in the infirmary right now, threatening to murder everyone that touches him."

Solara wished she could be surprised, but there was no way Roon would have passed on an opportunity to punish his son. "Where's Violo?" she said.

"He's also in the infirmary," Lunaro said. "The moment Tessan woke, Violo dropped. No one can wake him."

CHAPTER FORTY-NINE

Agathe's arrival interrupted their conversation. Roon was on her heels, but the physician unceremoniously shoved the king of the city out of the room and closed the door. It took half an hour of questions and prodding for her to deem Solara stable, and only then did she reopen the door. Roon was the first one in, and he sat down on the bedside and peered at Solara to ascertain her wellbeing for himself.

She started to ask what had happened with Samos, but Roon took her head in his hands and kissed her forehead, startling her silent. "I told Faisal I'd have his head if you didn't wake."

"That wouldn't have been fair, would it?" Solara said as he let her go. "It was my idea."

"I would have needed someone to blame, and it was him or your brother," Roon said. Solara frowned, and the man smiled. "I think I've grown a little fond of you, Miss Barthelme."

"What of Samos?" she said.

"The matter is being investigated by the court," he said. "Samos' man in the palace was apparently the second doctor who pronounced Tessan dead. That doctor is now also dead, so there's nothing to tie Samos to the crime unless you feel like testifying to all that occurred that night. Even then, it's your word against his.

"Most likely, we will argue back and forth for months on end about who is guilty and who committed unspeakable crimes, and in the end, we will come to no conclusion and pretend nothing happened because you were smart enough to leave no trace of your presence behind."

Solara breathed a laugh. "I'm thrilled for the state of law and order in the Diadem."

"You won, my dear," Roon said, and she met his gaze. "What else matters?"

Solara glanced at her doorway, where Lunaro leaned. *And Aliss? And Gaius and Mage?*

All safe, Lunaro promised. *Minds and bodies are all intact.*

"I take it you've already asked your brother about Tessan," Roon said. When she didn't answer, he said, "Would you like to see him?"

"Don't taunt me," Solara said.

"The terms of our agreement were simple, Solara," Roon said. "Keep Tessan in check and you can do with him as you wish. But he will not be lord of this city. Ensure that, and I have no interest in him."

"He's still your son," she said.

"Even I am not so arrogant, Sol. He never saw me as his father, only as his lord. And I should think the knife in his chest assured that will never change." He wasn't troubled by this fact. When it came to Tessan, he simply didn't care. "Are you prepared to accept responsibility for him?" Roon said.

"What about you?" Solara said.

Roon held her gaze, let her hear his every thought. "I have a beach house on the other end of the country that I've never seen," he said. "I intend to go see it."

He was going. His bags were already packed. He would leave her in charge of the Diadem and go see dolphins for the first time. Despite all the time he'd spent evaluating her and training her, there had been a part of Solara that was sure there was some wicked scheme up his sleeve that would become apparent the moment she let her guard down.

But he'd been honest. Brutal, but honest. He had groomed her to control the Diadem so that he could be free.

She darted a glance at Lunaro, who was unsurprised. He'd spoken with Roon, she realized. They'd had conversations at her breakfast table in the anteroom while they waited for her to wake.

"Enjoy your trip," Solara said.

"I will leave you to your visits, then," Roon said. "Faisal has been pacing the palace halls for days." He rose, placing a kiss on the top of her head. It felt final, and Solara didn't think she would ever see him again. "Don't overtax yourself, my dear." He left. She heard him informing Kylee that Solara could see the Casarriba siblings and no one else; she needed her rest.

"I think he's a psychopath," Lunaro said.

Solara nodded.

"You're going to do it? You're going to be lady of the Diadem?" Lunaro said. She could hear his skepticism. "What if people don't like it?"

"Tessan isn't going to give them a choice," she said. That was the use Roon had come up with for his son. It was the only reason he'd allowed Solara to know Tessan wasn't dead. "He's supposed to be my figurehead."

"And you think Tessan will give *you* a choice?" The skepticism got louder.

Solara hugged her knees to her chest. Tessan had never wanted to rule the Diadem, only to beat Nikara. She had to go talk to him. The thought made her nervous.

Faisal and Aliss came into the bedroom, the elder brother looking decidedly annoyed. "You look much better than at our last meeting," Aliss said cheerfully. "How's your head?"

"Intact, which is all I can ask for," Solara said. There was still blood crusted deep in her nose.

Aliss tipped her head at her brother. "He's not going to speak to you before you apologize for endangering our lives and running off with Mage when he said we had to leave."

The attitude in her voice made Solara smile. "Does your brother not know you and Mage are fearless women with their own free will?"

"We've been contesting my rights to have ideas." Aliss poked Faisal's arm, and he slapped her hand away. "I'll be doing penance for eternity, but you, his dearest Sol–"

"Act your age, Aliss," Faisal snapped.

Aliss winked at Solara. There was a blazing fire in her, a light so bright not even everything she'd suffered at the hands of Manfalon daughters had dimmed it. Aliss would not be coddled. Faisal could try to protect her, and she would chafe and rebel, and she would be too much for him to hold.

"I'm glad you're all right, Solara," Faisal said stiffly.

She wanted to tease him, but Aliss clearly had a handle on that. "Thank you," she said. Then she responded to the words he hadn't been able to form that night in the stable. "I love you, too."

Roon had kept her and Tessan apart specifically to make Tessan suffer, and it was cruel of her to prolong it, but first Solara went to see Violo. As soon as she walked into his sick room, she was aware of his thoughts, quiet but there. She laid one hand on his cool forehead and went into his mind. It was covered in mist, and she saw him wandering about, lost. *Come take my hand, Vi. I'll lead you back.*

The anxious sound of his breath steadied, and the worried wrinkles smoothed from his forehead. She didn't wait for him to wake before she left. It was strange to realize that she didn't know him, not really. Violo, the real Violo, had saved her from chewing glass. He'd blocked her escape when she would have left Tessan. And that was it. That was the history they'd shared. He wasn't her friend and her confidant and protector.

That had all been Tessan.

Now, she stood outside the door to his room in the infirmary and didn't know if she could face Tessan, either. How was she supposed to look him in the eye after everything? She'd bared her soul to "Violo," and now he knew every secret she'd kept from him. There was no running from the truth anymore. She pushed the door open and went in.

It was a spacious sick room with a large bed and a wash table beside it. A wall of windows looked out to the snow-coated gardens. Tessan was asleep, bathed in frosty light. He was coated in bruises and his hair lay wild across his pillows. He was bound by the wrists and ankles to the bed frame, and she could see angry red marks beneath the silk bindings.

The sight of the little wounds pushed her forward, and she swiftly untied him, tossing the bindings in a pile on the floor. They had probably needed to tie him down to make him submit to care, but it had been pure spite on Roon's part to leave him this way. It was incomprehensible to Solara that Roon could be so kind to her and so cruel to his son.

Solara gently touched the mark on his wrist with the pad of her thumb. He'd fought those bindings, fought for who knew how long, trying to get to her. "You're very stubborn, Tessan," she whispered. She did not envy his caretakers. She stroked his hair back from his face, resisting the urge to kiss the worried frown knotting his brow.

There were a thousand questions to be asked. Tessan was a stone mind. Nothing in, nothing out. But there were only two possible explanations for what happened. Either he had somehow performed a feat only recorded once before, when Scipia and Aine traded places. Or Solara had performed it when she ordered him not to leave her.

Against all the known rules of the gift, she had formed a connection with him. Even now she was aware of him in her mindscape: a clouded, distant presence but undeniably there.

Solara sat on the edge of the bed, then laid down beside him, resting her cheek against his shoulder. "You're very pretty when you sleep," she murmured. She'd never had this opportunity before. It was always the other way around, him watching her. As Violo, he'd told her he was content. That he'd be nothing to her but her bodyguard if it meant she was safe. Had he meant it? For all Roon's insanity, he was not incorrect. The Diadem had belonged to indifferent rulers for a very long time, and it was past time for that to change.

But would Tessan be willing to shoulder this burden with her? He'd backed her as Violo, her bodyguard, when he was powerless. Would he do it as Tessan, her husband, who outranked her?

Solara sat up on one elbow, looking down at his troubled expression. She gave into the urge and kissed his forehead, his eyes, his nose, his pursed lips. She put her face against his chest and breathed. The only scent on his clothes and skin was antiseptic, which was disappointing.

He stirred. "Sol?" His voice was ragged, as if he'd been shouting.

Solara lifted her head. His eyes opened, blinking at her in confusion and disbelief. She thought her chest would crack open from the amount of emotion it held.

Then she lifted her leg and kicked him in the shin as hard as she could.

He cursed and doubled over, almost flinging her off the bed. "Solara!"

"I thought Violo was going to warn you to expect that," she said. He shot her a vicious look, gripping his abused shin with both hands. "Don't look at me like that."

Tessan slowly let go of his shin. Solara fought back a grin. All her questions about how and why seemed irrelevant because she knew in that moment, even as he glared at her, that he'd do anything for her. She took his face in her hands and placed a kiss between his eyebrows.

"You shouldn't have come," he said gruffly.

"It wasn't enough," she said. "I wanted you. The *real* you." He stared at her. She could see him struggling with what to say. "Tell me," she said.

"You were my prisoner," he said. "And deep down I knew it, and I couldn't let you go."

"I lied to you," she said. "Over and over and over to get to Aliss, and I didn't think or care about what it would do to you."

"I turned a blind eye to her suffering because it was easier not to fight my sisters." He choked on the words. "I was so tired of protecting myself from them that as long as they pointed their cruelties elsewhere, I pretended not to see it." He swallowed hard, forcing himself to look her in the eye. "You should have been able to tell me about Aliss. I should have made them free her long ago."

Solara laid her hand on his chest, over the place Roon had buried his knife. "What happened that day?"

Tessan shook his head. "I was dying. I could feel myself slipping away. But then you told me I couldn't leave you." A smile softened his mouth.

"You clung to me, so I clung to you. And I was lost and confused, but it was another chance to stay beside you, so I took it."

She didn't know what any of this meant. Perhaps Lunaro, with all his research, would be able to make sense of it for her one day. For now, Solara just wanted to look at Tessan. Was it even surprising that he'd caught her eye three years ago? Solara had fought her feelings madly, imagining the taint of Nikara in every moment of it. But Solara had proven her superior strength again and again. Her mind was her own. Her feelings were her own. No one could have held her to an order for that long. No one.

"Why didn't you tell me?" Solara said. "Why did you pretend to be him and make me question everything I'd ever felt?"

Tessan looked down at her hands, which she'd folded into a knot on the sheets between them. It took her a moment to realize he was looking at her ring. "Regardless of my questions and any answer you ever gave me, I would have stood by your side and protected you until the day I died," he said. "But I had to know." He shook his head, frustrated. "You were close to me, and then you were far away. And at times you would laugh, and I'd know it was real, and then I could see it in your eyes while you lied to me." His voice softened. "I had to know what was true, and what was a lie, and why."

It was fair. All of his questions were fair. It must have been torment, to be on the receiving end of her grand performance.

"So, ask me," she said.

His mouth pursed. "Ask you what?"

"Ask me, Tessan," she said. "And when I give you my answer, don't you ever doubt it."

"Solara," he said, his voice thick. "Did you love me?"

He barely had the words out before she shook her head. "No, I didn't. You weren't my husband or my friend. You were my master, and you owned me, and my feelings were complicated, but I despised you for having that power over me."

Tessan's expression became eerily serene, as if he'd slipped a mask in place.

Solara moved closer to him, laying her hands on his shoulders. "But then you lost that power, and you were none of those things. You listened to me, and you were kind to me, and when I was at my absolute lowest, you were my friend." She willed the mask away, willed the clouds out of his eyes. "You protected me when I could give you nothing, and *that* is when I loved you."

Tessan looked away, his jaw working, but Solara turned him back to face her. "And if you will have me again, Tess, I will love you every day until the day *I* die."

He kept trying to compose himself, and Solara laughed, sliding her arms around his neck.

"Lord Manfalon," she said. "I have seen you lose your temper. Laugh. Cry. Sleep like a beautiful baby. Why are you always trying to hide from me?"

He bit the corner of his mouth, watching her lips form the words. "You can be very cruel, Sol."

Solara kissed the corner of his mouth, dislodging his teeth. "Tell me you'll have me."

"Is that an order?"

She closed her eyes, seeing that bank of clouds. Tessan shuddered. "You flatter me, Tess." She had never heard of a stone mind gaining psychic ability, not even this dim connection they shared. "Tess," she said, drawing out his name, and at last he smiled. "Tell me you'll have me."

"What will you give me in trade?" he said, and she knew he was hers. "I'm an expensive man."

"I'm an expensive woman."

"Yes, I seem to remember a costly trip into the city." He tugged the ribbon from the tail of her braid, letting her hair spill free as he turned them over, laying her back into the pillows. "Whatever happened to that hat with the orange roses?"

Solara smiled up at him innocently. "I have no idea what you're talking about."

He smiled back at her, and there was none of the timidity in it she had once seen, the smile of a man afraid to be happy. She hoped he would smile like this every day forever.

"Promise me," she said. "Promise me that you'll be a good man."

Tessan leaned close so they were eye to eye. "Promise me you will be a good ruler," he said. There was nothing but acceptance in Tessan's eyes. Maybe even relief.

Her anxiety melted, and she wrapped her arms around his neck and kissed him.

On the mindscape's third horizon, the black clouds began to lighten.

EPILOGUE

I just don't believe Nikara could have that much power over you," Lu said. "The things you've done are extraordinary, Sol. I don't think she could alter your mind. Not permanently."

He paced, gesturing with his arms as he spoke. "She can't have taken that memory. She must have buried it." He pivoted to face Solara. "Which means you can remember, if you try hard enough."

The longest day of the year had given way to night, and the night was brilliant. Lit with stars all the candlelight in the world couldn't drown out, the sky was ablaze. The *air* was ablaze with music that spilled from every bar and from every street corner where musicians played.

Solara hadn't even started drinking yet, but her skin tingled, fingertips numb, as if her body couldn't control its ecstasy. She wove her way down the street, dodging the drunken pedestrians: a well-dressed man stumbling along with help from a beautiful prostitute planning to rob him, two serving girls arm-in-arm on the hunt for their next drink, a harassed young man herding his wasted friends. He caught her eye and smiled grimly. They shared a moment of solidarity at being the only sober people on the street.

Not that Solara minded. She skirted left to make way for two burly men. One swung and tried to slap her ass, but she was too quick, and his friend laughed at him. "Sorry, pretty lady," he said. "He's already been kicked out of two bars."

"I wonder why," she said dryly.

They continued their way, and she continued hers. She was headed to the same place as always. A crowd of people blocked the door at the

Cider Jug, bellowing to be let in. The uproarious music thundered through the street tiles, humming through Solara's bones. At the door, Jonquin stood guard, the only thing grimmer than his blood-spattered club being the ferocious expression on his face.

Solara ducked under the barrier and popped up beside him, smiling. "Hello, Jonquin."

The men at the front of the line scowled at her.

"Hello, baby girl," Jonquin said. The look in his eyes alone kept the unruly line in check. His gaze swept her head to toe, and he tsked. He knew her well enough to know that the expensive dress she wore was not her own.

"I'm going to take it back unscathed," Solara said dismissively. "Don't be a bore."

It was so pretty. How could she have resisted? It was a beautiful, bold yellow cotton that cupped her body perfectly, flaring out around her thighs in a way that was going to look amazing when she spun on the dance floor. It had come in for a few alterations, and Solara had honestly only tried it on to see how her work looked on a proper body.

She smiled brilliantly at Jonquin and said, "Are you going to make me stand out here all night?"

He waved his club. "Get inside. And act right, baby girl!"

A chorus of protests went up from the line as she went through the door, but it was drowned out in the noise. The Cider Jug was packed with bodies, and they swept her up in their motion instantly. It wasn't just the plebeians out tonight. Solara knew her fabrics well enough to pick out who the richer patrons were.

Everything was color. Dresses in pastel pinks, blues, and yellows. Suits in cobalt, royal purple, and deep red. The air was thick with the scent of alcohol and sweat but also of the morning glories hanging in braided ropes from the rafters. Rose petals pounded underfoot. Daisy chain and rose crowns topping heads.

The server just inside the door, Maraki, dropped such a crown atop Solara's head. "The queen is here," she announced, leaning close to be heard.

Solara grinned. "Hello, Maraki." The crown smelled amazing. Solara couldn't help sparing a thought to how funny it would look on her brother's head.

"I was beginning to think you'd found somewhere else to be immoral." Maraki caught Solara's chin, inspecting her eyes. "Have you been drinking already?"

"Never in the street," Solara promised. "Is that all, mother?"

"Get out of my sight."

Solara just laughed. She was never out of Maraki's sight, as the older girl watched her like a hawk, and at the slightest hint of trouble, she was there at Solara's side, whether that entailed beating off an over-eager dance partner or telling the bartender that Solara was cut off for the night. She'd threatened on numerous occasions to walk Solara home and inform Lunaro just what his sister got up to on some nights but had yet to follow through.

The musicians in the corner were playing a two-step dance that Solara had learned standing on her father's toes in the kitchen years ago. She didn't like to dance it anymore. Every step was undercut with grief. She went to the bar, swallowing the sudden lump in her throat. Maraki's sister Taliah was waiting, laying out two shots of white whiskey.

Solara elbowed her way between two suited men until she could lean in, beaming. "Hi."

"Hi," Taliah said with noticeably less enthusiasm.

"Yes, hello," the man on Solara's left said.

Taliah jabbed a finger at him. "No. Leave."

He started to protest – he was a regular, a flirtatious but harmless man who had never noticed Solara before – and Taliah growled. The man winked at Solara and left, taking his drink with him.

"You don't have to be so rude," Solara said, picking up her shot.

"You could learn to be ruder," Taliah said curtly. "And then I wouldn't have to pick up your slack. The word is 'no.' Say it loud. Say it strong."

Solara rolled her eyes. When she reached for her second shot, Taliah put her hand over it. Stifling a groan, Solara met Taliah's eyes.

"I'm cutting you off at four," Taliah said. "I want your head clear tonight. There are a lot of people out. Do you understand me?"

"Yes," Solara said.

"Yes, what?"

"Yes, Taliah, I understand you," Solara said, enunciating each word. Taliah relinquished the drink and Solara downed it. She knew Taliah and Maraki only cared about her safety, but it was exhausting, being smothered by their good intentions. They seemed to think she was too reckless and too carefree. She wanted to explain that this was the only time she was ever like this.

At all other times, she was smart, silent, hardworking Solara, always with a book or some sewing in her hands, working hard, studying hard, feeding Lunaro, keeping her mouth shut, keeping her head on straight. She wanted to tell them that during the day, she felt stifled. Her thoughts, her emotions, her words... everything locked down inside of herself so she would never snap back at a rude nobleman or woman who pushed her off the sidewalk or ordered her to hold their umbrella; so that she would never admit to Lunaro that she was lonely and hungry and so, so tired.

The alcohol settled into Solara like heat in her veins. She looked up at Taliah, and she thought she saw a flicker of sadness in the woman's eyes, as if she'd heard everything that Solara had just thought.

"Go dance," Taliah said.

Solara pushed away from the bar and went. Amidst the dance floor, the thought noise was loudest, everyone's hold on their own mind loosened with alcohol and abandon. Loneliness, lust, sadness, and, despite it all, joy. Men and women jostled her, sloshing their drinks, shouting apologies. The floor was slick. The people were slick. Sweat ran down their faces, bare arms, and throats.

Solara closed her eyes and let the throng move her. It was dizzying, partially from the alcohol, partially from the thought noise. The man off to Solara's right was here without his wife's knowledge, chasing a pretty girl. The pretty girl knew his wife and was deliberately trying to catch him in his infidelity. A group of women had come together looking to blow off some stress, but they'd fought before their arrival and were now planning to end the night early.

Solara opened her eyes with a smile as the musicians launched into a new piece. She loved this song and its intricate sixteen-step dance. This one came with no emotional baggage. She'd learned it here in the Cider Jug one frigid winter night.

Someone caught her hand, a lanky young man with hair nearly as long as her own. His suit looked expensive, a definite red flag – always avoid the rich ones, Maraki would say. They don't know how to be told no. "Would you like to dance with me?" he shouted over the noise.

Solara could practically feel Maraki's eyes on her back.

"Please?" he added.

What did it matter, really? Solara nodded, and he laced their fingers and immediately launched into the steps so fast it snatched her breath away, and she broke into laughter. It didn't last long, because two dances in, Maraki came and separated them. He brushed his lips across her cheek before he left with a whispered, "I'll see you later."

Maraki scoffed. "No, he will not."

Solara mostly danced alone, trying not to laugh as prospective partners approached her and then were aggressively chased off by Maraki, who had had enough for one night. Two shots later and she was dizzy on euphoria, spinning and singing and laughing with a group of girls around her age.

It was just past midnight. Solara's buzz had worn off, and she was debating how inflexible Taliah would be about giving her a fifth shot when he came through the door.

Solara's dance steps slowed.

He was almost ridiculously tall. That was probably what caught her eye initially. The group of friends with him had catered to the occasion and worn colorful suits, so his black pants and white shirt were a shock to the eye. Lantern light glinted on the intricate silver embroidery on his cuffs and collar. It was casual wealth, not the kind trying hard like his friends' jewels and impractical brocade.

One of her new friends caught Solara's arm, trying to draw her back into the dance, but Solara watched the man approach the bar. He had glorious hair, thick and gold like a lion's mane, perfectly laid over his shoulders like he never paid any attention to it, and it was flawless just to spite people like Solara, who had spent an hour negotiating with hers.

Taliah served him and his friends, looking harassed now as the night and the patrons got wilder. He got whiskey, the top tier, and then turned and surveyed the room. His eyes were gray, like the sky before rain, framed by lashes as gold as his hair.

The girl tugging on Solara's arm put her chin on Solara's shoulder, nudging her hair out of the way. "He's pretty."

Solara's cheeks flushed. She didn't know why, as she'd shamelessly ogled attractive men all night long.

"Go talk to him! He looks like fun."

Solara turned around, mortified, and the girl laughed at her expression. Her friends tugged them back into the circle, and Solara picked up what dance they were doing and fell into it as easily as breathing, though her thoughts were elsewhere. She couldn't hear the man's thoughts, couldn't pinpoint them in the rush and crush, which was unusual for her. She didn't have the nerve to go strike up a conversation with a stranger, and besides, even if she did, what on earth was the point? A night of reckless flirtation before she retreated to her home and her work and another night listening to Lunaro's bad cough, wondering if her brother's body was going to give out?

Still.

Solara spun in a circle, searching for him. He and his companions had moved to a corner of the room. He leaned against the wall, looking bored, or maybe overwhelmed.

One of her own companions burst out laughing, and Solara finished her turn, embarrassed at being caught staring again.

"Do you want him to see you?" one of the girls demanded.

Yes.

Solara didn't have to say it. The girl caught her hand and spun her in a circle, so fast it made the lights blur. Solara's bright skirt flared around her, and she laughed, all thoughts momentarily vacating her head at the pure elation that filled her.

"Lift her up!"

She didn't know which of her companions said it, or who followed her order, but suddenly Solara was lifted by strong hands and set on a tabletop – Maraki would have her hide for this – and Solara just didn't care. All the prospective repercussions didn't matter. She spun and spun until her hair tumbled out of its pins. People on the ground cheered.

With every rotation, she saw him. Every time, she met his eyes, just for a second, for fractions of a second. *Who are you? I can't come to you.* She didn't dare, not with Maraki watching. *Come to me.*

Maybe he heard her. Maybe it was shamelessly obvious she was doing this for him. He pushed off the wall.

Solara stopped spinning, breathless.

He started toward her.

Maraki grabbed Solara's arm and wrenched her off the table. Half a dozen sets of hands reached to catch her, and Solara realized belatedly just how much attention she'd garnered.

"Solara Barthelme," Maraki hissed. "I'm going to murder you. Go. Home. Now."

"But–"

He was halfway across the room, but moving hesitantly, his head cocked slightly to the left. Maraki jerked Solara's arm again, hauling her toward the back door, snapping at her to be quiet as she tried, once more, to protest.

Solara twisted to look over her shoulder. He'd paused in the center of the room, a landmark amidst the dancers. *Come and find me,* she thought at him as Maraki wrenched her out the door. He'd lost track of her, scanning the crowd, brow furrowed. *I'll wait.*